by nancy thayer

summer
love

nancy thayer

summer love

a Novel

Ballantine Books
New York

Published in the United States by Ballantine Books, an imprint of Random House, a division of Penguin Random House LLC, New York.

BALLANTINE is a registered trademark and the colophon is a trademark of Penguin Random House LLC.

Hardback ISBN 978-0-593-35842-9
Ebook ISBN 978-0-593-35843-6

Printed in the United States of America on acid-free paper

randomhousebooks.com

2 4 6 8 9 7 5 3 1

First Edition

Book design by Alexis Capitini

For Charley,
a love for all seasons

Acknowledgments

Hello, everyone! I hope you made it safely and happily through the unsettling year of 2021. It was a little better than 2020, right? I survived by reading, writing, and watching way too much television. And *this* summer, I was able to spend time with my grandchildren, with summer friends, and even enjoy a few dinners out with island friends.

I also had lots of time to write. During the past two years, my mind has been crowded with ideas about summer love. Some people come to Nantucket for the summer months, fall in love, and in September, return to their normal lives. Sometimes their love lasts. Often, it doesn't. And that got me thinking about, and writing about, people who came to Nantucket as young adults in 1995, and what they were like twenty-five years later. Because people do change . . . or do they?

My editor, Shauna Summers, helped in so many ways to sort through the possibilities of my characters' adventures. She was astute and precise and absolutely brilliant, and I owe her a huge debt of gratitude. Thank you, Shauna.

People say that words are living things, and anyone who writes knows that it's true. Time after time, when I'm asleep, words that have been banished to an old draft in the computer will creep over, antlike, and insert themselves into the final draft, without my knowledge. Please forgive them.

Madeline Hopkins, who was the copyeditor for *Summer Love,* has an eagle eye for those pesky errors, and I'm grateful. And in this book, I discovered that Madeline and I have a special bond. I'm glad, and I'm especially glad for Madeline's awesome work as my copy editor. Much gratitude to my production editor, Jennifer Rodriguez, and special thanks to Belina Huey for the gorgeous cover!

I've been delighted to work with the Ballantine team who have managed to make the magic happen during unusual and often frustrating times. Allison Schuster, Karen Fink—thanks for all you do, and for making it fun. Much love and gratitude to Kim Hovey, and enormous thanks to Kara Welsh.

My agent, Meg Ruley, has kept me on track for many years now. I don't know what I'd do without her. I certainly wouldn't laugh as much! Thanks to all those who work for the Jane Rotrosen Agency, especially Jessica Errera, Christina Hogrebe, Sabrina Prestia, Hannah Strouth, and Julianne Tinari.

This was the year that my Christmas novel *Let It Snow* was made into a Hallmark Christmas movie called *Nantucket Noel.* It was a delight to watch, even though it wasn't filmed in Nantucket! I want to send enormous thanks to Josh Gray and Nantucket Dreamland for streaming the premiere showing of *Nantucket Noel* on the Dreamland's big screen. I'm so grateful to the wonderful audience who filled the theater with cheers and boos! *Nantucket Noel* might show up in Hallmark's *Christmas in July* special.

In 2020 and 2021, more than ever, writers reached out to one another, with fabulous results. I hope all readers have discovered the brilliant online group called Friends and Fiction, created by

Mary Kay Andrews, Mary Alice Monroe, Kristy Woodson Harvey, Patti Callahan Henry, and Kristin Harmel. Their own books will touch your heart *and* knock your socks off, and every week they interview other writers talking about their newest books. Check it out on Facebook or YouTube. It's a reader's goldmine.

The really lovely Brenda Novak not only writes wonderful books, but also has a monthly book club. Beloved Debbie Macomber also has a book club, and so does glamorous Elin Hilderbrand. We're all so lucky to have their books to read and their suggestions on what else would delight us. Viola Shipman has become a special friend and her heartwarming novels give us hope and good cheer whatever the season. Viola, whose grandson Wade Rouse writes in his grandmother's name, also interviews other writers on social media.

It's been a special pleasure to continue to work with the charming, ingenious Tim Ehrenberg, who performs his magic at Nantucket Book Partners. Mitchell's Book Corner is my hometown bookstore and their staff are dynamite at helping readers get the right book. Thanks to Christina Antonioni, Dick Burns, Wendy Hudson, and way over three blocks away, Suzanne Bennett of Bookworks.

My virtual assistant, Christina Higgins, has been great help in this wildly complicated virtual world. Chris Mason of Novation Media continues to be a technical champion, and Martha Sargent at Computer Solutions is miraculously calm and efficient when I have a fit of computer hysterics.

Tricia Patterson, I just love you. So does Charley. So does Callie. Tricia is a star in so many ways, especially when it comes to putting a twist in a plot or removing an unwanted twist elsewhere.

My blue-eyed, blond-haired, nine-years-younger baby sister, Martha, was diagnosed with breast cancer last spring, and she went through what she calls a "journey"—I would use other words! Now she's growing her hair back and getting a pedicure, and I want to send my special thanks to everyone at Sarah Cannon, the cancer center in Lee's Summit, Missouri. They took such good care of her and even had her laughing. Their optimism and skill were a godsend. Martha's husband, Chuck, and her sons, Andrew and Chase, were stars, and Josh Thayer and David Gillum helped from afar.

It's amazing to me that an entire book can be kept on a small flash drive, but even more amazing is how a nice long telephone conversation can make the world seem like a better place. Jill Hunter Burrill, Deborah and Mark Beale, Sofiya Popova, Dinah Fulton, Mary and John West, Antonia Massie, Gussy Manville, Curlette Anglin, Tanieca Hosang: They say that laughter is the best medicine, and *your* laughter is magic. And facetiming with my grandchildren? OMG! Heart heart heart heart! Special thanks and huge boxes of chips and chocolate go to Ellias, Fabulous, Emmett, Annie, Winnie, and especially my daughter, Sam, and her partner, Tom, who do all the hard work and still make me laugh.

Once again, electronic bouquets of flowers to my Facebook and Instagram friends and to all my readers. I love all of your posts of dogs, cats, grandchildren, children, food, more food, puns, flowers, and generally messy, wonderful lives. Jose Luis Borges said he imagines that Paradise will be a kind of library. May we all meet in Heaven someday and have an eternally glorious book club!

summer
love

1995

That Summer

The Sand Palace Four
Nick Volkov, 22
Ariel Spencer, 22
Wyatt Smith, 22
Sheila Murphy, 22

2020

This Summer

Nick, Francine, and Jade-Marie Volkov
Ariel, Wyatt, and Jason Smith
Sheila Murphy O'Connell and Penny O'Connell

one

That Summer

Nantucket Island was thirty miles out at sea, with no bridge or tunnel connecting it to the mainland. Often gale force winds cut it off from boats or planes, and even on mild summer days, fog could drift around the island, enclosing the small world in a shimmer that made Nantucket seem almost unreal, a fantasy made of salt air, mist, and dreams.

Most summer days were clear, bright, and beautiful. For a century, people had come to the island to enjoy the warm beaches, the sparkling ocean, and easy evenings under the stars, dining at restaurants with top-notch chefs.

The natives and the "washed-ashores" resided on the island year-round. Others came for the summer, filling Nantucket's guesthouses and hotels. The small town of Nantucket had a movie theater, library, amateur theater, classical concerts, and bookstores, all within walking distance from the hotels. A person could step off a ferry onto the cobblestones and walk to their hotel or house. In the 1990s, the super-rich summered on Nantucket, but no one knew who they were, because they didn't want to "stand out," considering it vulgar.

When first built in the seventies, a hotel named the Nantucket Palace towered in fake aristocratic grandeur at the corner of South Beach Street and Easton Street. Every islander knew that "the Nantucket Palace" was a ridiculous name for a hotel on an island settled by Quakers who believed in simplicity, but summer people flocked there because it was close to the shops, the yacht club, and the beaches.

In the nineties, the Palace was sold to an entrepreneur who wanted to make the hotel contemporary and cool. He hired Sharon Waters to deal with the paperwork. Sharon was a prim woman in her thirties who loved nothing more than adding figures on her desktop calculator. She had no problem working at a hotel that was in the middle of a renovation. Sharon had worked for the former owner. Now she was smoothly and happily dealing with the mounds of tedious paperwork for the new owners, who had demolished much of the hotel before being ordered to cease work until every form was signed, submitted, and approved. This fall and winter, the owners would build the new hotel and planned to name it Rockers. Sharon's office was just above the basement with its industrial-size laundry, four single bedrooms for staff, and one bathroom. Sharon was appointed to find tenants to rent the bedrooms in the basement of the one wing of the hotel that remained.

The word was out that there was summer money on Nantucket, and in the late spring, college graduates from near and far swarmed the island, looking for jobs and temporary living quarters. Of the many applicants, Sharon had awarded the rooms to the four people she thought least likely to hold wild parties or destroy them.

First, Ariel Spencer, who came from a good family, had just graduated from a good college, and lived in a pleasant Massachusetts suburb. Ariel had the quiet, sweet manner of a person who knows she's fortunate and wants you to be fortunate, too.

Second: Sheila Murphy. A good Catholic girl with bright red hair, she came from Ohio and had just graduated from Cleveland State University. Pretty but plump, Sheila was so shy Sharon Waters wanted to yell "Boo" at her for the pleasure of seeing her jump, but Sheila had worked as a maid at the Cleveland Renaissance and came with sterling recommendations.

Third: Wyatt Smith. Sharon took one look at him and thought: good guy. He looked reliable. Trustworthy. Sensible. A graduate of the University of Missouri in Columbia, he majored in geology, but he looked more like a runner than a geek. Lanky and tall, with tidy brown hair and nice blue eyes, he'd grown up in a small Missouri town. This summer he had a job at Cabot's Marine, repairing boats, selling parts. He was a quiet young man, respectful of Sharon, and she liked that.

Fourth, and a bit of a gamble, was Nicolas Volkov. With his curly black hair and sleepy amber eyes, he was more handsome than any guy should be, and obviously the kind who would flirt with anyone, probably to keep his skills sharp or maybe he just couldn't help himself. At his interview, he gave Sharon a sexy sleepy-eye look, even though Sharon was clearly in her thirties and not interested. He'd gone to Harvard, of course, and had a job at Fanshaw's, a new, posh men's clothing store run by a snobbish Brit. Nick was a descendant of an ancient aristocratic Russian family, he told Sharon, but they had fallen on hard times. His parents had had to sell their Fabergé Easter egg and some of their jewelry to afford his college tuition, which was why he was working this summer. Sharon gave him the final bedroom.

Ariel got to choose her room first simply because she arrived first. The four basement bedrooms were all dreary, with linoleum floors and small rectangular windows set high in knotty-pine-covered walls, but each had a closet, dresser, desk, chair, bedside table, and a bed that had an unstained mattress and clean sheets.

She'd brought her own sheets, actually, as well as her own pillow and quilt.

Ariel chose the bedroom farthest from the bathroom. Living in a dorm had presented her with more sounds of people vomiting than she'd ever expected to hear. She placed the small fuzzy teddy bear holding out a yellow silk flower on the bed in the room next to hers, hoping that a woman would take that room. Hoping that that woman would become a new friend.

It was the last day of May when Ariel entered her dull little bedroom, set her suitcases on the bed, and began to unpack. Her dresses and blouses were on quilted hangers brought from home. She wanted to look presentable at her job as receptionist at the real estate agency. She placed a large three-ring binder in the very center of her desk. Already it was filled with the beginning of a short story. She planned to write on weekends. She had been accepted into an MFA program at the University of Iowa. She would start this fall.

Someone knocked on her door, and Ariel turned to see a tall, slender, good-looking man standing on the threshold. "You're here early."

"Oh." For a moment, she could only stare. He was so unexpectedly, quietly attractive. She pulled herself together. "You're here early, too." Crossing the room, she held out her hand. "I'm Ariel Spencer."

"Wyatt Smith." Taking her hand in a brief, firm shake, he gave her a lopsided grin. "Looks like you'll have a female neighbor next door. She's marked her territory with a teddy bear."

Ariel blushed, caught out. "*I* put that there. It's not that I don't like men, I do. But they are . . . messier." She wanted to stand very close to Wyatt Smith. He had a double magnetism. Something about him made her feel safe . . . and sexy.

"Not me," Wyatt said. "I'm kind of tidy. Scientists have to be." He squinted his eyes, thinking. "Although I'm going to be working at Cabot's Marine, fixing boats this summer, so I'll probably come back covered in oil."

"You're a scientist, but you'll be working in a boatyard?" If she kept asking him questions, maybe time would freeze them like this so she could gaze at him forever. The more she looked at him, the more she liked him. She had to keep herself from drifting right up next to him.

Another lopsided smile. "My father is Benjamin Smith," Wyatt told her, unable to keep the pride from his voice.

"Okay . . ." Ariel smiled encouragingly.

"He's a scientist. He discovered smithonium. It's the one hundred and fourth element on the periodic table. It's named after him. It's used in building missiles. NASA uses it."

"Wow. Impressive," Ariel said.

"The University of Missouri has named a building after him," Wyatt added.

Ariel blinked. "Wow," she said again.

"Sorry," Wyatt said. "It's just . . . I'm going to work for my father's department and get my PhD."

"But you're here for the summer?"

"My mother pushed me to do this. She thought I needed to experience a completely different life for a while."

"Nantucket is certainly different." Ariel had decided that Wyatt was a sort of awkward American Hugh Grant, with his floppy brown hair and intensity.

"What about you?" Wyatt asked.

"I'll be a receptionist in a real estate office," Ariel told him. Should she invite him into her room? Where would he sit? On the bed? She felt slightly hysterical, in a good way.

"I've got to unpack," Wyatt said. "Let's get together tonight—"
Before he could finish, Ariel said, "Great!"

"—with the other basement dwellers," Wyatt continued. "We'll exchange all the necessary information."

Well, Ariel thought, that was a little dry. *Exchange all the necessary information?*

"I mean," Wyatt continued, "get to know each other." He shook his head. "I have all the social graces of a rock. But . . . I certainly would like to get to know you."

"Me, too." *I could love this man,* she thought, and blushed, and replied, "I mean I'd like to get to know you, too."

They moved to the corridor, smiling at each other.

"Well," Wyatt said.

"Well," Ariel said. "I'd better unpack."

"Me, too."

After Wyatt walked off down the hallway, Ariel quickly returned to her suitcase, in case Wyatt came back. She didn't want him to see her standing there like Cinderella with bluebirds on her wrists.

Even though that was what she felt like.

For the first time in her life.

Stop this! Ariel told herself. *You're going to be wanton for once in your life! You're going to have thousands of lovers. You can't be serious about the first man you see!*

She pulled out a drawer, filled it with ironed tees and a few light sweatshirts. She set a small pile of books on her bedside table. When she was thoroughly unpacked, she zipped her suitcase shut and put it on the shelf in her closet.

There! she thought. That's done. Now what? Would she have time to write?

She heard a series of clunks and peered around her door.

"Oh, dear," a girl whimpered. "I'm sorry. This suitcase is heavy."

A very pretty, plump, and rather amazingly buxom young woman in a sundress covered with butterflies stood at the entrance door with one suitcase next to her and another on the floor, just inside the hallway. It had popped open, displaying a variety of ruffled pastel undies, including lacy bras large enough to hold kittens.

Wyatt stepped out of his room. "Let me help." He went down the corridor and bent over to gather the clothing spilled from the bag.

"Oh, that's awfully nice of you, thank you," the girl cooed.

She had red hair tumbling down around her shoulders and skin as pale as cream. Her eyes were large and green, and they widened when she saw Ariel.

"Oh, thank heavens! Another woman!" She hurried down the hallway and held her hand out to Ariel. "I'm Sheila Murphy."

Ariel smiled. "Hi, Sheila. I'm Ariel Spencer. I left you a little present in your room."

"Really?" Sheila hurried into her room. She squealed and came out holding the teddy bear with the flower. "This is adorable! Thank you! I'm sorry. I didn't bring you anything . . ."

The light shifted and the three looked toward the open door at the entrance.

A tall, broad-shouldered man with pale skin and thick wavy black hair came toward them. A heavy duffel bag hung from one shoulder. He carried an impressive leather suitcase.

His eyes were an unusual and intriguing amber. His teeth were very white when he smiled. "Hello, everyone. I'm Nick Volkov, another winner in the basement room lottery."

Ariel and Sheila drifted down the hall toward him. Wyatt followed. The four shook hands, exchanged names, and sorted out whose room was whose.

"I have to report to work tomorrow," Sheila told them. "I'm a chambermaid at the Rose Hotel." She shrugged. "I guess I should get unpacked."

Nick snorted. "Are you kidding? We're not working today. The sun is out. We ought to hit the beach." He spoke with the confidence of a natural leader, the strongest, handsomest, boldest guy in any room.

"Good idea," Wyatt said.

Sheila glanced nervously at Ariel.

"It's a brilliant idea," Ariel said. "The perfect way to start the summer."

Nick clapped his hands once. "Okay. I'll change and be waiting outside."

Ariel went into her room, surprised that Sheila followed.

Sheila seemed worried. "Are you really going to put on your bathing suit? Now?"

"Of course! I can't wait to get into the water." Ariel took a moment to give Sheila her full attention, which was hard, because all she could think about was Wyatt. "Is something wrong, Sheila?"

Sheila clasped her hands nervously. "You're nice. It's just, I've never swum in the ocean before. And, well, the ocean is a few streets away. Are we going to walk there in our bathing suits?"

"Everyone does," Ariel assured her. "Or, mostly, they bike. Sharon Waters said we can pick up some old bikes from Young's Bicycle Shop to rent for the summer if we want."

"You want to ride a bike in your swimming suit?" Sheila's eyebrows rose.

"Sweetie," Ariel said, "Nantucket isn't like anywhere else. Let's go day by day, okay? Do you have a cover-up? A sarong? No? Okay, I've brought two or three, I'll loan you one."

"Thank you. I apologize for being so lame."

"Go put on your suit, I'll be in with something for you in a minute."

Sheila went into her room, shut the door, and undressed while leaning against the door—just in case the odd little button on the cheap metal doorknob didn't really keep it locked. She hadn't unpacked yet. She had to scurry to her suitcase to paw through it and find her bathing suit. It was a one-piece, with wire supports sewn into the bodice, and it was old, but looked new, because she hadn't gone swimming often. Swimming was what you did when you didn't have to work.

As she struggled into the unforgiving material, she held back tears. She had known it. She had *known* that she'd have to share space with perfect people, as relaxed and secure about their perfection as Nick, Wyatt, and Ariel.

Ariel. *Ariel,* for God's sake! What kind of name was that? It sounded like something out of Shakespeare. It probably *was* out of Shakespeare. And Ariel was absolutely lovely. She had bought a stuffed teddy bear and put it on a pillow for someone she didn't even know. Was she on the island to work for money? When she could afford to buy a teddy bear she wouldn't even keep? It was a small teddy bear, but still . . .

Ariel did seem nice. Sheila was well aware that she had a tendency to be envious and insecure, and that she often, as her mother said, cut off her nose to spite her face. Whatever she thought of Ariel, Sheila knew she needed to be friendly. After all, they were sharing quarters in this dismal basement for the summer. Maybe they would all be friends. She tucked a small camera into her beach bag, along with her wallet and sunblock, even though it was late afternoon.

A light tap on the door made Sheila jump.

She opened the door. "I'm sorry," she said to Ariel. "I didn't realize I had locked it. Oh, what a pretty sarong. Thank you for loaning it to me. I'm kind of nervous about the ocean thing. I grew up in the Midwest and I only swam in swimming pools."

Ariel put her hands on her hips. "Sheila, look at you! You're like the Venus de Milo with red hair. Honestly, I am *jealous*. You're going to drive men crazy."

Sheila blushed. "I'm kind of engaged. To my college boyfriend, Hank." She wrapped the sarong around her, tying it in a knot at her breastbone.

"Thank heavens," Ariel said, laughing.

Before Sheila could reply, one of the men yelled from the hall, "Come on, girls, let's go before the sun sets!"

Ariel took Sheila by the wrist and pulled her out of the room. Wyatt and Nick were at the end of the hall by the door leading to the outside.

"Shouldn't I lock my door?" Sheila asked.

Nick snorted. "Yeah, because someone will want to break into a room in the basement of a half-demolished hotel."

The bike shop was nearby. They rented ancient, dented bikes with baskets and headed down South Beach Street, single file. Nick led, steering with his knees, doing the kind of show-off tricks a teenager would do, every now and then glancing over his shoulder and flashing his movie star smile at the others. Wyatt's old bike creaked along under his comfortingly steady movements. Ariel went next, and behind her, Sheila rode with her hands tense on the handlebars, terrified she'd wreck the bike and herself at any moment.

A long, wide parking lot fronted the beach and the radiant expanse of water spinning from indigo into pale turquoise as it lapped onto the sand. An empty bike rack was waiting there, as if meant for them.

"Wow," Nick said as he slid his bike into the rack. "We've got the beach almost completely to ourselves!"

"Most people are getting ready for dinner," Wyatt said sensibly.

They propped their bikes in the rack, kicked off their shoes, and set their pale, bare feet in the sand. It was toasty warm.

"Aaah," Ariel sighed. "Summer."

"Yeah, summer," Nick agreed.

Sheila couldn't speak. She was overwhelmed by the luxurious golden sand and the sparkling blue water.

"Beautiful, isn't it?" Wyatt said.

"Let's get wet!" Nick said, and he began to run over the sand. The other three joined him.

They ran into the water at the same time. Near the shore, it was shallow and warm, but they kept on moving as the waves splashed up to their knees, then their waists—Sheila screamed at the cold— then their shoulders. Sunlight trembled over the water. It was as if they'd entered another universe, a new reality, where all they had to do was surrender to the embrace of the liquid blue.

Nick and Wyatt ducked under and came up far out, swimming freestyle away into the seemingly endless water. Ariel and Sheila were only a few yards apart.

"Relax," Ariel told Sheila, and fell backward into the water, letting it support her, floating faceup to the sun.

Carefully, Sheila did the same, sighing in pleasure at the coolness of the water on her back and the warmth of the sun on her face. She drifted. It felt like a blessing.

After a while, Ariel flipped over and began to swim a few yards. She returned to shore, shook her hair free of water, and sat down on the sand, her arms around her knees.

Sheila joined her.

"We should have brought towels," Ariel said.

"Next time," Sheila answered, still in a kind of trance.

They sat together, looking out at the men, who were now headed back. It was the time of day and the time of year when the sun remains high in the sky, shining down on the water, making it feel as if *this* was the whole world, the day would never end, they would always be young, and life would always be full of joy.

The men hit the shallows and stood shaking water from their hair, Nick's black as a pirate's, Wyatt's as brown as a seal's.

Ariel said, "How lucky are we to have two good-looking men for the summer? I'll take Wyatt. You can have Nick."

As if, Sheila thought. "I told you, I'm engaged to my college boyfriend."

Ariel laughed. "Then this is your last free summer. Make the most of it! Come on, I mean, flirt a little. Maybe kiss a few guys when you feel like it."

"A *few* guys?" Sheila studied the woman sitting next to her, so slim and cool, the epitome of a Barbie princess doll.

Ariel laughed and stretched out her arms. "Oh, yes, *lots* of men. Sheila, we'll never have this summer again."

The two men came toward them, tall and handsome, water glistening on their chests.

"It doesn't get better than that," Wyatt said, sitting down next to Ariel.

"Wait a minute," Nick said. "I'll get us some snacks." He dashed off toward the parking lot.

The three watched as Nick chatted to two women in a red convertible. Then he climbed into the back, and the car drove off.

"What's he doing?" Sheila asked.

"I wouldn't worry, he'll be back." Wyatt stretched out on the sand, hands behind his head, eyes closed. "This is the life."

Ariel studied Wyatt, taking in his messy brown hair, his handsome face, his tanned torso, his furry chest, his long legs, his funny bony feet. She wanted to touch him so much it hurt.

She glanced down the beach. Only a few steps away were a couple of plastic buckets left behind by children. Ariel put her fingers to her lips in a *sh* motion to Sheila. She rose, scooped sand into both buckets, and dumped the sand on Wyatt's legs.

Wyatt opened his eyes. "What are you doing?"

Ariel laughed, refilled her bucket, and motioned to Sheila to do the same.

Sheila hesitated, but she wanted Ariel to like her. She jumped up and joined in.

In no time at all, they had covered Wyatt up to his chest in sand. "You're acting like children," Wyatt chided, but he didn't move. As they were dumping sand on his shoulders, he said, "Actually, this is relaxing. It feels like . . . like a sand shower." He laughed. "Just don't dump any on my face."

"Oh," Sheila cried, "we would never do that!"

Ariel's eyes met Wyatt's and they both smiled.

"Hey! Look what I've got!"

The red convertible was back in the parking lot and Nick was in the process of climbing out while holding a six-pack of beer and a bag of chips. A striped beach towel hung over his shoulder. He kissed the girl driving right on the mouth. She grinned and drove away.

Nick came down the beach, waving his loot like a conquering hero.

"Beer and chips, baby!"

Wyatt rose from his sand blanket and ran back into the water, dunking his head and rinsing the sand from his hands.

Ariel took the towel from Nick's shoulder, beckoned to Sheila, and together they spread it out on the sand.

"Who's your daddy now?" Nick dropped to the towel and set the beer and chips in front of him.

"How did you do that?" Sheila asked.

"I asked the girls for a ride into town and back. I told them I was with my country mouse cousins who are here swooning at the sight of the ocean, which they've never seen before, and I wanted to supply us all with treats. Sweet girls. I'm taking Paula out for ice cream tomorrow night."

"What a wheeler-dealer you are," Ariel said.

"Be nice, children, and drink your beer," Nick replied.

Wyatt popped the tab on his beer and drank deeply. "You're a king, Nick. This is exactly what I need right now." He drank again.

"Come on, ladies, catch up," Nick said, swigging his own beer.

Ariel winked at Sheila. "Oh, don't worry, we'll catch up."

Sheila wasn't fond of beer, but she was thirsty, so she took a long drink, feeling the cool liquid slide down her throat.

"Nick," Ariel said, "you bought one six-pack, and there are four of us. What are you going to do with the extra two?"

Nick made an obvious sweep of his eyes over Ariel's body. "Why, darlin', we'll all have to share."

Pleasure fluttered over Ariel. Nick was such an obvious flirt, and he was—the perfect word came to her mind—*dashingly* handsome. He was playful. He was fun. Ariel touched her hand to her breast in an imitation of shock. "What? You mean our lips will have to touch the same can you big brawny males will drink from?"

Nick held Ariel's eyes. He was silent for one beat. Two. Three. "Tell you what. Wyatt and I will share one beer, and you and Sheila can share the other. Will that satisfy you?"

"It will," Ariel said. "Nick, you are a gentleman and a scholar."

When the four had swallowed the last drop of beer, Sheila jumped up from the sand, excitement all over her face.

"Look what I brought!" She held up a small throwaway camera. "I'm going to take photos of us. Someday we'll look at them and remember our first day on the island."

A woman with a child walking past overheard them. "Why don't you join your friends and let me take a photo of the four of you?"

"That would be great! Thanks!" Sheila handed her the camera and sat down next to Ariel.

"Lean together, for heaven's sakes," the woman said. "Look happy! Smile!"

The four obeyed, each of them thinking that they'd only just met. They weren't a group yet, and might never be.

The woman snapped several shots, tossed the camera to Sheila, and raced off to catch her child at the water's edge.

"I'll get these developed when the roll is full," Sheila said.

"Cool," Ariel said, just to be nice.

The long low moan of a horn alerted them to the sight of a ferry coming out of the harbor. The group went quiet, watching the large boat cutting smoothly through the water. Several sailboats were farther out, their sails white triangles on the blue. A family raced down the beach past them, the children screaming at the top of their lungs, the parents laughing. The family jumped into the water, dunking one another, splashing one another's faces, and the drops of water in the light of the low summer sun sparkled like sequins.

"I'm hungry," Wyatt said. "I need more than chips."

"Pizza," Nick said. "We can get it on Broad Street and eat it on Easy Street, looking at the harbor."

"Sounds like you've been here before," Ariel said.

"I've been everywhere before," Nick bragged.

"Don't we need to change clothes?" Sheila asked.

Ariel said, "Sweetie, for pizza on a bench, you're overdressed."

They biked from the Jetties beach over to South Beach and stopped at Broad Street, the long strip of pavement leading from the Steamship Authority's docks past the fast-food shops and on up into the expensive end of the street lined with classy restaurants and stores. Nick and Wyatt ordered a pizza each. Ariel and Sheila ordered one to split. They all bought Cokes from a machine and wandered down to the benches on Easy Street.

"I don't think I've ever been this hungry," Sheila said. She didn't want to be unladylike, but she tore into the pizza, savoring the thick cheese, the spicy sauce, the perfect crust.

They sat together, happily munching, watching a small red rowboat bobbing in the water and the duck couple paddling around muttering to each other.

"All right," Nick announced after he'd eaten his last bite. "Time to deal the cards. We're going to share close quarters for three months. Let's get to know each other. I'll start. Remember the kid in elementary school who couldn't sit still and started all the pranks that got us in trouble? That's me. I'm a social animal. When I attended Harvard, I worked nights at the Ritz, and I'm telling you, that is my world. I'm all about making people happy. I'll run six blocks to get someone just the right bagel. I enjoy meeting celebrities and sports stars, but just as much I get a kick from making a grumpy old dowager smile. I'm going to work at Fanshaw's, an upscale men's clothing store where I hope I make a lot of business contacts."

"You sound like fun," Sheila said.

Nick flashed his movie star smile at her. "Honey, I'll give you all the fun you want."

Sheila blushed.

Wyatt intoned slowly, "I'm a scientist. My father is Benjamin Smith, the discoverer of the one hundred and fourth element, smithonium. I'm going to study for my PhD and work for my father at the University of Missouri. My mother insisted I get my head out of a beaker for a while. She has a friend who told me Nantucket is totally different, so I came here to work at Cabot's Marine."

"Cool," Nick said. Like a television host, he directed, "Sheila, take it away."

Sheila was pulling a long strand of cheese off her teeth. Could she be any more gauche?

"Um, I, I'm from Cleveland, Ohio. I just graduated from Cleveland State University. I have a job as a chambermaid at a guesthouse here, the Rose Hotel. I'm going to marry my boyfriend, Hank, when I get back, but I wanted to make some money and have . . . a little adventure before I settled down." She sighed with relief and looked at Ariel.

"Okay, let me think," Ariel said, perfectly comfortable with people who were relative strangers. "I have a job as a receptionist at the Amos Longenecker Real Estate Agency. I'm from Boston, graduated from Emerson, and I'm not sure about my career path.

I want to be a novelist, but I know that doesn't happen without years of work, so I'm determined to enjoy this summer and not think of the future."

"I get you," Nick said.

In the distance, the church clock chimed eight times.

"We have to go home," Wyatt moaned. "I've got to be at my job at eight sharp tomorrow."

"We all need to shower," Sheila said, brushing sand off her arms.

"You mean *together*?" Nick asked, quirking an eyebrow.

"That would certainly be efficient," Wyatt said with a grin.

"Or not," Nick snickered, glancing at Wyatt.

Sheila was horrified. "Not together!"

"Stop it," Ariel said to the men. "Just for that, Sheila and I get the first showers. Separately."

They dumped their paper napkins and pizza boxes in a convenient bin and headed toward the site of the demolished hotel and its one standing wing. From a distance, in the fading light, the building looked almost romantic, like the ruin of a British cathedral.

"Are we going to be treated to the music of power saws and drills?" Ariel asked.

"Not for a while," Nick told her. "I spoke with Sharon Waters. The construction is all tied up in paperwork. Historic District Commission. The sewer and water companies. Stuff like that."

The four gazed at the lawn and the neglected flower garden around the hotel.

"Hard to believe this place was once called the Palace," Ariel said.

Nick put his hands on the waistband of his suit and shook it. Sand rained down his legs.

"I think we should call it the Sand Palace," he said.

"Absolutely!" Ariel agreed, clapping her hands and laughing.

"It's the only time in my life when I'll live in a palace," Sheila said mournfully.

"Oh, Sheila, *hush*," Ariel told her. Taking her hand, she pulled

Sheila toward the doorway. "You're not allowed to be maudlin this summer." She looked over her shoulder at Nick and Wyatt.

"You guys can shower after we have ours," Ariel said.

"Fine," Nick answered. "We'll be in our rooms, digging spy holes into the walls."

Sheila looked alarmed. "But—"

"Sheila, *hush*," Ariel said again, laughing as they hurried toward their rooms.

two

This Summer

The Lighthouse, previously Rockers, and before that the Nantucket Palace, had officially opened at the end of April. On June 10, Jade-Marie Volkov stood at the reception desk, eager for the day to begin. Like all the staff uniforms, hers was a light gray, with her name embroidered in red on the left breast pocket with a small lighthouse beneath it. Jade-Marie's long dark hair was swept back in a messy bun. She wore high-heeled peep-toe pumps and the elegant Chopard watch her father had given her when she turned twenty-one.

Her father, Nick Volkov, owned this hotel, among other properties. He had lived here once, years ago, when he was only twenty-two. Back then, the hotel had been undergoing renovation. Nick and three others had rented four basement rooms while they worked on the island. That summer they had become close, a kind of gang of four. Over the past twenty-five years, they had casually kept in touch with one another, mostly through the medium of what his wife, Francine, called Christmas brag-and-gag letters, but Nick was aware that some summers Sheila and her family went to visit Wyatt and his family or vice versa. Midwestern heat, backyard barbecues, hometown baseball games, the kids sleeping on air mattresses on the floor. They had never once invited Nick and his family. Probably the others thought Nick and Francine were snobs. Probably they were right.

Now Nick had bought and renovated the hotel where the four had met all those years ago, and Nick wanted a reunion with them at *his* place. *He* called it a reunion. His wife called it showing off. In spite of that, Nick had invited the other three, and their spouses and children, to be his guests at the hotel for a week in June.

Jade-Marie's mother, Francine, wasn't thrilled about this. That long ago summer, Francine had met them, had even given a small dinner party for them, but they had never liked her, never welcomed her into their little group. And *they* considered *her* snobbish. Still, she agreed to be here for the week, the wife of the owner, a pleasant presence backlighting Nick. Francine was beautiful, maybe even more so than when she was in her twenties, slight, elegant, with her blond hair bobbed to chin level. Jade-Marie thought her mother was bored, probably. She was such a private person.

Jade-Marie was thrilled about meeting the returning members of the gang. Her father had spoken of them often, his face lighting with pleasure as he talked. As an eternal optimist, her father was unable to sit down and rest, always rushing toward new ideas, new places. He had become wealthy that way. He had unerringly excellent instincts about which place or building was on the verge of huge success. But it wasn't about the money for Nicolas Volkov. It was about making the magic.

Jade-Marie thought she was a perfect mix between her mother's and father's characteristics. She had her father's thick black curly hair, her mother's sleek build, her father's confidence, her mother's caution. She had her father's fondness for all human beings and more than she'd like of her mother's snobbishness. Her aunt Celeste had often and loudly pitied Jade-Marie because her mother was so aloof.

Once, she'd heard Aunt Celeste saying, in French, to Francine that she was setting Jade-Marie up for a lonely life. No siblings. Practically raised by nannies and babysitters. *She will not know how to love!* Aunt Celeste had cried. Francine had answered scornfully that that was better than not knowing how to do anything *but* love.

"My daughter is smart, quick-witted, elegant, and strong. She will have other interests in her life than waiting for a man to marry her and tie her down to one small life."

Jade-Marie had held her breath, pressing her back against the wall outside her mother's room. She'd never heard such positive and slightly weird opinions of herself from her mother before.

Then she heard her mother continue. "Unfortunately, Jade-Marie is too much like her father. She is a dreamer. She thinks she can control her own life. She doesn't understand that life controls her."

Stung, Jade-Marie thought, *Well, then, I will be more like my father! I will make my own dreams come true!* At twenty-two, Jade-Marie's dreams were vague, complicated, and sometimes contradictory. She wanted to help the poor; she wanted to establish her own chain of environmentally ethical spas. She wanted to be considered beautiful, so that men would fall in love with her. She wanted to be a brilliant businesswoman. She wanted to have thousands of lovers until she met the right man. When she really fell in love, she would marry and have several children. She would never put her work before her children and she would never put her children before her work.

She wouldn't be *exactly* like her father. He liked the razzle-dazzle of dealmaking. The next big thing was always just out of reach. Jade-Marie liked the more domestic side of running a hotel, making people feel comfortable and safe. She knew this summer would prove to her—and her father—that she was good enough to run the hotel full-time. Jade-Marie knew she could do it. At the same time, she wondered whether she'd make any good friends or boyfriends on the island.

Jade-Marie had had crushes on boys when she was an adolescent. She had chosen to lose her virginity in college, to a boy she liked, and for a while they'd been a sort of couple. He was two years older. When he graduated, he went back to Nebraska to take an office job with Allstate. He tried to keep his relationship with Jade-Marie alive, but her father wanted her to see the world and be aware of all the possibilities now, while she was young. Last summer, Nick had brought her with him to Nantucket, when he bought the fading hotel and started plans for the restoration.

Jade-Marie had unexpectedly fallen head over heels in love with Nantucket.

She couldn't believe how wonderful the island was. The light! The ocean! The fabulous restaurants and shops! She didn't want to leave Nantucket even to finish college, but her parents insisted.

Her father had led her through the faded glories of the old hotel. He'd shown her the architectural plans for the renovations. He'd asked for her suggestions about chandeliers in the ballroom. Most of the hotel's public rooms had modern flush-mounted ceiling lights with three rows of glass prisms, a clean, almost mathematical look. Jade-Marie had pressed for the empress chandelier with tiers of Swarovski crystals for the ballroom. There would be weddings there, not only conferences, she reminded him. There would be graduation parties, reunions, celebrations. The ballroom needed a touch of romance, of history, even if the rest of the hotel was sleek and minimal.

Her father went with her choice. Jade-Marie had hugged him with tears in her eyes.

When she graduated from college this spring, she skipped the ceremony in order to be on the island for the opening of the hotel. She'd had weeks to familiarize herself with it all, the bistro with its large-screen TVs set into the wall, the offices behind the reception counter, the IT room hiding a humming supercomputer, the sleek, pale-hued guest bedrooms, the velvet lawn set out with tables and chairs and brightened with flowers.

"I'm going to run this hotel someday," she promised.

"Such dreams you have," her mother said, rolling her eyes.

In March, the Lighthouse was completed, with its 400-count Frette linens, luxurious terry-cloth bathrobes, and gorgeous photos of the island's lighthouses on the walls. In April, the hotel opened for Daffodil Weekend. Nick Volkov ordered masses of daffodils from Flowers on Chestnut. The lobby's urns were crowded with fresh daffodils and each guest room had its welcoming vase. Jade-Marie stayed by her father's side as they went through the day, solving problems. The Hudsons had booked a room for two and arrived with their three children. The supply of prosecco for the bistro had not turned up. One of the maids was caught on camera pocketing a batch of custom-made shampoo bottles.

By June, the workings of the hotel were in order. Jade-Marie was head receptionist, friendly and knowledgeable and professional. Beneath the counter, she kept her own laptop open. When she had time, she typed notes to herself about their guests—which ones complained, which ones held noisy drunken parties in their rooms, which ones leaned on the counter to try to flirt with her.

It was Sunday. Today her father's friends would arrive.

Jade-Marie was ready. She knew their names. Knew which rooms she was to give them. She was eager to meet them and she hoped her mother would return from her shopping stroll on Main Street in time to have dinner with them. Since her father had an important meeting with the chamber of commerce, he asked Jade-Marie to tell his friends he'd join them at dinner that night. Jade-Marie knew he didn't want to hang around the reception counter waiting for them to show up. He wanted *them* waiting for *him*. It was not an insignificant favor her father was asking of her. There was a slight sense of discomfort lingering around this reunion, and Jade-Marie had been chosen as the buffer person.

Now, across from her desk, the glass entrance doors slid smoothly open and a family entered.

A father. A mother. And another man, her age. A tall, dark-haired, stormy-faced, wide-shouldered Heathcliff of a man. He had to be Jason.

Jade-Marie's breath caught in her throat. She flushed. She couldn't take her eyes off him.

Jason seemed to sense her fascination. He looked up, saw Jade-Marie staring at him, and smiled.

For a long moment, they were the only two people in the room.

Then his parents surged toward Jade-Marie and the hotel counter. Mr. Smith and Mrs. Smith, the famous *Ariel,* the woman Jade-Marie's parents had admired all those years ago. Jade-Marie quickly took a mental snapshot, so she could review the woman's appearance in her mind later. She was not that tall, only about five-five, with blond hair—professionally lightened, Jade-Marie thought—curling to her shoulders. Bangs over her forehead, always good for hiding wrinkles—Jade-Marie's mother had given her thousands of style suggestions; that was Francine's standard form of conversation with her. Ariel's blond hair was short enough to show off her small turquoise earrings. She wore a sleeveless lavender linen dress and several gold arm bangles. She was seriously beautiful and much too glamorous to go by the name Smith. Wyatt Smith had dark hair, beginning to thin. Well, he was forty-seven. Still Jade-Marie's competitive father would be glad to see that while he still had a full head of hair, the other male from the Sand Palace Four had a bare spot at the crown of his head.

"You *have* to be Jade-Marie," the woman said. "You look exactly like your father."

Before she could answer, her husband spoke. "Hi, Jade-Marie. I'm Wyatt Smith and this is my wife, Ariel. We spent one crazy summer here with your father."

Jade-Marie turned on the professional charm. "Oh, yes, of course! Dad said you were arriving today. I'm so glad to meet you at last!"

Ariel said, "And this is our son, Jason."

Jason stepped forward and held out his hand. "Hello." His grasp was warm and firm.

"Hello." She could stare at him forever. His eyes were a magical gypsy blue with thick black lashes.

Wyatt cleared his throat loudly. Reluctantly, Jade-Marie pulled her hand away. Jason's mouth quirked up in a sideways smile, like a secret message between them.

Flustered, she clicked some keys on the desktop. Any keys at all, while she got herself calmed down. Deep breath, she told herself. *Focus*.

"You and Mrs. Smith have a suite on the third floor, and Jason"—she glanced at him with a professional smile—"you have your own room, also on the third floor, just down the hall. Mr. Volkov has comped your rooms and any food you might have at the hotel. We don't have a full-service restaurant, but we do have a bistro and a light breakfast buffet."

She handed the envelope containing the key cards to each man. Her fingers accidentally touched Jason's. For a moment, they let the touch linger.

Sudden laughter broke their connection. Two women walked in the front door, pulling their rolling suitcases along behind them. Obviously, they were mother and daughter. Both had red hair, creamy skin, and green eyes. Both were beautiful. Well, the mother was attractive, but her daughter was truly ravishing, in a Rita Hayworth way.

"Sheila!" Ariel Smith flew across the lobby to embrace her old friend.

"It's been too long," Sheila said, hugging her friend. She stepped back. "Let me look at you. It's been at least five years since you all came to visit. You look exactly the same. Wonderful."

Ariel Smith laughed. "You look wonderful, too."

Sheila's daughter stood nearby, waiting.

"Good Lord, Penny! Look at you, all grown up!" Ariel Smith kissed Penny's cheek and held Penny away so she could study her. "My goodness, you've become the most gorgeous woman I've ever seen!"

Mrs. O'Connell glowed with pride. "I'm sorry Hank couldn't

make it. He has some high school track competition. I didn't want the boys to come. Can you imagine the chaos? But I knew Penny would love visiting the island."

Mrs. Smith gently touched Penny's face. "When we last saw you, five years ago, you and Jason were such teenagers. Now you're both so . . . adult!"

Jason rolled his eyes and kissed Penny's cheek. "Hey."

"Hey," Penny said back.

"What's going on over here?" Wyatt Smith joined the group. "How's Hank?" he asked Penny.

As the others talked, Jade-Marie fussed around at her computer, getting their room cards ready, pretending it didn't hurt that she wasn't included in their group.

Finally, the exuberant Mrs. O'Connell swooped up to the desk. "Jade-Marie! I'm so happy to see you at last. I confess I've checked out your Instagram and the hotel's website. You're much lovelier in person than on the screen." She tried to reach over to hug Jade-Marie, but when that didn't work, she actually walked around the counter to pull her into a warm embrace. Jade-Marie was slightly embarrassed, but this was one of the fabulous four, so she made nice.

Mrs. O'Connell's daughter, Penny, came up to the counter. "Mom. You're intruding into her professional space. Stop it." Penny rolled her eyes. "Hi, Jade-Marie. Forgive my mother. She can be just a tad overbearing."

Jade-Marie instantly liked Penny. She seemed fun and unpretentious. "My mother can be that way, too," she fake-whispered. Mrs. O'Connell went back around to stand by her daughter. Jade-Marie held out a key card. "Your suite is on the third floor, with two double beds—"

"Oh, no," Mrs. O'Connell objected. "No, we have to have separate bedrooms. Please."

For a moment, Jade-Marie was surprised enough to hesitate. "My father chose the rooms himself. He wanted to give you all the best rooms, the best views."

"That's so thoughtful of Nick and I appreciate it," Mrs. O'Connell said, "but really, we need separate rooms. I have enough trouble sleeping as it is." When Jade-Marie still hesitated, she said, "I'll pay for the extra room."

"No, no," Jade-Marie hurried to respond. "I'm just checking to see what rooms are available on the third floor. Would you like a connecting door?"

"No," Mrs. O'Connell said.

Penny grinned at Jade-Marie. "Mom snores like a hibernating bear."

"I don't!" Mrs. O'Connell protested. "It's just . . . it's just what I prefer." Leaning forward, she spoke in a low voice, as if she didn't want the others to hear. "You see, we have four children, my husband and I, and the younger three are boys. They are absolutely Neolithic. You don't want details. I'm anticipating a week of utter luxury in a room of my own."

"Of course." Jade-Marie searched on the computer and found a room for Penny at the other end of the corridor. It wasn't as large as her mother's room, but it was nice. She gave them each their key cards, tucked into the envelope with special welcome notes from her father.

"My father will be serving drinks in his suite, Room 304, at six o'clock. He has reservations for dinner for everyone at eight o'clock at the yacht club across the street."

Mr. Smith said to Jason, "You see, I told you to bring a tie."

The Smiths and Mrs. O'Connell headed toward the elevator, chatting as they went.

Penny lingered behind, and when the elevator door closed on the four, she came to the front desk and slumped across it.

"Help me," she groaned, her tone ironic.

In a joking, overdone professional way, Jade-Marie asked, "And exactly what may I do for you, Miss O'Connell?"

"For starters, at dinner tonight, don't make me sit near my mother."

Jade-Marie grinned. She knew exactly how Penny felt. "I won't make you sit near *my* mother, either. How about next to Jason?"

Penny snorted. "He's gorgeous, isn't he? He was a sweet little boy when I last saw him. Our families got together several times, but the last time, Jason was off looking at colleges. Now he seems maybe a little, I don't know, *smug*?"

"Yeah, he does seem arrogant. He's probably pissed off that his parents made him come here with a lot of old people."

"Really? Gosh, I'm *excited* to be here. I've heard so much about the hotel and Nantucket."

"Let's get together after this reunion dinner," Jade-Marie suggested. "We can walk down to the harbor."

"I'd love that. And listen, I want to get a summer job. I need to make some money and I want to get away from my family. Does the hotel need anyone? It would be fun to be a receptionist!"

"I don't know. Let me check with Sharon Waters. She's our manager."

"Great!" Penny enclosed Jade-Marie's hand in both of hers. "Thank you!"

three
That Summer

By early June, the four inhabitants of the Sand Palace had developed a routine. They arranged to take the same day off so they could go to the beach together. They rode their rented bikes to the grocery store, returning with milk and food in the baskets. They set up a makeshift kitchen in a large empty storage closet. Sharon Waters had to give permission for the two-ring hot plate they bought, and with unusual generosity, Sharon sent in a small, used hotel room refrigerator that hummed constantly and shuddered as if offended when the door was opened. Ariel found several ragged bath mats with *The Nantucket Palace* embossed in gold on the white fleece. She taped them together to form a thick mat at the front door, so they could scrape the sand off their feet instead of tracking it down the hall and into the bathroom. Still, if they'd all been to the beach, sand rained down from their bathing suits as they trekked to their rooms.

Gradually, the four renters got used to the rhythm and demands of their new summer jobs.

Wyatt worked late at the boatyard most days. He was glad to do it. He liked his boss, Don Cabot. Don was a good guy, an island native with no desire to ever leave Nantucket. Wyatt admired how Don took his time checking out an engine and chatting with his customers, who all seemed to be good friends. Wyatt enjoyed tinkering with machinery, working on one engine for an hour, letting what he called his shallow mind do the work while his deep mind played with similarities or innovative slants on geological research. So many possibilities.

Wyatt liked all his basement friends. Nick was honest, open, up-front about being ambitious, wanting to make lots of money, and Wyatt respected that. Nick wasn't being hypocritical and pretending he wanted to save the world. He was funny, too, and imaginative in a way Wyatt had never learned to be.

As for the women . . . Wyatt wasn't a teenager anymore. He'd never been a romantic. But when he looked at Ariel, even the first time he met her, he experienced an immediate physical reaction. Like a volcano inside him, rumbling, threatening to spill over. As if when he saw her, who he was changed. He'd never felt this before. It was both alarming and comforting, as if all the cells in his body had said: *Here she is, at last.* He wanted to kiss her. He wanted to be with her forever, for God's sake. Impatience was a flaw in a scientist. He knew that. But his body and mind had gone behind his back, so to speak, to combine into a serious crush on a woman way out of his league.

Being a sales clerk at Fanshaw's was a perfect fit for Nick. The clientele was friendly and jovial, often complaining because their wives insisted on a new blazer or a pair of golf pants. Nick understood how clothes should hang on the body, and he wore them well himself. People trusted him. Privately, he was amused to see a distinguished silver-haired man, head of a city bank, purchase a pair of pink trousers embroidered with spouting blue whales. And the women! They entered the store intending to buy a tie or a scalloper's cap for a birthday present for their husbands or fiancés. Nick didn't have to do much more than smile to make them interested in a sweater or button-down shirt, and also a needle-pointed belt and some lizard-skin loafers. He liked talking to the other guys behind the counter, too, and often after work he went out for a drink with them.

Nick liked his roomies as well, but he tended to like pretty much anyone. The girls were gorgeous, but he wasn't here for that. He'd had his share of summer lovin' and he wasn't an adolescent anymore. He was here to work. His heart was filled with ambition, and his whip-smart mind kept him aimed at the best opportunities. He was here to learn how the upper five percent dressed, talked, joked, and treated women. His father was a high school teacher and he certainly didn't make the kind of money Nick was determined to have in his life. Nick wanted to travel, meet people, make people happy. Also, he wanted to make money. Own property. Lots of it. Part of the family lore was about Nick, at five, building rows of skyscrapers instead of sand castles on the beaches where the family vacationed and using small slipper shells as people. And at seven, he'd stolen all the houses, hotels, and money from the Monopoly game and set up his own bizarre real estate fantasy in his room.

He'd never lost that fantasy. But he needed money and experience, and he knew that summertime Nantucket was the place to find it.

The Amos Longenecker Real Estate Agency was located on Main Street, in a prime location, with a bright blue door in the center of two wide glass-paned walls. Much of the glass was covered with listings of houses for sale, but some was left open so that passersby could see the people in the office, typing, phoning, busy as bees. Ariel was given a desk at the very front, which made sense because she was the receptionist, but also because she was so elegantly beautiful she caught the eye. Ariel was happy with the buzz and rush of the office and with the realtors, who sat on her desk to chat. This was almost paradise, so much sunshine, salt air, and laughter.

Ariel hadn't spent much time with her fellow basement dwellers, but she liked them. She felt comfortable with them. Well, except for Wyatt. Just the thought of him made her pulse race in a way it never had with any other guy. Nick was handsome, clever, funny, and wickedly charming, but no current of attraction ran between them. He was ambitious; he had made that clear. Ariel respected that. Sheila, oh dear, Sheila. She was so naïve. If you told Sheila a marble was a pearl, she'd put it in a necklace and wear it. Ariel felt protective of her.

Sheila didn't exactly hate her job. The Rose Hotel was an older building with slanting floors and chipped bathroom tiles. She changed linens, dusted, vacuumed, scrubbed bathrooms, all tasks she'd done before at a large cosmopolitan hotel in Cleveland. There she'd at least had a chance of meeting a guy her age. Only married couples seemed to stay at the Rose, but the tips were good. The owner, Mrs. Reardon, was nice, but frazzled.

It was hard not to envy Ariel, who got to float off to work in some nice dress with her nails painted pale pink. Sheila didn't bother painting her nails. They'd only get ruined in scrubbing bathtubs and sinks. Really, Ariel was nice, in spite of her annoying perfection. As for the guys, the truth was she'd be thrilled to have either of them notice her. Nick was drop-dead gorgeous, and clearly he was a player, but that would be fun, not to get her emotions involved. Wyatt was maybe a little boring? That didn't matter. He was obviously infatuated with Ariel. Too bad Ariel didn't have pigtails, Sheila thought. Wyatt could dunk them into the ink bottle. As soon as she had that thought, she mentally slapped herself in the head. Who did she think she was, Anne of Green Gables? Why was she so old-fashioned? People didn't have ink bottles anymore, or pigtails. Sheila understood that she sometimes preferred reading historical romances because they made her feel more comfortable than this rarified world of Nantucket.

She knew she was, in a way, being unfaithful to her fiancé, Hank, but it was only in her thoughts, and why shouldn't she have a little fun before marriage? She'd never been a brave person, she'd never really gone wild. This summer was her chance.

Sunday morning, they woke to a cloudy sky and a gusty wind. This was the weather the shopkeepers loved, when the summer visitors couldn't enjoy the beach. The Sand Palace Four all had the day off. The guys slept late. Ariel and Sheila did their laundry, tidied their rooms, shampooed their hair, and tried each other's lipsticks. The four had become, if not friends, then comrades of a sort. After the guys rose and showered, they all went to the Downyflake for lunch.

Nick and Wyatt ordered eggs, bacon, sausage, hash browns, and pancakes. Ariel ordered blueberry pancakes and bacon. Sheila ordered the same. The food was delicious. For a while, they ate, groaning with pleasure, too focused to talk about anything. Finally, they sat back in their chairs, asked for another cup of coffee, and relaxed.

"I needed that," Wyatt said. "I got a beer last night at the Muse with Don Cabot. He introduced me to some of his friends, good guys, but when I got home, I realized all I'd had for dinner was two brews and a handful of peanuts."

"Want my bacon?" Ariel offered, holding out her plate.

"Sure. Thanks." Wyatt's hand touched Ariel's when she passed him the plate.

Nick, not one to be outdone, said, "I met Tinsley for drinks at the Club Car."

"Tinsley?" Wyatt asked. "You know someone named *Tinsley*?"

"Tinsley Carnegie," Nick said, arching an eyebrow. "She's rich. I think I'll marry her."

"God," Ariel said. "You are so shallow."

Nick snorted. "You won't be so critical when I buy one of the houses you're selling."

"Oh, please," Ariel retorted. "These houses are beyond your wildest dreams."

"Tell me about them," Sheila pleaded.

"Squash courts," Ariel said. "Indoor swimming pools with mosaic murals. Game rooms with pool tables. Oh, and one house—I've only seen it on the folders—one house has a master bathroom with the sink bowl made of glass etched with flowers. The floor and walls are marble. The bathtub is like a small swimming pool, in the middle of the room, with whirlpool jets and gold-plated fixtures."

"I'd love to see that," Sheila said longingly.

"I would, too," Nick said. "Take us there."

"What?" Ariel shook her head. "I can't do that."

"If these places are so fabulous, why are the owners selling?" Wyatt asked.

Ariel shrugged. "People get bored. They have other houses in Saint-Tropez and Aspen. They have a private jet with a personal pilot. They probably want to try someplace new."

"Are they here this summer?" Nick asked.

"No. The house is for sale. Transactions will be by their lawyers."

Wyatt asked, "So the tub is stand-alone? They must have run the pipes and wiring under the floor. I'd like to see it."

"Dude," Nick said. "You are so weird."

"I'd love to see the house myself," Ariel said. "But I'm only a receptionist. They're not going to give me the keys."

"I'll bet there's some real estate agent you could persuade," Nick said, waggling his eyebrows.

Ariel groaned. "You're disgusting. Plus, you're wrong. Longenecker Real Estate deals with some of the wealthiest people on earth. I live in the basement of the 'Sand Palace.' No way am I getting the keys to the place."

"Please, Ariel," Sheila said sweetly. "We only want to *look at* it. It's probably my only chance to learn how the one percent live."

"You are all asking way too much," Ariel said. "But I'll see what I can do."

———

By her third week, the realtors had learned to trust her. Ariel was cool, blond, classy. She never showed off her cleavage or wore too much perfume. She did her job perfectly. One Wednesday, when the realtors were racing off to attend soirees or show houses, Ariel coolly pocketed the keys for the Monet Lane house, shut down her computer, stepped out into the warm summer afternoon, and locked the office door.

She strolled along Main Street, gazing in the windows, admiring the flowers in the window boxes and the clothes displayed in the small, elegant shops. A dark gray Jeep waited in front of the pharmacy. She and the other three had pooled their money in order to rent the oldest, rustiest, most broken-down Jeep for the summer. The Monet Lane house was far out of town, overlooking Dionis Beach and Nantucket Sound, reachable by a long washboard dirt road. No way could the four of them bike out and back without being noticed. On the island, Jeeps were everywhere. Perfect camouflage.

Nick was driving. Wyatt was sitting shotgun. Ariel eased herself into the backseat next to Sheila. Nick drove them out of the small perfect town, into the wilds of the outer island.

The top was down, so their hair blew back and the sun was high enough to burn their faces. When they hit the dirt road with its roller-coaster ride over the ridges and dips, Sheila shrieked at each bounce. By then no one had to shush her because the landscape all around them was empty of people. Just acres of sand, scraggly bushes, small wildflowers, and more sand.

Who would want to live out here? Ariel wondered. When Nick brought the Jeep to a stop facing an enormous house with a stupendous view, she understood. The house looked out over Nantucket Sound, the water expanding forever, sparkling beneath the sun.

"Monet house," Nick said. "I think they mean Money house."
Sheila laughed appreciatively.

Ariel forced herself to stop gawking. She went to the front door and opened it with the realtor's keys. "Come on. No more than five minutes."

The others hurried in behind her. The house was built of wood, glass, and metal. Everything in it was oversized—the freezer, the sofas, the beds. Wyatt and Nick checked out the media room. Ariel and Sheila inspected the walk-in closets of the main bedroom. One large room held everything a man needed: suits, shoes, jackets, shirts, golf slacks, bathing attire. The wife's clothes and accessories required three separate rooms: clothes, shoes, jewelry. Three-way mirrors hung in each room.

"Feel how soft this is," Ariel said to Sheila, holding out a pashmina. "What do you think it's made out of?"

"Nun's hair," Sheila joked. She turned red and put her hand to her mouth. "I can't believe I said that."

"Don't worry. You're funny," Ariel assured the other girl. She sat down at a mirrored vanity and opened a silk-covered box. "Wow. Look."

A pirate's treasure of loot lay in a scrambled mess. Pearls twined around gold bracelets; diamond rings caught on the post of a diamond earring. Silver, turquoise, emerald, ruby, topaz. Rings, necklaces, bracelets, earrings.

"What a hoard," Sheila said. "Think how much jewelry she has if she can just leave this here."

"It's probably all costume jewelry," Ariel told her. "I've heard that when the rich travel, they have costume jewelry made to look like their real jewelry in case it gets stolen."

Sheila held up a necklace with emerald-cut diamonds sparkling from the heavy gold. "Don't you ever feel envious?"

"Sure, I guess," Ariel replied, walking back to Sheila. "Everyone does. But take a look at yourself in the mirror." Ariel took Sheila by the shoulders and turned her to face the full-length mirror. "How many women would sell their teeth to look like you?"

Sheila forced a smile. "If they sold their teeth, I don't think this bosom would help them."

Ariel laughed, too. "Come on. Let's join the guys."

"What did you think?" Nick asked as they bumped over the gravel drive and onto the dirt road.

Sheila admitted, "I'm in a state of shock. I've worked in some

pricey hotels, but I've never seen such luxury as in that empty
house in the middle of nowhere. It seems . . . wrong. Un-
American."

Nick laughed. "Honey, that house is as American as you can
get."

Ariel patted Sheila's arm. "You don't know anything about their
personal lives. Having all that stuff doesn't necessarily mean
they're happy."

"I suppose." Sheila could never tell them that it had taken all the
courage she possessed to come to this island for the summer, to
see a different part of the world, to see another kind of life, before
she married her college love, Hank. She had known she would
meet wealthy people, but she was seeing homes and places and
people whose lives she couldn't imagine. She would never have a
mansion as a summer home—she would never have a mansion!
But she was determined to have a summer to remember.

"Look," Wyatt said, after Ariel dropped off the keys at the
agency, "let's stop feeling sorry for ourselves. Who needs all that
crap. We're young, the sun's shining, we've got a Jeep for the summer. Let's go out to Great Point. I've heard it's amazing out there."

It was a long, rolling ride to the stretch of sand dividing Nantucket Sound from the Atlantic Ocean. Both sides of the water
were roiling dramatically, surging forward, crashing, and plunging
back. Along the shore, men cast their fishing lines, families lay on
blankets, and dogs wandered around, occasionally chasing a seagull.
The afternoon light glared steadily.

"We need a Frisbee," Wyatt said.

"Next time," Nick told him. He stripped off his polo shirt and
dove into the waves.

Wyatt did the same.

"Come on," Ariel told Sheila. She'd already taken off her shoes.
Now she removed her watch and earrings and piled them on the
back seat. "Let's have a swim."

"It looks cold," Sheila said. "And I'm not wearing a bathing
suit."

"We'll go in with our clothes on," Ariel told her. "The sun will dry us out in minutes."

Without waiting, Ariel raced barefoot down the sand and threw herself into the waves. The cold burned and the water was turbulent, smashing up against her with turquoise slaps. She swam underwater until she had to come up for air. Her eyes stung from the salt water, but she dove back down, kicking her legs and spinning, as the careless, powerful ocean lifted her up, pulled her down. A kind of ecstasy swept through her. This sweet abandon of herself, as a person, as a woman, as a dutiful daughter and ambitious spirit, all that simply vanished, and she was a creature of the sea, a creature captured by the sea. She laughed, taking in water and choking and arrowing up to the surface to cough. Getting her breath back, she floated for a moment, settling down, pulling in deep draughts of air. What had just happened? For a moment, she'd been transformed, body and soul. She had been terrified and euphoric.

"Ariel!" From far away, someone was calling her name.

She twisted into a dog paddle and spun around, searching for the shoreline. She was very far out. She hadn't realized she was so far away from the beach. She waved and began swimming hard back to the shore. After a moment, she realized the tide was ebbing, the currents fighting her every move to go forward. She plunged ahead, and gained several yards. Something black and round reared up in front of her, its dark eyes meeting hers.

"You're a harbor seal!" She yelled with joy and reached out to touch the creature, but it disappeared instantly, and she saw Wyatt swimming toward her. "I'm fine!" she called to Wyatt. "I'm fine! I just met a seal!"

Wyatt continued swimming until he reached her. "Hold on to my neck," he ordered, turning his back to her.

Ariel grabbed his neck, and then his shoulders, and allowed Wyatt to tow her through the water to the beach. For a few moments it seemed they were lovers, as his legs kicked up between her legs, and she felt his body moving and saw his head, his brown hair as slick and gleaming as the seal's. He had rescued her. He had noticed where she was and swum out to her. Ariel wanted to wrap her legs around him, clutching him to her, but when they reached the shallow water, Wyatt stood up. Ariel slipped off his back and stood next to him.

"Thank you, Wyatt," she said. They were both breathless.

"You're welcome." His look was intense when he said, "Wouldn't want to lose *you*."

Ariel met his eyes. "Wouldn't want to be lost." She wanted to hold him, kiss him, crush herself into him, but she couldn't, not here on the beach with people around. "I should give you a reward," she said teasingly.

"Like buying me a beer?" Wyatt suggested.

"Oh, I think you deserve much more than a beer."

Ariel saw his chest heave as his breath caught. She couldn't take her eyes away from him.

"Hey, shark bait," Nick called. "Let's go see the lighthouse."

Wyatt broke the spell, shouting, "On our way!"

Our, Ariel thought. Wyatt had said *our.*

Ariel caught her long hair and sluiced the water out, bending sideways. Her wet sundress clung to her. Sheila saw Nick and Wyatt surveying Ariel's body, her long legs, slim hips, small breasts with nipples hardened from the cold water. Sheila wished she'd gone in, at least for a few minutes.

The four trudged up the sandy path to the small open cabin holding the entrance to the towering lighthouse with its Fresnel lenses. The door to the winding stairs was locked.

"Come around to this side," Sheila called. "I've got my camera. I can get a shot of you all in front of the lighthouse."

"Sheila and her camera," Wyatt said with a sigh, but he joined the others, and then he took a photo of Sheila with Nick and Ariel.

They headed back to the beach, Sheila snapping shots as they went.

Two women, part of a nearby group, waved and invited the

four to join them on their beach blankets, beneath beach umbrellas. They'd anchored the ends of blankets with coolers holding beer, sandwiches, soft drinks. The women, Heidi and Jane, were with two guys, Roger and Bob, and they were working on the island for the summer, too. It was all spontaneous and friendly, everyone laughing, Heidi insisting Sheila use her sunblock and sit under the shade of the beach umbrella. Later, an older man and woman came over to offer them some of the striped bass they'd caught. Nick and the others regretfully passed—they had no way to cook the fish. But Heidi and Jane accepted. They wrapped the fish in sandwich wrapping and stuck them in the ice-filled cooler.

This is how it is for them, Sheila thought, *the wealthy ones. The effortless sharing and acceptance. Easy smiles and laughter.* The more they included her, the more Sheila knew, in her heart, she didn't belong.

A few nights after they'd gone to Great Point, a storm blew up from the northeast. It was sudden, like a cat pouncing, only a slight breeze shivering the trees and then torrents of rain swept sideways by a furious wind. Clouds layered the sky, making it blacker than it had been for weeks. The four had all worked hard that day, and were happily tucked into their beds when a high keening sang through the air. It wasn't in the basement, but it was nearby, as if someone on what remained of the first floor was chanting or singing. It stopped suddenly, then moments later began again. There was no rhythm to it, no sense.

Sheila crept out of bed, wrapping her robe around herself. She stuck her head out into the hall, which was dark. Sharon Waters had commanded them to turn off the one light at the end of the hall whenever possible.

"Sheila?" Ariel was just outside her bedroom. She'd shoved her feet into sandals and wrapped a blanket around her shoulders for comfort. "Can you hear that?"

Wyatt stepped out into the hall wearing a Mizzou tee and boxer shorts. He held a flashlight in his hand. "Someone's crying."

The high whining call rode through the air again.

"It's a ghost," Sheila whispered.

Nick entered the hall, clad in a blue and white striped cotton robe. "What the hell is that?"

"We don't know," Ariel told him.

"I'm scared," Sheila confessed.

"For God's sake," Wyatt swore, "let's go find out what it is."

He headed toward the door that led to the back stairs up to the first floor, what little remained of it. His flashlight wavered here and there.

"This is spooky," Ariel said. "Maybe this hotel does have ghosts."

Wyatt shoved the door open. A dim orange glow from a few ceiling lights illuminated the space.

They were in a hallway with a door that had once led to stairs to the higher floors of the hotel. Those higher floors didn't exist any longer. Plywood was nailed over the doorway, and yellow tape crossed the door warning NO EXIT. They turned left toward the stairs to the shell of the office area of the building. They climbed single file to the first floor where a couple of offices were untouched by the wrecker's ball. Here was Sharon Waters's domain and where the sound was coming from.

"Ariel, Sheila, stand back," Wyatt said. "We'll go in first."

Wyatt thrust the door open, exposing a faintly lit room filled with computers, copiers, desks, and desk chairs.

The other three crowded inside. Nick flicked a switch and an overhead light came on. They could see how the room fronted what had once been the lobby, empty now of furniture or baggage carts.

The keening was louder, and less steady.

"Maybe someone died here," Sheila said.

"Look." Wyatt strode to the other side of the room and pointed to a cracked window overlooking the lawn. Wind would shudder through it, scraping one edge of glass against another. "This is all it is. Nothing more." He held his hand over the crack and the noise stopped.

"You're brilliant, Wyatt!" Ariel ran to him, threw her arms

around his neck, and kissed him. "I thought we were about to be captured by aliens!"

"Find some tape," Nick said. "To cover the crack."

Sheila yanked open the drawer of a desk. A small roll of Scotch tape lay next to pens and paper clips. "I don't think . . ." she said helplessly.

"Here." Nick opened a cabinet filled with supplies, took out a thick roll of silver duct tape and a pair of scissors.

Together Nick and Wyatt taped over the crack, applying it from every possible angle until the keening had completely stopped.

"We'll explain to Sharon in the morning," Wyatt said.

Nick was searching through the desk drawers and cabinets. "You'd think someone would keep a bottle of whiskey here. I could use a drink."

"Nick, are you carrying a golf club?" Wyatt asked.

"It was all I could find," Nick answered. "I wanted to have some protection."

Ariel started laughing. Wyatt and Sheila joined her. Nick folded his arms in exasperation, still holding the golf club in his hand, trying to seem dignified in his striped seersucker robe.

"I'm so glad I provided amusement," Nick huffed. "I'm going back to bed."

Sheila followed, flicking off the overhead light as she went.

Ariel and Wyatt stood in the room, still as statues. Wyatt's flashlight hung loosely in his hand, pointed at the floor, and the room was dim.

"You were brave," Ariel said.

Wyatt laughed. "Not really."

They walked together to the top of the stairs. The flashlight made a golden tunnel down to the basement.

Ariel shivered a little and leaned against his body. They stood quietly, side by side in the darkness, breathing, sensing the rise and fall of the other's chest. It was intimate, and sensual.

"I want to know more about you," Ariel said.

Wyatt said, "I want to kiss you."

Ariel turned her face toward him. His lips met hers carefully, gently, and then they twisted toward each other and Wyatt cupped the back of her head in his hand, and their kiss became stronger, its sweetness deepening, and Ariel moaned.

When Wyatt spoke, his voice was husky. "I want . . . I want to spend time alone with you. I want to kiss you again, and not while standing at the top of the stairs. I want to know you, Ariel." He smoothed her hair away from her cheek. He said, as if praying, "Ariel."

"I want that, too." Ariel was trembling again, and maybe it was from fear but also it was from desire, and joy, and a kind of hope she'd never realized existed.

"We have the whole summer," Wyatt said.

"Yes." *I want more than the summer,* Ariel thought.

"What are you two doing up there?" Nick called.

"Admiring the view," Wyatt answered, laughing.

Wyatt took Ariel's hand and pointed the flashlight down the stairs. They descended carefully, not wanting this moment to end. Wyatt held Ariel's hand until she opened her bedroom door and disappeared, but only for the night.

four
This Summer

Sunday evening, their first night on the island, the five gathered at six o'clock, in Nick's suite, Room 304. It was Nick's wife, Francine, who welcomed them through the door, and Jade-Marie knew her mother was presenting the message her father wanted to convey: Nick was not only wealthy, he was married to the most glamorous woman in the world.

Francine wore wide-legged black silk trousers topped with a sleeveless black silk turtleneck. Four-inch high heels. Blond hair pulled back into a chignon, Lancôme Retro Rouge lipstick. Emerald-cut diamond ear studs. A gold Cartier watch.

Sheila wore a multicolor Johnny Was full-length dress that was too young for her but still worked, and dangling multicolored earrings. Between the day she'd ordered the dress from a catalog and tonight, Sheila had gained a few pounds. The dress was tight. When she moved, she bulged like a butterfly struggling to emerge from its cocoon.

Penny wore a green sundress that set off her coloring and an odd gold necklace with a small crown dangling from the chains. It looked silly, and Penny knew that, but she didn't care. Last Christmas, her three brothers had pooled their money to buy this necklace for her, because she was "the princess" to them. Over the years, her brothers had used the term angrily—"The princess always gets her way!" But now they were teenagers, impressed with their college graduate sister, and they remembered all the times she had covered up for something idiotic they'd done, and all the times she'd stuck up for them in a fight with their parents, and now they all completely and faithfully adored her. Penny considered it her most valuable possession.

Ariel, the always beautiful Ariel, was sleek in a little cream dress and pearls. Wyatt wore a suit and tie, and looked uncomfortable in them, always tugging at the shirt collar. Still, Jade-Marie thought, he was a handsome man.

Jason wore khakis, a polo shirt, and a blue blazer. His thick black hair fell over his forehead, and his black eyelashes made his blue eyes flash. He was tall, and Jade-Marie was glad. She was tall, too.

Francine assured everyone her husband would be there soon. He was on an important business call. Jade-Marie didn't miss the looks that shot between Mr. Smith and his wife. She glared at the Smiths. Jason grinned at Jade-Marie and rolled his eyes.

A waiter appeared with a tray of drinks: white wine, water, and vodka martinis. The group began to mingle and Jade-Marie let out an anxious breath. She wanted to like these people who had been her father's companions so very long ago, and she wanted them to like her. She really wanted Jason to like her.

"Francine, we're so tremendously happy to see you again," Sheila gushed, enclosing Francine's hand in both of hers. "And finally, our daughters can meet." Sheila beckoned to Penny to come stand next to her.

Francine murmured something in French to Jade-Marie, who came to stand next to Penny.

"Don't they look beautiful together?" Sheila pressed her hands to her breast. "Oh, Ariel, we were this lovely when we were their age, weren't we?"

"I suppose," Ariel answered. "It certainly caused us a lot of trouble."

"Really?" Penny's face lit up. "Tell!"

Sheila frowned at Ariel. "We don't need to discuss this now, or ever."

Jason and his father joined the group. "Are we already talking about that summer?"

Before anyone could answer, a door opened and Nick entered the room. He was still movie-star handsome. The silver glinting in his dark hair only made him more striking. His presence stopped the conversations. Everyone turned to look at him. He held out his hands in welcome.

"Nick!" Ariel called.

"My friends!" He went from person to person, hugging the men as hard as he hugged the women. "I'm so happy to see you all. How are your rooms? Are they big enough? Do you have everything you need?"

"It's fine," Wyatt answered.

"Fine?" Ariel laughed. "Our rooms are paradise, Nick. Thank you!"

Wyatt caught the look Ariel shot him. He had promised not to be sour. It would look as if he thought he was somehow less successful than Nick.

"I want to congratulate you, Nick. The Lighthouse really is first-class." Wyatt held out his hand.

Nick grabbed Wyatt's hand and pulled him into another tight hug. "It's a dream come true to see you here, Wyatt. God, you haven't aged a day."

Wyatt thought Nick was a phony, but the compliment pleased him. "Happy to see you, too. And this is not the only hotel you own, right?"

"Right," Nick said. "Even better, my daughter, Jade-Marie, the young light of my life, is going into the biz, too. She's the head receptionist this summer."

"But not for this week," Jade-Marie said. "This is a once-in-a-lifetime reunion. I don't want to miss a thing."

"Nick!" Sheila thrust herself forward between Ariel and Wyatt, tugging her daughter by the wrist. "Nick, I want you to meet my daughter, Penny!"

Nick responded by hugging Sheila and kissing her cheek. With a smile for Penny, he said, "Look at you two beauties. Penny, you look just like your mother."

Over the years, Penny had learned to take the remark gracefully. If she demurred, she knew her mother would go into some kind of *oh, no, I've gotten fat* nattering, which would mean everyone else had to tell Sheila she wasn't fat, and she wasn't, really.

To Penny's surprise, Sheila said, "Darling Nick, you're sweet, but I've changed. That's what a daughter and three sons will do to a person."

Francine dutifully remarked, "Sheila, you're gorgeous. Now come, everyone, let's have a drink before we go to dinner."

Nick stepped forward and lifted a glass of champagne from the waiter's tray.

"The rooms are different from our rooms in the Sand Palace, aren't they?" Nick prompted. "Jason, Penny, I assume your parents have told you about that summer."

"Maybe not everything," Sheila whispered to Ariel.

Penny spoke up. "Yes, Mom told me you all went to beach parties and danced on the sand by the light of the moon."

Ariel nodded. "That's right. It was so romantic."

Sheila said, "That was the summer I ate snails."

"Mom, *ugh*," Penny said.

Jade-Marie hastened to add, "In France, they're called *escargot*. They're served in the shell, simmered in a delicious wine broth, and they're a delicacy."

Nick said, "Our demolished hotel had been called the 'Nantucket Palace,' so we called it the 'Sand Palace.'"

"Right," Ariel agreed. "We called ourselves the 'Sand Palace Four.'"

Francine broke into the conversation. "And I eventually became part of the group, even though I never had occasion to stay at the Sand Palace."

"You were too good for the Sand Palace," Sheila said, with a touch of resentment in her voice.

"We biked all over the island," Wyatt said. "Seeing the moors, the ponds, the bluffs, and so on. Quite enlightening."

Ariel rolled her eyes at her stuffy husband. "What you mean to say is, we had so much fun!"

"I have pictures!" Sheila announced, her eyes bright with excitement. She opened her purse. "I've arranged them chronologically. I'll pass them around. Look! Our first day and our first time together at the beach."

The group crowded around, leaning over one another's shoulders, searching for a glimpse of the four of them at the Jetties beach.

"Mom," Jason said. "You look so young!"

"We *were* so young," Ariel told her son.

Wyatt fastened his eyes on his son's face. "We were your age."

"We all had such dreams," Ariel said.

"I remember!" Nick turned to Wyatt. "Hey, man, do you have a new element named after you yet?"

Wyatt's smile was more of a grimace. "No, and I don't expect to. My father's in his seventies and officially retired, but he's still head of our lab, comes in every day, assigns projects. Our work involves geology, more specifically the minerals in caves, and the research takes years. Jason will be the next Smith to name a new element."

"But only if he decides to remain in that field," Ariel was quick to add.

Jason said nothing.

Sheila quickly changed the subject. "Ariel, how is your writing going?"

"Sheila, how sweet of you to remember." Ariel's smile was genuine. "I've written some short stories that have been printed in university quarterlies, and actually one was just bought by an online magazine."

"Cool," Sheila said.

"So no novel yet, but I still have my hopes. When I was first married, I had no time for writing, really. Jason came along, we bought a house . . ."

"Faculty wives have certain responsibilities," Wyatt added.

"True," Ariel agreed, smiling at her husband. "I attended and even hosted many university occasions. Still, once Jason was in college, I managed to go to some writers' conferences. I write an occasional column for a local newspaper. And I do intend to begin a novel. But it's a huge time commitment." A shadow passed over her face. Ariel lifted her chin. "And, Sheila, what about you?"

"Oh, you know me," Sheila said. "I've got my gorgeous Penny and my three athletic boys, not to mention Hank. I basically cook and do laundry. The truth is, I love it this way."

"You're a lucky woman." Nick held out his arms. "This is *my* dream come true, having all of you here tonight. Penny, Jason, and Jade-Marie, I know you might be somewhat bored this week while the rest of us reminisce. On the other hand, you might be jealous . . . and you might learn something! Seldom have four people had so much fun."

Wyatt said, "Hear, hear!"

"After dinner, the Sand Palace Four will share dessert and our best memories in the privacy of this room. You young ones will be free to go off and enjoy the rest of the evening however you want."

Jade-Marie, who wore her long lustrous dark hair down, shook her head. "Don't worry, Dad. We'll be out making memories of our own." She stared directly at Jason with a *come on, I dare you* smile that sent dopamine racing through his body.

"We're all having dinner in the Governor's Room at the yacht club. I believe"—he glanced at his Rolex—"we should be going there now. So, freshen up, and my beautiful wife, Francine, and my gorgeous daughter, Jade-Marie, and I will lead the way. We'll see you in the lobby in five."

With that, he left the room.

"Oh," Sheila said. "That was abrupt."

"That was Nick," Ariel reminded her. "He always liked to keep everyone off balance."

The party filed out of the room and gradually regrouped in the lobby where the three Volkovs, father, mother, and daughter, greeted them and escorted them to the yacht club.

In the private dining room, a long table extended with a snow-white tablecloth, glittering crystal, and place cards. Nick Volkov, real estate tycoon and owner of the hotel, was at the head of the table, with Ariel on his right and Sheila's daughter, Penny, on his left. Sheila was in the middle, with Wyatt across from her. Jason sat next to Sheila, facing Jade-Marie. Francine was on his other side, at the foot of the table.

When the party had settled in, Nick summoned a waiter, who carried a silver tray with eight glasses. Another waiter brought a standing ice bucket with a bottle of Veuve Clicquot. The waiters filled the champagne glasses at each place, and Nick rose to speak.

"Just a brief history of what brings us together. In 1995, Jeff Mourton put his creaky old excuse for a hotel on the market. It was called, ironically, although I'm not sure Jeff had the brains to be ironic, *the Palace*."

Wyatt and Ariel groaned.

"Maybe call a hotel in Miami a palace," Nick continued, "but not on Nantucket. Big surprise, it tanked. Spencer Warren bought it and transformed it into *Rockers,* an equally inappropriate name. Nantucket is, basically, sand. Herman Melville called it 'a mere hillock, an elbow of sand; all beach, without a background.'"

"Woo-hoo!" Sheila cried. "Scholar!"

Nick continued, "But reality never bothered Spencer Warren. That summer, he had lawyers and architects working to get permits to transform the building into a nineties rock oasis. The basement of the building was left untouched, and the four of us rented what had once been the staff quarters. We all had just graduated from college. We were beginning our real lives!" He was aware that waitstaff had entered the room. "Now here we are, to celebrate!"

The waiters set out the starters of bluefish pâté and delicately salted bread. The diners became polite and formal. They chatted about favorite specialties at favorite restaurants, celebrity gossip, nothing serious or political. For a while it was all very pleasant. By the time the entrées had been served, the glasses had been refilled for the second or third time, and the group was relaxing, loosening up. The room became warmer. The artificial light in the room was low. Candles lit the long table, flickering as words floated past on breath, and people's faces were flushed and beautiful, almost otherworldly. Jason thought it was like seeing the parents as they had been when they were young.

Nick, at the head of the table, was being gallant to Penny, who was lovely and fresh and sweet. Ariel and Sheila chatted amiably, laughing now and then, like the old friends they were. Jason's father engaged Jade-Marie in conversation.

Francine leaned close to talk with Jason. She was from France, so for a while they spoke French, but Jason made so many hilarious mistakes they had to revert to English. Francine told Jason that this summer she was flying to Paris and driving down to Saint-Tropez with one of her friends. They would stay for two months, while Nick was involved with his "little hotel project."

"He always has to have a *project,* this one," Francine disclosed. "He does not know how to relax. To simply *be.* He's always trying to surpass a goal, conquer a challenge, win a prize."

Jason took a sip of wine. He glanced across the table. Jade-Marie was talking with Sheila, not looking Jason's way.

"Tell me about Jade-Marie," he said.

"What can I say?" Francine shrugged elegantly. "Look at her. She's beautiful. She's intelligent. I do not think she is a spontaneous, careless girl. She adores her papa. She'll be working at this hotel all summer, and who knows? Maybe this will be her vocation. Certainly, the island is full of natural beauty, and much of the population is cultured and cosmopolitan."

Jason asked, "Is she engaged? Or . . . with someone?"

"Oh, my darling, no. She is only twenty-two. She's only finished college. She needs to explore the world." Francine lowered her voice. "But do not be fooled. Jade-Marie is a very smart girl. Very smart. If she wishes, she will one day run this hotel, and then own it."

Jade-Marie overheard her mother and turned away from Sheila. "Are you talking about me, Maman?"

Francine smiled. "But of course! I have no other topic of conversation."

Wyatt joined in with Francine and Jade-Marie, which allowed Jason to study Jade-Marie while she wasn't aware. The waiters had quietly brought more wine and Jason could tell he'd had enough to destabilize his common sense. Jade-Marie's cheeks were flaming, and Jason guessed she, too, was well into a happy hour.

Sheila interrupted his thoughts. "Tell me about your father and mother," she burbled. "The flawless Ariel and the brilliant Wyatt. Are they happy?"

Before Jason could answer, Sheila continued.

"Oh, Sheila!" She slapped one hand with the other, playfully reprimanding herself. "Don't ask such a silly question! Of course, his parents are happy. They are Ariel and Wyatt! And my, you are such a beautiful son for them. Yes, they are fortunate."

Jason noticed that from across the table, Penny was watching her mother carefully.

"I think you're even more fortunate," Jason said. "You have a gorgeous daughter." He caught Jade-Marie's sharp glance. She was listening to him. His heart caught as their eyes met. He wrenched his attention away.

Sheila was talking. "She is lovely, isn't she? You're right. Also, I have three sons!" Sheila brightened, as if she had just realized the fact.

"Tell me about them," Jason said.

It was the perfect question. Sheila almost floated off her chair with pleasure. As she described each son, Jason glanced across the table. Penny was smiling gratefully at him. Jade-Marie's eyes were fastened on him now, captivating him. Jason could almost touch the current of attraction Jade-Marie was sending his way. For a moment, he ached with desire.

Sheila gripped Jason's arm, forcing his attention back to her. "But Sean, he's my baby, and already he's becoming a man. Sean means 'God is gracious,' you know, and God was gracious giving him to me, ten years after my first child."

Jason frowned at the intensity of Sheila's unexpected grip.

Penny leaned across the table. "Mom. Drink some water."

Laughter broke out at the top of the table. Everyone looked at Nick, who explained, "Ariel and I were remembering the party out at Cisco Beach, where we did shots of tequila and danced in the light of the full moon."

"Awww," Penny said. "What a wonderful image."

Ariel cut in. "Yes, but when we finally left, Nick got into the old Jeep and said, 'I can't find the ignition.' And Wyatt said, 'That's because you're in the backseat.'"

The parents howled with laughter.

"Yeah, and remember the night—"

With fluid grace, Jade-Marie rose. "I think it's time for dessert. That means we young ones are set free to roam the island. If it's all right, I'll lead the way."

Her announcement set off a flurry of people pushing chairs back, parents hugging children as if they were setting off on an adventure, and at last, Jade-Marie going through the door of the private dining room and down the stairs. Jason gestured for Penny to follow Jade-Marie, and he went behind.

"Alone, at last," Nick quipped, rubbing his hands together. "Now we can talk."

Ariel spoke first. "Francine, what I want to know is what *you've* been doing all these years."

Francine looked very pleased to be included. "Ariel, thank you. I know my husband is the bright red cardinal and I am the small wren in the background. But my father owns several hotels, mostly in Europe now. I sit on many of the boards. I attend many meetings—"

Nick broke in. "Yes, and to be clear all the family meetings are held someplace like Monaco or Martinique."

"True," Francine said, with a smug smile at her husband. "My husband knows because he joins me at these meetings. My personal interest is in art. I help my family obtain art for the walls of their most prized hotels. Here at the Lighthouse, for example. And hotels in Bermuda, Saint-Tropez, and Jackson Hole. Possessing an art collection adds to their reputation and appeal."

Sheila cut in. "Will Jade-Marie be a hotelier like Nick or will she work with your family?"

"Ahh." Francine responded with glowing pleasure. "That is the thing, Sheila. Jade-Marie will have both. She knows about hotels, and she knows about art, and she knows about money. What about Penny?"

Sheila sat back in her chair, as if she'd been pushed. She'd never liked Francine, and she knew very well that was because she was jealous of the Frenchwoman, who had remained pencil thin over the years, while Sheila had, if only slightly, ballooned. Sheila felt that Francine's question was some kind of attack on her, because Penny hadn't yet discovered her calling. But Sheila admitted to herself that she was the one who had asked about Jade-Marie, so this was only fair.

"I don't think Penny knows what she wants to do. It's possible she'll want to be like me, marry someone she loves, have lots of children, and enjoy family life."

"I agree with Francine," Wyatt said. "When you do important work, your child should follow in your footsteps."

"I didn't actually say that, Wyatt," Francine said sweetly.

Ariel spoke up. "And here we are, everyone, staying at a hotel Nick owns, with our beloved children, twenty-five years after our meeting at the Sand Palace. I propose a toast!"

She had transformed the mood of the room. Everyone toasted,

and Sheila, her cheeks rosy with champagne, said giddily, "Let's talk about our weddings! Francine, were you married in Paris?"

While the parents discussed their pasts, their children discussed what to do with the warm summer evening.

"Let's go to the Brant Point lighthouse," Jade-Marie suggested. "It's a short walk from here."

Jason shrugged. "Sure."

"What a good idea!" Penny said, smiling up at Jason as if it had been his idea.

As they went out the door of the club, a man their age was coming in.

"Hey, Jade-Marie!" He was very tall, with black hair and dark eyes. He wore Nantucket red shorts with an untucked striped shirt. "Nice to see you again."

Jade-Marie said, "Hey, Liam! Are you here for the summer?"

"Off and on. I'm going to sail every hour I can find."

Jade-Marie smiled. "Liam Miller, sailing addict, meet my friends, Penny O'Connell and Jason Smith."

Liam offered his hand to Jason. Liam's hand was hard and calloused. Jason watched Liam take Penny's hand and almost laughed out loud at Penny's expression. She seemed innocent, naïve. If she ever met a rock star, she'd explode.

Liam said, "I'm off for a sail now. Why don't you all come with me?"

"At *night?*" Penny almost squeaked.

"Yes, at night! Look at that moon. It will light the way." Liam waved a hand at the sky, which was only now, at ten o'clock, losing the last of the sunlight.

"I'd love to!" Jade-Marie said.

Penny shrank back, just a little. "I don't know . . ."

Jason said, "Come on, Penny. You'll be fine."

"You will, I promise," Jade-Marie said, putting a warm hand on Penny's arm.

"Do you know how to sail?" Penny asked.

"I do," Jade-Marie said.

Liam stepped close to Penny. "Penny, if we capsize, I promise I'll save you."

"Okay," she agreed, looking starstruck, "if you say so."

"I say so," Liam said. "In fact, I promise." He took her hand and kissed it.

Jade-Marie shot a glance at Jason. They smiled, knowing they were having the same thought.

"This way, then." Liam kept hold of Penny's hand and headed down the side of the yacht club and onto the brick sidewalk to the boardwalk to the harbor. The club launch waited by the ramp and the club driver reached out a hand to help them on.

"Oh, I'm wearing heels," Penny said, drawing back.

"Take them off, Penny," Jade-Marie suggested sweetly. She glanced over at Jason with another smile, as if she felt she and Jason were some kind of team.

I'd like that a lot, Jason thought.

"Here, Penny, lean on me, you'll be fine," Liam said.

Once they were all on board and seated, everyone wearing a life jacket, the launch driver steered them between yachts tied to moorings to Liam's sailboat. It was a trim boat decked out with teak, and when Liam raised the mainsail, it skipped sweetly over the water, blown by the easy night breeze.

Liam deftly steered his boat between the others in the harbor, where the lights from the boats' cabins cast blurry reflections in the water. Bits of music flashed through the air. When they reached Nantucket Sound, fewer boats were in sight.

"The water looks black now," Penny noticed. She leaned over the side, gripping the hull tightly.

"Well, the sky is dark, so the water is reflecting the sky," Jade-Marie said sensibly.

Jason didn't mention it, but out here on the sound, the wind swept the waves along more swiftly. The waves made a slapping noise as they hit the hull. The boat rocked, not dangerously, but slanting back and forth enough to make it feel like a funhouse ride in the dark.

"There are probably all sorts of creatures swimming beneath us," Penny whispered, as if to keep the creatures from hearing her.

"There certainly are," Liam agreed. "Seals, sea bass, and even bluefish."

"And sharks, too," Jason said.

"Don't be mean," Jade-Marie told him.

"Oh, I can handle it," Penny told Jade-Marie. "I have three brothers at home."

"Where are you from?" Liam asked.

"Cleveland, Ohio. We're on the shore of Lake Erie, so I have been sailing, but not at night. And my brothers have Jet Skis, and Dad has a motorboat so they can water-ski."

"Do you water-ski, Penny?" Jade-Marie asked.

"I *can*. It's not my favorite thing."

"What's your favorite thing?" Liam asked her.

Penny smiled up at the tall sailor. "I don't know. I don't think I've discovered it quite yet." She stared up at Liam, as if Liam might be it.

Penny may not be naïve, after all, Jason thought.

For a while, no one spoke. They settled into the rhythm and music of the waves.

Jason broke the silence. "I live in Columbia, Missouri. My parents have a place on the Lake of the Ozarks. We've got a couple of boats. One of them is my mom's pontoon boat that we take out on hot summer days so we can dive in the water, cool off, and then eat a steak hot from our grill."

"Do you sail?" Liam asked.

Jason shrugged. "Not really. I have friends with sailboats, but we don't have one. Your boat is awesome."

Liam nodded. "Thanks."

"Look at the moon," Jade-Marie said.

The silver moon, not quite full, tilted drunkenly on its side.

Stars speckled the sky. In the distance, a large car ferry was making its way toward the island, like a castle moving on the sea.

For a while, they went along in silence, each person, finally even Penny, relaxing into the softness of the air, the rhythmic rocking of the boat. The Great Point lighthouse flared at them every few seconds, and when they were only a hundred yards or so from the coast, Liam dropped the sail and the anchor. It was warm, very dark, like a dream.

Liam broke the silence. "Missouri, you said. Why there?"

Jason spoke without enthusiasm. "My dad's an important scientist and professor at the University of Missouri in Columbia. His father, my grandfather, discovered an unknown mineral in a cave and had an element named after him."

"And what about you?" Jade-Marie asked.

"I like the area fine," Jason said. "But I'd like to live somewhere different for a while." After a moment, he looked at Jade-Marie. "I like this, now."

"I know how you feel!" Penny exclaimed. "I love my family and my friends, but I want to go places, see new things, have some adventures."

"What was your major in college?" Liam asked.

Penny answered with enthusiasm. "Technology. I seem to have a knack for it. It's like my brothers got all the athletic genes and I got all the tech genes. Probably that's because to be a techie, you have to sit still and focus. My brothers really can't do that. They like to play sports, throw balls, knock things over."

"Wow, Penny," Jade-Marie said. "If you're good in information technology, you can live anywhere."

"I suppose that's true, although my parents are really hoping I'll stay in Cleveland." Penny sighed.

"You ought to travel now, while you're young," Jade-Marie said. "Or you could live someplace like Boston. You'd have an IT job in a snap. Then you could take weekend trips to nearby cities like New York or Montreal. Or even to Nantucket."

"Or," Liam said, "you could meet a new friend with a sailboat who could take you down the entire East Coast. Spend warm summer nights on the boat, sleeping under the stars." He looked right at Penny as he spoke.

Penny's heart did a backflip. She was glad it was dark so no one could see her blush. She looked right back at Liam and said, "You make it sound so easy. I mean, leaving my home. My family would be hurt."

Jade-Marie chimed in. "Hey, they'll have to get over it. You're an adult. You have your own interests and talents. Your parents have three other children, right?"

"Jade-Marie's right. You're lucky," Jason said. "Your parents have other kids. I'm an only child, and my dad is so passionate about his research, he thinks it's the single most important thing in the world. He almost hit me when I said I wanted to think about doing something different. We're headed for a major argument after this week."

Jade-Marie said eagerly, "Because you want to stay on Nantucket for a while, right?"

"I'm not sure," Jason said, meeting her eyes. "This is the first day I've been here."

"I saw some of the island last year when I came with Dad," Jade-Marie said. "That's when I met you at the party at the yacht club, Liam. I didn't have a chance to learn about your work."

"I work for my family's company, Zephron. Our family is based in Florida, but we've got a house here," Liam said. "I guess, over the years, I've seen a lot of the island."

"Will you show us around tomorrow?" Jade-Marie asked.

"I'd like that," Liam said, looking at Penny. "But now we should be heading back."

The group was quiet as they sailed into the harbor. Jade-Marie and Jason lay on the deck, gazing up at the stars. Penny sat with her elbows back on the rail, looking at the stars, and at Liam.

When they were just inside the harbor, Penny said, "What is Zephron, Liam?"

"It's a company that makes wind turbines. My job's involved with, no surprise, turbines in the ocean."

"That sounds awesome," Jason said. "Good for you."

"Boring for me, actually. The paperwork is ridiculous. Our company has to have approval from the Bureau of Ocean Energy Management, which is part of the Department of the Interior. Right now, we're trying to get approval to put up a wind farm twelve miles off Nantucket and twelve miles off the Vineyard."

Jade-Marie said, "Wow."

"We've got lots of resistance. Lots of hate. Fishermen say we'll keep the fish away, birders say we'll kill birds. And yet, it's a source of green energy, and we need wind farms."

"Does that mean sometimes you're in a suit and tie?" Penny asked, almost licking her lips.

"It does. But I get away as often as possible. I sail by myself for a week or two. I go down to the Caribbean and crew on racing boats." He paused and stared at Penny. "Now and then, I take a friend with me."

Penny said, "That must be so fun."

"It can be," Liam told her.

The boat slipped into the harbor. Liam found his mooring and dropped his painter over it, then took his phone from his pocket and signaled the launch. When it came, Jason helped the women step off Liam's boat and onto the launch, and he followed.

"Where are you sleeping?" Penny asked Liam.

"On my boat, of course. I'll be rocked like a baby in a cradle." He gave Penny a daring look. "Want to join me?"

"Oh, I couldn't. I mean, my mother would be upset if she knew . . ." Penny took a deep breath and squared her shoulders. "But maybe another night."

"I'll count on it," Liam said.

They said their goodbyes and walked back to the hotel. Jason had a woman on each side. Penny was babbling about the warm night, the zillions of stars, the salty air, and she knew she was

really talking so the other two wouldn't tease her for liking Liam
so quickly and completely.

Jason and Jade-Marie weren't thinking about Penny. They wer-
en't really thinking at all. They were touching. They were holding
hands.

five
That Summer

Sheila was well aware that her job as chambermaid at the Rose Hotel was less cool than Ariel's as a receptionist at the real estate agency. After all, Sheila was scrubbing toilets, changing stained sheets, emptying overflowing waste baskets, and gathering up empty bottles, cans, and candy wrappers. But she was also smoothing fresh, sweetly scented sheets over beds with beveled walnut headboards carved with lovebirds and flowers. She was putting out fresh rose-shaped soaps and shampoos and clever small kits of sewing necessities. She was peeking, accidentally, of course, at what young women carried in their vanity bags. Joy or Chanel No. 5 perfume. Face cream, hand cream, body cream. Eyelash curlers, mascara, eyeliner, and expensive lipsticks in sunset colors that begged to be tried on . . . so she did try them on. They did wonders for her pale skin, and felt like silk on her mouth. She blotted her lips, carefully tucking the tissue into her apron pocket, before she left the room.

Mrs. Reardon, the owner of the small hotel, could be fierce if Sheila did something wrong, but in general she was sweet, and occasionally daffy. The overabundance of roses in the curtains, carpets, vases, linens, and dishes was eye-popping and almost disturbing.

"You do have a lot of roses around," Sheila said during her second week, when she felt more comfortable with her older, plumper boss.

"Ah, well, you see, I'm not as daft as I am clever," Mrs. Reardon said. "No one ever forgets this place. You'll hear newlyweds squealing with laughter over the rose shower curtains, and isn't that lovely? I've given them something to make them smile and talk about in years to come. I don't need a brochure."

It was happy people who came to stay at the Rose, and they were well-off and generous, too. They tipped lavishly, especially the newlyweds, so much so that after three weeks, Sheila took the ferry to Hyannis and bought herself a new dress and lipsticks at the mall.

On Sundays and some especially alluring late afternoons, Sheila went out with her three friends to beach parties. The guys carried six-packs of beer in their bike panniers. Sheila and Ariel took crackers and cheese. Somewhere among the crowd was a table set up in the sand with a keg weighing down one end and Styrofoam buckets of ice holding beer and Cokes and a variety of snacks on paper plates. It was kind of what Sheila imagined heaven would be like, with all newcomers welcome, easily joining the group, swimming, flirting, laughing, and drinking. Often a guy with a guitar found a perch on a bit of driftwood and sang lusty sea shanties. People, girls mostly, danced to his music, swaying their hips, the sun turning their high-held beer bottles into glowing lanterns. Women wore short shorts and T-shirts, or a man's unbuttoned shirt over a bikini, and lots of bangles jingling on tanned arms, long hair flying as they danced in the sea breeze. At the top of the dune, where the sand became a dirt road, piles of sneakers and flip-flops were abandoned. Everyone went barefoot in the sand, still warm from the summer day.

During that magic season, there was sunlight until after nine o'clock, and soon the moon and stars flashed their reflections onto the sea, and someone set up a portable radio or CD player, and they milled around with one another, laughing and whooping like schoolchildren at recess. Some went off to sit on the beach and have long, confessional conversations. The dancing got personal. People paired up and kissed while they slow-danced. Often a woman would go home with a guy, and just as often a couple didn't bother to leave the beach but walked down to the privacy of a convenient dune. Sheila had offers, but she refused. She had promised Hank she would stay true to him, and she had meant that when she said it. But Nantucket was so . . . seductive. As if desire were carried in the air.

Tall, handsome Nick was always surrounded by swarms of girls. His pale skin was charmingly sunburned and he had one of those Hollywood smiles that made your heart stop just to see it. He never brought a woman back to the Sand Palace, but he often didn't return home until morning, when he'd shower and dress for work. Sheila admitted to herself that she was slightly in awe of Nick, but that wasn't the same as being in love. Sometimes he'd wrap an arm around her shoulders, pull her against him, kiss the top of her head, but they were only chums. Someone like him would never love someone like her.

One sultry evening when the sticky heat of summer made Sheila's shorts and tee cling to her, someone set up a boom box playing a soft rock station. A big, football-player kind of guy lumbered over to where Sheila stood chatting with some girls from the Midwest.

"Hey," he said.

Sheila looked up at him. Cute. Maybe even sweet. His right eyebrow was sliced in the middle by a scar.

"Hi," Sheila said.

"Are you Irish?" he asked. "I mean, red hair."

Sheila's friends made cooing, chuckling noises like pigeons and watched, amused.

"I'm not," Sheila told him. "But my mother's parents were from Ireland."

"I want to go there," he said.

"I'd like to do that, too." Sheila held out her hand. "I'm Sheila."

He took her hand in his catcher's mitt of a hand. "Robin."

Sheila grinned. "Robin?"

"I know, right? Parents. I usually say Rob. But something about you." He didn't seem to like long sentences.

"Where are you from, Rob?" It hurt Sheila's neck to look up at him.

"Pittsburgh. Let's dance." He pulled her against him, as Sheila glanced around, looking for somewhere to set her beer.

"I've got it," one of the Midwestern girls said, slipping the bottle from Sheila's grasp.

Rob wasn't much of a dancer, and it was difficult on sand. Her head came to his chest. He pulled her closer. Sheila moved back, wanting to put some space between them, but his hand on her waist was as strong as an iron bar. She was locked against him as they swayed.

"You're pretty," Rob said.

"Thanks." Sheila leaned her head back as far as she could, trying to see his face. "Rob, you're kind of crushing me."

"Sorry," Rob said, but he pressed himself tighter against her.

He slid his hand down, forcing his pelvis against hers, and his erection strained between their soft cotton clothing. Sheila panicked enough to forget the languorousness of the summer evening as she began to try to figure out how to get away from him. On nights like this, the music never stopped, and Rob's version of dancing was rubbing himself against her.

"Rob, I'm not comfortable." She tried to pull away.

He kept her clasped to him.

"Rob, let go or I'll yell," she said, loudly enough for others around them to notice, if they could hear anything above the music and the chatter.

He held her tighter.

I'll knee him in the groin, Sheila thought. She'd never done that before, but the only other thing she could think to do was to scratch his face with her car keys—she'd learned that sometime in high school—but she didn't have her car keys with her. She didn't want to make a scene. They were in a crowd, so he couldn't actually rape her, but the way he was rocking his pelvis against her was disgusting, and when she looked at his face and saw how glazed his eyes were, it was creepy, almost frightening.

"Please, Rob, let me go," Sheila said, more loudly.

And then Nick was there, shoving Rob away from Sheila so hard all three of them stumbled in the sand.

"She asked you to let her go," Nick said.

"Who the hell are you?" Rob yelled. "I don't know you." He tried to shove Nick aside.

Sheila was aware a crowd had gathered around them to watch. She was secretly thrilled that two men were fighting because of her.

"Get lost," Nick said.

"I'll get you lost," Rob said, and swung his hand.

All Nick had to do was to step back. Rob fell over, facedown, in the sand.

People laughed. Nick took Sheila's hand. "Come on." He pulled her away from Rob, who was struggling to rise.

"Thank you, Nick," Sheila said, both pleased and embarrassed.

"No problem," Nick replied. "The guy's an asshole. Stay away from him." He stopped at the edge of the crowd and looked down at Sheila. "You okay?"

"I'm fine."

Girls surrounded Sheila, asking if she was okay, and Sheila knew what they really wanted to know was who Nick was. Nick wandered away toward the beer table.

"Is that your brother?" one girl asked hopefully.

"Yeah, kind of," Sheila said. She never could understand why Nick rescued her. He hardly noticed her when they were at the Sand Palace. He never tried to kiss her or even joke with her about being alone together. She knew he wasn't romantically interested in her, but at least they were becoming friends, and she'd never really had a man friend before.

———

Sometimes, Ariel or Nick would be invited by someone they worked with at the real estate agency or Fanshaw's to a party at a summer person's house and all four of them would go. Maybe they'd have to listen to a brief fundraising speech, but the food and wine were always what Nick called top-notch. If they were lucky, it rained, and then the party was in the house. Sheila got to gaze at fine oil paintings, weird sculptures, furniture covered in silk, tables covered in silver-framed pictures of laughing families on the beach, or on their yacht, or the tennis court. Almost always, the guests at these parties were older and gave Sheila and the others a fake dismissive smile as they sauntered past. Sheila didn't mind. She felt as if she were in an extremely exclusive museum, at a onetime-only showing.

Once Wyatt approached her when they were in someone's game room. Ping-pong table, pool table, a table set with marble chess pieces, a sofa in front of a screen with video games.

Sheila was leaning against the pool table, sipping her cocktail.

"What do you think?" Wyatt asked.

"I have no words," Sheila said.

"And they're here only two weeks of the year."

"I can't imagine living in a place like this."

"You never know," Wyatt said. "You're pretty. You could snag a rich guy."

"*Snag* a rich guy? Because I'm pretty? Wow, thanks for such a charming thought!" Sheila's face flamed.

She started to walk off, but Wyatt caught her arm. "I didn't mean to insult you."

Sheila yanked her arm away and walked down a hallway until she found a bathroom. She went inside, locked the door, and sat on the edge of the bathtub. Pulling a pristine white washcloth off the rack, she held it against her face, ashamed. Maybe Wyatt didn't mean to insult her, but he did.

Someone knocked on the door. Sheila held her breath.

"Sheila? It's Ariel. Let me in."

Oh, no. Ariel had seen Sheila walk away, biting her lips to keep from crying. Sheila knew that if she didn't let Ariel in, the whole insulting scene would seem even worse than it was. When she rose and opened the door, Ariel quickly entered, shutting it immediately. They sat side by side on the edge of the tub.

"Wyatt told me he was a jerk."

"Wyatt told you?" Sheila's heart plummeted. How humiliating that he and Ariel had talked about her.

"Sheila, get over yourself. Guys are idiots. I'm surprised he didn't say you'd catch a guy because you have big boobs."

"It's so easy for you, isn't it?" Sheila said scornfully.

Ariel took a moment. "It's easier because I don't have big boobs, I guess. I wish I did."

Sheila was shocked. She didn't think Ariel was teasing her. "I can't believe you'd wish for anything but to be yourself."

"You'd be surprised," Ariel replied softly.

"What?" Sheila was curious. "What could you possibly want?"

"Truthfully? I'd like to be a writer, but there are so many good writers out there, it's nearly impossible to get published." She looked down at her hands. "Anyway, that's me. What do *you* want to be?"

"Just something normal," Sheila said. "A wife. A mother. I'll marry Hank. We'll have a nice house and several kids."

"Really." Ariel slid down to the floor, facing Sheila. "That's all you want for your entire life? Don't you want some excitement, some crazy fling, something special, just this summer?"

Sheila couldn't meet Ariel's eyes when she admitted softly, "I don't want to lose Hank. He's all I have."

"Sheila! Don't be such a coward. You don't have to tell Hank or anyone what you do this summer. This is your life. Probably the only time you have left to be wild, to make some delicious memories for the rest of your life."

"I suppose . . ." Sheila bit the end of a fingernail. Someone like Ariel couldn't understand.

At that moment, a guy pounded on the door. "What are you doing in there, making out?"

Ariel rolled her eyes. "Hang on!" She stood, held out her hand, and pulled Sheila up. "You know, Sheila, you have gorgeous eyes. You need to use mascara and eyeliner. And your lipstick is the wrong color for you. We'll experiment the next rainy day."

"That's so nice of you," Sheila said.

Ariel kept hold of Sheila's hand. "Listen, I need you to know. I was jealous when I saw Wyatt talking to you at the pool table."

Sheila was astonished. "Jealous of me?"

"I really like Wyatt. I mean I *really* like him."

"We've been here about three weeks and you're already in love with Wyatt?" Sheila asked.

"I was in love with him the moment I saw him," Ariel said.

"Okay, yeah, it is starting to look like you two are a couple."

"Let's keep it that way, okay?" Ariel asked, smiling, but her eyes were serious.

"Of course," Sheila agreed. She wanted to laugh and tell someone that the goddess Ariel thought Sheila was any kind of threat.

The two girls walked out of the bathroom together. The game room was crowded and noisy.

Wyatt came up to them. "Sheila, if I offended you, I apologize."

Sheila forced a smile. "I overreacted. No problem."

Nick emerged from the mob. "I think we should leave. It's getting kind of out of control."

He led the way, cutting a path through couples kissing, guys hooting with laughter, past a bar crowded with empty glasses and, at the far end, several people rolling up dollar bills and snorting white powder. Outside, the air was warm and humid and quiet. They hurried to the old rented Jeep and drove away. Boys in the front seat, girls in the back. Quickly the lights of the party house disappeared behind them.

Wyatt yawned. "What time is it? I'm beat and I've got to work tomorrow."

"It's only one-thirty," Nick told him. He steered off the Belgium block lane onto the main road leading to town. "Hey, did you see that blonde I was talking to?"

"I did," Ariel yelled from the backseat. "She's out of your league, Nick. Too old, too rich."

"She's smart," Nick yelled back. "She's got an MBA from the Wharton School. I could be the vision man, she could be the money, and someone like Sharon Waters could be the tent peg."

"You'd be the tent peg," Wyatt joked.

"Seriously. I like business. I want to do something big. Own a chain of hotels, malls, whatever, and Carey speaks my language."

Ariel laughed. "Ugh, Nick, you're going to *date* her?"

Nick snapped, "Ariel, it is possible to be *friends* with a woman."

"Oh, excuuuuse me," Ariel said, still laughing.

They arrived at the Sand Palace and spilled out of the Jeep. Security lights were on at the three exits and in Sharon Waters's office. All four had a key to the basement door, and Nick, at the head of the group, unlocked the door and, with an Edwardian flourish, bowed the other three inside before entering and locking the door behind him.

By now it was routine for the guys to wait until the girls had used the bathroom. As Sheila and Ariel padded in their flip-flops back down the hall to their rooms, Ariel said to Sheila, "Tomorrow we'll have a makeup session in my room. I think we should work on your eyebrows, too."

Two days later, Sheila knocked on the door of the Grandiflora Room—all the Rose Hotel's rooms were named after specific roses. No one answered, so she unlocked the door and stepped inside, carrying the fresh pile of sheets and towels in her arms.

The queen-size bed had been slept in. The covers were mussed. Other than that, the room was surprisingly tidy. Most guests dropped clothes, books, maps, and lotions on the chairs and desk and bedside tables.

Sheila pulled back the heavy dark green duvet.

"Hello," a man said, steam clouding around him as he walked out from the bathroom. He had only a towel wrapped around his hips. His chest glistened with drops of water.

Sheila bit back a shriek of surprise. "Oh, I'm so sorry, I didn't realize you were in the bathroom. I did knock." She was pleased with her composure and silently grateful that after living in a dorm, she'd gotten used to seeing men in various states of undress. Although this felt different, here in the private room.

The man smiled. He was broad-shouldered, in his late thirties, with ebony black hair and eyes and a four o'clock beard that accentuated his strong jawline. He looked a little bit like Satan, if Satan were a Calvin Klein model.

"Don't be sorry. It's great to have such a beautiful sight to start the day."

Sheila knew she was blushing. "I'll, I'll, um, I'll just come back." She retrieved the new pile of linens and went toward the door.

"Could I invite you for coffee?" he asked.

Sheila was speechless.

He shook his head. "Forgive me. Of course, you can't stop working to join me for coffee. Maybe I could buy you a drink tonight?" When she hesitated, he added, "My name is Frank Johnson. I work for a New York ad agency. I'll give you the phone number. You can call them and check me out."

"I'm not sure . . ." She thought of Hank, steady, reliable Hank.

"I know it's odd that I'm at this little B&B. It was the only reservation I could get at the last minute. I'll be here off and on during the summer."

Sheila's heart thumped with delight and terror. "I don't finish here until five o'clock."

"Well, then. Could you meet me at the Brant Point Grill at five-thirty?"

That would give her time to hurry home, shower, and change. "Yes. Yes, I could. That would be . . . lovely."

"I'll see you then."

six

This Summer

Monday morning, Jade-Marie woke early. She threw back her covers, sat up, put her feet over the side of the bed, and suddenly remembered that because of her father's weeklong reunion, she had today off. She fell back into bed, pulled up the sheet, and snuggled into her pillow.

Her father had asked her to "entertain" Penny and Jason, as if he thought she could take them for ice cream at Children's Beach. She hadn't expected to feel so twitterpated over Jason, and she was irritated by the power of her feelings. *She'd* fallen in love at first sight, but she couldn't get a clear read on Jason. He'd held her hand as they walked back from Liam's boat last night, but when they'd entered the lobby, he'd released her hand and said good night to her and Penny. Then he'd walked off to the elevator alone.

Still, Jade-Marie's father wanted her to be hospitable and she would be. Jade-Marie rose from bed, crossed the room, and drew back the curtain. She didn't have a water view, but the charming eccentric mansions along Hulbert Avenue seemed to glow beneath a clear blue sky. It would be hot today. She'd take Penny and Jason to the beach. For now, she showered, slipped on a pretty sundress and lip balm, and headed downstairs.

In the morning, until eleven, the bar was turned into a serve-yourself Continental breakfast room with a long buffet table holding urns of hot coffee, hot tea, hot water, and all the accessories. Bagels and muffins were piled on plates, and bananas and apples were in a bowl. They'd had a toast-it-yourself area, but guests had complained that it was hard to use, or they had burned their fingers, so that part was eliminated.

Jade-Marie found two four-tops pushed together. Penny and her mother sat there, along with Jade-Marie's father and the Smiths.

"Good morning!" she said, with a great big smile, and a chorus of greetings answered her.

Jade-Marie made herself a cup of coffee and sat down at the table. Her mother wasn't there, preferring breakfast in her room before preparing herself to meet the day. Francine was so unlike Jade-Marie's father that Jade-Marie couldn't imagine why they got married. Although, there was that saying, opposites attract. Nick was sociable, energetic, realistic. Francine was laid-back, dreamy, and not shy but private. Jade-Marie's mother was as gorgeous as Jade-Marie's father, but Francine wasn't as bold. Nick wanted to be charming. Francine didn't care. She preferred listening to opera while doing needlepoint, and going to the ballet. She did have close friends in New York, and she participated in several charities.

Francine had not been happy about the week with Nick's old buddies. The family had been home in their apartment in the city when Jade-Marie overheard them arguing.

"You expect me to spend a week of my life with people who never liked me," Francine had said, her voice murderously low.

"Be fair, Francine. You weren't exactly friendly."

"For twenty-five years, your only contact has been their brag-and-gag Christmas letters."

"Which are addressed to me *and* you."

"They visited each other's homes during the summer. Never once did they invite us."

"First of all, you wouldn't have wanted to go. True?"

Sullenly, Francine admitted, "True."

"Second, oh, the hell with the numbers. You're right, Francine. I *want* to show off. It would mean a lot to me to have the people who knew me when I was living in the basement of a destroyed building see me now, the owner of a first-class hotel."

Jade-Marie hadn't heard how they resolved the issue, but last night at drinks and dinner, her mother had been elegantly beautiful, and pleasant to everyone. She hoped her mother wasn't hiding away this morning.

Across the table, spreading cream cheese on her bagel, sat Sheila. She was sparkling in the light of day, her auburn hair contrasting with her pale creamy skin, her green eyes bright, and all of her so voluptuous. She wore white clam-diggers and a loose, pale green tunic that dipped in a V at her chest, so that some of her large cushiony bosom was revealed.

Penny was sipping coffee, and she gave Jade-Marie a brilliant smile.

"This island is so beautiful," Penny said.

"It is. You haven't been here before, have you, Penny?" Jade-Marie asked.

"No. My mother raves about it. I've always wanted to see it."

"I have the day off, and it's gorgeous weather. I thought I'd take you and Jason out for a day at Surfside Beach."

"Is it far away?" Penny asked. "I mean, do they have cell service out there? I mean, in case I get a phone call?"

"Oh, are you expecting a phone call?" Jade-Marie asked, widening her eyes in pretend innocence.

Penny blushed. "Maybe."

"Good morning, everyone." Francine appeared, wearing a classic Lilly Pulitzer dress, short and sleeveless. Her blond hair was held back by a headband. Small diamond ear studs. Effortlessly elegant. She slid gracefully onto the empty chair next to Ariel.

"Mom, want me to bring you some breakfast?" Jade-Marie asked.

"Just coffee, darling. Lovely, thank you." Francine smiled at Ariel. "Do you swim?"

Ariel smiled. "I do. I was like a mermaid the summer we all lived together." She glanced around the table. "We were all part fish. Tanned as horses, well, except for you, Sheila. You were our little palomino, so pale."

"More like a little Appaloosa," Sheila said, "covered in freckles and spots!"

Francine asked, "What did you do if it rained on your day off?"

Ariel shrugged her shoulders. "We all slept in. That was a real luxury. Often, I wrote. Small scenes, ideas for a short story." A sadness swept over her face. "Haven't got far with that yet."

Sheila added, "And we'd get all our weekly chores done. Laundry. The minimum of cleaning. Men and bathrooms . . . I have three sons, and I don't think men are capable of something as challenging as *aiming*."

"Mom," Penny said reprovingly.

Wyatt cut in. "Come on, Sheila, you know what our living conditions were like that summer. A pit in the basement. Four bedrooms, one grungy bath. A corridor filled with mold and mildew."

Nick nodded. "Right. It's a wonder we didn't all get some obscure lung disease."

"What's the basement like now?" Sheila asked.

"Completely different," Nick said. "If you want, we can take a tour after breakfast."

"Or not," Francine said bluntly. "It is, after all, a *basement*."

"That's right. You came to our hovel for dinner one night," Sheila said, cocking her head to the side like a little bird. "But then you . . . disappeared?"

Francine said, "I had to go to Paris for a wedding."

Jade-Marie tuned out. She fixed her gaze on Jason. She lowered her eyelids slightly, holding her gaze, willing him to meet her eyes.

And Jason looked at Jade-Marie. For a few moments, they

couldn't tear their eyes away from each other. Jade-Marie couldn't breathe. He felt it, too, she knew. The sensation was electric, overpowering. She gave him the slightest smile.

Penny sat quietly at the table, watching the others talk, picking at her croissant, thinking her own private thoughts.

Penny had gone through her life knowing she was pretty. Not beautiful, and not to everyone's taste, but sweet and soft. She hadn't chosen to have the bosom she carried around and she couldn't imagine why women would purposefully have breast implants, because large breasts were, frankly, such a bother. She couldn't wear a dress because if it fit over her breasts, it was too large in the hips. She couldn't walk anywhere without men and boys and women, too, gawking at her chest. She wasn't a *freak*. She was just well endowed, and she did everything she could to camouflage her round bosom. As she grew older, she understood that her breasts weren't necessarily a curse. That she could use them to her advantage.

Penny and Sheila both looked like the romanticized Victorian Irish washerwoman with ruffles on her low-cut blouse and rosy cheeks and lips. Penny's mother's hair had faded from red to auburn, but they still had the same green eyes and hourglass body.

When the invitation to stay at the hotel in Nantucket arrived, Sheila was thrilled. She took them both shopping for summer dresses and had their hair styled at an expensive salon. She had their suitcases out and packed and repacked them days before the trip.

Penny couldn't blame her mother. Sheila's three sons were like baboons, thudding through the house, shoving everything that even looked like food into their mouths, making fart jokes, knocking lamps and tables over while wrestling one another. Their father was a big, muscular man. He was the athletic coach at the high school, and well aware of the rampant energy his sons carried, never mind the rampaging hormones. He kept his three sons involved in sports, running extra laps, lifting weights, and racing

one another in swimming contests, so that when they were con-
fined to the house, they were exhausted and their monkey energy
muted.

Penny knew her mother loved her sons, even though sometimes
when Brodie broke a window playing baseball in the house or
when Patrick knocked over the pot of stew while he was ladling
some into his mouth, Sheila sat down and cried. For a while, then,
the boys would be contrite. They'd slump into the family room
and murder one another on video games.

But now, here on Nantucket, sipping coffee at a long table with
the others, Penny watched as her mother and Ariel talked about
all boys' clumsy, muddled, crazy adolescence, and Ariel and Sheila
were laughing about it until tears fell down their cheeks. They
were trying to explain it to Francine, but Francine almost cringed,
looking horrified. Francine was elegant, Penny decided. Ariel was
elegant, too. But Penny's mother? She was pretty, but never elegant. Penny slumped at the table.

Of course, Jason and Jade-Marie were already, so soon, crushing on each other.

Jade-Marie. What a stupid name.

A movement caught Penny's eye. Swiveling in her chair, she
watched as Liam Miller strode to the counter, asking a question
that made the desk clerk smile.

Liam turned, saw Penny in the bistro, and waved as he approached the table.

Penny gave a little wave back. Was he waving at her or at all of
them?

He pulled out a chair and swiveled it around so that he could sit
next to Penny. "May I join you?"

"Sure," Penny said, her heart jumping madly inside.

Penny smiled at Liam. He smiled at her. For a moment, no one
else was in the room.

Then Jade-Marie leaned forward. "Hey, everyone, I'd like you
to meet Liam Miller. He's the guy who took us sailing last night.
Dad, I think you know his dad from the yacht club."

"Of course," Nick said. "Hi, Liam. Welcome."

Sheila leaned forward with a smile. "Do you live here, Liam?"

"I wish. No, I work for a company based in Florida, and I travel a lot. But my parents have a summer home here, and I come as often as possible."

"Would you like some coffee?" Jade-Marie asked. "Or a cinnamon roll? Help yourself."

Penny wished she'd thought to offer him coffee.

"Thanks," Liam said. "I'm good." He turned to Penny. "Do you all have a plan for today?"

"Oh," Penny said, "didn't you suggest showing us the island today? I mean, last night . . ."

"Yes, I'd love to, if you're up for it," Liam said.

Jason asked, "You're not sailing today?"

Liam shook his head. "It's dead calm out there and supposed to be all day."

"Good!" Jade-Marie said. "Here's what we'll do. We can use the hotel bikes, and pick up some lunch somewhere, and bike out to Surfside and swim, and—"

Nick interrupted. "It might be too cold to swim."

"We'll see." Jade-Marie rose. "I'm going to get ready. Meet you back here in ten minutes."

Penny thought that this was one of those perfect days a person gets only three or four times in their lives. The four of them sped along on the bike paths, sometimes single file, sometimes two by two. The day was bright with sun, but not too hot, and there was not enough wind to push or pull them in any direction. She'd been nervous for the first few minutes, knowing she could ride a bike but unable to remember when she last had actually been on one. Going over the cobblestones on Main Street was a challenge, and she knew any biker would look ridiculous being wobbled around, but once back on a street or a bike path, she relaxed. It felt good to move, to be in charge of her bike. The island streamed past, now forest, now open moorland, now a flash of blue water, now hedges of arbor vitae and picket fences smothered in clematis. She wore her most daring bikini with a long T-shirt over it. She felt like she was in a movie of herself.

Their first stop was Surfside. They parked their bikes and ran down the dune to the beach where the ocean lazily waltzed against the shore. It was early in the season, and the beach wasn't crowded. They all went into the water, screaming, laughing, daring one another to swim farther out, but the water still held on to its winter cold, and they didn't stay in for long.

"Your lips are blue!" Liam said, and wrapped her towel around her and pulled her to him, skin to skin, rubbing her back to warm her up.

Penny thought she might faint with joy.

The four sat on the beach, enjoying the slow sweep of the waves, letting the sun dry them enough that they felt warm. Then they trudged back up the dune—the sand was so deep it was impossible to do anything but trudge. They got back on their bikes and followed Liam to the bike path to 'Sconset, the small village at the eastern side of the island. They bought sandwiches from Claudette's and sat on the wooden deck eating them, sharing insignificant information with one another. Jade-Marie didn't like pickles, Penny didn't care for onions in her sandwich, Jason had once eaten a potato chip sandwich, Liam would eat anything. Afterward, they strolled along a lane lined with small, ancient, rose-smothered fishing cottages. They went single file along the bluff path leading between millionaires' mansions and the wild greenery overlooking the steep cliff falling down to the ocean.

They returned to town, bought ice cream cones in the small Sconset Market, and trailed down the steep road to the beach. Here, on the east end of the island, the waves splashed against the shore. The sun shone down on the sprays of water, turning the drops into prisms and crystals. Farther down the beach, a man threw a Frisbee for his yellow Labrador, small children wielded toy spades and buckets as they built sand castles, and an older couple walked hand in hand at the water's edge. No one was swimming. They sat in the warm sand, and the sun fell on their shoulders and the rainbows in the spray mesmerized them. Overhead, gulls flew and dipped and called. Far down the beach, tiny sandpipers raced around on their long, thin legs, pecking at the sand in frantic movements.

"They look like me when I can't find my car keys," Penny said, and they all laughed.

"Want to swim?" Jason asked.

"Maybe not. The currents here are strong," Liam told them. "A person can get carried out to sea."

Penny stood up. "I'm going to search for seashells."

"I'll join you," Liam said.

"I want to walk around this funny little village," Jade-Marie said. "It's called Codfish Park. Guess why."

"It's where the codfish come for recreational purposes?" Jason said.

"Ooh, really bad joke. Just for that, you have to walk with me." Jade-Marie reached out her hand to Jason's.

The two couples waved and went their separate ways.

Penny and Liam walked west, along the lonely stretch of shore speckled with angel's wings, moon shells, slipper shells, and spiraling whelk shells, each shell striped or spotted differently.

"It's like snowflakes," Penny murmured.

"Right," Liam agreed. "An infinity of patterns."

Penny smiled at him. He was tall, and walking on the upper side of the slightly slanting beach, so he seemed even taller. He was an unusual sort of person, at least to her. She'd never thought that a man who owned such a beautiful sailboat might walk and talk with her. Might say something so, well, poetic.

Liam stopped to bend down and pick up a smooth shard of pale lavender sea glass. He handed it to Penny. "For you."

They stopped walking as she took the glass and tilted it this way and that, so that it became pale or dark with the light and shadows. This was a moment she would always remember, Penny thought, this pause on the sand with the waves dancing at their feet like the frilled skirts of ballerinas and the sun circling the two of them as if they were enclosed in a spotlight, and this tall man's large hand touching hers as he gave her the glass that had been shaped by the sea.

"It's beautiful," Penny said.

"You're beautiful," Liam said.

Penny was breathless, and slightly on guard. How easily he'd given her the compliment, as if he did it all the time. Still, her heart sped up and desire sparked in her blood.

"I'm going to kiss you," Liam said. And he did.

His kiss was tentative and tender, a greeting. Penny stood on her toes and put her hands on his chest because he was so tall, and even with him leaning down, they were apart. She wanted him to know she wanted this kiss. Beneath her hands, his chest was hard and warm from the sun.

Liam put his hands on her shoulders to steady her when the kiss ended.

"Hello," he said.

"Hello." Penny smiled up at him and didn't want to look away.

Liam held hands with Penny as they walked back toward their friends.

"Nice walk?" Jade-Marie asked.

"Very nice," Penny told her.

Together the four sat lazily watching the waves.

Jade-Marie sighed. "I don't want to go back to the hotel. Or to the Associated Society of Parental Jolliness."

"Come to my place," Liam said. "Mom and Dad might be there, but all we'll have to do is say hello. I've got a flat-screen TV and lots of snacks, and if you feel restless, we've got a volleyball setup in the backyard."

"The question is, Liam," Jade-Marie said, "do you have air-conditioning?"

"We do," Liam said.

"What are we waiting for?" Jason asked, jumping up from the sand.

They had to bike back to town, only a matter of ten miles or so, but the afternoon sun was strong and while no wind pushed at their bikes, neither did the wind send cool breezes across their sunburned skin.

Liam's house was in the middle of town, on Orange Street, built in 1840 and added onto here and there in the following decades. The "English basement" had its own door off the street, which led to an open space big enough to have a ping-pong table at the far end and a small galley kitchen at the other end. The television was enormous, and the curve-around sofas were plump with down-filled pillows, all upholstered in some sort of miracle cloth that felt like silk and retained no stains. The air was cool and dry.

"Make yourself comfortable," Liam said. "I'm going to run up and tell Mom we're here."

He quickly returned. "All good."

The group decided to watch *Jaws,* the classic shark movie. They'd all seen it before, and they yelled out to the woman on her surfboard, warning her to go back to shore. Jason fell asleep, snoring slightly, and Penny was still too hopeful, confused, and elated to feel hungry, but Jade-Marie and Liam ate a bowl of popcorn and a tub of cut-up watermelon.

This house, Penny thought, as the Hollywood version of a New England fishing village gathered to solve the shark problem, was perfect. It was simply a big old white-clapboard house, tall and narrow, with no ostentatious displays of wealth, instead a sense of deep comfort and hominess. It gave her an insight into the parents who'd raised Liam, and she realized she was eager to meet them. Then she scolded herself for even thinking that. This wasn't a *date.* It was just friends hanging out.

During the movie, Jade-Marie's phone pinged loudly, waking Jason up.

"Sorry," Jade-Marie said. "That's from the parents. Must take."

Liam paused the movie, and they all listened to Jade-Marie say where they were, and that the three of them would be home soon.

"They're going to Dune for dinner and wanted to know if we want to join them," Jade-Marie told the others.

"No, thank you," Penny and Jason said at the same time.

"I'll be glad when we don't have to check in with them," Jason said. "We are technically adults, and in the past four years we've already done some stuff we wouldn't want them to know about."

"I don't think *I* have," Penny objected.

Liam chuckled. "Well, then, Penny, I think it's high time you do."

Someone clicked the remote and they returned to *Jaws*.

When the movie finished, Jade-Marie said, "I have to go home and take a shower. I still have sand between my toes and in my hair."

"You look sunburned," Jason told her.

"So do you." Jade-Marie stood up and stretched, yawning at the same time. "We biked miles and miles today."

Reluctantly, Penny joined her. "I'm tired, too. The thought of getting on that bike one more time makes my thighs ache."

"I've got bike racks on my Jeep," Liam said. "I'll drive you home."

"That's not necessary," Jason said.

"Actually," Penny said, feeling brave, as if she were standing naked in the room declaring she wanted to spend more time with Liam, even one more minute, "I'd love to be driven back to the hotel."

Jade-Marie and Jason pedaled away from the house as Liam lifted Penny's bike onto the rack.

Penny climbed into the Jeep and pulled her door shut. And suddenly it seemed as if she and Liam were closed in their very own small, dark room with no one to see them or hear them.

"Liam," she said, her voice almost a whisper.

Liam pulled her toward him and kissed her, a sweet, gentle kiss. "I need to take you home. I want to . . . do more than kiss you, but not in a Jeep in my parents' driveway. I want to take things slow with you. I think it's right between us, and I want to keep it that way."

"I'm here for only a week," Penny told him.

"We'll make it a week that matters," he said, and started the engine.

He drove to the hotel with his hand on Penny's thigh.

seven

That Summer

Sheila almost canceled her drink date with Frank Johnson, but that would mean calling the Rose Hotel and asking Mrs. Reardon to let her speak with him, and Mrs. Reardon would demand to know why Sheila wanted to speak to one of their guests and she'd remind Sheila that the maids weren't allowed to "fraternize" with the hotel's guests, and maybe Sheila would end up being fired before she ever spoke to Frank again.

Sheila knew Frank Johnson was older, and much more sophisticated. She felt a little frightened, a little excited, as if she were preparing to dive off one of those high cliffs in Mexico. But it wasn't as if she would be betraying Hank. She would only be having a drink with someone and how different was that from chatting with a guy at a party?

Still, she almost didn't go. She didn't have anything appropriate to wear. The two dresses she'd brought from home were hopelessly sweet and the one she'd bought at the mall in Hyannis was

too Jimmy Buffett. One of her dresses had a pattern of butterflies. The other was a pale green cotton shift. That, at least, didn't
look totally bargain-basement.

It was a complete blessing that none of the other Sand Palace
residents were around when she showered and dressed. Ariel
would insist on doing something with her hair, or using some of
her eye shadow. But Sheila's coloring was totally different from
Ariel's. Sheila's red hair and pale skin made any makeup look like
she'd decided to become a clown.

Should she wear high heels? She'd brought one pair, a neutral
pump, the kind of thing she could wear to church.

But no. This was summer on Nantucket. Everyone was casual
and carefree. Sheila slipped on her sandals, and they were pretty,
with beads on the straps that crisscrossed over her arches.

It's only a drink! Sheila reminded herself as she walked from
the Sand Palace to the Brant Point Grill. But her heart was flutter-
ing inside her like a hummingbird's wings.

She entered the bar. Immediately, she saw him, sitting at one of
the tables by the window.

He stood up as she approached. "Hello. I'm so glad you came."

She managed a nervous smile. "I can't stay long." Why did she
say that? she wondered. She could stay all night if she wanted.

A waiter approached.

"I'm having a martini," Frank told Sheila. "What would you
like, Sheila?"

She pretended to consider the question. "A cosmopolitan,
please." She'd had one before, in college. Actually, she'd had quite
a few in college and she knew she could handle one or two before
making a fool of herself.

"I'm glad to see you," Frank said. "You look beautiful tonight.
How do you like working at the Rose?"

She almost said, "I've had worse jobs, believe me," but she
shrugged her shoulders and said, "I like it. Mrs. Reardon is a doll
and it's easy work, and I get to meet such *interesting* people." She
smiled coyly. *Dear Lord,* Sheila thought, *am I flirting? I'm flirting!*

Frank laughed. "I'm glad you're meeting interesting people. In my line of work, I'm supposed to be the interesting one, and sometimes that's exhausting."

"Why don't you do something else, then?" she asked, as if she thought people could easily change their careers.

"It runs in the family, I guess," Frank said, and his face soured just a little, and he slugged back his drink.

She'd finished her own drink, and a soft, rosy halo surrounded her. Or did it come *from* her? She asked for another cosmo.

"Advertising runs in the family?" Sheila was genuinely surprised. She could understand being a doctor or a lawyer running in a family, but advertising?

"Oh, you'd be surprised." Frank signaled the waiter. "I'm talking at least a hundred years ago. For example, salesmen in my family went to county fairs to hawk 'medicines.' They advertised a soothing potion for a teething baby. It contained morphine." He laughed and shook his head. "Can you imagine that? Or creams for obesity? Or cocaine for asthma?"

"Wow," Sheila said. "That's crazy." She sipped her second cosmo, and sighed as she relaxed. How sophisticated she was, talking about cocaine.

"My grandparents used to buy Carter's Little Liver Pills. Have you even heard of those? They contain bisacodyl, a kind of laxative. Even back then, advertising was important."

"Of course," Sheila said. It seemed the right thing to say.

"You've probably never heard of 'iron-poor blood' and Geritol," Frank said.

"Iron-poor blood" made Sheila think of having periods, and even as relaxed as she was feeling, she wasn't going to talk about that. Frank nattered on some more. Sheila put her elbow on the table and leaned her chin in her hand, listening to him. His words swept by her in waves. The cosmos were stronger than what she was used to.

"Tell me, what do you want to do after the summer?" Frank asked. He had to ask her twice before she understood the question.

"I'm not sure," Sheila said, lying easily, because the drink made her believe that anything was possible. "I have a degree in education from Cleveland State University, and my fallback job would be teaching. But now that I'm here, on this funny little island few people have heard of unless they've read *Moby-Dick*—" She grinned and was delighted to hear Frank chuckle. She was not only sophisticated, she was witty! "I think I'd like to travel more. I'd like . . . could I have another cosmo, please?"

"Of course." Frank signaled the waiter and in only minutes Sheila had a new one in her hands. "You were saying?"

Frank was so handsome. Her cocktail was so intoxicating. Sheila felt she could do anything, be anyone. "I'll tell you a secret. I've never told anyone before. I want to be a photographer. I took courses in college, and the teacher said I was good."

"You should be a photographer's model. You're so beautiful," Frank said.

Sheila realized she was leaning over the table toward him. She'd been whispering to him, as if anyone else in the room was interested in her future.

"I think I may be drunk," Sheila told Frank.

He smiled. "I think you may be, too. Let's get you some food and water."

Sheila lounged in her chair, letting her thoughts drift. Did she really want to be a photographer? Maybe. After all, she'd brought a camera with her and taken some pictures. But she had to find a way to make a living first.

The waiter put a plate of cheese, crackers, olives, and peanuts on the table. He set a glass in front of Sheila and poured it full of water. When Frank nodded, the waiter put the pitcher on the table.

Sheila drank the entire glass of water and poured herself another one. After a moment, she said, "Well, this is embarrassing."

"The drinks here are maybe stronger than what you're accustomed to," Frank said.

"Tell me about your job," Sheila said, drinking the water and pulling herself together. "Do you like it?"

"I do, actually. It's creative, and I like traveling. Some clients are more pleasant to be with than others . . ."

Sheila ate the olives, cheese, and crackers as Frank talked. Gradually, the rosy glow around her faded. She didn't feel bad or good. She needed to sleep.

She interrupted Frank. "I have to go home."

"Are you okay?" Frank asked. "Are you going to be sick?"

"No, no. I'm so sorry, but I think I need a little nap."

Frank signaled the waiter and paid the bill. "I'll walk you home."

"But you don't know where I live," Sheila protested.

"True. But I'm sure you do," Frank said.

Sheila thought that was hilarious. When she finished laughing, she said, "It's only about a block away. The old hotel being renovated. We call it the Sand Palace."

Frank took her arm and steadied her as they walked. With every step, she became a little less drunk, a little more stable, and by the time they were at the hotel, she was almost sober.

"Don't come in," she told Frank. "It's only a hall and four rooms."

"That's fine," Frank said. "Keep drinking water."

Sheila looked up at the tall, handsome man standing before her. "Do you know something?" She put her hands on his shoulders. "You're a remarkable man. You could have taken advantage of me, as drunk as I was. We could have gotten a room at the White Elephant . . . Instead, you got me water and food. You're a true gentleman."

Frank inhaled sharply. "Well. Thank you. But believe me, I hope I have a chance to take advantage of you this summer."

"I hope so, too," Sheila told him, her heart racing.

Frank smiled. "Let me take you to dinner at the Club Car Saturday. I promise I'll be a gentleman."

"I'll see you then," Sheila said, and kissed his cheek, and went inside to her room.

———

It was Ariel who initiated the Hump Night dinners. One of the real estate agents presented her with a pound of scallops. She stored them in the office's refrigerator along with her lunch yogurt. She called Sheila, who had told her Mrs. Reardon would allow her two calls a day on the Rose Hotel phone. Sheila agreed to buy rice and a lemon and tomatoes. Mrs. Reardon overheard and advised Sheila to buy some chorizo to chop and sauté with the scallops to add to the rice.

"Scallops are sweet but like eating thin air. Believe me, they won't satisfy a man's appetite," Mrs. Reardon said. "Buy a Chardonnay to pair with the meal."

"Thank you, Mrs. Reardon," Sheila said, wondering why in the world her boss thought Sheila could afford wine.

Later, as Sheila was leaving, Mrs. Reardon came to the back hall.

"Here," the hotel owner said, handing Sheila a bottle of pale gold wine, "this will be perfect. Add just the smallest drop to the scallops and chorizo."

"Thank you, Mrs. Reardon!" Sheila practically curtsied.

That night, on their two-burner hot plate, Sheila cooked the rice while Ariel sauteed the scallops and chorizo, and when Nick and Wyatt came in, they were astonished. The girls had set a table up on the first floor in the small vacant office next to Sharon Waters's, and found four old metal folding chairs. Ariel had put a hydrangea from a bush in the hotel's unkempt garden in a small jar in the middle of the table.

They had wisely cooked a lot of rice, and Ariel had picked up vanilla ice cream and fresh blueberries, so it was a memorable feast. They relaxed during the delicious meal, and instead of rushing off to get a beer or collapsing in bed and reading books or walking down to the water, they stayed at the table and talked about their jobs or bosses or former bosses and laughed as their cheeks grew rosy. It was that simple: Sharing a home-cooked meal together made them a kind of family. They knew one another better, in ways that seemed insignificant, but were the invisible threads of life.

"We should do this each week," Nick declared as they rose to carry their plates and glasses down to the small kitchen sink.

"We?" Ariel asked sweetly.

"Okay," Nick said. "I get what you're saying. Wyatt, are you up for cooking a decent dinner next week?"

"Sure," Wyatt said.

"*Not* pork and beans or hamburgers or hot dogs," Ariel said.

"And there must be a fresh vegetable," Sheila added, secretly amazed that she could tell these two guys what to do.

Sometimes when the night was rainy, Ariel and Sheila had makeup and hairstyle sessions. Ariel had changed the starkness of her plywood bedroom walls by putting up pictures she'd found at the Thrift Shop. Sheila, not wanting to copy Ariel, had taken home magazines left behind in the Rose Hotel, cut out photos she liked, and taped really clever collages to the walls. Ariel had screamed when she saw them.

"You're so talented!" Ariel told Sheila. "You're an artist!"

"Not really," Sheila protested, but she was pleased.

Some nights the guys went off to the Atlantic Café to drink beer and watch baseball. Those nights Sheila and Ariel turned into their own spa nights, soaking in perfumed bubble bath, washing each other's hair, getting into their robes, and painting each other's nails. Ariel showed Sheila how to wear eyeliner and blush. Sheila French-braided Ariel's long blond hair. Ariel had a bottle of Baileys Irish Cream she'd been given at some party.

One night, they talked about guys.

"I've met a man," Sheila confessed. She was lying on her bed while Ariel painted her toenails.

"Oooh, a man! Tell me everything!"

"Well, it doesn't mean anything. I mean, I *am* engaged to Hank. But this man is so fascinating, and handsome, and nice, too."

"What's his name? Where did you meet him? Have you kissed him? Details, please." When Sheila didn't answer immediately, Ariel tugged her toes.

Sheila said, "Stop! Okay, okay. His name is Frank Johnson. He's an advertising man. He's staying at the Rose Hotel. I met him for a drink, and he was a perfect gentleman. No, I haven't kissed him. I want to, though."

Ariel put the brush back in the small bottle of coral nail polish. "Frank Johnson? That's kind of a phony name, don't you think?"

"What? No! It's a perfectly normal name."

"How old is he?"

"Are you my mother? I don't know. Maybe early or middle thirties. Ariel, he's really nice."

"Why is he staying at the Rose Hotel? That seems kind of off."

"He said it's the only place he could find a room. He's staying for several weeks. Don't be so suspicious. I know what I'm doing. I like him."

"You have been with a man before, right?"

"Of course!" Sheila sat up, insulted. She swung her legs over the side of the bed and studied her toes. "This looks so pretty. Thanks." Sheila took a deep breath. "Okay, listen. I've only slept with one guy. But it was Hank, and I love him, and he loves me. We both went to Cleveland State University, and I think at first Hank and I latched on to each other because we knew each other from high school. We were goldfish in an ocean of whales and sea turtles. So, well, we liked each other, and the more I saw him, the more I liked him. We made love. He asked me to marry him before I left for Nantucket. I said yes. I guess I never experienced the supreme rapture the books talk about, but it's nice."

"Maybe the books exaggerate," Ariel said.

"What about you?"

Ariel shrugged. "I haven't been with many men. To be exact, two. I was in love with a guy my sophomore year and we got serious, but he broke up with me my junior year so I slept with his best friend in revenge, not that it was even pleasant, and forget *rapture.*" Ariel shivered. "I'm absolutely *not* looking for a serious relationship this summer." Ariel paused, thinking of Wyatt, and how her heart bloomed when he was near. But she was worried about her friend. "Sheila, you should be careful. You don't want this Frank Johnson to break your heart . . . or worse."

"I'll be careful." Impulsively, Sheila leaned over and hugged Ariel. "We're on Nantucket and it's summer and we're only serious about having fun."

"You're right." Ariel stood up. "We should get some sleep. Work tomorrow."

"Right." Sheila checked her watch. "The guys aren't back yet."

"We're not their mothers." Ariel grinned. "And thank heavens for that!"

It was Wednesday night a couple of weeks later. The women had cooked. The four sat down to enjoy chicken parmesan that Sheila had inventively made in the skillet on the two-burner hot plate. It was a hot day, and even though they had small windows in their rooms to let in fresh air, the basement was beginning to smell of mildew and mold. Sheila and Ariel burned scented candles when they were in their rooms. Wyatt was much more sensible. He bought small circular fans for everyone, and they were a great help.

The four Sand Palace occupants had been living there for over a month, and they'd become increasingly comfortable with one another. Both Ariel and Sheila wore tank tops, shorts, and flip-flops at the dinner table. They carelessly pulled their long hair up into ponytails or buns on top of their heads. The men wore shorts and tees, and Wyatt smelled of oil from the boat shop and Nick smelled of a heady men's cologne from Fanshaw's.

The men had brought beer, which they slugged down immediately. Ariel and Sheila chose ice water. For the first few minutes, everyone ate as if starving.

Nick broke the silence. "So, children, how was school today?"

"Exhausting," Sheila grumbled. "Mrs. Reardon's hotel is full and some people treat their rooms like a giant wastebasket, dropping stuff all over."

"I'm good," Wyatt said. "Mr. Cabot is a great guy, seems to know everything and everyone on the island."

"I like where I work, too," Ariel told them. "Although I'll admit, my face hurts from smiling. Tonight, I'm going to curl up with a book. Plus, I've got a date with the washing machine. Sheila, if you want to give me your laundry, I'll throw it in with mine."

"Thanks, Ariel. I haven't had time to—"

Nick interrupted. "Doesn't anyone want to know what I'm doing?"

"Nick," Ariel and Sheila chanted together teasingly, "*please* tell us, what are you doing?"

Wyatt snorted.

"One of Mr. Fanshaw's customers asked me to help tend bar at a party on the Morecombs' yacht tomorrow night. The big one in the harbor. Check it out. Her name is *MORE*."

"I've noticed that yacht. It's enormous," Wyatt said.

"Fanshaw's giving me one of his white shirts so I'll be appropriately dressed. I'll serve drinks and cocktails. I'll make a week's worth of pay in one night."

"Maybe you'll meet a woman," Ariel suggested.

"Maybe I will," Nick agreed.

The next evening, as Nick showered, shaved, and dressed, his hands shook. *This* was why he'd chosen Nantucket. He wanted to meet people with money. Big money. He'd work for them, he'd marry them, whatever it took. He was determined to change his life.

His older brother was a physicist at MIT working on dark matter. He lived with a pretty woman named Ursula, also a physicist. When the two were talking about their work, Nick had no idea what they were saying.

His sister, Anya, had married a banker. They had a huge house in Ipswich and four children whom his mother worshipped. The only way Nick, the youngest child, could excel would be to make a lot of money while making an obvious and substantial difference in the real world. Nick was determined to do just that.

He'd worked for Brooks Brothers in Boston, and here on Nantucket at Fanshaw's, he assisted the kind of men he wanted to emulate. They carried themselves with ease and importance, and they were always automatically polite to Nick. They didn't have to *act* powerful. They *were power.*

Nick walked down Straight Wharf to the end of the pier where a longer pier extended for the big yachts. *MORE* was the first of five superyachts at anchor. Every window glowed gold. Nick went past the first boarding ramp, which was meant for guests, and down to the last boarding ramp, meant for crew. He was met by a tall, tanned man wearing the yacht's uniform of navy blue and light blue.

"Name?" the man asked, looking down at a clipboard.

Nick gave his name.

"Lower deck, midships," the man said.

"Give me a break," Nick said.

The man pointed to a door. "Take the stairs down two flights."

Nick went through the door and down the narrow steep stairs to a long, narrow room where guys dressed like he was were opening bottles of wine, filling buckets of ice from an ice machine, and polishing trays.

A man with a name tag that read JOE stepped in front of Nick.

"Well, aren't you a pretty boy," Joe said. "Lucky for you. You can take drinks around. Phillip has a tray. Champagne. Mortlach 18—that's Scotch, pretty boy. Sparkling water. Go on, they're starting to arrive."

Nick had worked for caterers before, during his college days, and he'd learned how to balance a tray. He knew how to place the heavier drinks in the middle of the tray, the lighter ones on the outside, how to hold it with his fingertips, his wrist angled slightly while keeping his shoulder straight, how to hold it below shoulder level. He was tall, strong, and young.

As he stepped onto the foredeck, he was reminded that he was also handsome by the way the women's heads turned, by the way they smiled.

"Darling, thank heavens you're here," an older woman said, slinking toward him. "We're parched."

He walked around the deck, making eye contact, smiling, nodding, saying nothing but "You're welcome." He knew better than to flirt with the guests.

An hour later, the deck was crowded and loud with talk and laughter, and they still accepted more drinks from Nick's tray. Impressive, he thought, how much these people could drink. At Joe's request, Nick opened the doors to the lounge with its soft leather sofas and fine paintings on the wall. Immediately, several of the older women swept in, dropping around the long coffee table with cries of pleasure.

Nick waited by the door to see if they wanted more drinks. They ignored him.

"God, I couldn't have stood up for another minute," a glamorous woman said, putting her feet on the short table. "My Louboutins are killing me."

"But they're so gorgeous," another woman countered.

"The things we do for our husbands," a red-haired lady dripping with emeralds chimed in. "They get to wear deck shoes. We have to torture ourselves for beauty."

Nick surveyed the room. All the guests held full glasses. He quietly left and headed back to the serving galley.

At the top of the stairs, sitting on the stairs, leaning against an inner wall, her long legs stretched out across a step, with a cigarette in one hand and a paperback book in the other, was a beautiful woman with long blond hair and a very short dress.

Nick gave himself a moment to compose himself. She was much younger than the other guests. Must be someone's daughter, he decided.

"Excuse me," he said.

She looked up at him. "*Mon Dieu,*" she said. "Aren't they the most boring people on the planet?"

She was exquisitely beautiful, her frame delicate and slender, as if she were a ballerina lost on the ship. She did not move her legs.

Nick sensed the spark between them, and that gave him the courage to say, "But aren't you one of the guests?"

That made her toss back her head and laugh. "You are correct. I'm here with my father. My mother is with the angels, so I have to be his accessory. But I've fulfilled my duty, so I'm escaping."

"The stairs don't seem like a comfortable place to sit," Nick said.

"Again, you are correct." The blonde smoothly twisted her legs down to the next step and rose. "I am Francine Bruel."

"Nick Volkov."

"Do you live on the island?"

"For the summer."

Loud baritone laughter exploded from the front deck.

"Take me somewhere else." She moved close to Nick, gazing up at him with crystal blue eyes. There were only inches between them.

"I wish I could," Nick said. "But I'm working here tonight."

Francine made a sweeping gesture with her hand. "Who cares. Let's go into town."

Nick shook his head. "I'm afraid I care. I'm working because I need to, but I would like nothing more than to take you someplace."

"*Lâche,*" Francine said, glaring at him.

"I'm not a coward," Nick told her, and was rewarded with her eyes widening when she realized he understood French. *Score one for me,* Nick thought. His education had been helpful, after all. He wasn't fluent in French, but he did have a working ability. *Working,* he thought.

He said sternly, "I am here working, and you are here playing." He stepped closer to her, towering over her so that she had to tilt her head back to look at him. "And I am not a toy."

Before he could control himself, he hurried down the steps to the next deck and the next.

The galley was wild now that the party was almost over. The waiters drank champagne from half-empty glasses, ate the slightly burned hors d'oeuvres that hadn't been served, and did mincing imitations of some of the more colorful guests.

Nick gave himself a moment to stand outside and catch his breath. He was trembling and he knew his cheeks were burning. The last thing he'd expected tonight was to experience such intense emotion. Francine had stepped out of his wildest fantasies.

And Francine was sophisticated and filthy rich, he reminded himself. Any man would want her, and she would consider Nick entire tiers beneath her. For a long moment, Nick was swept with shame. He was handsome, he could probably take her to bed, but she would never consider him her equal, and what he had felt for her in those few moments had not been love, but infatuation, sexual attraction, lust. And a powerful exhilaration that such a beauty would even speak to him.

Yet, helplessly, he knew he would hold the sight of her, her long blond hair falling back past her shoulders and her blue eyes daring him, like a treasure in his heart.

He hit his fist into his hand. "Fool!" he whispered to himself angrily.

Nick pushed his way into the galley and joined the other caterers, who were laughing as they washed trays, loaded the dishwasher, and tossed out lipstick-blotted napkins. This was where he belonged now, but this was not where he would stay.

eight
This Summer

Tuesday morning, they all gathered in the bistro for coffee and croissants. Nick rose, clapping his hands to draw everyone's attention to him.

"I hope you've all had a good breakfast. Now, I've made plans for us today. Don't worry, I won't schedule your every day here, but I want you kids to see what your parents saw when we were your age."

Penny leaned forward. "If you don't mind, I'd like to stay here. I'm, um, expecting a phone call."

"Oh, come with us," Jade-Marie said. "It won't be as much fun without you."

Sheila said, "You're coming with us, Penny. You had all day yesterday to be with Jason and Jade-Marie."

"All right, Mom." She turned to Nick. "Thank you very much, Mr. Volkov. It will be wonderful to see the island."

Someone kicked Penny's leg softly. She looked across the table at Jade-Marie.

"Like we didn't see it yesterday," Jade-Marie whispered, rolling her eyes.

Penny's smile was genuine, conspiratorial.

Ariel leaned on the window, gazing out at the passing scenery. Nick was driving the Jeep, and Sheila had been given the passenger seat. Wyatt had the other window in the backseat and Francine, so slender she could easily fit between them, had the middle seat. Behind them, Jade-Marie drove the other Jeep, with Penny next to her and Jason in the back.

They were headed out to Madaket on the west end of the island.

"I'm amazed at all the houses that have been built," Wyatt said. "It wasn't this crowded when we were here."

"It's been twenty-five years," Nick told him. "Nantucket has become the playground of the super-rich."

"Which explains why you've built a hotel here," Wyatt said.

"Well, of course," Francine said. "My husband would hardly build a hotel in an ugly location."

Ariel zapped a look at her husband. Ariel believed Nick deeply loved Francine, and she was certain that now, this week, he would like for them to be, if not friends with her, at least friendly. Nick might be an ambitious man, but he had a deep heart.

Ariel ran her eyes over the back of Nick's beautifully shaped head. His hair had the crisp glossiness of a professional cut, and it was as black as it had been when she first met him. Only a few silver hairs glittered here and there, probably, knowing Nick's vanity, a hairdresser's magic touch to give Nick gravitas. He hadn't put on weight in the past twenty-five years, and his muscles seemed to be honed from work at the gym.

Even though Wyatt had grown a slight paunch, Ariel still loved her husband's body. Loved her husband. That was why she had learned to be happy stuck in a small town in the middle of the country when once she'd dreamed of living in a loft in New York, writing novels, or typing chapters at a desk in her compartment on the Orient Express. Wyatt knew she loved him. He never doubted it. She understood that his real passion was science, but he did love her and their son, and that was an abundance to her.

Also, she met with a small group of other struggling writers twice a month, and their advice, frustrations, and laughter were invaluable to her. She wanted to start an online writers' club, but needed money to set up a website. She'd mentioned this to Wyatt, but he didn't take her seriously. All he'd said was *you'll figure it out.*

When she returned to Missouri, she'd take a job, any job, until she'd compiled a few thousand dollars to have someone build an enticing website.

They arrived at the end of the road, at the end of the island. A large sand dune rose in front of them, but they could hear the sea.

Jade-Marie, in the other Jeep, now pulled up next to them. Penny, Jade-Marie, and Jason tumbled out.

"I'm giving you the grand tour," Nick told them. "We'll see the far west end of the island, and then I'll take you to the east end for lunch."

"You would be wise to take off your shoes," Francine advised.

The group did as she suggested, and they climbed up the high dune in their bare feet, huffing and puffing and laughing at themselves, until finally they reached the ridge at the top and the Atlantic Ocean in all its sparkling blue beauty came into view.

"It goes on forever," Jade-Marie said.

"It goes on until it hits Portugal," Wyatt said.

"We've got sharks showing up here now," Nick said. "Great whites."

"Really? Why?" Penny asked.

"Warming seas have brought the seals, and great whites love seals," Nick explained. "The town has built higher stands for the lifeguards so they can search the water for fins. It's the same out at 'Sconset. And fishing at Great Point can get dramatic. Sometimes sharks will fight to get the fish a guy has on his line."

Francine put her hand on Nick's arm. "Darling, let's simply enjoy the view. Please."

Jade-Marie spoke up. "Mother and I often spend time in Saint-Tropez or Nice. The beaches are beautiful there, and we know there are sharks in the Mediterranean, but so far they haven't been spotted near shore."

"It must be beautiful," Penny said. "I'd love to go there someday."

"I'll go with you," Jason joked. "Those are the beaches where women go topless, right?"

Everyone laughed, and Jade-Marie was both grateful to Jason for bringing some humor into the moment and hurt that he said he'd go anywhere with Penny. Although, Jade-Marie thought ruefully, Penny without her top would be a sight to see.

Nick clapped his hands. "Okay, group, back to the car. We're going to drive all the way to the other end of the island."

They drove along the Madaket road, turned onto Prospect Street so they could see the Old Mill where settlers had ground their corn, zigzagged through the busy shopping areas, and flew along Milestone Road, past the vast plains of the moors, to the small village of 'Sconset. They saw mansions and one-room fishing shacks. They walked on the beach as the ocean sprayed them with each wave. They oohed and aahed over the fishermen's cottages, and were properly impressed as they walked along the bluff path by the extravagant summer mansions facing the Atlantic.

Finally, they got back in their cars and drove down Polpis Road and over the Wauwinet road until they came to the inn and restaurant. A brick path bordered by a lavish display of hydrangea and roses wound up to the front door. The building was shingled, in keeping with the island's architectural choice, and the trim on the windows and porch was glossy white.

"If we go any further," Nick told them, "we'll be on sand roads. We have four-wheel drive and if we wanted to, we could drive all the way out to Great Point."

"I'd much rather sit in the shade with a cool drink," Francine told her husband. Then, surprising the others, she smiled at them and asked, "Don't you all agree?"

Wyatt immediately said, "Absolutely."

Ariel put her hands to her heart. "It looks like heaven."

Nick smiled, pleased at her reaction. "The restaurant here is called Toppers. It has a view of the end of the Polpis harbor. We can eat on the porch, or if you'd prefer, in the dining room."

"Porch, please," Sheila said.

The group followed Nick into the lobby, elegant in its simplicity. Immediately, the manager appeared to greet Nick and meet his guests and chat as charmingly as if they were the highlight of his day. They were shown to their tables on the back porch, a long stretch overlooking a velvet lawn leading to the bright blue harbor and a private beach with kayaks, canoes, and Sunfish waiting.

"I want to live here," Sheila said. "Right here."

A waiter appeared. "Would you like one long table or several smaller ones?"

"The long table, please," Nick said.

The group mingled around, finding their seats. Nick, Wyatt, and Jason became almost courtly when they said they'd sit facing the hotel so the women could have the water view.

They studied their menus, and for a while the group was quiet.

"What's Wagyu beef?" Wyatt asked.

"It's from Japan," Nick began.

Jade-Marie interrupted, laughing. "It's beef that has been massaged. I mean the cows have been massaged. Therefore, the beef is supposed to be especially tender."

"I become very tender when I'm massaged," Jason joked, looking at Jade-Marie.

"Twenty-seven dollars for a hamburger?" Wyatt shook his head.

"It's my treat, mate," Nick said. "Go crazy and order the fries, too."

"I remember a time when you couldn't afford an expensive meal," Wyatt told Nick.

"Ramen noodles, dude," Nick said, laughing.

Sheila, intent on her menu, asked, "What is bottarga?"

"It's a kind of roe, darling." Francine lifted one eyebrow and smiled slightly when she saw that Sheila didn't understand. "Like caviar. Roe are fish eggs. Bottarga is similar. Very salty."

"Thanks," Sheila said, her smile genuine.

"What are crudites?" Jason asked. "And why would we want to eat them?"

Francine laughed, a musical sound of pleasure. "I agree completely, Jason. *Quelle horreur!* But it only means raw vegetables. They're served with dips or sauces."

"I'm having the hamburger," Wyatt said stubbornly.

Ariel reached across the table to touch her husband's hand. "Maybe seafood? You can have a hamburger anywhere, and you've got to think of your cholesterol."

The waiter arrived to take their orders.

"Should we have wine at lunch?" Sheila wondered. "It doesn't seem right."

"Ooh-la-la, such a fuss!" Francine said. "A glass or two of wine for lunch is ordinary for me."

Stop it! Jade-Marie thought, her eyes flashing a warning at her mother. Jade-Marie hated it when her mother went into her *I am French and therefore better than all of you* mode.

"I'll have a soda," Jade-Marie said. "I never drink at lunch. You're right, Sheila, liquor at lunch can make a person drowsy."

"No wine for us, thank you," Ariel said.

Jason studied his mother and father. His mother had never seemed dissatisfied with her life married to an absentminded scientific professor. But he had always understood how much it meant to her to take her solitary trips back East to visit her parents or, more often, to writers' talks in Kansas City or St. Louis or Chicago. He wished she could do more. She always came back so happy after a writers' conference, so enthusiastic. Email and Zoom provided some conversation for her, but it wasn't the same as being with other writers in real life. He knew his father didn't make the kind of money that would fund more trips. That was the thing about scientific research. Professors weren't paid much, and if they were awarded grants, most of the money went to equipment or lab assistants.

Jason knew his father wanted him to follow in his footsteps. He knew his mother appreciated his presence and humor and he worried about what would happen when he left. Because he *would* leave. He was young, and he wanted to be his own man. It was even possible that he would never return, not for good. He wanted to find a world where *he* fit, where he felt at home.

Nick cleared his throat and began a brief history lecture. "This area of the island was settled by Wampanoag tribes in the seventh century. They lived on berries and fish, and the men even hunted whales in canoes made out of trees. The name Wampanoag means 'Easterners' or 'People of the Dawn.'"

"How poetic," Ariel said. "People of the Dawn."

"The land on the other side of the harbor is called Coskata-Coatue. It's a barrier beach and a wildlife refuge owned by the Trustees of Reservations. We can drive there or walk there later. Spectacular views."

Wyatt said, "Nick, you're a walking encyclopedia."

Nick shot back, "And you're the next Einstein."

A kind of tension shivered between the two men, for just a moment, and then Nick continued with his history lecture, stopping only when the waiter arrived with their meals.

After a moment, Ariel said, "This is sublime, but I don't think anything will ever taste better than that pizza we shared that first night on Easy Street."

Wyatt agreed. "I remember it, too. But we were young and literally hungry then."

"And before that, our first time on the beach," Sheila reminisced, "Nick got us some chips and beer. He convinced a couple of girls to drive him into town and bring him all the way back."

"Why didn't you drive into town, Dad?" Jade-Marie asked.

"It was our first night on the island. We only had bikes."

Before Nick could continue, Ariel said, laughing, "While you were gone, Sheila and I covered Wyatt up to the neck in sand!"

"No way," Jason said. "I can't believe my father would allow that."

"Oh, Wyatt wasn't as important as he is now," Ariel told her son, reaching over to squeeze Wyatt's shoulder.

Wyatt grinned, accepting the teasing. "At least I didn't try to save us all from a serial killer with a golf club."

Penny gasped. "A serial killer with a golf club was in your building?"

The four Sand Palace inhabitants roared with laughter.

"No," Sheila told her daughter. "Nick had the golf club. There was a room above us, and we were in that grotty basement late at night when we heard this creepy shrieking noise. We were almost asleep, and we all came out of our rooms—"

"You should have seen us," Nick said. "We were huddled together like a clump of teenagers from a Freddy Krueger movie, scared out of our wits. We figured out the sound came from upstairs, but remember, most of the building was demolished. We had a light in the corridor, but no light on the stairs, and we had to pass through a kind of nightmare passageway to get to Sharon Waters's office and the light switch."

"We were brave," Wyatt added. "Nick and I went first, protecting the women."

"It was like someone screaming from the grave," Ariel whispered. "I get goosebumps thinking of it. Nantucket has always had houses with ghosts, and I thought maybe an old grave had been opened when the hotel was destroyed."

"What was it?" Jade-Marie asked, terrified.

The Sand Palace four grinned at one another.

"A cracked window!" Wyatt answered. "Nothing but a cracked window with the wind blowing through. I found some tape in Sharon's cabinet and fixed it."

Nick laughed. "I went through all of Sharon's desk drawers, trying to find a bottle of Scotch or bourbon. I was about to have a heart attack."

"But she didn't have any liquor, so we laughed at ourselves and went downstairs," Sheila said.

Ariel said dreamily, "And Wyatt and I fell in love."

"What?" Jason looked embarrassed.

"We stood on the top step and talked," Ariel said. "We kissed. It was so—"

"All right, all right," Jason said. "I don't need to hear the details."

Wyatt and Ariel shared a private smile.

The waiter came by with dessert menus.

"I shouldn't," said Sheila.

"You absolutely should," Ariel told her. "When will you have this chance again?"

"Okay, if you insist," Sheila quickly agreed.

They all leaned back in their chairs, reading the menu, feeling the warmth of the sun, hearing the gentle sigh of waves on the shore.

"How fortunate we are," Ariel said. "This is lovely, Nick. Thank you."

"Yes," Jade-Marie echoed, gazing at Jason. "How lucky we are."

After a moment, Jason asked if he and Jade-Marie could walk back to town on the beach.

"Sorry, no," Nick said. "The beach gives way to marsh and swampy areas. It's not quite quicksand, but it's composed of dead sea creatures. Makes wonderful fertilizer, but it's hard to move through and the smell is repulsive."

"Let's walk back on the road, then," Jade-Marie suggested. "Penny, want to go with us?" *Say no,* Jade-Marie silently begged, *say no.*

"No, thanks," Penny said. "I want to go back in case Liam stops by."

After the others had driven off toward town, Jade-Marie and Jason strolled away from Wauwinet, down a narrow road bordered with pines and tupelo and an occasional house. They turned right onto the Polpis road, also two-lane and narrow. On the south side was a bike path. They crossed over and walked toward town.

For a while, they didn't talk. It was enough to be near each other, alone.

"That's a cranberry bog," Jade-Marie said, pointing. "It doesn't look like much now, but in the fall, all the cranberries turn bright red."

"You know a lot about the island," Jason observed.

"I do. I think it's my favorite place in the world."

"Why?"

Jade-Marie took his hand and pulled him up a rutted dirt road. When they'd reached the crest in the small hill, she waved her arm. "Look at all that. It's called the moors. Like Scotland's moors. Heather grows there, and all sorts of wildflowers, and there are several beautiful clear ponds, and deer live here, and rabbits, and probably voles, and lots of birds nest in the trees." She laughed at herself. "I sound like a third-grade teacher."

"I like hearing this. Tell me more."

"Well, the moors are about four thousand acres, most of it owned by the Nantucket Conservation Foundation, some by Mass Audubon. Some single-lane dirt roads for people driving, lots and lots of paths for walkers, and no houses allowed. It's wild. It's not taken over by corporations. It's its real self."

"I guess you're a nature lover," Jason said.

"Guilty as charged. You're not?"

"I like the ocean. I like being on a boat or swimming, or simply staring at the horizon."

"I could live here," Jade-Marie said. She ambled back toward the road and the bike path.

Jason followed. "You know, I think I could, too."

Jade-Marie glanced over her shoulder at him. "I assumed you had joined your father in his scientific research."

Jason nodded, looking sad. "My father assumes that, too. And my famous grandfather. They'd like a scientific dynasty. I've been working at the university since I graduated."

"That is kind of cool," Jade-Marie said hesitantly.

"It would be, if I liked science," Jason told her.

They walked quietly for a while.

"Actually," Jason said, "it's not the science that I dislike, it's the repetitive research and documentation. But really, I don't want to be like my father and grandfather. Their entire lives are science. They're always, *always* living in their heads. No other profession in the world matters to them. They are certain that they're superior to everyone else. My father's entire connection to nature is through chemical analysis. And he expects everyone to cater to him. He's not mean to my mom, he doesn't hit her, but he treats her like a servant. He looks down his nose at her writing. He ridicules her for having her head in the clouds. She's had fiction published, and he's never read one word she's written. And if I don't make A's in science, he's furious. And the worst thing is, he's always competing with his father and he knows he can never win, but there's the entire world around him and he doesn't even see it."

Jason drew a deep breath. "Sorry."

Jade-Marie held his hand and leaned against his arm. "Why don't you tell me what you really think?"

"You must think I'm an asshole. I mean, you and your father have a perfect relationship."

"Not perfect at all," Jade-Marie said. "I don't think any two people have a perfect relationship. I mean, look at my parents. My father's a classic extrovert, plus he always needs more. My mother is an introvert. She does some charity work in Paris, and sometimes Dad will show up for one of her occasions, and sometimes she'll show up for the opening of a new hotel, but mostly they just let the other get on with it."

"You seem to want to follow in your father's footsteps, though," Jason pointed out.

"I kind of do. I like the idea of running a hotel. But I also want a husband and children. And I don't want to travel the way my parents do. I really want to be settled."

"Is that okay with your parents?"

Jade-Marie laughed. "If I wanted to drive a dogsled, they'd be fine with it. I'll bet your mother would be fine with you doing what you want."

"I'm not so sure. A few months ago, I told Mom I wasn't sure

I wanted to be a scientist. She told me that I've got science in my blood. That I'm going to continue my father's research. That I'll feel better in a few more years."

Jade-Marie shook her head. What could she possibly say?

"I realized then that my mother would always be on my father's side. That she loved me, kept me safe and healthy, but she wouldn't protect me from my father's wishes. That she couldn't even *see* how I might yearn for a different life. Just as she wouldn't stand up for her own worth as a writer."

"I'm sorry," Jade-Marie said. "Really."

They'd come into town as they talked, and had to walk single file along the busy two-lane road to the airport. They came to Marine Home Center. Suddenly, Jason took Jade-Marie's hand and stopped.

"I apologize for dumping all that on you," Jason said. "I'm not always such bad company."

"I liked talking with you," Jade-Marie said. "Why don't we go out to Cisco Brewers tonight. That will be an entirely different world, and I know you'll enjoy it."

"Yeah. I'd like that. I think . . . maybe I'll walk down to the beach."

She could tell he needed some space. "Of course. I'm going to call Penny and see if she wants to go shopping."

"Good idea," Jason said. He hesitated, then said all in a rush, "I don't blather on like this to just anyone. In fact, you're the first person I've talked to so honestly."

"I like that," Jade-Marie said. "I'd like to be your first person in a lot of things." She quickly kissed his cheek and walked away, her face blushing red, her heart beating fast.

nine
That Summer

Wednesday was the first true hot day of the summer.

At least, people on Nantucket complained that it was hot. They had no idea, Wyatt thought. They hadn't experienced the breath-stopping humid heat of Missouri where the air plastered itself against a person's face like damp gauze.

It was in the caves of the Ozarks where Wyatt's father had discovered a rock streaked with a mineral that would earn him fame and admiration and a raise in salary. Wyatt was ten when that extraordinary event took place. Suddenly his father, who Wyatt considered boring and way too strict, was being interviewed on television and visited by scientists from around the world. Wyatt flew with his famous father to visit the NASA headquarters in Washington, D.C., to meet important people, some in military uniform covered with ribbons and metals. Wyatt was taken on a special tour of the National Air and Space Museum and spent the evening in the Hay-Adams hotel, eating room service and watching television while his father went to a dinner given in his honor.

It was on that trip that Wyatt realized he was doomed. In all the photos taken of his father, Wyatt was invited—forced—to stand at his father's side. His father joked, with a serious undertone, that his son was his assistant. Wyatt would carry on the exciting scientific work that began with Dr. Benjamin Smith's discovery of a rare mineral that would help NASA send men to the moon and Mars. That was what his father announced to the world, and Wyatt watched his fate laid out for him without one word about what he thought of the plan.

Wyatt majored in science at the University of Missouri where his father taught. He lived with his parents—why spend money for dorms when his mother's food was so good? By the time he entered his final year, he was depressed and angry. He was restless. His mother understood. She suggested that he take a summer job "back East" before spending the rest of his life in the same town where he'd grown up, so he'd talked with friends who'd traveled, and here he was, in a landscape like nothing he'd ever known.

He was beginning to feel what happiness was.

He liked his job at Cabot's. Wyatt was good at fixing mechanical things. Not so good at personal relationships, but at work Don Cabot talked almost incessantly, and his stories were entertaining.

And there was Ariel.

Wyatt knew from the moment he set eyes on her that he was in love with Ariel. Ariel had grown up just outside Boston. She'd been to Paris. She was head-turningly beautiful. She was friendly with everyone, and her laughter was magical.

Why anyone so lovely would be interested in him was a mystery. Wyatt was smart enough to know that he was a good-looking guy. He'd had plenty of girlfriends in his life and any one of them would have married him in an instant. Ariel, for all her sophistication, always brightened when she set eyes on Wyatt, and sometimes, when they were walking and their arms brushed, her face would flush pink. For all her beauty, she was not a snob. As the days passed, Wyatt realized Ariel was not interested in the party scene, in rich people, fabulous venues, expensive jewelry.

Ariel read a lot. She seemed like someone who would be content in a university town. So Wyatt thought he might have a chance. It was hard to get personal when they were all together, during either Hump Night dinners or beach picnics or parties. He wanted to spend some time alone with her. Getting to know her, letting her get to know him. He knew better than to ask her out on a date. Nick and Sheila would tease them mercilessly.

He had an idea. A spur-of-the-moment kind of thing, and he told Don Cabot he was leaving for his lunch hour, but he'd be right back.

Ariel usually spent her lunch hour at her desk at the Amos Longenecker Real Estate Agency. This made all the realtors happy, because she was there in case someone dropped in or called. Also, Ariel was frugal, wanting to save her money. She brought a perfectly satisfactory peanut butter, lettuce, and mayonnaise sandwich from her basement kitchen.

Serious heat arrived on the island. The sidewalk bustled with people in shorts and scallopers' caps or short tank tops and flip-flops. Ariel always wore a pretty dress and sandals to work. She wanted to look professional. She changed the moment she got home, usually into one of her bathing suits and a T-shirt.

It was just after noon when the agency door opened and Wyatt walked in. Her heart jumped.

"Wyatt! Why aren't you at work?"

Wyatt smiled. "I'm on lunch hour. I walked into town to get a sandwich and I thought I'd stop by and see if you wanted to go kayaking with me after work."

For a moment, Ariel was speechless. "Kayaking?"

"It's easy. Mr. Cabot at the boat shop said we could use one of theirs for free. They have two-seaters. Also, life vests."

"I've never kayaked," Ariel said weakly.

"It will take thirty seconds to show you. Basically, you sit and paddle. We could go around the inner harbor, and the cool thing is it's so quiet. No motor. No sails."

"It sounds wonderful. I'd love to do it."

"Great! You know where I work, right? Down on North Washington across from the senior citizens center."

"I'll be there. As soon after five as I can get there." *I will run,* Ariel thought. *I will shoot myself out of a cannon. I will fly.*

"Don't go to the Sand Palace and change. I mean, because Nick or Sheila might be there, and we only have the one kayak." Wyatt's ears went pink as he talked.

He wants to be alone with me, Ariel realized.

He wants to be alone with me.

"I mean, your dress might get wet, but not soaked. We won't capsize or anything. You can leave your purse or whatever in Cabot's office."

Wyatt is *babbling,* Ariel realized. She grinned at him. "Good. That's all good."

"So, well, I'll see you there."

"Yes. See you there right after five."

Their gaze was a lifeline, tying them together.

"Okay," Wyatt said, smiling, "I'm leaving now."

"Okay," Ariel said. "Drive safely."

"I walked. The Jeep's at the Sand Palace."

Ariel thought they could be speaking in Mandarin as long as they could stay connected like this.

"Right," she said. "Walk safely."

"I will. And you, um, work safely." Wyatt's eyes were twinkling now, his cheeks as pink as his ears.

We are stinkin' adorable, Ariel thought. *We can't leave each other.*

Wyatt stepped outside and shut the door. As he walked past the agency, he waved. Ariel waved back and then didn't move. She sat smiling, afraid to break the spell.

Suddenly, Wyatt was back at the wide window. He held up his hand, pointed to his five fingers, and mouthed "Five!"

Ariel nearly lifted off her chair with joy. "FIVE," she called.

The agency phone rang. She had to pick it up. When she did, it took her a moment to remember what to say. "Amos Longenecker Real Estate Agency, Ariel speaking." She waved again at Wyatt, who waved back at her and disappeared.

What does this mean? Ariel wondered. It was a question that floated like a banner through her thoughts as she spent the afternoon answering the phone and sorting files.

She left the office at five and walked through the town down to the street leading to the end of the harbor, the town pier, and Cabot's Marine. She swung her purse as she walked and hummed a tune about flowers from *Alice's Adventures in Wonderland.* People smiled at her. Little children smiled at her. She felt like Julie Andrews in *The Sound of Music,* except did Maria ever have sex? Did Julie Andrews? Ariel let her thoughts bounce around like silly rubber balls.

The boat shop was on the end of the harbor beach. It looked like an old barn with weathered shingles and a sailboat weather vane atop the slanted roof.

Wyatt was leaning against the door, waiting. He pulled Ariel into the shadowy coolness of the boat shop and led her past shelves of rope and strange metal things over to the counter.

"Don?" Wyatt called. "We're going out in the kayak now."

From somewhere in the depths of the shop came a sound that was very much like the voice of God. *"Fine."*

"I'll put these behind the counter," Wyatt said, reaching for her purse and her sandals.

Their hands touched when she handed them to him. Wyatt seemed so calm and matter-of-fact about it all that Ariel began to worry that his invitation didn't mean anything, really. Maybe he'd already asked Sheila and Nick and they were too busy working or had other plans.

"Here." Wyatt gave her a yellow life vest.

"I don't need that, Wyatt. You know I can swim."

The voice of God roared, *"PUT THE VEST ON."*

She put the life vest on.

Wyatt took her hand and led her toward the water. The town pier had boats tied to every available floating dock. In the harbor, sailboats and motorboats bobbed next to their large white buoys.

The yellow kayak was waiting on the beach. It had two seats and four double-ended paddles.

"Which one should I take?" Ariel asked.

"The front. Great view. Here, wear this." Wyatt handed her a scalloper's cap with a long bill.

"I have sunglasses," Ariel told him, tapping her frames.

"You'll want as much protection from the sun as you can get," Wyatt told her.

"Oh. Thanks."

Now that they were so close to each other, they were awkward. Gathering the skirt of her frilly summer dress around her knees, Ariel stepped barefoot into the boat, lowered herself onto the yellow vinyl seat, and slid her legs into the enclosed deck. Wyatt handed her a double-ended paddle. The kayak rocked as Wyatt shoved it into the water and jumped into his seat behind her.

"Don't paddle," he told her. "I'm going to steer us between all these boats. Don't worry. We won't hit any of them."

The water made gentle rippling sounds as Wyatt paddled. They went around a wooden sailboat and between two motorboats, all tied to buoys.

"You can paddle now," Wyatt said. "See if you can get into my rhythm."

After a few attempts, Ariel's paddle was in sync with his. All around them, the water was clear and blue and cool.

"I feel like a duck!" Ariel told Wyatt, laughing. "I mean, we're almost in the water. This is really sea level."

"I'm going to steer us between the gap and into Polpis Harbor. The ferries don't go there and neither do the big stinkpots."

Ariel concentrated on paddling. The sensation of sliding through the water without engine or sail was a kind of freedom, a kind of opening up. In the wide blue waters of Polpis Harbor, only a slight breeze blew, cooling Ariel, wrinkling the surface of the water, transforming the colors from indigo to turquoise to deep blue. Nothing was pressing on her. No phone was ringing, no customer or agent needed her attention, the ducks and geese they slid past didn't even fuss at them. She could hear Wyatt breathing and sense the movement of his body as he paddled. It was intimate. She couldn't stop smiling.

They bumped up against someone's wooden dock. The house was obviously empty, so they felt no sense of trespassing.

"Let's take a swim and cool off," Wyatt suggested. "Be careful, don't dive here. The water's shallow."

It was impossible to be graceful, getting out of the kayak and into the water, but once there, Ariel floated with her eyes closed, her dress sopping wet all around her, her hair hanging down into the water, and the only sounds she heard were of Wyatt moving. It was a very quiet adventure. She was completely happy.

"Your nose will be burned," Wyatt said, treading water next to her.

"Don't bother me," Ariel told him. "I'm having a moment of bliss."

"I'll give you a moment of bliss." Reaching around her shoulders, he pulled her face up from the water and kissed her.

Ariel didn't take her lips away from his as she kicked herself gently into a standing position so she could put her arms around him and pull him close to her. After a long time, Wyatt pulled back, keeping his hands on her arms.

"I can't stop thinking about you," he said.

"I know," Ariel replied. "Me, too."

"Let's head over to Coatue." Wyatt hoisted himself up on the old weathered dock and held the kayak steady while Ariel climbed in.

They were silent as they paddled across the blue water to the long stretch of beach covered with wild roses and poison ivy. They slid out of the kayak, pulled it up onto the sand, and collapsed on the beach.

It was quiet. No houses, no cars. The town itself seemed far away, another place. They heard only the lapping of the waves against the shore and the occasional cry of a bird.

Ariel expected Wyatt to put his arms around her and kiss her again. Instead, he sat up, drew his knees to his chest, wrapped his arms around his legs, and said, in that serene way he had, "I want to know everything about you."

Ariel was surprised. "Oh! Well. I mean you know a lot about me already."

"Not the real stuff. The deep stuff. Like, which do you prefer, the city or the country?"

Ariel lay back, taking a moment to enjoy the sensation of the hot sand against her cool back. "I don't think anyone's asked me that before. I'd have to give it some thought. I mean, I've seen a lot of cities, London, Paris, and so on, and I have dreams of living in a loft in New York, and . . ."

After a moment, Wyatt prompted her. "And what?"

Ariel sat up. Softly, she admitted, "I'm trying to write a novel."

Her voice was so low Wyatt could barely hear her. "Cool."

Ariel turned to him, holding his arm. "Don't tell any of the others, please. I tell people I want to be a writer, you know, generically. But I have an idea for a novel . . . I write with a pencil in a spiral notebook. When I'm around people, like at college or when we're all in the Sand Palace, I can't seem to write. I'm inhibited, I guess, by the fear that someone will barge into my room and catch me and want to read what I've written and they'll pull my notebook away from me and read a few lines and then laugh at me."

"That is one very specific fear," Wyatt said, keeping his tone serious. "Ariel, I won't tell anyone. Trust me."

"I do trust you." Ariel flushed, removed her hand, looked down at the sand. "The thing is, I have this kind of daydream that I go somewhere quiet, where I can concentrate, where no one will interrupt me. Where I can walk—walking helps me think—without stopping to say hello to people or hearing other voices. When I'm writing, well, I'm already hearing other voices, and I know that sounds moony, but it's true. When I'm writing, I'm with that world, *in* that world. I want everything else to be far away for a while. Just a while."

"I get that," Wyatt said.

Ariel shrugged. "It's silly. I know some writers who can write while they're sitting in coffee shops. And I know I'm crazy to think I could ever get a book published, but I did take a creative writing course and the instructor told me I showed promise as a writer." Ariel suddenly stood up. "Want to walk? Let's walk."

They strolled down the beach, wandering in and out of the water onto the warm sand, stopping to pick up an interesting shell or sea glass.

Wyatt didn't speak. He was full of the honor Ariel had paid him, telling him her secret desire to write, and he thought, maybe he was stretching it, but he thought that just maybe this would mean that Ariel wouldn't mind living in the middle of nowhere. After all, it was a university town.

Ariel broke the silence. "What do you want, Wyatt? I know you're all into science."

He didn't want to scare her off. "I guess. I mean, I'm an assistant to my father, who's a really big deal. I've been given an assistant professorship at the University of Missouri. I start in September. I'll be a lecturer. And a researcher."

"That sounds wonderful, Wyatt! How lucky you are to know what you want to do and to already have a job."

"I'll never be as important as my father," Wyatt replied.

"You don't have to be. You're *you*."

"Columbia, Missouri, is a nice town to live in. Probably lots of writers around. Because of the university and the journalism school."

"It sounds nice." Ariel gazed at Wyatt.

"Maybe you'd like to see it," Wyatt suggested.

"Maybe I would." Ariel put her hand to her forehead. "The sun's getting low."

"Yeah. We should be getting back."

They swam for a while in the cool water then maneuvered themselves back into the kayak. Wyatt and Ariel paddled. They didn't speak. They were so low to the water, and there was no wind, so when the sun flashed lights all around them, the water reflected the colors. It was like a dream.

Back at the boathouse, they returned the life vests and chatted with the owner. Wyatt walked his bike as he and Ariel headed back to the Sand Palace. They talked about movies they liked, and television shows, and music, and let the dream go, for now.

Nick was helping a customer, a portly gentleman who enjoyed wearing suits with vests, when Francine Bruel walked into Fanshaw's. Before Nick could excuse himself, Steve, the other assistant, came from around the counter to greet her.

Francine shot a sideways glance at Nick before speaking with Steve. Nick finished helping his customer, taking his time to chat with the man, who was actually extremely interesting and jovial. All the time, he was piercingly aware of Francine's presence. Had she come in specially to see him? But how would she know where he worked? And why would she even care?

"That silver cigarette case is very nice," Francine said to Steve. "Of course, my sister shouldn't smoke, but if she's going to, she might as well be elegant about it."

By the time Nick reached the counter, Francine's transaction was done. The silver case was wrapped in black paper and placed in Fanshaw's signature black-and-gold bag.

Francine was wearing a white dress that clung to her body. Thin straps went over her shoulders from the very low bodice. She was extremely tan. Her blue eyes flashed.

"Hello, Nick," she said, smiling.

Next to him, Steve gulped in unabashed surprise that Nick knew Francine.

"Hi, Francine. It's nice to see you again." He stood casually, smiling down at her. Inside, he was trembling.

"My father knows Mr. Fanshaw," Francine said.

"Why does that not surprise me," Nick told her, letting his tone verge on the sarcastic.

She liked that. She stepped closer.

"I wonder, would you buy me a drink?"

Nick checked his watch. "My shift is over in—"

"Don't worry, Nick," Steve said. "I'll manage. It's only an hour. We're not that busy."

"Thank you." Francine threw Steve a sparkling smile. "It's so kind of you."

"Thanks, Steve," Nick said. As he followed Francine out the door, he looked back at Steve with a big smile and raised eyebrows.

They stood on the sidewalk for a moment.

"Where would you like to go?" Nick asked.

Francine shrugged. "Someplace dark and gloomy, where we can huddle together and whisper secrets."

"It's early," Nick said. "Let's see if we can get a booth at the Brotherhood." Without thinking, he put his hand on the small of her back and gently turned toward Broad Street.

It was only five o'clock when they entered the historic brick building. Few customers had arrived yet, so they were allowed to occupy the booth at the far back, sheltered and private. The lights were low. A small candle in a glass flickered from the middle of the table between them.

Francine ordered a martini, dry, with an olive.

"Like James Bond," Nick observed.

"He preferred three olives," Francine said. "And shaken, not stirred."

At the same time, Nick said, "Shaken, not stirred," and they smiled at each other with delight, as if they'd done something remarkable.

"And for you, sir?" the waiter asked.

His usual tipple was beer, but today he said, "The same."

Francine leaned back in her booth, raised her arms high, stretched, and yawned.

"Hard day?" Nick asked.

She dropped her arms. Her breasts moved beneath the silky white of her dress. Four slender gold bangles circled her arms.

She wore a heavy gold ring embossed with what had to be a family crest on her little finger. Her fingernails were cut very short. No polish.

Francine noticed him observe her hands.

"Long nails are a bother," she said. "Plus, they catch on things."

"I want to know all about you," Nick said.

Francine laughed. "What else could you possibly want to know? You've seen me on the yacht, you know I'm the carefree, and some would say worthless, daughter of a wealthy man. I do what I want when I want."

"Where did you go to school?"

She laughed again, sarcasm in her tone. "School? Where did I go to *school*? Will you grade me according to where I went to college? If I say the Sorbonne, will you like me more than if I told you I didn't attend college? Ah, now I've confused you. Did I go to the Sorbonne or not?"

"You like to play games," Nick said sharply.

Francine's eyelashes lowered, and her smile became knowing. "Yes. I like to play games." She reached over and lightly touched the tip of her fingers to the back of Nick's hand as it lay in a loose fist on the tabletop. She swirled her fingers to his wrist.

Nick sat entranced. He couldn't swallow. He wasn't sure he could breathe. He wasn't certain it was even a cerebral thought that forced him to suddenly turn his hand over and catch her small, smooth one in his grip.

He said, "Do you want to have sex with me? Because I can certainly willingly and, you'll find, extremely skillfully have sex with you. But more than that, I want to have a relationship with you that is not only sexual."

Her eyes dropped. She pulled her hand away.

The waiter delivered their martinis, making more of a fuss about it than necessary. Francine waited until the waiter went away before lifting her head to face Nick.

"Sweet boy, you don't want to have a relationship with me. I'm crap at relationships." Francine lifted her martini glass toward Nick. "*Santé,*" she toasted.

"*Santé*," Nick responded. He drank in silence. The martini was perfect, ice cold, so cold and clear he could scarcely taste it, and a moment later he felt his chest warm. Ice to heat, Nick thought, and gazed at Francine. *Ice to heat.*

"And you?" Francine said. "Tell me about you."

Nick took another sip before he spoke. The gin worked immediately, loosening his control, causing his fear to vanish.

"I'm the son of Russian aristocrats who have no inheritance to speak of. I attended Harvard. I'm smart, but not wealthy. Well, obviously I'm not wealthy if I'm catering on your friend's yacht." He took another sip. It was amazing to him how such a small amount of clear liquid could loosen him up. "Although, actually, I do live in a palace. We call it the Sand Palace."

"We?"

Nick wanted to please her. From the moment they met, he wanted to please her, and so he told her about his three housemates, their jobs, the half-demolished hotel, the owner's fancy plans.

"And what do you want to do?" Francine asked.

"I want to make money," Nick told her, all his inhibitions gone. "Not just work to have an ordinary life. I want to make a *lot* of money. I want to own a chain of hotels. I want to travel to cities because I own real estate there. I want to have so many employees I can't possibly know all their names, and I want to hold an annual party where my employees drink champagne and cheer because they've received a Christmas bonus."

Suddenly it seemed to him that Francine was looking at him indulgently, like a mother watching her baby take its first step, or a schoolboy reciting a poem.

"Why are you humoring me?" Nick asked. "Why did you come to Fanshaw's? To see me, or was it a spur-of-the-moment decision to play with me because you were bored?"

Francine set her half-drunk martini to one side. She crossed her arms on the table and leaned toward him. She said, "I attended the Sorbonne. I have a degree in art history. I am embarrassed to prefer the Impressionists. I have no skills. I can ski well.

I can swim. I think I was born to play, like a little dolphin in the ocean."

"Not a dolphin," Nick said. "A mermaid."

Francine blushed at his words. "For you, Nick, I will be a mermaid."

Sunday morning, Nick and Wyatt slept late. Ariel and Sheila spread newspapers on the floor around a chair facing the mirror in Ariel's room and took turns trimming each other's hair. They were both in bathing suits and flip-flops. Even with the fan, it was hot and muggy in the basement.

Sheila's red hair had a slight but determined curl to it. Ariel kept dipping the comb into a bowl of water on her desk.

"So," Ariel said, "tell me about your date last night."

"It was lovely," Sheila said, and could not hold back a smile.

Ariel paused, holding the scissors above Sheila's head. "Get out. Did you go to bed with him?"

"Of course not!" Sheila was indignant. The evening had passed with the swiftness of a dream, and Frank had not pressed her to have sex with him. "Frank took me to dinner at the Club Car. We had a crisp Chardonnay and broiled sea bass with lemon. It was so delicious I wanted to lick the plate."

"A *crisp* Chardonnay?" Ariel echoed. "Since when have you been able to judge a Chardonnay?"

Sheila turned red. "Oh, God!" She buried her face in her hands. "I am the most unsophisticated woman in the entire world!"

"I'm not sure that's true," Ariel said, adding with a smile, "but please stop moving your head like that. I almost cut off your ear."

Sheila sat straight, still blushing. "Don't make fun of me, Ariel. I know I'm naïve, but with Frank, I feel . . . more grown-up. Last night we spoke about books, and music—he wants to take me to one of the Musical Arts concerts, but they're always on Tuesday nights, and I'm always tired after working. But anyway, he told me he's reading *Couples* by John Updike. I'm going to get it from the library and read it, too."

Ariel whistled. "I doubt they have a copy at the library."

"I *know* it's got a lot of sex in it!" Sheila declared. "Frank isn't going to corrupt me."

Ariel said, "Stop moving your head. I never said he was. But you admit he's older, and he told you he's divorced, so it's only natural he'd be a little more . . . experienced . . . than you."

"He's a nice guy," Sheila said firmly. "He walked me back here, and he only kissed me good night. He didn't suggest, well, going to his room, or anything like that."

"Of course he didn't, you dope. If Mrs. Reardon saw him take you into his room, she'd throw him out and fire you."

"Couldn't you try to be nice about this?" Sheila asked.

"I'm not sure." Ariel snipped the split ends on the back. "Why don't you ask Hank what he thinks. I mean, I thought you were going to marry him. Yeah, ask Hank about Frank!" Ariel sing-songed the words, chiming the names. "And have you told Frank about Hank?"

"You're obnoxious," Sheila said. "It's a good thing I've already trimmed *your* hair."

Sheila took the last load of sheets from the dryer, plopped them on the laundry table, and began folding them. Her workday was almost over. She could leave when the sheets were done. She was moving slowly, lingering, hoping Frank would come bounding in and up the stairs to his room and she could catch him to say hello. To see if he was still interested in her, or if he'd decided she was too young and silly to spend time with.

In her pocket, she had a letter from Hank. She'd picked it up from her box in the post office this morning on her way to work, and she hadn't bothered to read it yet. She knew what it would say. He missed her, it was hot, he had some potential winners on the high school team he was coaching all summer in preparation for the fall.

Sheila owed him a letter, but she'd gotten so dreamy since her dinner with Frank, as if she'd fallen off a rock ledge and landed in a flower garden. So what if the flowers were poppies, like in *The Wizard of Oz,* and the garden would evaporate the moment she left the island? She still wanted—*something*—from Frank. With Frank. Even if it turned out not to be real.

She went up the stairs from the basement, through the hall and up to the linen cupboard on the second floor. She laid the fresh sheets on the shelf and shook the lavender sachet that Mrs. Reardon kept in her closets so that the delicate fragrance would, for a moment, float free. Really, she might as well be living in her grandmother's house.

In the kitchen at the back of the house, she looked at the wall clock and wrote the time on Mrs. Reardon's schedule. She stepped into the downstairs half bath and changed in to her shorts and tank top, putting her uniform in a tote. She did not want to walk down the streets in her maid's uniform.

If she went out the front door, she might have a chance of running into Frank, but by now she was frustrated and slightly hurt that she hadn't seen him, so she headed to the kitchen.

"Sheila?" The front door slammed and a man called her name. She turned.

Frank walked toward her. He was carrying his briefcase in one hand and his suit jacket in the other. He looked tired and unbearably handsome.

"Hi, Frank." She couldn't hold back her smile. She knew she glowed with delight to see him.

Frank scanned the area for a sighting of Mrs. Reardon.

"She's at a chamber of commerce meeting," Sheila said.

"I'm sorry I haven't spoken with you, but I've been working and it's damned hard trying to get you on that business phone. I don't think that Mrs. Waters likes being *your* secretary."

"It's understandable. She takes dozens of work phone calls every day. Probably doesn't want to have to run down to the basement to leave messages. But it's the only phone in the building." Sheila ran her eyes over his handsome face. "You look hot."

"It's the humidity that gets me." Frank took out a handkerchief and mopped his forehead. "Listen, I know we can't talk here. Will you let me take you out to dinner Saturday night?"

"I would love that."

"It's a date, then. I'll pick you up at seven."

"I'll be ready." Sheila was spellbound by the look in Frank's black eyes. "I'll sit on the bench outside."

"I'll take you to 'Sconset," Frank said. "I'm taking you as far away from this town as we can get without leaving the island."

"Good." She quickly kissed him on his mouth and smiled and hurried out the front door.

ten

This Summer

When they arrived back at the hotel after their lunch at Topper's, they went their separate ways. Nick had to check his email, Wyatt had to check *his* email, Sheila, Ariel, and Francine went off to take naps, and Penny went to her room alone.

Liam had not stopped by or left a message or texted. She decided to tour some of the island's museums and was opening the door of her room when her phone buzzed.

It wasn't Liam. But it was Jade-Marie, so that was cool.

"Hey, Penny, listen, Jason stopped to check out Cabot's Marine and I'm about five minutes from town. Want to go shopping?"

"God, yes!" Penny cried.

"I'll meet you by the library. See ya."

It was the glimmer of sunstruck blue that caught his eyes. Jason walked through the parking lot and behind Marine Home Center to an expanse of marshland, as Nantucket Harbor ended in small fingers of water curving through seagrass. He had to step carefully or get sucked into the swamp, but quickly he was on the long sandy beach leading to the heart of the town.

It was early in the summer, but sailboats were already tied to moorings, bobbing in the gentle waves beneath a beaming sun. It felt good to walk in the open air, to stretch his long legs, to take deep breaths of the salty air. Birds flew overhead, calling to one another, and he stopped to watch them, these common gulls, who could fly in their own universe of light and wind, who could be close enough, almost, to touch heaven. A tall white heron stood on one leg, as still as a statue. He had to step onto pavement to go around the Great Harbor Yacht Club, but a few strides later, he was back on the beach, passing a stand where you could rent a kayak. In the water, a man rowed out to his boat, slowly dipping and lifting the oars. In the distance, two mothers watched their toddlers carefully fill their buckets with sand, and why, Jason thought, could he not have had this?

He was spoiled. He was crazy. He wished he could talk to someone who would understand. His parents certainly wouldn't.

Jason arrived at the town pier. The harbormaster's headquarters were here in a building facing the water. On the other side of the pier was a boat shop. Cabot's Marine.

Cabot's Marine. He knew his father had worked here the summer he lived on the island.

The sight of it tugged at him. God, he was twenty-four! He should be able to choose his own life.

Suddenly, he was slammed with exhaustion. Turning away from the boat shop, Jason walked on toward the town, and passed the busiest streets, and found the Lighthouse. He was glad he saw no one he knew in the lobby. He went to his room, fell on his bed, and was instantly asleep.

Penny and Jade-Marie strolled up Main Street while convertibles and SUVs rumbled along on the cobblestones near them. It was a warm, sunny afternoon, and most people were at the beach, but the shops were still busy.

"The island has a population of around fifteen thousand in the winter," Jade-Marie said. "In the summer, eighty thousand."

"Wow. All tourists?"

"Some come for the day. Many are summer people, who own houses here, or rent for a month every summer. Some are seasonal workers, bartenders, waitresses, house cleaners, event planners. We had *sixty* weddings here last August."

"How do you know all this?"

"I came here last year with my father when he was in the process of buying the hotel. Mom knew some people who were having galas. We met lots of people. And our family spent Christmas here last year. It's a small town with big money."

They paused in front of a real estate agency across from the modest brick post office building.

"Wow, houses are expensive here!" Penny said. "I could never afford to live here."

"No," Jade-Marie said bluntly. "I couldn't if I didn't work at the hotel."

"Do you have, like, a suite?"

Jade-Marie rolled her eyes. "I have, like, a *room*. I eat breakfast at the bistro and bring takeout to my room when I'm done for the day."

"Will you live there this winter?"

"Probably. I mean, I don't need a kitchen to cook meals in. I don't *want* a kitchen to cook meals in. Don't look so wide-eyed, Penny." Jade-Marie linked her arm through Penny's and talked as they continued walking. "You and I grew up in such different ways. You had a backyard where your father barbecued hamburgers, right?"

"That's not a bad thing," Penny said.

"I didn't say it was. But my family has never lived like that. We've lived the longest in our apartment in the city—"

"The *city*? Oh, I guess there's only one city in the world?"

Jade-Marie rolled her eyes. "New York. You knew what I meant."

Penny pouted sweetly. "Why, no, I didn't. I'm only a country girl."

Jade-Marie snorted. "Enough with the act. Be yourself."

"I'm not sure I know who *myself* is," Penny confessed. "I'm not being coy, either. How did I turn out so differently from my family? I swear, it's all about football in our house, and there I am, wanting to escape."

"Where do you want to go?" Jade-Marie asked.

"The saddest thing? I don't even know. I want an *adventure*. I want people back home to think I'm *glamorous*. *I* want to think *I'm* glamorous! I want to find out *who I can be,* and I don't want my mother to tell me what to do and where to go and how to make the lasagna the way my brothers like it."

Jade-Marie laughed. "I get that. I kind of wish the opposite. I mean, I want to stay in one place. My parents fly to Paris or Miami or Denver without a thought. I want to be in a place where I know people, where I have a home."

"Well, at least I made it to Nantucket," Penny said wistfully.

"Yes, and we're going shopping." Jade-Marie stopped in front of windows displaying flamboyant dresses. "Look at this place. It's new this year. Let's check it out."

Penny followed Jade-Marie into the store. It smelled like cinnamon. The dresses were summery, cute, and irresistible. They tried on several, asking each other for an opinion. In the end, they both liked the sundress with silver discs dangling in odd places.

"We'd be so cute in these," Jade-Marie said.

"Have you even looked at the price tag?" Penny asked in a whisper.

"Don't be such a baby. I'll buy both. We can wear them when we go out tonight."

"You can't buy me a dress!" Penny protested.

"Why not?" Jade-Marie shot back.

"Don't you dare! I can't repay you," Penny snapped.

"We'll figure it out," Jade-Marie said. Then she took Penny by the wrist. "Shoes! We have to go to Murray's Toggery."

They cruised through the shop full of iconic Nantucket red shirts and headed to the second floor. Jade-Marie stopped at the Jack Rogers silver espadrilles. "Let's get these. You'll thank me, I promise. These brick sidewalks and cobblestone streets are killer if you're wearing stilettos. I've seen women break their ankles."

"I think you may be the devil," Penny said as she slipped into the marvelously comfortable and still kind of sexy shoes. "I want these. And, Jade-Marie, I'm totally paying you back."

"I know that. Now. What else?"

They window-shopped up and down Main Street before buying ice cream cones at the Nantucket Pharmacy. Outside, they sat on a bench under a towering elm tree and for a while they were quiet, watching people stroll past.

"I like it here," Penny said. "It's a small town, but so fabulous."

"I like it here, too. That's why I'm staying here through the winter, to run the hotel."

Penny licked a curl of raspberry chocolate ice cream off her cone. "Will anyone come in the winter?"

"Absolutely. We have a brilliant Christmas season. The Stroll and New Year's Eve and, in the winter, lots of events, bird-watching, and library programs."

"So you got the job because of your dad?" Penny asked.

"Stop it." Jade sniffed. "I studied hospitality management in college. I've worked in hotels all my life and I like it. Plus, Nantucket is where I feel at home. And frankly, I want to stay in one place. My father is so restless, we've moved more times than I can name."

"But he's rich, right?" Penny asked.

"So what? I'm an adult. I intend to make my own fortune. What are *you* going to do?"

Penny said proudly, "I want to travel. Live all over the world. Since I'm a star at IT, I can take a job with a big company on either coast. The truth . . . I want to make my own fortune, too. I need to get away from my family."

"God, I hear you. *Ma mere* wants to go back to Paris. She's tired of my father moving us wherever his newest passion takes him and hates being alone in the New York apartment. I think she stayed with him only until I graduated from college." Jade-Marie leaned back in her chair. "They're so different. I can't imagine why they married in the first place."

"My parents will always be together," Penny said. "I'm the one who hates that my mom is like a servant to my father and the boys. She's smart, she could get all kinds of jobs, but no, she has to be home, cooking for four huge males, doing their stinky laundry, cleaning up after they track mud all over the house. I was so happy when I was away from them at college."

"Good for you," Jade-Marie said emphatically. "You're an adult. You have your own life to lead, your own path to follow. Your own choices to make. With your degree, you can go anywhere."

Penny nodded eagerly. "I *want* to go everywhere. I want to be adventurous, maybe even wild. I've been a good little girl all my life."

"Let's start your adventure tonight," Jade-Marie suggested.

Someone was knocking on his door. Groggy, Jason sat up, ran his hand through his hair, checked the time. It was almost seven o'clock.

"Jason Smith! Get up!"

Jason yawned, shuffled to the door, and opened it.

"Sweetie," Ariel said. "Nick told us we're on our own for the evening. I thought we might walk around town and have dinner at Cru, the restaurant down on Straight Wharf. Want to join us?"

"Um, no thanks, Mom. I think I'm going out to Cisco Brewers with Jade-Marie and Penny."

"I've heard that place is fun," Ariel said. "Maybe your father and I should go there, too."

"No, Mom." Jason shot his mother a look.

Ariel's mouth quirked up sideways. "Gotcha," she said. "We wouldn't dream of going there." She kissed his cheek and left.

Jason headed into the shower. When he was drying himself off, he noticed he was developing a healthy tan. He pulled on some board shorts and a rugby shirt.

"Jason! Jason Smith!"

More pounding on the door.

"What are you doing?" Jade-Marie had changed clothes since he'd seen her earlier. Now she wore a silver dress, which was, in Jason's opinion, unnervingly tight.

"I fell asleep."

"Wake up," Jade-Marie ordered. "Slap some cold water on your face, and meet us downstairs. We're going out to Cisco Brewers."

Jason nodded. "Five minutes."

He used the john, brushed his teeth, and couldn't be bothered to do more. He was hungry.

He met Jade-Marie and Penny in the lobby. Now he noticed Penny. She wore the same silver dress, but on Penny it looked . . . different. Jade-Marie looked sleek. Penny looked—he tried to find the right word—voluptuous. Or bulgy, but he wasn't sure that was a word. Her breasts were only partially contained in the low-cut top, and when Penny made the slightest move, the entire dress shifted alarmingly.

"Wow." That was all he could say.

"A bus goes out to Cisco," Jade-Marie said, "but it's quicker if I drive the Jeep."

The two women sat in front. Jason rode in back, watching the lush green fields roll by. Jade-Marie turned on the radio and a Taylor Swift song came on. She rolled down the windows of the Jeep instead of putting on the air conditioner and Jason liked that. In front of him, the two women sang and shimmied and laughed. They rode away from town, toward a rural area with, in the distance, the Atlantic Ocean crashing. Here, the air was different.

Dozens of cars were there already. Jade-Marie parked in a field next to other cars. They could have found the brewery with their eyes closed, purely by the sound of people laughing and music from a live band. The place was packed. Couples with children, families with dogs, a gaggle of girls, a clump of guys, all, except the children and dogs, drinking beer or cocktails. They got in line for the bar, bought Whale's Tale Pale Ale to start with, and Jason wandered off to one of the food trucks, knowing if he didn't get something to eat, drinking alcohol might put him right back to sleep.

He bought a bowl of curry from the Big Hug Dumplings truck and ate it leaning against one of the walls, just watching. The party was out on the patio, open to the stars. The gypsy band Coq au Vin was playing wild romantic music, exotic mixed with popular, and the crowd was dancing out in the open air. The picnic tables were full of people, and dogs sniffed the cobblestone floor looking for any food that had been dropped. The sun was low in the sky, the air smelled of the sea, and right at this moment, happiness was everywhere. Jason checked out the guys tending bar. They were cool. Easy, relaxed, joking, listening. At the far end of the yard where the cobblestones ended, a couple was kissing passionately, carelessly. Probably they were drunk, but it would be easy to get drunk out here, with the wild Atlantic winds so near and the rest of the world so far away. He wondered if he could be a bartender here. He ate another bowl of curry and drank another beer. Jason wandered through the crowd, looking for the girls.

Suddenly, Jade-Marie was right in front of him. The way the lights rippled across her dress, shimmering the silver discs, made her look magical. He'd never seen a more beautiful woman.

"Want to dance?" she asked. Her voice was teasing, but her eyes were serious.

"I'm a terrible dancer." His heart was flipping out.

"I doubt that." She began to sway with the music, which had gotten slow and easy. She put her arms around his neck and moved against him.

Jason put his hands on her waist. Jade-Marie let her head fall back so she could gaze up into his eyes. Her dark wavy hair tumbled down her back. She pressed herself against him. She fit easily, perfectly, in his arms.

She rose on her toes, her breath moving against his neck. She kissed him gently, slowly, on his throat. She pressed her hips against his. For just one moment, Jason closed his eyes and sank into the sensation. For just one moment, he was in a place, a world, he'd never known.

Jade-Marie brought her hands up along his neck, his jaw, and curled her fingers in his hair. "God, you're handsome."

He pulled her tighter and whispered, "You're beautiful."

Jade-Marie smiled—he could feel her lips against his neck. She moved slowly, driving Jason mad. They continued to sway to the same steady rhythm, a beat of their own, no matter what music the band played. All around them, people laughed, sang, danced, with the gypsy band's music coming on louder, wilder, bewitching them all. Jason took Jade-Marie's cheek in his hand and gently moved her lips toward his. He kissed her for a long time, and it was sexual, but it was deeper than that.

In the distance, the ocean crashed.

eleven

That Summer

Tuesday morning, Sheila woke to the sound of an argument. Wyatt and Nick were in the hall, yelling.

A light knock came on her door. Sheila opened it to find Ariel there.

"They're fighting. Come help me. Maybe we can sort it out."

Ariel was in a pretty nightgown. Sheila wore a T-shirt that hung almost to her knees. She stepped out into the dim corridor with Ariel.

"Come on, man," Nick was saying. He was wearing a striped seersucker robe and flip-flops. "You know how important this is to me. It might be the night that changes my entire life. I swear to God I'll pay you back."

Wyatt crossed his arms over his chest and leaned back against the wall. "I don't trust you." Wyatt was dressed in shorts and a wrinkled shirt.

"Well, Wyatt, you're just *sad*."

Ariel stepped close to the men. "What's the problem, guys?"

Nick snorted and waved his arm at Wyatt. "I asked him to loan me three hundred dollars for tonight. I want to take Francine to dinner, and I know she's got expensive tastes. *My* money is in the bank, because I trust banks, but today I have to work during my lunch hour, and Wyatt won't loan me the money."

"That's a lot of money," Ariel said quietly.

"Well, this is an important night for me. I like Francine. *A lot.*" Nick paced up and down the hall as he spoke. "Plus, her father is Jean-Paul Bruel. He's an important hotelier. I'd give my left kidney to work for him. If Francine mentions to her father that she's met me, that she likes me . . ."

"How romantic," Ariel said dryly.

Nick turned on Ariel, fists clenched. "Maybe it *is* romantic. I like Francine. She likes me enough to search me out at Fanshaw's. That means *something.* When I saw her on the yacht, we—clicked. I wanted to ask her out, but I was only the caterer and she's the daughter of a millionaire. But I think we really did"—he searched for the word—"*connect.*"

"If you're right," Wyatt said, "she won't care if you don't have money."

"That's true," Nick agreed. "But her father will. He won't want her spending time with me."

"Nick, man," Wyatt said in a friendly tone, "you're a great guy. But I don't know you well enough to hand over three hundred dollars."

"Three hundred dollars?" Sheila said. "Where are you taking her? Paris?"

With obvious patience, Nick said, "I want to take her to the Chanticleer. I want to buy good wine and leave a big tip. I want to impress her, all right? This is my chance to show her who I am."

"With someone else's money," Wyatt muttered.

"I told you I'd pay it back!"

"I don't believe you," Wyatt said. With a face like stone, he turned away and went into his room, shutting the door softly.

———

In her room, Ariel slowly dressed, pulling on a high-necked sundress. She twisted her long blond hair up into a knot at the back of her head. It was cool in her basement room, and the fan helped immensely, but the humidity was pervasive.

Quietly, she walked down the corridor to Nick's room. She knocked lightly. When he opened the door, she put her finger to her lips in a *sh* sign. She handed him an envelope. When he tried to embrace her, she shook her head and hurried back to her room.

After a while, she heard Nick leave. She heard Sheila go into the bathroom and run the shower.

Ariel went to Wyatt's room, knocked on the door, and entered. Wyatt was lying on his bed, reading a John le Carré book. When he saw Ariel, he closed his book.

"Let's talk," Ariel said, sitting at the foot of his bed.

Wyatt sat next to her. "I knew when I came here that Nantucket was a playground for the wealthy, but I didn't think someone my age would be so obsessed with money."

"Nick would have repaid you," Ariel said softly.

Wyatt didn't answer right away. "If you believe that, if you can afford to lose three hundred dollars, you and I come from different worlds. Someone like you would never want to be with someone like me."

"Someone like *me*? Someone like *you*? What does that even mean, Wyatt? I'm working on the island, too, but I don't have ambitions like Nick has. I want to be in love with the man I marry, and know that he loves me, and I want to have children, at least one, and I want to write, I want to create a space for me to write. That is who someone like me is."

As she spoke, she sensed Wyatt closing down.

"Ah," Ariel said, "I've said the marriage word, and freaked you out."

Wyatt faced her. "The thought of marriage does freak me out. I'll never have a lot of money. I'll probably make full professor and get tenure, but I'll never be able to give you everything you want."

"But I thought . . ." Tears came to Ariel's eyes. "You mean that whatever we have between us now is only, in your mind, a summer affair."

"No, that's *not* what I mean." Wyatt ran his hands through his hair. "Ariel, I want to be with you. I think of you all the time. I think about you . . . seriously. But I want it to be right."

"I think it already *is* right," Ariel told him. "Let's talk later. I have to get to work."

"Yes," Wyatt said. He kissed her mouth softly. "Later."

Nick and Francine sat at a table in the Chanticleer, near the window, sipping their martinis. They'd given their orders—mussels and salmon for Francine, salad and steak for Nick—and an expensive bottle of cold white wine, because that was what Francine preferred. Still, Nick thought, he might make it out of here for less than three hundred dollars.

Their drink at the Brotherhood after she came to Fanshaw's had not lasted long. She'd had a dinner engagement. But she had searched him out, Nick thought, and that was important. She'd said that for him she would be a mermaid—and then a group of her friends approached her, chattering away excitedly, and their private conversation ended.

But Nick remembered thinking: *ice to heat.* And he could sense the electricity between them.

"The maître d' knows you by name," Nick said.

"They ought to," Francine said. "I drop enough money here."

"Money is important to you," Nick said, smiling.

"Is that wrong?" Francine spoke as if she were so exhausted it used her last breath to speak. As if the conversation was already boring her.

"Not at all." Nick sipped his wine. *I like this woman,* he thought. *I think I can be honest with her.* "Money's important to me, also. I just don't have as much as I want, but I intend to get it."

Francine lifted one perfect eyebrow. "Really? Before, you said you want to own a chain of hotels. How will you make that happen?"

"I'm willing to work hard and kiss ass to get it."

His last few words brought a genuine laugh to Francine. She leaned back in her chair and applauded. "Bravo! I like this, that you are a practical man."

"Are you a practical woman?" he asked.

"God, no!" Francine said, making her eyes big as if he'd shocked her. "That's why I need to be with a practical man."

"You could get any man you wanted," Nick told her.

"Maybe. Probably. But the trouble is, there are so few men I find attractive."

The waiter set their first courses in front of them. Now Nick wished he hadn't ordered a salad. Lettuce was difficult to eat elegantly. He watched Francine use the two-pronged mussel fork to lift the small meat from its shell and slide it between her barely open lips. She delicately deposited the shell in the small bowl set beside her. She was elegance itself.

Francine met his eyes. "You want to meet my father, do you not?"

Nick felt his face redden. "Of course I want to meet your father. I read about him long before I met you. I know he's an international hotelier. But I didn't ask you to dinner in order to charm you into introducing me to your father. Don't insult me. Don't insult yourself."

"I love how you blush when you're angry," Francine said, lowering her eyelashes. "I apologize for insulting you. I promise not to introduce you to him."

"That's fine with me, Francine. I mean it. You and I—" Nick put down his salad fork and laid his hands on the table, making himself calm down, taming his swirling thoughts.

Francine continued to enjoy her mussels, moaning lightly with each one.

Nick finally said, "Francine, forget your father. I think there's something, I don't know, I hate using the word 'special'—"

"'Interesting'?" Francine suggested.

"Yes, fine, *interesting* between us. It's not just lust, although it is partly lust. You have a drop of wine on your lip and it makes me want to sweep away the plates and throw you on the table and ravish you."

"Oh, please do!" Francine laughed. "I would enjoy that immensely."

"I know you would. But I've said it before. I want more than sex with you. I want—" Nick hesitated. More than once in his life his impulses had driven him into trouble. "I want you to know that I had to borrow money to bring you here tonight. I want you to come to the total crash pad where I'm living for the summer and have dinner with me and my friends tomorrow. On Hump Night. And don't dress like you are now, all chic and diamonds. Try to dress like a normal person. I didn't choose the people I live with for the summer, but I like them, and they are *real*. And it seems to me you could use a little reality."

Francine stared at Nick, and she seemed to be on the verge of crying. She looked like porcelain, as if she could shatter. Then, before he could speak, her face changed. Her shield was up. That Mona Lisa half-smile was back in place.

"I would love to meet your friends," Francine said. "I am honored by the invitation. But tell me, what do you mean by Hump Night?"

"It means that Wednesday is the 'hump' day of the week. Like a camel's back. Meaning it's sort of the mountain we have to trudge up and then it's smooth sliding downhill to the weekend."

"Ah. Clever." Francine was concentrating on her mussels.

"Sheila and Ariel started it. We're all working so hard that our nutritional decisions are usually potato chips and ice cream, with some V8 juice to give us some vitamins. On Wednesday, Hump Day, we set the table nicely—it's not in the basement, it's on the first floor in an air-conditioned, civilized area. Well, not really civilized, given that the hotel is mostly a wreck. The builders are waiting on permission from the powers that be. Still, it's nice. We have wine with our meal, and we actually have conversations."

"It sounds *darling*," Francine said. She reached across the table and touched Nick's face lightly. "I can't wait to come."

twelve

This Summer

Nick had given the Sand Palace Four a daylong tour of the island, including an extravagant lunch at the famous Chanticleer restaurant in 'Sconset. They had strolled the idyllic lanes of the eastern end of the island, remarking on the changes in shoreline and residences the past twenty-five years had brought. They'd sat at the 'Sconset beach, watching the tides roll in and out, talking idly about this and that, until they were sun-dazed and so relaxed they were almost limp.

When they returned to the hotel in the late afternoon, Nick told the others everyone was free to do whatever they wanted. Ariel and Wyatt went off to their room for a nap, promising Sheila they'd get in touch later about evening plans.

Sheila took a long soaking bath and creamed lotion on her skin, which was already freckled from the sun in spite of her sunblock. She pulled on her robe and lay down on her bed, the bed a maid had made up with fresh linens, leaving a chocolate in gold foil on her pillow. She swirled the chocolate slowly in her mouth, loving its rich silkiness. This room, the luxury, the silence, the views, made her feel as if she were in a posh spa. Thank heaven there had been availability for Penny to have her own room. Penny was, after all, an adult, but it was hard for Sheila not to worry about her.

Sheila didn't want her daughter to feel like the outsider Sheila had been twenty-five years ago. And that caused her to think about Francine. If anyone was an outsider this week, it was Nick's wife. Francine was snobbish and aloof, but maybe that was the way she dealt with being around the Sand Palace Four. It would be nice, Sheila thought, to get to know Francine better. If Francine had lived with Nick all these years, she would have some interesting tales to tell.

On the spur of the moment, Sheila called Ariel.

"Ariel, I've had an idea. Let's invite Francine to go out to dinner for a girls' night out. I don't want her to feel ignored."

"That's so sweet," Ariel said. "Hang on, let me ask Wyatt what he thinks." After a few mumbling noises, Ariel said, "Wyatt wants to watch the Red Sox. Let's do it!"

"Great, I'll call her right now."

Francine accepted their invitation and Sheila made a reservation for three at the Languedoc, which she assumed Francine would prefer because the restaurant's name was French.

They met in the hotel lobby at seven-thirty. Ariel wore a blue silk sheath with a violet shrug that set off her blue eyes. Sheila wore a white piqué sundress with a pink paisley shawl, a rather exotic and daring accessory for her, and an expensive one, too. Francine met them in the hotel lobby wearing cream-colored slacks, a matching cream long-sleeved T-shirt, and around her neck, an Hermès scarf in cream printed with gold buckles and black riding crops.

"Why doesn't she just wear a sign that says 'I'm French,'" Sheila whispered to Ariel.

"Because she doesn't have to," Ariel responded.

The restaurant was only a few blocks away, but the sidewalks were crowded with tourists, mothers pushing double baby strollers, small children skipping along oblivious to anyone else, and gaggles of girls window-shopping. They were delighted to be shown into the upstairs back room, a chamber of quiet and elegance.

The moment they settled into their chairs, a handsome man appeared in front of Francine.

"Darling, they didn't tell me you were coming," he said, bending to kiss Francine's cheek.

"I would have called you myself, but it was all spur of the moment." Francine turned her head toward the others. "Ariel, Sheila, this is my very close friend Jimmy Jaksic."

"Delighted to meet you," Jimmy said. "Of course, Francine would have beautiful friends."

Before anyone else could speak, Jimmy said, "Francine, I'm bringing you a bottle of Louis Roederer Cristal for the table."

"You're too kind," Francine cooed. Jimmy went away. Francine said, "This man knows *everything* about food and wine. If the Lighthouse had a restaurant, I would make Nick steal Jimmy away. He is the most charming man in the universe."

"He must be French," Sheila said.

Francine laughed. "No, he's an American. But yes, he seems French, doesn't he?"

Jimmy brought the champagne to the table, uncorked it with a flourish, and poured it into beautiful crystal glasses.

"Enjoy," he said, and hurried away.

"Cheers," the three women said, and sipped the champagne.

At first, they were formal and terribly polite, but as the champagne worked its magic and their appetizers appeared, the three women became more comfortable with one another.

Francine said, "You two seem so close. Do you keep in touch? Letters, emails, photos?"

Ariel and Sheila exchanged tense glances.

"Yes, in a way. Christmas letters," Ariel said, laughing a little. "Life was so complicated that fall, actually the moment we stepped off the ferry into the real world. Wyatt and I had a quick wedding in Boston, with only our families attending, no friends, and we moved to Missouri right away because Wyatt started work at the university. I got pregnant immediately, probably on our wedding night. We had to find a house, we had a baby, Wyatt was devoted to his work . . . it was a crazy time."

"Hank was waiting for me when I got off the boat in Hyannis." Sheila was relaxed and happy in her reminiscence. "It was very romantic. We got married in October. Hank had a job coaching the high school football team, and he was all about football. I had a premature baby at the beginning of April, little Penny. She was perfectly healthy, only small. Hank was disappointed when the baby was a girl, but a few years later I gave birth to a boy. And if that wasn't enough, I had two more sons. This week is the most blissfully quiet time I've had in twenty-five years."

"What about you, Francine?" Ariel asked. "Did you want more children?"

"Oh, no!" Francine looked askance. "I'm not really a lover of babies. Also, I'm involved with my family's hotels." She glanced up. "Oh, look, our dinner. Bon appétit!"

The waiter set oysters and pan-roasted lobster before them.

Francine took a bite, then put down her fork.

"I was not strictly truthful."

Ariel and Sheila stared at her, fascinated.

"Nick wanted to have more children. He wanted very much to have a son. But I dreaded the thought of another pregnancy and childbirth, so I stayed on the pill."

"He didn't know?" Sheila asked.

"No. Someday I'll tell him. Or not. Remember, Nick was ambitious. Is ambitious. He was always working, traveling, giving orders, solving problems. He spent very little time with Jade-Marie when she was small. Now, of course, he adores her. She is his mini-me." Francine turned to Ariel. "What about you? You have only one child."

Ariel toyed with her food for a moment. She put down her

fork. "I wanted more children, but I couldn't have them. I had a hysterectomy, for health reasons—don't be alarmed, it was not serious. But yes, Francine, we have only the one child."

"You could have adopted," Sheila said.

Ariel laughed ruefully. "Wyatt wanted only children who carried his brilliant DNA. His father is such a huge deal, and Wyatt is still trying to catch up with his father's accomplishments. Sadly, that might be impossible."

"Maybe Jason will carry on the tradition?" Francine suggested.

"Maybe." Ariel sipped her wine. "I don't think he wants to. I sense a rebellion on its way."

"And what about your own accomplishments?" Sheila asked.

"*My* accomplishments?" Ariel looked puzzled.

"Yes, tell us about the short stories you've had published."

Tears filled Ariel's eyes. "Do you know, no one has asked me that before?"

"Wyatt must have," Francine said.

Ariel shook her head. "Wyatt hasn't read my work. He thinks fiction is useless. I have a small group of friends at home who write. I'd like to take a course in creative writing at the university, but Wyatt is dead set against that. He's afraid I'll write something that will embarrass him."

"That's terrible," Sheila cried. "He's not your boss!"

"He is the breadwinner," Ariel admitted. "He says that once I start making money with my writing, he'll take me seriously."

Completely deadpan, Francine asked, "Would you like me to kill him now or later?"

Ariel laughed. "Thanks for your support, Francine. Actually, after this trip, I'm determined to take more time to write. I've started a novel. I'd like to attend one of the writers' retreats. I could write all day and at night I'd have a meal in a lodge with other writers. We could discuss our work, and how technology is changing the writers' world—" Ariel caught herself. "Maybe someday."

"Why not now?" Sheila asked.

"Writers' retreats are expensive. Getting to them is expensive. Don't worry. I'll get there."

In the moment of silence, the waiter discreetly opened another bottle of champagne and set fresh glasses before them.

"I truly hope so," Francine said. She gently touched Ariel's hand, then lifted the conversation away from Ariel. "Tell me, Sheila, have you ever worked? I mean other than when you were a chambermaid on the island."

Sheila flushed, but held back her anger. "I think anyone who manages to feed, clothe, and keep four children relatively healthy could be classified as a worker."

Francine nodded. "That was your vision, growing up? To have a large family?"

"Yes," Sheila said stoutly. "It absolutely was. I come from a large Irish family, and I wanted the same for my children. I complain about being overwhelmed, and I am. Anyone with three hulking teenage boys would be. But I love being a mother. Hank and I have known each other since high school. We were college sweethearts and we are still in love."

"After all these years?" Francine asked, laughing.

Sheila squared her shoulders indignantly. "Why is that so funny to you, Francine? Yes, I did marry him because I loved him so very much. I still do."

"I'm not laughing at you, dear Sheila. I'm delighted you are so happy."

Ariel leaned forward. "Did you ever tell him about . . ."

"Heavens, no!" Sheila went pale.

"Oh, this sounds very interesting," Francine said.

"I don't want to talk about it. I can't talk about it," Sheila insisted.

"It sounds like a romantic liaison," Francine cooed.

"It was." Ariel quickly rescued Sheila. "She slept with another man when she was engaged to Hank."

Francine performed a delicate shrug. "Oh, we've all done that." Reaching into her small jeweled evening bag, she pulled out a credit card. "This is on me."

"Francine," Ariel objected, "we really meant for this to be *our* treat."

"Ah, but it has been *my* treat, to get to know you two. Nick has talked about the Sand Palace clique so often."

The waiter returned with the bill, and Jimmy Jaksic came over to thank them for coming, and after many compliments, the three women walked out onto Broad Street. Darkness had fallen, but the shops were brightly lit, and the air was full of laughter.

"You can step out of your real life when you're on Nantucket," Francine said.

"Sometimes you can begin your real life here," Ariel told her.

Francine linked arms with both women. "Darlings, you are teaching me so much."

"Really?" Sheila asked.

"Of course. For example, that you can be elegant without wearing high heels. And completely inelegant if you wear high heels on these cobblestones."

At that moment, a young woman in front of them almost fell when her heel was stuck between two cobblestones. She had to squat down and pry her shoe loose. She was fine, not hurt. She slid the shoe back on and walked carefully to the brick sidewalk.

Francine, Sheila, and Ariel laughed together, feeling just for the moment, part of a club.

It was almost one in the morning when the three walked from the brewery through the field to the Jeep.

"Are you all right to drive?" Jason asked.

"I'm good." Jade-Marie slid behind the steering wheel.

Jason crawled into the backseat, his long legs pressing against the back of Jade-Marie's seat.

Penny collapsed in the passenger seat. "This won't work!" She couldn't get her seatbelt to catch.

Jade-Marie reached over and fastened it.

"You guys were dancing so slow!" Penny yelled.

Jade-Marie changed the subject. "Who was that guy you were dancing with?"

"Wasn't he cute? He was so cute!"

"Penny, if you're going to throw up, roll down the window. No barfing in this car."

"His name was Jade-Marie," Penny said.

"Penny, that is *my* name."

Penny laughed so hard she couldn't speak for a few minutes. "I meant Jamie. Or was it Jacob? Or Jason?"

"Penny, you're drunk."

"No, *you're* drunk!" Penny yelled.

"I'm not drunk. I drank two beers. That's all. I've had my share of hangovers and I never want another one." Jade-Marie steered the car carefully into the line of traffic leaving the brewery and heading back to town.

Penny began to cry. "I'm going to have a hideous hangover. And I'll never see Liam again and I liked him so much. I told you I want to work on the island this summer. Have you found out if a job's available?"

"Penny, working on the island isn't glamorous. It's not like sailing and partying all the time. I did check, and I'll tell you, not that you'll remember any of this tomorrow, but the hotel is fully staffed. But if you looked for a job at one of the shops in town, I'm sure you'd find something."

"That would be *fabulous*, Jade-Marie. I like clothes. I'd be a great saleswoman." Penny tried to hug Jade-Marie, but her seatbelt prevented that. "You are my very best friend."

"I sincerely hope that isn't true."

"Well, that's mean." Penny sulked for a few minutes. "I'm not as drunk as you think. And I see things. Like you and Jason dancing."

Jade-Marie sighed. "Penny, Jason is right here in the backseat."

"Hi, Jason!"

"Hi, Penny," Jason replied.

Penny's hair flew as she turned to Jade-Marie. "If I get a summer job here, can I live in the hotel?"

"What? No. Of course not."

"But *you* have a room there."

"Penny, my father owns the hotel and I work there. I'm in charge of the front desk five days a week. Dad gave me this week off because you all are here."

Penny leaned as close as she could to Jade-Marie and spoke in a sweet voice. "Then let me share your room. I'm sure it's big enough for two. Just think, we'll be like my mother and Ariel."

"My room is small. One queen bed. It's for employees."

Penny huffed, making certain Jade-Marie knew she felt rejected. "All right, I'll find my own room."

"Good luck. Get a job first and the owner might help you find a place. Penny, summer here isn't all beach parties, not for those of us who work here."

"I know that! Mom told me what it was like, being a chambermaid. But honestly, this place is amazing. I'm serious about wanting a job here in the summer."

"Fine," Jade-Marie grumbled. She turned in to the hotel parking lot and pulled the Jeep into a place marked STAFF. "I'll see what I can find out about possible jobs." She looked at the backseat. "Jason, we're here."

Jason waited while the women got out. Penny leaned against the car, her head sagging.

"Hey, Penny," Jason said. "Let me help you into the hotel." He put his arm around her.

Jade-Marie slipped her arm around Penny's other side. Together, Jade-Marie and Jason kept Penny upright as they walked and carried her to the hotel.

At the entrance, Penny rolled her head toward Jade-Marie. "You're, like, my sister."

"I'm, like, exhausted," Jade-Marie said. "I've got to check with the front desk to see how everything's going. You should drink four glasses of water with two aspirin and go right to bed."

"All right, sis," Penny said, wandering off to find the elevator to her floor.

"Good night, Jade-Marie," Jason said. He hesitated.

Jade-Marie nodded toward the elevator. "Perhaps be sure she gets to her room?"

"It's not her I care about," Jason answered.

"I know. But it's late. She's your friend." Jade-Marie kissed his cheek. "See you tomorrow."

She walked over to the check-in counter, pretending to check a computer while she calmed her racing heart.

What was she thinking? She couldn't fall in love with Jason for so many reasons. There was her career, which she was excited about and committed to. And Jason lived in Missouri. He had to carry on his father's and grandfather's scientific work. Jade-Marie liked Ariel a lot, but she thought Jason's father was arrogant in that quiet, cerebral way where the very tilt of his head indicated he couldn't be bothered to listen to you. Ick, Wyatt Smith would be the worst father-in-law in the world!

That she was even imagining this made her want to bang her forehead into the wall.

But when she finally rode the elevator to her floor, and entered her room and got ready for bed, when she lay down with her head on her pillow, all she could think of was that long kiss with Jason while they danced.

thirteen
That Summer

A riel and Sheila were in the basement, cooking feverishly.
"Nick should have asked us first," Sheila grumbled.

"It's fine," Ariel said soothingly. "Look, Sheila, it's all done. Boeuf bourguignon, rice, salad. Nick promised to bring wine."

"You were crazy to make a French dish. You know she'll be critical."

"She's not a monster, Sheila." Ariel was sweating through her clothes in the humid basement cupboard where the hotplate was. "We're doing this for Nick, remember? He likes her. Let's carry it upstairs."

"If she's late, the food will be cold."

"Too bad," Ariel said. "Don't worry so much."

But Sheila did worry. It was bad enough to be the least chic of the Sand Palace group, and now she had to spend what was usually a fun evening with a Meg Ryan clone with a French accent?

Then she thought of Frank, and her mood improved.

Today, after work, she'd met Ariel at the Thrift Shop. They'd bought two slightly yellowed tablecloths and linen napkins. Five wineglasses. Ariel had bought a white porcelain soup tureen that she said she'd keep for herself, for whenever she got married. The Thrift Shop did have quality antiques. They'd picked some roses from a yard overflowing with flowers where no one seemed to be occupying the house. Sheila said they were wrong to do it, but Ariel said it was a crime to have those roses and not be there to enjoy them.

They heard noises from upstairs. Wyatt and Nick had brought wine and Nick had gone into Sharon Waters's office to unlock her door. It was better, the four decided, to have Francine enter from a workspace than the humid basement corridor.

As Ariel and Sheila carried the food upstairs, they heard noises. A door opening and closing. The rumble of Nick's voice. A musical laugh that had to be Francine's.

Then they were all five in the room, smiling, greeting, hugging. Francine kissed everyone on both cheeks, of course. Sheila rolled her eyes at Ariel. Nick beamed. Everyone was extremely cordial.

Nick gave them each a glass of wine and for a while they stood in a loose circle, as if they were at a cocktail party. Francine wore jeans and a white T-shirt, no jewelry. Ariel and Sheila wore sundresses, because it was so hot cooking in the basement, but Ariel had worn only small gold studs in her ears, and Sheila had put on her best dangling silver earrings, a silver chain with a single pearl on it, which she considered very elegant, and a silver bangle bracelet. Now Sheila hated herself for being so wrong, wearing jewelry. She hated Francine for being so beautiful and so slender. Francine was a celery stick; Sheila was a watermelon.

"We should eat," Ariel said. "We don't want it to get cold. Francine, Sheila and I have prepared a French dish in your honor."

"Oh, *merci beaucoup*," Francine exclaimed, sounding surprised and genuine, and Sheila liked her a little better for that.

The five sat at the table, and Sheila spooned the rice onto the plates, and Ariel ladled the beef stew on top of the rice, and Ariel said, "Bon appétit!" and Sheila rolled her eyes again.

Delicious food and good wine can work wonders. Everyone complimented Ariel and Sheila, and Ariel didn't point out that she was the one who had made the stew. As they ate, they spoke about normal things, weather, movies, music. Sheila and Ariel noticed the way Francine and Nick looked at each other, almost dreamily in love. Sheila noticed the way Ariel looked at Wyatt, and she felt like the loner, the outsider at the table, the one without a lover near her. Then Sheila thought of Frank. She had a date with him this Saturday, and she really was kind of in love with him, and now she didn't feel so bad.

"Sheila," Francine said. "You wear such a beautiful pearl. There must be a romantic story behind it. Can you tell me?"

Sheila went paralyzed for a moment, simply from having Francine's crystal gaze focused on her. Her grandmother had given it to her, but that would sound kind of pitiful.

"Oh, thank you," Sheila said. "My boyfriend, well, he's almost my fiancé, but he couldn't afford a ring, and he gave me this when we talked about what would happen after college."

"His taste is sublime," Francine cooed. "Tell me about this boyfriend. What is his name?"

"It's Frank," Sheila said, then gasped at her own mistake, and giggled. "I mean Hank. *Hank.* A nickname for Henry. He was christened Henry, but his father is also named Henry, so they call Hank, Hank."

"And what does your Hank do?"

"He's a football coach at our high school. I mean, the one we went to. When he was there, he was captain of our football team, and he was amazing. He was written up in all the papers, even the Cleveland *Plain Dealer.*"

"Is he very handsome?" Francine seemed truly interested.

"Oh, he *is*!" Immediately, Sheila wished she hadn't been so enthusiastic. She glanced around the table to see if anyone was smirking at her, but the guys were eating and Ariel was smiling. "But he's also very intelligent, and a wonderful leader."

"Football," Francine said. "He must be muscular." She winked suggestively.

"Come on, ladies," Nick interrupted jokingly. "Wyatt and I can't sit here while you all drool over this Hank fellow. The two of us have good qualities, too, you know."

Sheila let the conversation roll on. She tried to hold on to the warm happiness spreading through her from her conversation with Francine. Well, Sheila thought, Francine *was* really a nice person.

The name Francine made her think of the name Frank. She hadn't done anything with him, really, and even though she was going to dinner with him Saturday, she vowed to herself that she wouldn't even kiss him.

When dinner was over, Ariel said, "For dessert, ladies and gentlemen, we're going out to forage for ice cream cones!"

"I don't think I could eat another thing," Wyatt said.

"We'll walk by the water on the way," Ariel told him. "I'm sure you can work up an appetite."

The group, including Francine, carried the dishes down to the small makeshift kitchen. The guys had to wash them because the women had done the cooking, so Ariel, Sheila, and Francine freshened up in the bathroom, reapplying lipstick, brushing their hair, and it wasn't until they walked out the basement door of the Sand Palace that Ariel realized the classy Francine had seen their summer quarters. The three women waited in the unkempt garden outside the partly destroyed hotel.

"Francine," Ariel said, "I'm sure our basement pied-á-terre isn't what you're used to, but the four of us are trying to make money here this summer, and this place was the best and most inexpensive option."

"Ah, I see." Francine nodded. "And the four of you met here?"

"We did," Ariel answered. "Surprisingly, so far we've all gotten along just fine."

Sheila, not wanting to be left out, added, "We call it the Sand Palace."

Francine looked surprised. "The Sand Palace?"

Ariel and Sheila explained the history of the hotel and its summer name. Wyatt and Nick came out, and they all headed toward town. Summer songs drifted through the air from passing cars, and the closer they came to town, the more people they saw, holding hands, laughing, enjoying ice cream cones. The summer night was perfect, warm, calm, and bright from the moonlight. A long line of customers stretched from the popular Juice Bar, and the five joined the end of the line. Nick and Francine stood together, talking softly, and Ariel linked her arm through Sheila's so she wouldn't feel left out.

Sheila wanted very much to prove to Francine that their little group was special. She said the first thing that came to her mind.

"Francine, did you know that Wyatt's father has an element named after him?"

Francine smiled. "I did not know that. Are you a scientist, too, Wyatt?"

Wyatt seemed both pleased and irritated to have the spotlight on him. "Yes, but I'm hardly in my father's category. This fall I'll be teaching freshmen about methods of field investigation for geological engineering studies, how to collect data, geologic mapping, soil formation, soil chemistry, and ion exchange, and so on."

Francine wrinkled her nose. "I'm so glad I asked."

Ariel came to his rescue. "Francine, it's all really interesting when you think about it. I mean, we can use a telescope to see the stars, but how do we find out what is going on right beneath our feet?"

Sheila did a quick shuffle, lifting her feet up from the sidewalk. "I don't think I want to know!"

To their surprise, Francine remarked, "Ah, Sheila, but you know in France, we have the most famous cave drawings, done thousands of years ago, proving how even in the Stone Age, humans kept records and made art from their lives. Les Combarelles is my favorite. It has ancient drawings of bison, reindeer, bears, lions. So beautiful and so precious."

"I've always wanted to see Lascaux," Wyatt said.

Suddenly, they were first in line to order. It was an achievement to buy a Juice Bar cone on a crowded summer night. They strolled off with their ice creams, feeling oddly triumphant.

"I think," Nick said when they settled on benches by the water, "that Francine should be considered an honorary member of the Sand Palace group."

"She did use the bathroom," Ariel said, laughing, "so she's certainly had her initiation."

"All in favor?" Nick asked with fake pompousness.

Everyone raised his or her cone. "Aye!"

"It's unanimous," Nick said. He shook Francine's hand. "Welcome to the most specialized club in America."

"I'm honored," Francine said.

They laughed together, and that night they felt *together,* people at the beginning of an adventure, beautiful people who drew envious looks, happy people sharing this romantic moment in time.

When the town clock at the Unitarian church struck ten, Nick said, "I should go home. I have to be up and out the door by eight tomorrow morning."

"So do I," Ariel said.

"Walk me home," Francine said softly to Nick. "It's nearby, on Upper Main Street."

"Sure." Nick took Francine's hand, and everyone said goodbye.

And Sheila knew that Ariel and Wyatt would want some time to walk and talk and kiss without her trailing behind.

"You two go ahead," Sheila said. "I'd like to sit here awhile longer."

After the others left, Sheila did sit alone on a bench by the water, but she didn't feel sad. Really, she was still riding high from Francine's attention, from the sense of friendship they all shared that evening. She'd not had much of that in her life. Oh, she'd always had a best friend, but Sheila had never been a cheerleader, or part of a choral group or band. She'd never been to a sleepaway camp because her parents couldn't afford it. She worked all during high school and college, mostly at the Cleveland Renaissance. She was friendly with the other housekeeping staff, but they never saw each other outside of work. She'd gone to parties. She was pretty, she knew that, and she was always invited to lots of parties, and she'd had fun, but she'd never been part of a group. Tonight, sitting with her friends on an island, Sheila was warm and happy and more hopeful than she'd ever been.

When Ariel and Wyatt arrived at the Sand Palace, Ariel said, "It seems a shame to have to go to bed so early."

They sat together on the bench in the forgotten garden where flowers grew among the weeds. Wyatt put his arm around Ariel and drew her close.

"When I was young," Wyatt said, "I'd lie in our yard in the dark and look up at the stars."

"You are a secret romantic," Ariel murmured.

"More romantic than a scientist should be," Wyatt said. "If you meet my father, you'd know what a true scientist is like."

"The important thing to me is that I met *you,* Wyatt," Ariel said softly.

Wyatt shifted uncomfortably. He felt like a traitor if his father was criticized in any way.

"My father is a great man," Wyatt said.

Ariel yawned. "I'm sure he is. And now I need to go to bed. I've got work tomorrow." She rose and walked away. Over her shoulder, she said, "Good night."

Nick's shift at Fanshaw's ended at five and Steve Stapleton took over for the evening. In August the men's clothing store stayed open until eleven. Nick had done the evening shifts a few times and was impressed at the amount of business done then. People came from dinners all rosy-cheeked and convivial, "just looking," they said, and they'd buy shirts and golf shorts and butter-soft wallets and navy blazers, running up five-thousand-dollar bills without blinking an eye.

He was behind the counter of watches and wallets when Jean-Paul Bruel walked in. He had been in before, when Nick didn't know who he was. Bruel was always impeccably dressed in a three-piece suit, no matter how hot the weather was, and no one wore a three-piece suit on Nantucket unless they were going to court.

"I think you are Nick," Mr. Bruel exclaimed, coming up to the counter. "You are the man my daughter told me about?"

Nick's heart raced. The man standing before him was everything Nick wanted to be: a wealthy, cosmopolitan hotelier who was at home anywhere in the world.

Nick extended his hand. "I hope I am that man, Mr. Bruel. I certainly am Nick."

"In that case, please join me for a drink," Mr. Bruel said. "I would like to talk with you. Perhaps make a proposition . . . a job offer."

Nick hesitated. During college, he'd worked nights at the Ritz Boston. After the summer, he was to work there again, starting off as clerk, with the position of hotel manager eventually assured.

Still, Jean-Paul Bruel was here in real life, offering a drink and a proposition!

Nick checked his watch. "I'm off work at five. Is that too early for a drink?"

Mr. Bruel laughed. "It is *never* too early for a drink."

Steve Stapleton entered from the back. He had obviously just showered. His hair showed comb tracks and his face was strawberry-red.

"Day at the beach?" Nick asked.

Steve groaned. "I fell asleep in the sun."

Nick laughed. "Are you okay to take over?"

"I'm fine," Steve said.

Nick often stayed to chat with Steve about the store, their customers, beach parties they'd heard were on for that night, and women, but this evening Nick said, "Steve, I've got to leave now. See you tomorrow."

Outside the shop, Mr. Bruel said, "It is nice to drink in the open air as we do in Europe, so we could go to the Boarding House, but today is extremely hot. The Tap Room is a brief walk away, and it is air-conditioned. Much better for concentration."

Once seated in the dimly lit, brick-walled room, they ordered their drinks—Mr. Bruel a Pernod, Nick a dry martini.

"I will not waste your time," Mr. Bruel began. "I own a line of luxury-class hotels."

"Hotel Rex," Nick said. He had done his homework. He'd spent hours in the library, researching the clients of Fanshaw's.

"Indeed. I am in the process of building more hotels, and I need an assistant manager for the hotel in New York. I like the cut of your jib. That is how you put it on Nantucket, yes?"

Nick had never heard anyone say that, but he was not going to argue.

Mr. Bruel continued, "You went to college in Boston, I believe."

Nick's heart thumped. "Yes. My father was a history professor in Boston."

"Your father taught history at the Williamstown High School," Mr. Bruel corrected. "We need to be accurate when talking with each other, no?"

"Absolutely." Nick had been foolish to think for even one moment that Bruel had not done as much background checking on him as Nick had done on Bruel.

"How many languages do you speak?" Mr. Bruel asked.

"Only two, I'm afraid. English and French."

"No Russian?"

"I could buy a bottle of vodka," Nick joked.

"You Americans. So proud to be so ignorant." Mr. Bruel held up his hand. "Wait, I apologize. I did not mean to say ignorant. Anyway, let's move on. You have the right personality and intelligence to run a hotel. You have charisma. But you need more specific information. You will need a few months working with my hotel manager in New York. I assume you are free to leave Nantucket on September first."

"Are you offering me a position?" Nick asked.

"I am offering you a chance to earn that position. Appearance and charm can go far, but you need knowledge, and I've watched you. You learn quickly."

Nick took a long time to sip his martini. Did he really want to give up his position at the Ritz? But to be on the ladder at Bruel's hotel was an incredible opportunity, leapfrogging several rungs up.

"This is very appealing," Nick said. "Would I be paid for my work with your hotel manager?"

"But of course!" Mr. Bruel made a gesture with his hand as if letting a bird fly free. "You would need to work hard, but I think you are a quick study. I think you might be exactly what I want."

"Then I'd be delighted to work for you."

"I, also, am delighted. I'll be in touch with details. I'll send you a check to cover your transfer to New York and all such pedestrian matters."

"Mr. Bruel, sir, I am honored." And he was, Nick thought. He really was. This might be the offer he'd been working toward. Dreaming toward.

fourteen

This Summer

Penny woke with a dry mouth and a pounding headache, but a long shower and several cups of in-room coffee brought her back to normal.

Her phone pinged. Liam had texted: *Good morning Penny see you at the dock in thirty?*

She texted back a thumbs-up emoji. Tapping her weather app, she saw that the day would be hot and sunny, with winds at twenty miles per hour. Not perfect, but nice.

Her family had never been much for sailing, or any sport that didn't involve a ball. But she'd gone sailing on Lake Erie with friends and drifting on a pontoon boat on the Lake of the Ozarks with Jason and his parents. She slipped on a bikini, a long sweatshirt, short shorts, and deck shoes, pulled her hair back into a ponytail, gathered her ball cap, phone, and room key, and went down to the bistro. It was almost ten o'clock, and all the bacon and eggs were gone, but Penny found a lovely chocolate croissant and a tall glass of cranberry juice.

She knew that the oldies were off touring museums today. After she'd left the hotel, she texted her mother and Jade-Marie that she was going sailing with Liam.

At the dock, Penny found Liam waiting on the launch. When she boarded, he held out his hand to help her, and kissed her cheek.

"It's nice to see you," Liam said.

Penny grinned, as if they had a secret, and she thought they did, one they shared, one they would show each other. "Nice to see you."

They didn't talk as they were motored out to Liam's boat, and once on the boat, she did what she could to help make the boat ready to sail.

Finally, they were driven by a lazy wind from the harbor out into the seemingly endless blue waters of Nantucket Sound.

"We're going up to Great Point," Liam told Penny. "Where we went the other night."

"Isn't that where the seals congregate?" Penny peeled off her sweatshirt and shorts and slathered sunblock on her legs and arms and face.

"We won't get that close to the point itself. I have an Ocearch shark tracker app on my phone. We're good."

The day was glorious. The wind picked up out on the sound, and they went at a steady clip through the blue water, beneath the cloudless blue sky. Other sailors were out, and they saw in the distance the distinct shape of fishing boats.

They didn't talk while they sailed. It was enough to simply be there, hearing the splash of the water against the hull and the whipping of the sail in the wind, feeling the boat rock and the sun warming her body, smelling the fresh salt air. After a while, Liam dropped the sails and let down the anchor.

"Let's swim," he said.

"Okay," Penny answered, hiding her nervousness.

She dove into the water, immediately aware of the salt stinging her eyes. Instinctively, she swam back up to the surface and treaded water, gasping from the cold, checking to be certain she was close to the boat.

Liam came near and shouted, "Okay?"

"Okay!" she answered.

"I'll be back," Liam yelled. He struck off in a rhythmic crawl away from the shore.

For a while, Penny bobbed in place, admiring him. He was fast and steady and he made it look so easy, she thought he could swim to Hyannis. She didn't feel so at home in the water. Part of her was still nervous, but she made herself free-stroke away from the boat to prove to herself she was brave, and she wished she could put a marker to show Liam how far she'd gone. Occasionally the wake from other boats splashed her in the face. For a moment fear seized her as the water rocked her one way and another and she realized no one could see her and help her if she yelled. She used the fear to fuel her energy to swim back to the boat. When she had hold of the boat's ladder, she dangled in the water, catching her breath, and for only a moment, she felt exhilarated, ready to go out again.

Huffing and puffing, she pulled herself up into the boat, shedding water as she went. She sat on the bench and squeezed the water from her hair, patted her face dry, and put on more sunblock. Exhausted and pleased with herself, she climbed onto the bow, stretched out, and napped.

It had taken her years to feel comfortable in a bathing suit around other people. Bikini or Speedo, her body was so revealed. Every freckle, mole, and birthmark right out there for anyone to see. Four years of long soul-searching talks with the women she came to know at college had helped her take pride in herself, however she was. She was also toughened by having three brothers in the house, overhearing the various ways they talked about girls.

Liam was older than her brothers, obviously. He seemed content with himself. At home in his skin.

She heard him arrive back in the boat, towel off his hair, and then there he was, water sparkling from his arms and chest, and she thought how very handsome he was.

"Want a Coke?" he asked.

"Sure." She sat up and watched him go to the cooler, lift out two Cokes, and bring them back. He sat on the bow with her. "Thanks," she told him.

"You're welcome." Liam put his hand on her knee. "I'd like to take you on a longer trip. Up the coast to New Brunswick and the Bay of Fundy where gems lie among the rocks in the mud when the tide is out. Or down the coast, to Florida where the manatees live."

Penny couldn't breathe. This man and his world were past her imagining.

"I'd bring you back here, of course," Liam said teasingly.

"I don't know if I'm brave enough for a trip like that," she managed to say.

"Understood. Let's start with a short sail to Boston. If you'd like, we could make it an overnight stay."

"Where would we . . . sleep?"

"I have a cabin below deck. It's got a nice big bed, and a small kitchen, big enough for morning coffee. We could take cheese and bread and champagne."

"Champagne?"

"To celebrate your first adventure. Later, if you enjoyed sailing, we could go down the coast and see new sights, new coastlines. I could catch sea bass and cook them for us. You could see porpoises and whales. At night, we'd lie on the bow and look up at the stars. It makes you believe in magic, seeing all those stars from the ocean. It makes you believe in God."

"*You* make me believe in Fate," Penny told him, and she was privately proud of herself for saying something clever. "How soon would we go?"

"Today? Tonight?"

Penny almost choked on her Coke. She cleared her throat. "But I think I want to get a job here," Penny told Liam. "I've talked to

Jade-Marie about it and she said it's a possibility. It's only June. The stores need help."

"If there's a job waiting for you, it will still be here in a couple of days," Liam said.

This was getting real. "I . . . I should check with my mom."

"How old are you?" Liam asked, smiling to show he wasn't being mean.

"Well, I can't just vanish! I'm supposed to be enjoying Nantucket and we came on this trip together." Penny huffed, and crossed her arms over her chest.

"It will be a twenty-four-hour trip. We'll have Wi-Fi connection all the way there and back. You'll see the coast of Massachusetts."

"And we'll sleep on the boat?" Penny asked.

"We'll sleep on the boat," Liam told her. Rising easily, he held out his hand. "Come with me. I'll show you the cabin."

Thursday morning, Jason allowed himself one of his grizzly-bear deep, long sleeps. In high school, he could stay in bed until afternoon, coming out of his bedroom with a scratchy beard and body odor his mom said she could smell three rooms away. Since graduating from college, Jason spent the days in bed as long as he could, wanting to avoid his father.

His dad accused him of "being good at avoiding things" and Jason knew that was true. Mostly he wanted to avoid any awareness of his life choices. He should just surrender to his father's wish and slot himself into the science conveyor belt.

But that was *not* what he wanted to do. He could never surpass his father, and he didn't even want to try. He didn't want to see life through test tubes and equations, passing his days and nights inside of textbooks. He'd tried to explain to his parents why he wanted to live somewhere else, at least *try* living somewhere else. When he spoke about his plans, his father got impatient and angry and his mother spent all her time soothing his father. Now that he was here, away from the university and coursework and tests and computer graphics, now that he could see how normal life could be lived, he knew he seriously needed to make that break with his parents.

Finally, about two, Jason got up, showered, and dressed. When he got to the lobby, no one except the receptionist was there. The bistro was closed. He had no messages on his phone. A rush of guilt ran through him—had he forgotten to show up for something? He stepped out into the day. The sky was sunny, with a light breeze drifting through the air. He walked down to the strip, bought himself a slice of pizza and a Coke, and sat on a bench on Easy Street, watching the boats come and go in the harbor.

He liked the action of all the boats. The hulking car ferry, the trim schooners, the ostentatious yachts, the authentic fishing trawlers. His dad had told him that he'd worked at Cabot's Marine that summer on Nantucket, and Jason had seen it just yesterday on his walk back to the hotel. It was only five minutes away.

Jason started walking. He crossed Main Street, staying as close to the water as he could. He walked past small clothing shops and the Handlebar Café and was at the town parking lot when he realized that Cabot's Marine was right across the very narrow street. He crossed over, walked up the drive, and looked in. The garage was open, and a small motorboat sat on a trailer inside.

"Help you?" a guy said. He was fiddling with an Evinrude outboard motor.

Jason hesitated. The man he was talking to seemed about sixty, wearing worn, grease-stained clothes and thick glasses. Jason hated the way he looked in comparison, all shiny in his new board shorts. If he were the boat guy, he'd walk right over to Jason and punch him in the face, just because.

"Um, my dad used to work here. Twenty-five years ago. Wyatt Smith."

The other man's face lit up. "I remember Wyatt! Man, he was smart! You're Wyatt's boy?"

"Yeah. Jason Smith."

"Don Cabot." He stood up and held out his hand. "Come in. Have a beer."

Jason didn't often drink beer at three in the afternoon, but Don reached into a freezer, pulled out a Bud, and tossed it to him.

"Thanks, Don." Jason stepped in and looked around.

Don returned to the outboard motor. "People don't pay attention. They could have saved themselves a lot of aggravation and money. Now it's *my* aggravation and *their* money." He laughed.

Jason walked around the shop. Along one wall ran a glass display case and counter with a computerized cash register and a credit card scanner. Basic metal shelving held cables, ropes, foul weather gear, chains, mooring buoys, and other navigational tools. At the far end, just outside the building, facing the water, was a fiberglass skiff and an inflatable dinghy. Anchors, pennants, and electronic devices hung from one wall.

"You sail?" Don asked.

"I can. More jet ski. We go down to the Lake of the Ozarks."

"How's your dad?"

"Good. He teaches science at the University of Missouri."

"Nice. He was a smart guy."

"Yeah." Jason slugged back his beer. He liked the atmosphere of this place. Both ends of the boathouse were wide open to the harbor and sky.

Don said, "Listen, I need some help. See those cardboard boxes? Open them for me. Put the invoices on the counter by the cash register and you can figure out where the stock goes."

"Great." Jason headed over to the pile of boxes.

"Utility knife on the top box."

Jason opened the first box easily, slicing the wrapping tape down the middle and folding back the four cardboard flaps. "Flashlights," he called.

"Next to the display case," Don yelled. "Flatten the box when you're done."

Jason focused. It was an easy enough task, but the shop was crammed with objects. He dealt with the task, flattened the box, opened another.

"Garmin GPS," he yelled. "Display case, right?"

"Right."

He unpacked first aid boxes, map-tech charts, muck boots. Boat trailer winches, tongue jacks and dollies. Metal tools he had no name for. It felt good to be moving with a purpose. His mind respected the equipment that made boating possible. When a phone rang, Don ignored it, and mostly he didn't talk. An old radio sat on a shelf playing soft rock. The sun streamed in the wide garage door.

Jason carried the flattened boxes around to the side of the shop where the wooden dumpsters sat, and returned to Don.

"Anything else I can do?" he asked.

"Want a summer job?" Don replied. He stood up to face Jason. His face was weathered and lined, but his body was lean and looked fit.

"A summer job," Jason repeated, as if his mind couldn't translate the words into meaning.

"I'd use you into the fall," Don replied. "It's the three summer months that are killing me. I need more help."

"I'm not a mechanic," Jason said.

"You could take care of the other stuff. I need three full-time workers. Bobby's off-island today. He's a mechanic."

Jason squinted, staring down at his feet. He could be here, instead of in a cubicle with a computer under his father's supervision.

"I'd have to find a place to stay."

"You could rent the apartment over the shop."

Jason tried not to act like a total dope. "Your apartment over the shop?" This shop sitting right practically in the harbor?

"It's small. One room, galley kitchen, and head. And in all honesty, it's a dump. I've got to say that when there's a gale, the windows rattle and the bed shakes. Go up and check it out. The door's in the back."

Jason went around back, opened a door, and went up the steep, narrow stairs that led directly into a room. Don was right. It was a pit. Old, unstained, splintery wooden floors and walls, a twin bed against the back wall, hooks on the wall instead of a closet, a small tilting chest, and a bathroom with a shower, toilet, and sink, all rust-stained. The bathroom floor smelled of mildew. Next to the bathroom door was an old metal cabinet with a chipped porcelain sink. A two-burner hot plate sat on a metal filing cabinet.

But two windows faced the harbor, and from where he stood, Jason could almost jump into the blue water glistening under the sun. The town pier extended out into the harbor next to Cabot's Marine. A long sandy beach ran along both sides of the pier. Fishing boats, sailboats, Boston Whalers, dinghies, and inflatables rocked neatly in their slips. Beyond the pier, Jason could see the opposite shore with its beaches and private docks, and farther out, a long sandbar extending out of sight. He couldn't tell exactly where the water turned to sky.

He took a deep breath, the first deep breath he'd had in a year. This was freedom. This was—the world! As he watched, a Sunfish with a bright red sail zipped between boats tied to their moorings. A gull dipped, dropped a shell on the wooden pier, and dove down, screaming, to extract the meat. Flags fluttered from boats tied to buoys and from houses across the water. He could stand here forever and the scene would never be exactly the same.

His heart opened. Tension evaporated from his shoulders. He didn't have to be the mini-me his father wanted. He could be far away from academia. He could be on an island!

He held back a gigantic whoop. He didn't want to seem totally childish. He ran back down the stairs and into the boathouse.

"After I paid rent, would I make any money?" he asked.

"I always give my guys a deal," Don said. "You'll make money." He held out his hand. "I think you'd like it here and I could sure use you. Tell your dad I said hello."

"I'll take the job," Jason said.

"Good. Can you start tomorrow?"

"I'd like to wait until Saturday. I'm here with my parents for a reunion with old friends. It's kind of a big deal for my parents. They leave on Saturday."

"Fine," Don said. "Be here at seven Saturday morning. Boat people start early. I'm here at five. We'll do paperwork tomorrow morning. Bring coffee. My machine's broken. You can pick some up at the Handlebar Café on your way here."

Jason caught himself whistling as he walked back to the hotel. His father would be furious, but Jason didn't care. He had found his own job and his own place to live. He sensed that his real life was beginning.

Jade-Marie went to the back office where Sharon Waters was at her desk, working on her computer. Jade-Marie threw herself into a chair, reached over to Sharon's bookshelf, and took a double-size Butterfinger for herself.

"Lunch," she said to Sharon.

"I made coffee," Sharon said, without taking her eyes off her screen.

Sharon was in her early sixties, trim, attractive, and calm. She'd been with the hotel twenty-five years ago when it was caught in the turbulent process of renovation. She had worked then with jackhammers, electric drills, and hanging electric cords in the old hotel space, and she worked just as efficiently now in her sharp, modern office with all its zippy technology.

"What are you doing?" Jade-Marie asked.

"Tax stuff. Numbers. My happy place."

Jade-Marie laughed. "Are you going to come out and meet the old gang?"

Sharon answered without removing her fingers from the keyboard. "I don't think so. I didn't really know them. Hardly ever saw them. They were so young."

"You weren't much older."

"True. But I was obsessed with order."

"And probably *order* wasn't the highest priority for the Sand Palace group."

"That's for sure. I remember that they did have Wednesday night dinners here. In the room that's now used for storage. They set up a card table and used paper towels for napkins and paper plates and cooked fancy meals and drank wine. And they cleaned up after themselves." Sharon stopped typing and swiveled in her padded, high-backed executive chair to face Jade-Marie. "They were all so beautiful. And hopeful."

"Happy?" Jade-Marie asked.

"No one is ever happy all the time." Sharon leaned back in her chair, closing her eyes.

"Did they fight?"

"Not *fight*, no. In August there was a week when everything seemed topsy-turvy."

"Why?"

"Jade-Marie, I don't know. I did my best not to intrude. As long as they didn't damage their rooms, I stayed out of their way."

"I have a crush on Jason," Jade-Marie confessed.

"Jason," Sharon said, nodding. "Wyatt's son. Is the crush mutual?"

"We danced out at Cisco last night, and the chemistry was off the charts, but he'll be here only for a week, plus the son of my parents' friends? Weird."

Jade-Marie could see Sharon's eyes darting back to her computer screen. She knew Sharon could deal with only a small shot of gossip.

"I'll let you get back to work. Thanks for the candy bar."

Sharon had swiveled back to the computer before Jade-Marie was at the office door. She went down the hall and into the foyer. Rosa, a pretty middle-aged woman, was behind the reception desk.

"How's it going, Rosa?"

Rosa shrugged. "Okay. Your father had the *What to Do on the Island* brochures printed up. Everyone's checked out on time and the girls are making up the rooms. Nothing exciting."

"Right." Jade-Marie knew that Rosa had five children at home, four of them teenagers. Rosa was probably glad for the lack of excitement.

"Jade-Marie!"

Both women turned to look at the main entrance door. Penny was almost flying through it.

"Penny! Are you okay?"

"I'm wonderful!" Penny said. "I'm going sailing with Liam tonight. Overnight! We'll sail up the coast to Boston and back tomorrow."

"You are? Why?"

"Because I want to! Jade-Marie, this is probably the most exciting thing I've ever done in my life."

"The chances of getting a job go down every day you're not on the island," Jade-Marie reminded Penny. "Lots of people want to work here for the summer."

"I don't care. I'm in love with Liam, and I want this adventure."

Jade-Marie took Penny's hand. "Penny, I don't know you well. I've only just met you. But aren't you behaving kind of recklessly?"

"You're right, I *am* being reckless for the first time in my pathetic life. My brothers get away with everything, so I'm the good child who never gives them trouble. But I'm not a child anymore. I'm going with Liam."

"What about your mother?"

"I have to pack. If I don't see her before I go, I'll leave her a note. And we can always phone."

Penny stood up again, and this time she hurried to the elevator, leaving Jade-Marie confused, worried, and happy for her new friend.

Ariel was only slightly surprised when the caller ID indicated that it was Sheila.

"Hi, Ariel." Sheila's voice held a slight note of tension. "I was wondering if you'd like to go on a bike ride with me. Now. It wouldn't be a long ride."

Ariel understood at once. She'd been waiting for something like this. "Of course. Let me put on my sneakers."

They met at the front desk and checked out two bikes.

"We need to wear helmets, too," Sheila said.

Ariel said, "Seriously? You know they've built bike paths since we were here last."

"We need to wear bike helmets," Sheila said stubbornly.

"All right, all right. We'll wear bike helmets."

Sheila led with Ariel right behind her as they cautiously steered their bikes through the parts of town that had no bike paths and only a few inches at the side marked for biking. At the rotary, they walked their bikes, turning west. A proper bike path had been built going out to 'Sconset, but they had biked only a half mile when Sheila stopped.

"It was here," she said, nodding her head at the turnoff to Polpis Road.

The two women waited until the traffic cleared, then walked their bikes across the street and down the bike path to Polpis.

"Look," Sheila said. "There wasn't a bike path there twenty-five years ago."

"They must have added this left-turn lane," Ariel suggested.

Tears came to Sheila's eyes. "Maybe there were too many accidents at this intersection."

Ariel gave Sheila a few moments, then said, "There's still a woods here. Want to walk in it?"

"Yes," Sheila said. "Good idea."

Behind Island Liquors lay several acres of wild land, part of it a dump site for building machines, much of it thick forest bordering the Milestone road. The trees and tall weeds were very green. No walking paths existed. The area was thick with scruffy bushes fighting other bushes for air and light. It was all innocent and natural, untouched by man.

"It's just as I remember," Sheila said.

"Do you regret it?" Ariel asked.

"Oh, I do regret the accident. I'd give anything to undo that. But the truth is, Ariel, there have been days in my life when I was stuck at home in a blizzard with sick children, and wiping up vomit and rocking crying babies. Then, I remembered my few hours spent with Frank Johnson on the island, and I don't regret it at all. Really, the memory sustains me somehow."

"Have you ever talked to him again? Googled him?"

"Oh, no. I'd never do that. He was like a dream I had." Sheila looked around and held out her hands. "I thought I might feel something here, because what happened here was so huge in my life, it seemed something might be etched here forever. But no, this place doesn't remember me."

"That's a good thing, Sheila." Ariel wrapped her arms around her friend and held her as she cried. "Let's bike back into town and get ice cream!"

Sheila sniffed back her tears. "Yes, let's!"

fifteen
That Summer

Wyatt whistled as he loped home from working all day at the boat yard. He was making good money. He was in love with Ariel, and he believed she loved him. Soon they would be back in Missouri, and Wyatt would have this beautiful woman waiting for him at home while he focused on his work. In his mind, he organized his classroom lectures. He couldn't wait for Ariel to meet his father.

The Sand Palace was quiet. Wyatt went down the hall and took a long shower. That was one good thing about working with boats. It felt so good to stand under hot water, washing off the grease and oil and dirt. He brushed his teeth and shaved, so he wouldn't have to in the morning.

He wrapped a towel around his middle, stepped into his flip-flops, and opened the bathroom door. Steam billowed out into the hall. He was returning to his own room when he ran into Ariel.

"You smell good," she said. She was all dressed up in her work clothes, and she was beautiful.

He smiled down at her. "You smell sexy." He was insanely aware that he was half naked next to her. He almost couldn't think. His voice was husky when he said, "I've been working my fingers to the bone."

"Let me kiss them better." Ariel turned her head slightly and kissed the tips of his fingers.

Her kisses were like matches to fire, so small to start something so huge and wild. Wyatt pulled her to him, cupped her head, and kissed her sweet mouth.

Ariel melted against him. Wyatt lifted her off her feet, kissing her as he carried her into his room, slamming his door shut with one foot. He fell on his bed, pulling Ariel on top of him. He wanted to make love with her, but he didn't want to pressure her and he didn't want to crush her under him, making her feel trapped.

Ariel wrapped her arms around his neck and wriggled against him, and that nearly made him crazy.

"You're so handsome," Ariel whispered, kissing his neck, his shoulders, his chest. "You're the most wonderful man I've ever met."

"Marry me," Wyatt told her. "Marry me tonight."

Ariel laughed. "We can't marry tonight, silly. But someday. Soon."

He didn't want to frighten her with the heat of his desire for her. He wanted to do this right. "Well, then, let's pick up some fish and chips and go watch the boats."

"A perfect idea," Ariel said.

It was happening. Sheila was ready. This was her third date with Frank, and this was the night she would go to bed with him. They hadn't talked about it, but Sheila knew it was going to happen, and she couldn't wait. Frank told her he was taking her to the Chanticleer, the famously expensive and classy restaurant out at the east end of the island.

Sheila worried about what to wear. Her butterfly dress was too silly. Ariel loaned her a simple black dress and swept Sheila's red hair up into an elegant chignon.

Entering the restaurant was an experience in itself. The white gate and the roof of the building were covered with hundreds, if not thousands, of small pink roses, and on the front lawn stood a beautiful merry-go-round horse. Inside, the floors were polished wood, the tables covered with snowy white linen, and the atmosphere was hushed, as if they were in a place of worship.

The maître d' approached. "It's good to see you again, Mr. Johnson."

"Thank you, Mark," Frank said.

They were seated at a table overlooking the garden. Immediately, Frank ordered a bottle of champagne, which soon arrived in a standing ice-filled bucket. The waiter expertly removed the cork and poured the pale gold liquid into their glasses, then discreetly disappeared.

Sheila took a sip. "This is heavenly."

"I'm glad you like it," Frank said, keeping his eyes steadily on her face.

"How has your work been going this summer?" Sheila asked. She had sat in her bed last night with a pad of paper and a pen, working out what she could ask Frank to help her get to know him.

Frank leaned back in his chair. "It might not look like work to you. More of a drink or dinner with friends. I've brought several accounts here for lunch or dinner."

"That's why the maître d' knows you," Sheila said.

"Yes. I tip well. Over our food and drinks, I ask about his wife, his children, a vacation in the planning stage, if their dog recovered from being hit by a car."

"They must be pleased that you remember them so well, as if you were a friend."

Frank poured them each another glass of champagne. "It's not an act. I like my clients. I reciprocate. I tell them that I miss my daughter, now that my divorce has gone through, that my wife is marrying her lover and they want to move to New Mexico, but our custody arrangement says she cannot take Amy out of the state. I tell them I live in a one-bedroom apartment in Newark, and will stay there until I decide where to live permanently. The airport is nearby. Some clients offer sympathy, some have also been divorced and share their complaints."

"How old is your daughter?" Sheila asked.

The waiter approached to take their order, putting their conversation on pause. Sheila ordered the tuna tartare and the halibut. Frank ordered oysters and a steak.

When the waiter stepped away, Frank continued as if they hadn't been interrupted.

"Amy is six. I do love her, but the truth is that with my traveling, I haven't been home often to be with her. That, I regret."

Sheila could hear the melancholy in his voice, see the sorrow in his eyes.

"Tell me about Amy," she said.

Frank shook his head and smiled ruefully. "Not tonight, Sheila." Reaching across the table, he took her hand and said, "When you are as old as I am, you will learn to live in the moment. In this moment, I am here with a beautiful young woman and we are about to be served ambrosia."

Sheila blushed as he held her hand. She didn't know what to say. She was relieved when the waiter set their appetizers before them.

Dinner rolls and butter were on the table, and Sheila broke a roll, buttered it, and took small bites to help her swallow her very pink raw tuna. They chatted about the island weather, a play the Theatre Workshop was performing, and Mrs. Reardon's decorating scheme. Sheila spoke about her nice Catholic family, her parents' old-fashioned ways, and the rather daring friends staying at the Sand Palace with her. Their entrées arrived. As they ate, they discussed their food, and the extravagant barbecues Sheila's father had in their backyard in the summer, and Frank spoke of unusual treats he'd tasted on his travels: rattlesnake, frog legs, haggis.

When the waiter asked if they'd like dessert, they looked at the menus and then at each other.

"The chocolate mousse looks good," Sheila said.

Frank said, "Just coffee for me, thanks." He gazed at Sheila, and suddenly it was as if the atmosphere had changed, and just his eyes on her made Sheila's face warm. The noises of the room disappeared. She was alone in the universe with Frank.

"How fortunate you are," Frank said.

"Oh?" Sheila asked, slightly worried.

"You can eat dessert and not worry about gaining weight. I'm older, and desserts are forbidden if I want to keep my lovely figure." Frank laughed and patted his firm belly.

"You look perfect," Sheila blurted. "I mean, you do have a lovely figure. I mean, I guess men don't actually have *lovely figures,* but you are muscular and broad-shouldered and handsome."

"I'm flattered that you think so." Frank paused, and then he said in a low, serious voice, "Beautiful Sheila, I want nothing more in the world than to put my muscular figure next to yours."

Sheila sat back in her chair, refolding her napkin. His words had set her alight. Flames seemed to flicker in her belly and she knew they would only be extinguished if she could press herself against this eloquent man. She told herself to be brave. To live in the moment.

She sat straight and met his gaze. "I would like that, too."

"Now?" he asked.

"Now," she answered.

Frank pushed back his chair and stood up. He took his wallet from the breast pocket of his suit, removed a few hundred-dollar bills, and put them on the table.

"I know where to go," Frank said, and he reached for Sheila's hand.

Sheila thought that he would take her to his car. Instead, he led her to a small cottage on a side street of the small village. They walked up a brick sidewalk bordered with flowers. The house was dark. Frank slid a key out of his pocket and opened the front door.

"It's all right," he told Sheila. "The owners are away."

He kept his hand on hers as they went down a hall and into a bedroom. The curtains were pulled and no lights were on, but Sheila could make out the shapes of a bed, a dresser, a bedside table. Frank turned Sheila to face him. She was trembling.

"Don't worry," he said in a low voice. "I've had a vasectomy. You can't get pregnant."

"I'm on the pill," she told him. She wanted to say, *Stop talking.*

Finally, he put his arms around her and pressed himself against her. She was almost paralyzed with fear and anticipation. She put her hands on his back. Frank kissed the side of her neck and down the tanned bare skin of her shoulders. Then he kissed her mouth.

The kiss tasted like champagne. Sheila nearly fell to the floor with intoxication. He kissed her for a long time, slowly, determinedly, the kiss becoming more forceful with each moment.

"How do you get this dress off?" he asked.

Sheila smiled. She slipped one strap off her shoulder, then the other, and the slide of the silk against her skin seemed unbearably erotic. She shimmied the dress down to the floor and stepped out of it. She wore only lace panties. Her tightest, strapless bra.

Frank exhaled. "My God," he said.

He kissed her breasts, her belly, the small bump of pubic bone. Sheila shook so hard she said, "I can't stand up."

He carried her to the large bed, lay her down, and undressed while keeping his eyes on her. When he was naked, he was clearly ready, but he continued kissing her, touching her, telling her she was beautiful here, and here, and here. When he entered her, she cried out.

They stayed in the small house the entire night. At one point, Frank got them each a glass of ice water. They slept into the small, deep hours, waking to make love when they were barely conscious. His need for her astonished her. She'd never felt so beautiful, so alluring, so necessary.

When morning came, blaring its light through the closed curtains, they left the house, walked to Frank's car, and drove back to town.

At the Sand Palace, Frank asked, "Will I see you again?"

Sheila, drunk on power, laughed. "You bet. You'll see me when I'm in my tidy uniform working at the Rose Hotel."

"You mean more to me than you can imagine," Frank told her. He looked sad, and tired, and angry.

Sheila said, "I'm glad." She hurriedly shut the car door and went toward the Sand Palace, and quietly slipped down the hall to her room.

Nick cut himself shaving, and cursed. He was anxious about the dinner at Francine's tonight. Francine and her father were so elegant and sophisticated. Nick didn't want to show up with a shaving cut on his chin. Plus, would one of his Sand Palace friends embarrass him? It was only his love life and his professional life at stake.

After Francine had extended the dinner invitation, Nick had said to them all, "Look, you don't have to go if you don't want to."

"Don't be silly," Ariel had said. "We're all dying to go. We can see how your classy inamorata lives."

"All right," Nick had conceded. "Just don't—"

"Don't what?" Wyatt had interrupted. "Don't fart at the table? Don't talk with our mouths full?"

Ariel had hit Wyatt on the shoulder. "Stop it. Be nice."

As the four walked along Upper Main Street, Nick admitted to himself that his friends at least *looked* nice. Wyatt had scrubbed the boat oil off his fingernails and put on a summer weight blazer Nick didn't even know Wyatt possessed. Ariel always looked perfect. Tonight, she wore a Lilly Pulitzer dress and small gold ear studs. Even Sheila, who often wore low-cut tops—and why shouldn't she, her figure was a gift to mankind—even Sheila had worn a sleeveless dress with what Ariel called a boat-neck collar, so that much of Sheila's gorgeous pulchritude was not on display.

They all looked fine, Nick decided.

"This is it," Ariel said. "Twenty Main Street."

"Wow," Sheila whispered.

"Good Lord, Nick, you've picked well," Wyatt said.

The house was an antique two-story, brick Colonial with stunning white trim and on the roof, two brick chimneys and a white widow's walk. It was impressively large, and it was situated at a rise in the land, so it looked formidable.

"Gird your loins, boys," Ariel said. "We're going in."

Francine opened the tall front door with a welcoming smile. She wore a simple navy-blue silk dress, no jewelry, and no shoes.

"Mes amies!" she cried. "Come in, come in."

She led them into the front room, asked them how their day had gone, prepared Pernod cocktails in antique etched glasses so fragile Nick was afraid to touch his.

"Is that a Renoir?" Ariel asked, gazing at a painting of a sweet, plump, young girl holding roses.

Francine said lazily, "Yes. My mother acquired it years ago."

"Your house is lovely," Ariel said, sinking into a burgundy and cream striped silk sofa.

"Merci, but it is too much, I know, too much. My mother loved excess."

"It's stunning," Sheila said, blinking several times as she took it all in.

The walls were papered silk with male peacocks' tails at the full moment of their display, presenting a confusing glory of different colors in fan shapes, with large indigo eyes in the middle. The room was crammed with furniture, some delicate French antiques, some new chairs and sofas, so fully stuffed it was difficult to sit upright in them. The desk and tables were covered with silver objects that splintered the light, throwing it back in their eyes.

"Is your mother in France?" Ariel asked.

"No, I'm sorry to say, she died a few years ago. Lung cancer. Too many Sobranies." Noticing Sheila's confusion, Francine added, "Cigarettes made from a secret Russian formula for the elite, the heads of state, the monarchies, the kings. The oldest cigarette brand in the world. The cocktail cigarettes were delightful, different colors, pink, green, violet . . . I always longed to smoke them, but when my mother died of lung cancer, I decided not to smoke." Francine shrugged playfully. "I changed my mind."

"I'm sorry about your mother," Sheila said.

"Thank you. She was joyful, flamboyant. She had many passions. Do you know her worst obsession?"

"Tell us," Ariel said.

"Opera!" Francine laughed. "Screeching and bellowing throughout the house. The more dramatic, the better. I mean, she played recordings. She couldn't sing, and she knew it, thank the Lord."

"My mother loves ventriloquists and their dummies," Sheila said. "They frighten me."

Nick cringed. "I'm sure—"

"Ooh-la-la!" Francine cried. "I also dislike those dummies. They seem malevolent."

"I'm afraid of clowns," Ariel admitted. "And mimes."

"Mimes are the worst!" Francine agreed. "People blame the French for mimes, but it is an ancient form of acting, Greek or Roman, I think."

A woman appeared at the door. She wore simple black trousers, a black shirt, and white apron. Her auburn hair was twisted up at the back of her head.

"Dinner is ready, Francine," she said.

"Oh, Natalie, thank you. Everyone, I want you to meet Natalie, my friend and companion."

Introductions were made all around. Nick didn't know whether to rise like a gentleman or offer to shake her hand, but Natalie didn't actually enter the room, so he stayed put.

They followed Francine into the dining room, where the walls were papered with silver, the tablecloth and napkins were of antique intricate lace, and the chandelier blazed above the table. The meal was simple. Escargot in a wine and butter broth, rack of lamb, asparagus, and a salad to finish. Fresh strawberries in cream in a crystal bowl for dessert.

Conversation was light. Ariel spoke about her trip to Paris, which led Francine to ask exactly where Ariel went and what she saw. They were served with two different wines, one white, one red, and by the salad course, Sheila's face became very pink.

"I haven't been to Paris, but I've been to Quebec," Sheila announced. "Our French class went on a trip."

"Did you stay in the Château Frontenac?" Francine asked.

"Ha! Sure we did." Sheila touched her napkin to her mouth, instantly aware that she'd been rude. In a more pleasant tone, she continued, "I'm afraid that was too expensive for us. But we were able to use our paltry French now and then. When a Quebecois understood us, we were thrilled."

"You are admirable," Francine said. "Americans are lazy about other languages. They think everyone should speak English."

"Some of us have trouble doing even that," Nick joked.

Natalie brought them small cups of strong espresso. Sheila went into a coughing fit. The men threw the thick black liquid back as if chugging liquor. Ariel sipped hers, her eyes watering.

"We should go for a walk," Francine said, rising.

It was almost dark when they left the Bruel house. Francine linked her arm with Nick's. Wyatt took Ariel's hand, and Sheila trailed behind, pretending to inspect roses or a small sculpture.

"Sheila, join us," Ariel called.

"No, thanks," Sheila answered. "I'm thinking of Hank." She was thinking of Frank.

They strolled through the town, down to the harbor to look at the yachts. The lights inside the cabins cast radiant silver on the water, which shimmered when the wind stirred. It seemed like a moment out of time.

They had work tomorrow, which meant sleep tonight, so they walked Francine back home and returned to the Sand Palace. The evening was cool and fresh, the air fragrant with flowers and salt. Without planning it, they dropped to the ground on the unkempt lawn and lay back, staring up at the stars.

Ariel said, "Thank you for taking us tonight, Nick. Francine is lovely."

"You'll have a hard time keeping that one happy," Wyatt said.

"Why would you say that?" Ariel demanded.

"Look at the way she lives," Wyatt responded. "All that fancy, unnecessary stuff. I was afraid to move, afraid I'd break something."

"She's not like that," Nick argued.

"I agree with Wyatt," Sheila said.

Ariel raised her head to stare at Sheila, surprised. "Why?"

"I'm not such a redneck I'd insult her to her face," Sheila shot back. "But come on, no wonder there was a French revolution. I'm surprised Francine didn't serve us cake."

Wyatt laughed. "Clever, Sheila. Yes, it was all very Marie Antoinette."

Nick argued, "It isn't French to be wealthy."

"No," Sheila said, "but it is certainly *Francine* to display her wealth."

"I agree," Wyatt said. "Peacock feathers on the wall? And *frigging* escargot? How ostentatious is that, to serve us *snails* as a delicacy."

"You two are not being very nice," Ariel scolded. "She is who she is, and she took us as we are, as we were serving her a Hump Night dinner. She didn't drop Nick because all of us are so middle class."

"Speak for yourself," Nick said, trying to joke, trying to ease the conversation, which had gotten strangely out of control.

"We're not joking," Sheila said, her voice heated. "How much clearer can it get than here on Nantucket? The world is divided into two separate kinds of people. The rich and the poor, or as you say, Nick, the *middle class*. I'm quite happy to stay in the middle class."

"Me, too," Wyatt said.

"You're making something out of nothing," Nick said.

Ariel didn't speak.

They lay quietly for a while, their own thoughts tumbling inside them.

"Ariel, your silence speaks volumes," Wyatt said, after a while. "Don't tell me *you* side with Francine."

Ariel sat up, leaning back on her hands. "I don't side with anyone," she said quietly. "I had a spectacular evening, and I enjoyed every moment, the food, the wine, the beauty of the house. I don't hate anyone simply because they're wealthy. And I don't envy them, either. But I can tell you that living here on this island, working at the real estate agency, I'm seeing how pleasant money can make life, and I do not want to be poor." She stood up. "Good night, everyone. We have work tomorrow." She walked, alone, into the Sand Palace.

sixteen

This Summer

Thursday evening, Jade-Marie looked at her watch. It was almost five-thirty, about the time the Sand Palace Four gathered at the bistro for a drink. Jade-Marie was nervous. This was her father's special week and she wanted everything to go well. She felt protective of Sheila because Sheila had once been part of the Sand Palace group. Plus, she liked Penny a lot and hoped Sheila was okay with Penny going off with Liam. Jade-Marie trusted Liam to be good with Penny. She wasn't sure she could trust the seas.

Her father, Sheila, and Wyatt walked through the sliding glass doors, into the foyer. Jade-Marie hurried over to greet them.

"Hi, guys, good day?" Jade-Marie kissed her father on the cheek.

"Out at the new police and fire station," Nick said.

Jade-Marie snorted. "What? Why don't you take them to the dump, too?"

"Actually, we went there first," Wyatt told her. "I asked Nick to show me the changes in the infrastructure of the island. When we were here in '95, the police station was in town and the fire station was by Stop & Shop. It's great how it's all been modernized."

Nick led them to the bistro. "Let's have a drink and call the wives." Speaking to Jade-Marie, he said, "I'm taking everyone out to Millie's and then to watch the sunset on the beach."

"Nice," Jade-Marie said.

"Come with us," Nick said.

"I might do that."

They ordered their drinks and sat at the long table by the window overlooking the pool.

Sheila kept tapping her phone and looking worried. "Has anyone seen Penny?" she asked. "I've been trying to reach her, but she's not answering her phone."

"Didn't you find her note?" Jade-Marie asked.

"What note?" Sheila demanded.

"She told me she'd leave you a note. Or call you." Jade-Marie took a deep breath. "Penny told me she's going sailing with Liam overnight."

"What? Penny's on a sailboat overnight? I don't understand."

Oh, no, Jade-Marie thought. She hurried to reassure Sheila. "Mrs. O'Connell, Penny will be fine. Liam's an experienced sailor and no storms are forecast. It's an *adventure.*"

"She should have asked me!" Sheila was red in the face.

Francine and Ariel stepped out of the elevator and strolled across the foyer to their table. Francine wore clam-diggers and a gray silk T-shirt. Ariel wore white shorts and a blue boyfriend shirt.

"Hi, everyone. I hope I haven't kept you waiting." Francine leaned over to kiss Jade-Marie. "We oldies are going out to Millie's for dinner and to watch the sunset. Want to join us?"

Nick rose. "Babe, I'll get you a G and T. Ariel, what can I get you?"

Ariel slid into a chair next to Wyatt. "I'd love a prosecco."

"And so it shall be!" Nick replied, bowing at the waist before walking back to the bar.

Francine slid into a chair next to Jade-Marie. She scanned the faces around the table. "What's wrong?"

"My daughter is gone!" Sheila cried. "Jade-Marie let her go off with that Liam person. Overnight!"

"Lucky Penny," Francine said. "I wouldn't mind spending the night with Liam. Have you seen him?"

"*Mom,*" Jade-Marie said, smiling, amused and only slightly embarrassed.

Sheila's mouth tightened. "You think it's *funny*? Penny is my *only* daughter. She's less—less sophisticated than the rest of you. If something happens to her, I'm holding you personally responsible, Jade-Marie."

"I wasn't laughing at you or Penny," Jade-Marie said.

Wyatt shook his head. "Sheila, you're catastrophizing."

"I'm what?"

"You're predicting dire events without sufficient information."

Ariel nodded. "He's right, Sheila."

Sheila sniffed. "I'll be glad to be wrong when my daughter returns."

"Hold on, hold on." Nick set Ariel's prosecco before her. "Sheila, look, I know Liam. He's a champion sailor."

The sliding glass doors opened, and Jason stepped into the foyer. He caught sight of the others sitting around the long table in the bistro and waved. He started walking toward them, then paused.

"Please come join us," Jade-Marie said. "We've got a crisis."

"Really?" Jason walked toward the group. "Well, *I've* got—"

Sheila interrupted him. "My daughter has gone off with Liam on a sailboat overnight!"

Jason turned on a dime and went to the bar.

The oldies, as Jade-Marie now thought of them, kept trying to reassure Sheila. Had Sheila always been such a drama queen?

Jason returned with a beer in his hand.

"Sit here," Jade-Marie said, patting an empty chair next to her.

Jason sat. Lowering his voice, he said to Jade-Marie, "Penny went sailing with Liam overnight? Wow. I wouldn't have believed she had the guts."

"It is a surprise. Sheila seems to think it's a catastrophe."

"Wait till I break my news," Jason told her.

"What news?" Jade-Marie leaned toward Jason, as if they were conspirators. She was close enough to see the sunburn over his nose and cheeks, close enough to sense the fresh salt air on his shirt, warmed by his chest. Close enough to touch that chest. Close enough to kiss.

Softly, Jason said, "I have a job at Cabot's Marine for the summer."

"You're kidding."

"Not kidding." He moved his hand from the back of the chair to her shoulder, gently urging her closer to him. "Because of you, Jade-Marie. You gave me the courage to do it. When we talked today, I knew what I wanted to do."

"Remain on the island and be free," Jade-Marie whispered.

"Yes. And spend as much time with you as I can. You're changing my world, Jade-Marie."

Tears welled in her eyes. "I'm so proud of you," she said softly. "Oh, I really want to kiss you now."

"Darling," Ariel called. "Could you share your secret with us or is it only for Jade-Marie?" Her voice was sweet and slightly shaky.

"I've got a job at Cabot's Marine," Jason told his mother. "For the summer and maybe longer."

"Here on the island?" Ariel asked, her hand at her throat.

"You can't work here," Wyatt said angrily. "You've already got a job, in case you forgot, at the university!"

"I don't like working there," Jason said, his voice mild. "I've mentioned this before, about fifty times."

"Get over it," Wyatt argued. "No one likes their first job. You have to start in the basement, like I said, and slowly make your way up."

"Dad, first of all, you were never in the basement. Plus, *you* like geology. I don't. I never have."

"Don Cabot is a good guy—" Nick interjected.

Wyatt turned on him. "No one asked your opinion."

Francine stood up. She was very slight, but she radiated power. "Let's allow Jason and his family to discuss this matter. Sheila and Nick and I—and Jade-Marie, if you'd like—are going out to Madaket. We'll go in Nick's Jeep. The hotel has another car you can use when you follow later."

"Thanks, Mom, but I'm doing something with Jason." Jade-Marie turned to Jason. "I'll wait for you on the bench outside."

Jason reached up and gripped her hand. Still holding it, he rose.

"Jade-Marie and I are going to the Jetties to eat. We'll walk."

Jade-Marie gave her mother a little wave as she was towed to the front door by Jason. When the sliding glass doors opened, she and Jason stepped through into the hot summer evening, and Jade-Marie was exhilarated, as if they'd been released from prison.

For a few moments, they walked in silence. Jason gripped Jade-Marie's hand hard.

"Um, Jason," she said, "your hand . . ."

"Oh, sorry. I guess I wasn't thinking."

"Oh, you were thinking. But share it with me. Don't keep it inside. Let's talk about it. I mean, it is extraordinary, what you've done. Leaving a full-time job at home for a short-term job on an island? I mean, *wow*."

Jason raised his eyes to meet hers. "Okay," he said. "I'm thinking I made an impulsive decision."

"But not necessarily the wrong one," Jade-Marie said.

"Right," Jason said. "You're right, Jade-Marie. It's odd. I felt at home at Cabot's Marine. I felt—challenged. I mean, an outboard motor is complicated. It's not like studying anomalous precious metal occurrences, but it's real. Somehow, it's more real. It's here, now. Don showed me the transom clamp bracket, and swivel bracket, the screw threads, and the lubricant to grease them. Some of the stuff I already know, the spark plugs, the fuel filter. I want to take apart an outboard motor and put it back together again. I would *like* to do that. I never knew before that I'd like to do that. I like to—move."

"If you worked on the island for the summer, you could learn stuff that you could use anywhere," Jade-Marie said quietly.

"True. But you know what? I want to live through a winter here. I want to see more of the island. I've only been here four and a half days, and it's like I stepped into a whole new world."

"I know what you mean," Jade-Marie said.

"I'm glad Penny went with Liam. It will change her life. The day we biked around the island was a revelation for me. I sound like I've joined a cult, I know, but honest to God, it's a kind of magic. I mean I don't want to worship it or write songs about it or anything. I just want to be there. Be *here* on this island."

"It will be difficult to find a place to live in the summer," Jade-Marie said.

"No! That's the thing! Don has a small apartment above the shop. It's kind of a pit, but it's right on the harbor. I can see everything!"

"That's amazing. I'm surprised Don hasn't rented it out."

"You should see it. The sink has rust stains, and the mattress you don't even want to know about. The windows have a great view, but they're really old, and get this, to keep a window raised, you have to prop it up with a stick."

"That's an old Nantucket custom," Jade-Marie said.

"Really? How do you know that? How long have you lived here?"

"I was here for a few weeks last summer, when Dad was thinking of buying the place, and we spent Christmas here. I've been here this year since April. I like it a lot. I've toured the whaling museum and gone to some talks and made a few friends."

"Will you be here this winter?" Jason asked.

Jade-Marie smiled. "I will."

Jason asked, "So how do your parents feel about you staying here?"

"They're fine with it. They'd be fine if I said I was going to become a kangaroo trainer in Australia. Not that they don't love me, they do. But we have moved so many times in my life because of Dad's work. They get that I want to stay in one place. Mom's going back to France for a few months for her fundraisers. Dad will be here for the summer. A group in Switzerland wants him to invest in a ski hotel, so he'll go out there at some point, and rendezvous with Mom in Switzerland for Christmas. I'm invited, but I'd rather stay here and see what a Nantucket winter is like."

Jason said, "Tell me about your dad. He's an interesting person."

"That's one way of describing him," Jade-Marie said. She sighed. "You've seen him, and what you see is what you get. He's energetic, brilliant, charming, impulsive, and fun. He's a good guy. He's always excited about the next project, and he loves solving problems. Bad side—he's impatient. With my mom and me, he's unreliable."

They reached the parking lot for Jetties Beach and the Mobi-Mat to the water and the Sandbar outdoor restaurant and bar. Jason bought them each a beer and they scuffed through the sand down to the water. In the daytime, the beach was crowded with families because the water was shallow for a long way out. Now families had left for dinner. It was easy to find an isolated spot to sit.

They watched in silence as a yacht with a helicopter and Jet Skis floated into the inner harbor. One of the fast ferries drifted past, heading for the mainland. White sails hovered in the far distance like mirages.

"I wonder how Penny is," Jade-Marie mused.

"I bet she's in heaven on the open water. It's amazing out there."

"Liam isn't bad, either," Jade-Marie said, trying to get a rise out of Jason. "He's a sexy guy," she added.

"But he's a good guy, right?" Jason asked.

Jade-Marie laughed. "Don't worry about Penny. She's more likely to attack him than the other way round."

After that, they were quiet. It was that time of evening when it seemed the earth and ocean paused to take a deep breath. The light changed and dimmed. The sky drifted from blue into lavender. The temperature dropped as a light breeze swayed over the water and onto the land. This far away from the restaurant, no noises interrupted the delicate evening sounds. The waves lapped musically against the shore. A gull cried. The moon rose, sending a shimmering lilac-hued veil around the island.

"Nice," Jason said.

"Nice," Jade-Marie agreed.

"It's immense," Jason said.

Jade-Marie remained quiet, giving him space to think, to feel.

"My dad is going to be so angry. And so hurt. But the world is larger than his science. This"—Jason held his hands wide—"this can't be captured."

"No," Jade-Marie said. "Only enjoyed."

"Right!" Jason smiled at Jade-Marie. "Right."

Jade-Marie said softly, "You must feel like an astronaut stepping out of the spaceship onto the moon."

Jason nodded. After a moment, he said somberly, "I feel like someone stepping out of a boarding school into my real home."

"That's a lot," Jade-Marie murmured.

"Do you know what I like about you?"

She cocked her head. "What?"

"You know how to be quiet."

Jade-Marie peered up at him from under her lashes. "I can be noisy, too." She couldn't believe she was behaving like this, but she could tell by the way his pupils dilated and his breath hitched that he wanted her, too.

Jason stared at her, as if trying to figure out the answer to a puzzle. He bent toward her, pulling her to him, kissing her hard and then harder, as if some wall inside him had broken and his feelings were rushing out.

A child cried out in a high little voice, "Mommy, what are those people doing?"

Immediately, Jason and Jade-Marie pulled apart.

"I guess *all* the families haven't gone home," Jason said.

"Also," Jade-Marie remarked, readjusting her clothes, "kissing on a beach is difficult."

"Then let's go back to the hotel," Jason said.

He stood up and held out his hand. She took it, and rose, and walked by his side as they headed toward the Lighthouse.

Liam had caught a bluefish, cleaned it and grilled it while Penny stood in the tiny galley kitchen, tossing a salad of the arugula and romaine Liam had in his toy-size refrigerator. They had sat on the deck chairs next to the hibachi, eating as the sun set, licking their fingers, not needing to talk.

They were in open water, no land in sight, when Liam dropped the anchor. The sky was cloudless, and Penny had never seen so many stars. She lay on the bow of the boat in her sweatshirt and shorts and life vest, a glass of prosecco in her hands, propped on her stomach, and marveled at the sky.

Liam lay next to her. He was in shorts and a sweatshirt and held a glass of whiskey in his hands.

Now Liam stood up. He leaned over Penny, his legs wide apart for balance. He held out his hand.

He said, "Let's go to bed."

Penny said, "I'm not sleepy."

Liam said, "We're not going to sleep."

Penny's heart tripped. She wanted this. She had known this would be part of their trip, and she was eager and nervous. She took his hand and he pulled her up. She followed him to the stern and down the steps into the cabin. Beneath the bow, where they'd just been lying, a wide bed stretched out, with pillows and sheets and small windows on each side. She lifted her arms to take off her sweatshirt—she had nothing on underneath because she'd hung her bikini top up to dry.

"My God," Liam said. "You're beautiful."

The attraction between them was so intense, Penny was trembling. Liam stripped down until he wore only a shark's tooth on a rope around his neck. His chest was lightly furred with black hair, and along his arms, the hair was bleached white. A scar ran from his neck to his navel. Penny could imagine him wearing a pirate's hat and boots, a parrot on his shoulder.

Liam embraced Penny, and they lowered themselves onto the bed, and making love was so sweet, Penny wept.

Afterward, they slept, curled together. They both woke in the night, shifting positions. The portholes were still dark. They made love again, and slept again.

It was early morning when Penny woke with the sun streaking across the bed. She yawned lazily and rose. She could hear Liam walking on the deck. She pulled on her bikini and joined him. He'd made coffee and offered pastries he'd bought the day before at the Downyflake. For a long time, they had breakfast and gazed at the sea and sky, both calm, both blue with streaks of rose and violet.

"It seems like the world is brand new," Penny said. "Like it was created only today."

Liam nodded. "I know."

He poured them both another cup of coffee, and together they sat basking in the early sunlight.

"Your phone's been buzzing," Liam said.

Penny rolled her eyes. "I know. Probably my mom. Are you still alive? Have you been eaten by a whale? Are you stranded on an ice floe?"

Liam laughed. "You should let her know you're okay."

Penny read aloud as she tapped a few words into her phone with her thumbs. "I'm fine. We're close to Boston. Have fun today." She sent the message and then turned her phone off. "Families! I love my mom, but I don't want to be like her. I want to travel. I want—experiences."

Liam grinned. "I'd say you're off to a good start."

Penny stretched her arms and lifted her face to the sun. "Absolutely." She took another sip of her coffee. "I saw the photo of you and your family in the media room. Your sister is pretty. She looks like your father and you look like your mother."

Liam nodded. "You're perceptive, aren't you?" He leaned back in his chair and gave a long sigh.

"What?" Penny asked.

"So, I don't tell many people this. It's a private thing and what's done is done and it's fine."

Penny waited silently.

"My father isn't my biological father. I mean, the man I call my father now. When I was a toddler, around two years old, my parents and I were on Nantucket for the summer, and we were driving to 'Sconset, and . . ." He paused, as if gathering strength. "When I was a toddler, my parents had a serious car accident with another car at the turn on Polpis Road. My mother was all right, and I was trussed up like a turkey in my car seat in the back, but my father was killed."

"God, Liam. I'm so sorry."

"Ah, I was too young to know what was going on. My grandparents came to the island and took care of me while my mother went through the business of dealing with her husband's body and the paperwork and the memorial service." Liam swallowed the rest of his coffee. "They say you don't remember anything before you were five years old. It's true, I don't remember the accident. I don't even remember my father. I don't remember my mother's grief, but she has told me about it. When I was six, my mother married Gus Miller, and she legally changed my last name to Miller."

"Do you know your birth father's name?"

"Yeah. It was Harrison." Liam laughed harshly. "How many thousands of Harrisons are there in the world? Anyway, Miller is my last name now."

"Do you get along with your . . . your father?"

"We get along as well as any son and father," Liam said. "He's all right. My mother's happy and it's nice to have a sister."

"What about the man who ran into your father's car?"

Liam shook his head. "The judge ruled that both drivers were at fault. My father was turning before he should have, and the other driver was going too fast. Both drivers had been drinking."

"Do you know what happened to him?"

Liam's face grew dark. "I do not know, and I don't want to know. My mother is happy and I wouldn't trade Grace for anyone in the world."

Penny said nothing.

After a while, Liam said, "I would have liked to know my birth father. You know, to meet him, to hear him speak." With a kind of growl, Liam stood up, stomped down the stairs into the galley, rinsed his cup, and came back to the deck.

"Time to get sailing, if you want to see Boston," he said.

seventeen
That Summer

The late July heat and humidity was so intense that the Sand
Palace Four decided to get sandwiches and soft drinks and spend
the Hump Night dinner at the beach. They rode their creaking
bikes to the Jetties beach and walked down to the water. Behind
them at the concession stand, music was blaring and crowds were
shoving to get drinks and hot dogs.

Sheila said, "Let's go further down the beach. I don't want to
listen to all that noise."

Nick said, "You sound like a cranky old lady."

"I *am* a cranky old lady," Sheila shot back. "The Rose Hotel is
full, and Mrs. Reardon is constantly in hysterics about sand in the
rugs and dead lightbulbs."

"Dead lightbulbs," Wyatt said and laughed. "Sounds like a kind
of bug."

"A lightning bug!" Ariel said, laughing.

"Yeah, a firefly," Nick agreed.

"You're all crazy," Sheila told them, joining in the laughter. "It's a sixty-watt glass bulb of light and I have to get a ladder and climb up and replace it. It's not fun."

"A glowworm," Wyatt whispered.

Sheila batted him on the arm.

"Doesn't Mrs. Reardon have a handyman?" Ariel asked.

"She's got a plumber and an electrician, but she's not going to pay an electrician to change a lightbulb. I don't mind, really. It's just one more thing in addition to all the shit work I'm supposed to do."

"Someone's in a bad mood," Wyatt said.

Ariel wrapped her arm around Sheila. "She deserves to be. I get to prance around in nice clothes all day, but my feet hurt at night, if that's any consolation. And I've got to say I meet some of the world's snottiest people. This week when a couple came in to talk with a realtor, the wife looked at me and said, 'Hey, you, go get me an iced coffee, with sugar.' I ran down to the Hub for coffee, and when I returned, she snatched it out of my hand without saying thanks."

Nick laughed. "We get some pompous customers in Fanshaw's, too. Yesterday a mom came in to buy clothes for her son who's going to boarding school. She kept saying Groton, Groton, my son needs this for Groton. What a pain she was, and I was totally polite, practically bowing and scraping. As they were going out the door, she said to her son, 'You can tell *that* man didn't go to Groton.'"

"Ouch," Sheila said.

"It's okay," Nick told her. "I yelled, 'No, I went to Exeter.' And her son gave me a thumbs-up!"

"Did you go to Exeter?" Ariel asked.

"No, and I don't care if that woman ever returns to the store. Someday I'll own a hotel and she'll walk in and I'll tell her all our rooms are taken."

"I like working at Cabot's," Wyatt said. "Don is a good guy, and he interacts with the customers. He knows all of them, really."

Ariel said, "I have an idea. A good one. Not this week, but sometime in August, before we all go our separate ways, the four of us should go out to dinner. It doesn't have to be Toppers or the Chanticleer, but maybe the Boarding House. Something nice. We'll be our own guests."

"It wouldn't be cheap," Sheila reminded her.

"I think it's a good idea," Nick said. "We'll eat peanut butter on crackers a couple of nights to balance out the cost."

Ariel said, "Sheila, you don't want to go to a nice restaurant because someone else is taking you to them now."

Nick sat up. "Whoa! Sheila! You've got an island boyfriend?"

Wyatt grumbled, "I thought you were engaged to what's his name, Hank, back home."

Sheila shifted nervously on the sand. "He's not a boyfriend. He's just a friend."

"What's he doing here?" Nick asked.

Sheila hesitated. "He's staying at the Rose Hotel. He's in advertising."

"You mean he's a traveling salesman?" Nick raised his hands in a triumphant gesture. "*Go,* Sheila!"

"It's not that way," Sheila protested. She sat up and started building a sand castle with her hands, turning her back to the others.

"Hey," Nick said, "I'm not criticizing. I think we should all have a last-minute fling before we return to the big bad adult world."

Wyatt stood up abruptly and stalked off down to the water.

"What's with him?" Nick asked. "Why has he got his panties all in a bundle?"

"I don't know, Nick," Ariel said. "Maybe he takes sex more seriously than you do."

Nick shook his head. "It's too hot to argue." He walked down the beach, away from the group.

When both men were far enough away, Sheila murmured, "I slept with Frank."

Ariel made a small gasp of surprise. "Was it okay?"

"Okay? It was *beautiful*." Sheila spun away from the sand castle to face Ariel. "He told me he loves me."

"But what about Hank?" Ariel asked.

"I don't know. It's too early, too fresh. I've got the rest of the summer to figure it out." Sheila put her hands on Ariel's arms, as if pleading. "It's possible we could be together. He's divorced. I could find some kind of work. Maybe here, on the island, and Frank and I could buy a small cottage—"

"With a white picket fence and a rose garden?" Ariel shook her head. "Sheila, get real. And think of Hank. Maybe invite Hank here to visit? If you see him again . . ."

Sheila sighed, disappointed. "I know you're trying to help, but you don't understand the enormity of our feelings for one another."

"Oh, I do understand," Ariel said. "And I don't think it's necessarily a good thing."

Nick and Wyatt were walking back to them, tossing a grimy tennis ball they'd found in the water. To Ariel's surprise, Wyatt threw the ball at her, and to everyone's surprise, she caught it.

"Come on, ladies. Let's have a game. Boys against girls. Like tennis or volleyball without a net."

Ariel laughed with delight. She took Sheila's hand and pulled her to her feet. Nick drew a line in the sand.

"Baseball on the beach, winner take all!" Nick announced.

"What's the prize?" Sheila asked.

Ariel tossed the ball over the line and over Nick's head. Wyatt caught it. "No prize, Sheila. Just play."

They threw the ball back and forth, moving farther apart each time. The guys could throw the farthest, so Ariel and Sheila conspired and threw the ball just over the line, making the guys run and dive. They each jumped to catch the ball, often falling on the sand, or stumbling in a hole, screaming, laughing, and a family stopped to watch them, applauding each time one of them caught a tricky throw. The tide was coming in, quietly slipping up toward their sand line, and the sky gently faded from bright blue to pale blue to gray.

A couple holding hands walked past. The man yelled, "Zen tennis?"

Nick gave the man a thumbs-up, and Sheila threw the ball and hit Nick in the head and couldn't stop apologizing.

Too soon, it was too dark to see the ball. They gathered up their gear and walked across the sand to the parking lot, where they all stopped to slip on their sandals. As they walked, Nick began to sing the Irish ballad "Molly Malone." He had a strong true baritone voice, and while he sang, the others were held spellbound.

They reached the Sand Palace, threw their sandy towels over the bench outside, and shook the sand off their sandals.

"That was beautiful, Nick," Ariel said. "I didn't know you could sing."

"There's a lot I can do you don't know about," Nick said, giving her a look.

Wyatt punched Nick's arm. "There's a lot I can do *you* don't know about."

"You guys," Sheila said, and went into the Sand Palace to get ready for bed.

Sheila considered her talk with Ariel. She knew Ariel was right. She should be more careful with Frank. True, she was on the birth control pill, but Frank was older and more experienced.

And of course, Sheila had to remember Hank, waiting for her in Ohio.

Still, Sheila thought, the damage was done. She'd already cheated on Hank. She'd had sex—glorious, grown-up, complicated, imaginative sex—with Frank. Would it make her transgression even worse if she did it again?

Who was a person, really? Everyone was defined by their circumstances: where they were born, what they looked like, how smart or attractive they were. Maybe life was like the theater. She could be one person in one show and a completely different kind of person in another. She hadn't thought these sorts of things before. She wondered if this was what it felt like to be on drugs.

Saturday night, Ariel went to see a movie with her real estate friends. Wyatt was working late and Nick was off with Francine.

Sheila had another date with Frank. As she slipped on the violet silk slip dress Ariel had loaned her—the violet was all wrong for her own coloring, that flaming red hair, but it fit her like a dream—Sheila played with the idea that she'd break off with Frank tonight. It would be the right thing to do. Also, it would keep her from having a broken heart when he left the island.

A year ago, at college, a friend had given her a cute little evening bag for her birthday. It was small, just big enough to hold a lipstick and some cash, in case, her friend had laughed, she ever needed to buy some condoms. She wore long dangling rhinestone earrings she'd found at the Thrift Shop. She thought she looked glamorous when she put them on, but really, were they too much? Kind of slutty?

She hurried out of the Sand Palace before she could change her mind. Frank said he'd pick her up from the bench in front of the building, and there he was, waiting, the top down on his rented convertible.

"Hi," she called, unable to keep the good old Midwestern cheer from her voice. "I'm so glad to see you." She slid into the passenger seat. She didn't try to kiss him, not in public.

"You have no idea how glad I am to see you," Frank said.

She studied his face as he focused on pulling away from the curb and heading toward Orange Street, the long road that led all the way out of town. Frank somehow looked older, with dark circles under his eyes and his mouth set in a somber line.

"Are you okay?" she asked gently.

Frank heaved a sigh. "I need a drink. I need many drinks."

"Have you made dinner reservations?" Before he could answer, Sheila said, "Because we could cancel them. We could buy a six-pack and go to the beach and relax."

Frank laughed, a bitter sound like a dog's bark. "A six-pack. You *are* an innocent."

Sheila blinked, wounded. She stared straight ahead and didn't speak.

"We'll stop at the Muse first," Frank said. "Our reservation isn't until eight."

"That's fine," Sheila said, although that kind of wasn't fine. The Muse was a bar with excellent pizza, strong drinks, and an enormous and devoted group of regulars. She'd look overdressed in there, or cheap. She quietly slipped off her dangling earrings and put them in her purse.

Frank didn't speak as they rode, and when he parked in the gravel parking lot, he didn't open Sheila's door for her as he usually did. She followed him into the large, dimly lit space. It was early, but the place was still crowded.

They sat at the bar. Sheila didn't like sitting at a bar, not simply because she thought she looked like she was trying to pick someone up, but also because her feet didn't touch the floor but dangled a few inches above it. She ordered a ginger ale, wanting to wait for the taste of wine at the restaurant. Frank ordered a shot of bourbon. When it arrived, he tossed it down and ordered another.

Sheila felt uncomfortable. Worried. This man was not the Frank she was used to, not that she'd seen him enough to know what the normal Frank really was.

"Frank, we don't have to go out tonight. Let's just relax," she said quietly.

Frank turned to her. "I'm sorry, Sheila. I'm acting like an ass. I apologize. I've just had a bad day and I didn't have a chance to shake it off before picking you up."

She put her hand on his arm. "Want to tell me what happened?"

Frank leaned over and kissed her cheek. "No, sweetheart, I don't. I want to forget today. I want to be with you, dine with you, make love to you. You're my medicine. My reward."

If a warning bell sounded in her mind, it was drowned out by the rush of pleasure Sheila felt as Frank spoke. She was his medicine. His reward.

Before she could speak, Frank said to the bartender, "Another."

The bartender, a tall man with major muscles, quickly shot a look at Sheila, raised an eyebrow, and clearly indicated he wanted her to weigh in on whether Frank should be served another shot. It would be his third in perhaps seven minutes.

Sheila could only smile sweetly, giving him permission. She'd seen Frank drink cocktails and wine at dinner. He was a large man. He had the capacity. Besides, she didn't want to be the one to question his order.

The bartender set a third shot glass of golden liquid before Frank. He slammed it back.

"So, Frank," Sheila said conversationally, as if this were a normal evening, "do you watch baseball? Everyone roots for the Red Sox here, but I've got my hopes up for the Cleveland Indians."

Frank paused before speaking. "Yeah, that's good." He stepped off his stool, took Sheila's hand, and helped her down. "Let's go to dinner. We've got reservations at Toppers."

"Wow," Sheila said, unable to hide her enthusiasm. Toppers was the most revered—and expensive—restaurant on the island. She would have been happy to work there. She'd never dreamed she would dine there. The hotel and restaurant were hidden away, far from town, on a winding lane off the Polpis road.

As they walked across the parking lot to Frank's car, Sheila watched his gait, his steadiness. He seemed absolutely normal, as if the three quick shots of bourbon hadn't affected him at all. He helped her into the car, gently shut her door, went around the front, and slid into the driver's seat.

He drove through the side streets that led to the Milestone road, and he didn't say a word. It made Sheila nervous.

She put her hand on his arm. "Frank, something's wrong, I can tell. Can you talk about it?"

Sheila meant to calm him, but her words did the opposite. She could see his jaw clench.

"You think you can sweet-talk me and make me all better? Not in my world, babe."

"Look out, Frank!"

They'd arrived at the rotary where cars came and went to and from Old South Road and the Milestone road and Sparks Avenue. Traffic was heavy here, at the height of the summer. When Sheila warned him, Frank slammed on his brakes just in time to keep from running the STOP sign. Sheila was thrown forward and bounced back.

"Sorry," Frank muttered.

He waited impatiently while a cement truck barreled through, then hit the gas, making the car lurch. They sped onto Milestone Road, and Sheila braced herself, holding on to the door handle. It was silly, she knew, to be afraid of their speed, because the fastest a car was permitted by law to go on Nantucket was only forty-five miles an hour.

The Milestone road was two-lane, and both lanes had heavy traffic. Forests of pine and tupelo bordered the road, providing an immediate sense of countryside, of escape from a busy commercial town out into a green wilderness.

Sheila was worried now, and almost afraid. She didn't know whether Frank had passed the Polpis road turnoff on purpose or by accident.

Softly, she said, "Frank, we passed the road to Polpis."

"Shit!" Frank yelled.

He slammed on the brakes, yanked the steering wheel hard, making the car spin into a U-turn that narrowly missed hitting a contractor's truck in the other lane. Horns up and down the road blared.

"It's okay," Sheila said, alarmed. "We don't have to go so fast—"

"The road is right here," Frank told her.

He spun the steering wheel, veered to the right, and slammed hard into a small station wagon turning from the other direction without stopping at the Stop sign.

The noise was apocalyptic. Metal shrieked against metal as the two cars collided. The hood of the station wagon flew up. The station wagon driver's door crumpled.

Sheila heard screaming. It took her a moment to realize the scream was coming from her.

Sheila was propelled forward, the dashboard punching into her abdomen. She had instinctively thrown her hands up, and she thought that one, if not both, wrist was broken.

Someone in the station wagon was wailing. Sheila glimpsed a child in the backseat of the other car.

"Frank?" She turned toward him, dazed.

Frank had been propelled toward the steering wheel. Blood streamed down his face.

"Get out!" he yelled at Sheila. His face was ugly with anger. "Run! Get out of here, Sheila, *go*!"

"I want to help you," Sheila cried.

"Then run! I mean it! Go into the woods. Now, goddammit!" Frank shoved her, hard.

Sheila said, "Okay."

The passenger door was crumpled, so she climbed out over the door, landing on the tarmac of the road, losing her balance, and falling into the wild greenery of bushes and Queen Anne's lace on the side. She heard sirens. She heard someone screaming from the station wagon. She heard cars stopping all around them. People yelling.

She scrambled to her feet and ran across the grass and weeds on the roadside, right into the protective dimness of the crowded trees. Her ears were ringing. Her wrists were on fire, but she had pushed herself off the ground with them, so she knew they weren't broken. She didn't think anything was broken, although her abdomen hurt. She kept running into the interior of the woods.

When she was far enough away from the road to no longer hear the screaming, to no longer spot even a blur of metal or the blue flash of a patrol car, she fell to the ground, sitting with her back against a tree, her skirt becoming sticky with pine needles, her lungs gulping for air.

What hurt most were Frank's words, yelling at her to run away.

Maybe she had passed out. *Fainted,* her mother would say. When Sheila opened her eyes, the woods around her were darker. The quiet seemed ominous. Her first thought was of something attacking her, a bear, a coyote. Then she remembered the only wild animals on the island were deer and rabbits. Shakily, she rose to her feet, leaning against a tree for support. Fear washed over her. Was Frank okay?

Were any of the passengers in the station wagon hurt?

The police would give Frank a Breathalyzer test, and he would fail it.

She had to get back to the Sand Palace. She had to pretend she knew nothing about the accident. Sheila wanted to call her mother, but her mother would only scold her for going anywhere with any man other than Hank. Sheila wanted to call *someone,* but she had no idea where a pay phone was or even a building with people who had a phone, and if she could get there from here, she shouldn't go into the building, any building, because people would ask her if she was okay, was she in that terrible accident on the Milestone road?

She knew she had to walk home. First, she had to find a road, and from either of the two roads it would be only a two-mile walk to the Sand Palace. She slipped off her heels, amazed that she'd been able to run so far in them. Carrying them in her hands, she decided on a direction and stumbled forward, tripping over fallen branches as she went. In only minutes, she saw the blank wall of a building, and a minute later, she realized she was approaching Island Liquors from the back. The shop sat off Polpis Road, just a short way from the Milestone road. Soon she was on pavement, in the large parking lot of the liquor store. The soles of her feet were hardened from walking on hot sand, so she kept her shoes in her hand.

She was almost at the road when the sounds of sirens alerted her. She jumped behind a tree and peered around toward the accident site. Two ambulances were racing away from the crumpled cars. *Two,* Sheila thought. A line of cars streamed back from the accident toward Polpis. Two police cars were parked on the verge of the road and as she watched, a state trooper climbed off his motorcycle. Policemen were stationed at both sides of the wreck, directing traffic. Lights were flashing, people were yelling, and at the back of the stalled line of cars on the Polpis road, someone began to honk his horn in irritation at the holdup.

Frank would be okay, Sheila told herself. He had been talking to her after the accident. Maybe he'd broken an arm or a leg, or simply had his ribs bruised. She tried to remember who had been in the station wagon, but she wasn't sure she'd even seen the person. She was grateful that Frank had forced her to leave. Their romantic evening would have become a nightmare of sitting in a police station—or even the hospital.

Once again, she slid down against a tree and closed her eyes. She was still trembling and her fingertips were cold. She wanted to cry, but her entire body seemed frozen, blank.

After a while, she heard the sound of traffic moving near her. Rising, she dared to look and saw the cars moving in both directions past the liquor store. A tow truck was slowly dragging the station wagon away, and Frank's convertible was already gone. She began walking toward the main road, her shoes in her hand, her cute little evening bag over her shoulder as if nothing had happened. The sky was that beautiful shade of lavender that happened just before dark. Sheila wove in and out of the line of trees along the road, not wanting to be noticed. At the intersection where the accident had happened, she paused, waiting until no cars were in sight. Then she hurried across to the other side, noticing shards of glass and metal littering the pavement. She heard herself moan, but remained dry-eyed, focused, thinking of nothing but getting back to the safety of her bedroom.

It was a short hike to Orange Street. Here, along the verge, thick grass carpeted the ground. It cushioned Sheila's steps. It felt heavenly. Soon she was crossing the parking lot of Marine Home Center, and then she put her heels on and trotted up Orange to

Main and past Main out to South Beach and the Sand Palace. All around her, families ate ice cream cones and window-shopped, couples held hands, people stopped to let the dogs on their leashes sniff greetings. It was normal. Safe. One-way streets. Slow traffic. Some people saw her and looked away, grinning. Sheila knew they were thinking she'd had an argument with her boyfriend, or gotten way too drunk.

Finally, she saw the odd silhouette of the Sand Palace. She almost ran toward it. No one else was there. She entered her room and collapsed on her bed, and she was so cold she pulled the covers up over her shoulders all the way to her ears, as she had when she was a child, trying to hide.

eighteen
This Summer

The oldies, as Francine had called them, went to Madaket, walked the long white satin beach, and watched the sun sink, flaming, into the sea. They didn't talk, laugh, reminisce. They walked alone, thinking their own thoughts, stopping now and then to toss a pebble into the ocean. The blue water slowly darkened until it was as black as the sky. It was a spectacular sunset, but it didn't lighten Wyatt's or Sheila's moods. If anything, they became more somber, as if the sunset were a curtain closing down on their lives.

Back at the Lighthouse, no one wanted to go out for an ice cream. First Sheila, and then Ariel and Wyatt, said good night and went off to the privacy of their rooms.

When Francine and Nick entered their suite, it was only ten o'clock, and outside their windows, the town was vibrant with voices, music, laughter.

Francine slipped off her clothes and slithered into her short silk nightie. For a moment she remained at the closet door, considering whether to pull on her kimono and settle into bed with a book she was eager to return to, or to stay in her nightgown, often a visual flag that she'd be interested in sex.

Nick came out of the bathroom in his boxers, looking preoccupied.

Francine pulled on her silk kimono and went over to the small sofa by the window.

"Nickie, come. Sit here with me."

Her husband settled next to her. "It's odd, isn't it, being with them all again."

"I suppose. I never knew them as well as you did. I think they're enjoying themselves."

"I guess. It's just so odd, seeing their children as adults. I worry about them. I mean, Wyatt is awfully hard on Jason. It's as if he expects Jason to be a mini-me, to be an important scientist like he is."

Francine shrugged. "Fathers are often that way. Look at you and Jade-Marie. She wants to run a hotel, just like her father."

That made Nick smile. Jade-Marie often made her father smile. "That's true." Reaching over, he took her hand. "Jade-Marie really is the best of the two of us, isn't she? She loves hospitality work and she's good at it. At the same time, she's got your tranquility, the innate ability to remain serene, to assure others."

"Also, she can spot a situation and manage it immediately, which is one of your many talents," Francine said. With a sigh, she snuggled into her husband's arms. "I worry about how Jade-Marie acts with Jason."

"What do you mean?"

"I think she's fallen a bit in love with him."

"Why do you say that?"

"I see the way she looks at him."

"Francine, it's only been a few days."

Francine chuckled. "I fell in love with you instantly, twenty-five years ago when you were catering on a yacht."

Nick nuzzled his chin into her hair. "I remember. You were the most impossibly sophisticated woman I'd ever seen."

"I can do impossibly sophisticated things," Francine murmured.

"I know I'm a lucky man." Nick kissed her cheek. "But I feel responsible this week. What if Penny doesn't make it back tomorrow?"

"Worst-case scenario, my darling, Penny loves sailing and calls Sheila to tell her she's spending the summer with Liam. Sheila will have a very public nervous breakdown, we'll let her rant, then we'll put her on the plane so she can return to her husband and her three sons. Penny and Sheila will be fine."

"I hope you're right. I know that if Jason really does remain here this summer, working for Cabot's, quitting his university job, Wyatt will never forgive me."

Francine laughed. "Darling, why do you care about Wyatt? He's such a dull stick. He's handsome, yes, but I really don't know how Ariel can stay with him. If anything, Wyatt should understand. Wyatt worked at Cabot's twenty-five years ago, and maybe it's a compliment to Wyatt that his son wants to do the same."

"What if Jade-Marie wants to marry Jason?"

Francine's laugh was like a peal of bells. "What if our daughter wants to marry the man she loves? We'll have the reception here at the hotel and they can honeymoon in Paris."

"You're impossibly cheerful tonight."

Francine slid her kimono off, letting it puddle on the sofa. "I've been a good wife and hostess for several days. Is there any chance you and I could think about ourselves for the rest of the evening?"

Nick let his eyes linger on his lovely wife. Running a hotel chain was a constant plague of disasters, complications, late night phone calls, frustrated guests, and weeping employees. This week he'd instructed his vice president, who was in Jackson Hole, to take all calls and deal with all problems. He'd insisted this was his vacation, when he would reunite with old friends.

He didn't need to ruin this beautiful evening with his gorgeous wife. He traveled so much that a night like this was unusual. He knew that the excitement of challenges and disasters was what kept him fulfilled. But everyone needed to rest now and then. To refuel and revive with the pleasures of life—which was what he'd been trying to provide for his old Sand Palace friends. He liked making other people happy.

He shouldn't forget—and Francine would not let him forget—that sometimes he needed to indulge in a little pleasure himself.

He took Francine's hands and pulled her up against him. He kissed the side of her neck. They were apart so often that even after twenty-five years they weren't bored by each other. Sex between them was always new, and always loving.

Francine wrapped her arms around his shoulders and pressed against him, and everyone else in the world, and the world itself, disappeared.

Sheila prepared for bed, brushing her teeth, creaming her face and hands, slipping between the crisp expensive sheets and heavenly soft quilted duvet, and picking up the e-reader she'd left on the bedside table.

She couldn't concentrate. She worried about Penny. Would Liam dock at a harbor tonight, or would they be out in the dark on the open waters? The Pilgrims had done it, after all. Were there sharks back in the 1600s? There must have been. What would they eat? What if Penny got drunk? Liam was such a large man, he would have a capacity for alcohol far beyond Penny's. What if—

She had to stop this. She needed to think of something else. After all, unlike everyone else from the Sand Palace, she had more than one child. She had four!

She picked up her phone and called home.

"Sheila!" Hank answered, sounding glad to hear from her. "How's it going out there on your golden island?" The warmth of her husband's voice, his enthusiasm for life, his love for her, was like an embrace.

Sheila burst into tears. "I miss you," she said. "I miss you all."

"*We* miss *you*. You're having fun, right? Sun and old friends, freedom from housework for a week?"

"Yes, yes, but, Hank, Penny's gone off sailing with a strange man."

"Well, what man? Does Nick know him? Is he a good sailor?"

"His name is Liam. Nick does know him, and he's apparently a prizewinning sailor. He's sailed across the Atlantic."

"Is he taking Penny across the Atlantic?"

"No, no, he's taking her up along the East Coast. All the way to Boston."

"Wow, Sheila, that's terrific! What an adventure for our little girl. She's breaking out, don't you see, Sheila, and it's about time, isn't it?"

"Oh." Sheila was stunned. She and Hank rarely talked about Penny's temperament, or about the boys'. There never was time to sit down and discuss their children, and Hank wasn't the kind to probe into his children's psyche anyway. Hank was all about action. "I never thought of her that way."

"Well, now you can. She's an adult, after all, Sheila."

Sheila was still weeping slightly. "How are the boys?"

"God Almighty, I was going to phone you! Sean hit a grand slam in the ninth inning! The crowd went crazy. He ran the bases like he was ten feet tall, and his whole team yelled and hollered and carried him on their shoulders, and Brodie and Patrick can't stop congratulating him. We went out for pizza, I took the entire team, but you know Ernie Castleton, he coaches the team, he came along, too, and paid for half of it. I think Sean's floating a few feet over his bed even now, he's so proud of himself."

"Oh, Hank, how wonderful." Sheila broke into a smile, which brought on more tears. Her youngest, smallest, least athletic son, Sean, was fourteen, still short, and getting that pre-pubescent chubbiness that boys got before they shot up tall. Sean had a cowlick at the back of his head that would not stay down, and he had freckles. He looked like Norman Rockwell had invented him. His older brothers, fifteen and seventeen, teased their younger brother terribly, but they all teased each other unmercifully. "I wish I'd been there," Sheila said.

"Don't you worry. We've got it all on video. We'll watch it a dozen times when you get home. Now tell me, Sheila, what have you been doing with all your old mates?"

It took Sheila a moment to switch from the image of her young freckle-faced boy—had she paid him enough attention? Had she paid any of her boys enough attention? She had read to them often when they were young, and made cookies with them, but as they got older, it seemed they were always at some kind of athletic event, which she hated attending because it made her nervous. All that yelling and booing. She hated the competition. Once at the dinner table when the guys were talking about a game, Sheila had said, "I wish they would all just play until they had the same score, and then go home." How the guys had laughed!

"You still there?" Hank asked.

"I am. Sorry. I miss the boys. I miss you."

"But you're having a good time, right?"

Was she?

"Yes, I'm having a great time. Exhausting. Nick has all of us bumping in Jeeps over the sand to lighthouses and walking beaches at sunset. Everyone's nice. But I'd rather be home. It's crowded with tourists here."

Hank laughed. "Sheila, *you're* a tourist there."

"I know, I know. I suppose I mean the tourist population must have doubled if not tripled since I worked here. And the shops! Sweaters for two hundred fifty dollars. Necklaces for thirty thousand. Houses for ten million. It's extremely upscale now, very posh. Ariel and I took Francine for dinner Wednesday evening, and the restaurant was wonderful, but the bill for three people was over three hundred dollars without a tip!"

"Jesus," Hank said. "You're going to have to get a job when you get back here, just to refill up our bank account."

"No, Ariel and I meant to split it, but Francine knew everyone there and insisted on paying. I need to think of something to give her to show appreciation for this week."

"It was Nick who invited you, wasn't it?"

"True. But Francine has been great. Kind and generous. I can't buy her a gift here—I couldn't afford it."

"Tell you what. I'll overnight you a couple of Wildcats baseball hats."

Sheila blinked, hesitated, then grinned. "Hank, that would be perfect. I think Francine would carry off a Wildcats cap beautifully."

When they disconnected, Sheila realized she was smiling. Hank's prodigious energy wasn't often focused on her, and she still felt nervous when he was scolding one of their sons. But he was a generally optimistic, happy man, and he still loved her. The boys loved her, too. She knew that. But they didn't need her as much.

They didn't need her as much. She let the thought tumble in her mind. This could be a good thing, as well as a sad thing. She could have little adventures of her own. After all, she was having one now.

Please, God, not like the adventure she'd had the summer she worked here. For years, Sheila had managed to keep Frank Johnson and the terrible car accident out of her thoughts. As a wife and mother, she'd had more than enough to worry about. But here on the island, as hard as she tried, she couldn't help but remember those days of her youth when she went a little bit wild, and how it all had ended.

She'd never told Hank about it. It would hurt him too much and destroy the trust between them. She'd put that memory at the farthest reach of her mind, but now, with Penny out on a boat with a man she'd just met, the memory of those traumatic summer days came flooding back. She was driving herself mad with worry about Penny and Liam. Maybe, when they returned, Sheila would take Penny somewhere private, and tell her about that car crash, and convince Penny to be more careful.

That idea was unsettling. Now she'd never get to sleep. She decided she was just a tad hungry. She threw on her raincoat, which made her look slightly, if oddly, dressed, and left the room.

When she got into their hotel room, Ariel said, "I'm going to take a shower." Without waiting for a response, she stepped into the bathroom and shut the door firmly behind her. She leaned against it, catching her breath, slowing her heart.

How angry she was, at both her men. Jason, for taking a job on Nantucket without bothering to consult with his parents. Wyatt, who was in one of his black dog moods because his twenty-four-year-old son wouldn't do exactly what he wanted.

She stripped off her clothes, let them lie where they fell, pulled a shower cap on over her hair, and turned on the water.

Ahhh. She could adjust the water temperature to her exact pleasure, something that never happened at home because their old plumbing was inefficient at best and disastrous at worst. The soap the hotel provided was citrusy, and she sighed. She'd read somewhere that citrus fragrance was psychologically soothing. She let her head fall back as the water streamed over her, and felt the tension in her body float away.

Here, on the island, it was easier to get some perspective on her husband. When they married and set up house in Missouri, Wyatt had been more affectionate. When she met Wyatt's father, the great Benjamin Smith, she understood why Wyatt allowed himself to follow the same path. Wyatt's father wanted nothing less than to change the world through science, and Wyatt was his replica, his assistant, and his acolyte. As the months passed and she met the other department wives, she came to understand that the scientists, each and every one of them, thought they were doing the most important work in the world. They considered themselves superior to everyone. They were always focused on their work, and nothing else really interested them.

Fortunately, Ariel gave birth to Jason, and her world centered around her son's every breath. As the years went along, her friends, "the Wives," as they called themselves, kept her sane and happy. Margot, Bitsy, and Carolyn had become friends years ago, and ever since Jason was nine, Ariel had met with her gal pals on Friday nights for dinner, drinks, and gossip. In the early years, it had been Applebee's or Shakespeare's Pizza, but as they all grew older and were less financially strained, they chose fancy restaurants and filet mignons and custom cocktails. Their conversation early on focused on parenting, soccer games, and the joy of a new household appliance. Now they talked about celebrity crushes: movie stars and hunky athletes, cruises they wanted to take together, and if wearing a French maid's outfit complete with high heels and a thong would revive their sagging sex life. They told dirty jokes and howled with laughter. They went shopping for sales and came away with four-hundred-count sheets and a Keurig as triumphant as if they'd won first place in a marathon.

They often criticized their husbands, but they never mentioned divorce.

A few years ago, Ariel had apprehensively posted on Facebook that she wanted to start a writers' group. At first, few people responded, but she continued to post and even began a blog, and now five women and two men met once every two weeks to talk about writing and read and critique one another's work. Her group praised her short stories and urged her to dig in and write a novel.

Ariel had a seditious thought: If Jason stayed on Nantucket, she would have even more time to focus on her writing.

Wyatt didn't have friends, Ariel realized. He had *colleagues*. They attended departmental holiday parties, but as Wyatt chatted and chuckled, Ariel knew it was a front. His department at the university was fiercely competitive with other departments, and within his particular section, he was competitive with the people he worked with. His father was now professor emeritus, slowly developing memory loss but never losing his arrogance. When they had Sunday dinners, Benjamin talked the entire time. Ariel could understand why Wyatt's mother had divorced his father and moved far away.

And Wyatt now had no one with whom he could share his frustrations and triumphs.

No one except Jason.

All these years, Wyatt had relied on Jason to be his personal cheerleader, to be intelligent enough to understand how brilliant Wyatt was, but not so smart Jason could compete with Wyatt. If Jason left the university, who would Wyatt have to adore him? Ariel loved Wyatt, and sometimes she admired him, but sometimes she thought he was a selfish, introverted spoiled baby. Wyatt's father had told them he had begun a scientific dynasty, and Wyatt had dutifully and happily gone along with that thought, but Jason was breaking the chain. And it was Jason's right to do that.

Ariel dried off from her shower, took her robe down from the hook on the bathroom door, and tied it at the waist. She brushed her hair. She was going to have a serious, *significant* talk with Wyatt right now.

She opened the door and stepped out into the room.

Wyatt wasn't there.

Wyatt was restless and cranky. Plus, it didn't take a psychic to predict that the moment Ariel stepped out of the bathroom, she'd be ready for one of her "discussions" that always ended in tears for her and exhaustion for him.

Tonight he didn't want to argue. Jason was a traitor and Wyatt was not going to let him get away with it. Wyatt hadn't spent weekends helping his son do his homework and learn the complicated mysteries of science only to have him become a manual laborer.

He knew the bistro wasn't open this late, but next to it was a small alcove with soda and snack machines. He'd get something, a Snickers, anything, just to leave the room and walk in impersonal air. He called to Ariel that he'd be right back. He wasn't sure she heard him with the water running, but he'd probably return before she got out of the shower.

He carefully pulled the door shut and hung the DO NOT DISTURB sign on the door. As he walked to the elevator, he decided that Nick had really done a fine job with this hotel. The plush carpet, the teak and beveled glass elevator, all first class.

The elevator doors slid smoothly open. He headed for the snack alcove.

"Hi!" Sheila said. Her face was crimson. She was in a raincoat, holding a pint of ice cream.

Wyatt smiled. "Stress relief?"

Sheila nodded. "I'm so worried about Penny."

"She'll be fine." Wyatt sighed. "I wish I could say the same about Jason."

"He'll be fine, too," Sheila assured him. "He's a wonderful boy. Much more, um, personable than you were at that age."

"I have great plans for him," Wyatt said.

"Well, it looks like Jason has his own plans." Moving closer to Wyatt, Sheila said, "They're *fine,* Wyatt. Our children have made it through adolescence. I remember when we all used to say we'd be happy if our kids ended up alive and not in jail."

Wyatt forced a chuckle. "I don't think I ever said that."

Sheila gave him a wry look. "No, I suppose you didn't." Sheila looked down at her hands, turning her wedding ring, watching the small diamond in her engagement ring sparkle. "You know, you're not an easy man, Wyatt."

"You're saying I should let Jason spend his life doing manual labor?"

"You might consider it. If that's what makes him happy."

"Then *you* should *consider* letting Penny sail off with that nitwit," Wyatt snapped.

Sheila laughed. "I don't think people say 'nitwit' anymore. Plus, you're right. I agree with you. I should let her go. I mean, really, I can't *not* let her go. She's gone." Sheila cocked her head. She reached out and took Wyatt's hand.

Wyatt looked down at her hand on his, shocked. Sheila felt him fold his hand around hers, clasping their hands together. They hadn't changed much in twenty-five years. For a moment they were together again, young, eager, hopeful, clueless.

"We thought we knew everything," Sheila said.

"We still don't," Wyatt replied, with a grin.

"We know enough to let our children choose their paths," Sheila said softly.

Wyatt pulled his hand away. "Next, you'll be telling me to try yoga."

"It would be good for you," Sheila observed. "Relieve some of your tension."

Wyatt sighed. No one respected his work. "Good night, Sheila," he said, and headed back to his room.

nineteen
That Summer

When Sheila opened her eyes, the morning sun was streaming through the small high window.

She sat up, feeling a burning pain in her abdomen, and it all came back to her, the night before, Frank's anger, the accident, her bizarre barefooted walk in the forest.

In the bathroom, as she showered, she saw the plum-colored bruises on her rib cage, and a long scrape on her ankle—she couldn't remember getting that—that had bled and clotted. The soles of her feet were blistered and torn. The moment of the crash came back to her in blips. She couldn't seem to focus.

She started to dress for work at the Rose Hotel, then realized it was Sunday. All the doors to the others' rooms were closed. She was sure everyone was sleeping. Sheila pulled on shorts and a tank top and got back in bed.

This time, she couldn't slip into the oblivion of sleep. Her mind raced. How was Frank? Why had he told her to run? The only phone number he had was for Sharon Waters's phone on the first floor, and on Sunday, no one answered it. The island had no local television news, and the island newspaper came out only once a week, on Thursday. Maybe someone had reported it on a radio station, but she had no access to a radio.

Throwing back her covers, she paced the floor. A shroud of guilt clung to her. She couldn't think, she couldn't breathe. She had been the one to tell Frank they had taken the wrong road. Had she shouted too loudly and alarmed him? But he had already been in a strange, agitated state.

Finally, desperate, she knocked on Ariel's door.

"Come in," Ariel called.

Sheila found Ariel lying in bed with a book in her hand.

"You look awful," Ariel said, sitting up and tossing the book aside.

"I feel awful," Sheila said. "Ariel, I don't know what to do."

"Sit here." Ariel patted the bed. "Tell me."

Sheila sat. She needed to talk. "I went on another date last night with Frank. We were on Milestone Road. He was going to take me to Toppers! He missed a turn, and circled back, and when he made the right turn, another car was coming right at us. We crashed. It was terrifying, Ariel, the crash, the noise, and then he yelled at me, told me to go away, he looked angry and *mean*. So I did run, I hid in the trees. I heard sirens, and I saw tow trucks, and I walked home, and I haven't heard from him."

"Are you okay?" Ariel asked, gently touching Sheila's arm.

"I'm fine. I have a bruise on my chest from hitting the dashboard, but that doesn't matter. I don't know how Frank is. I can't call the hotel and ask to speak to him because Mrs. Reardon would know it's me. I don't know what to do."

"That must have been so scary." Ariel put her arm around Sheila's shoulders and hugged her.

"I don't know what to do," Sheila repeated.

Ariel said, "Let me think." She got up and walked to her dresser, put on her watch, nodded to herself, and finally said, "How about this. Let's go to the Rose Hotel. If you see Mrs. Reardon, you can tell her you've lost something—a bracelet, maybe. If she's not there, well, you can peek into Frank's room."

"That's a good idea." Sheila was wonderfully cheered. "You are so smart! And you'll go with me, right?"

"Sure. Let me put some lipstick on. And you need to brush your hair and work on your face, put some blush on so you don't look so deathly pale."

The Sunday morning town was quiet. The air smelled like coffee and cinnamon.

Sheila and Ariel entered the Rose Hotel by the front door. They stood for a moment in the foyer, listening for noises. Nothing.

"His room is on the second floor," Sheila whispered.

The women walked up only two steps before, with a clatter and a rush, Mrs. Reardon appeared from the kitchen into the foyer.

"Sheila! Oh, my dear, how good of you to come over! I'm at my wits' end! Did you hear about Mr. Johnson? The police came to my door!" She clutched her hands to her chest. In a trembling whisper, she added, *"The police."*

Sheila put her hands in her pockets to hide their trembling. "What's happened?"

"There was an accident. A terrible accident," Mrs. Reardon said. "Mr. Johnson was in his car, heading to the Polpis road, and he collided with another car that was turning left. You know how impatient our summer drivers can be."

"Is he . . . is Mr. Johnson okay?"

"He's in the hospital. Some injuries, not life-threatening, but bad. I have his information on file, so I told the police I would call his wife, and I did."

Sheila sagged against Ariel. "His wife."

"Yes. Her name is Bethany. Isn't that just the prettiest name? She told me she'd fly in as soon as she could arrange it."

"I thought Mr. Johnson was divorced," Sheila whispered, more to herself than anyone else.

Mrs. Reardon looked confused. "Why would you think that?"

Ariel spoke up. "The people in the other car. Are they okay?"

"I'm not sure. Agnes, my best friend, is a nurse at the hospital. I phoned her right after the police left. She couldn't say much, everything is confidential, you know, but she did say a man came into the emergency room with a broken arm and other injuries."

"No fatalities?" Sheila asked.

"Oh, dear, I don't know." Mrs. Reardon wrung her hands together. "Maybe," she whispered.

Ariel said, "I'm Ariel Spencer, Mrs. Reardon. Sheila's told me so much about you and how beautiful your inn is. Sheila thought she'd left a bracelet here, but as we came in the door, she remembered where it is. We're so sorry to bother you—"

"It's no bother at all. Sundays are quiet. Would you both like to have a cup of tea?"

"No, thank you. Perhaps another time." Ariel linked her arm through Sheila's and walked to the front door.

Sheila managed to give the landlady a normal smile. "I'll see you tomorrow, Mrs. Reardon."

"Yes, yes, have fun on your day off." The older woman looked at them with a bit of envy in her eyes.

Ariel and Sheila hurried down the stairs and onto Centre Street.

"I want to see him," Sheila said. "I'm going to the hospital. It's only a short walk."

Ariel put her hand on Sheila's arm. "Wait. Don't. That's a ridiculous idea."

Tears stung Sheila's eyes. "I don't believe he's still married. He told me he loved me. I want to ask him myself. I want to see that he's okay. Mrs. Reardon gets confused. I'm going even if you don't go with me." She pulled away from Ariel.

Ariel sighed. "Okay, okay, Sheila. Hang on. I'll go with you."

Sheila was already racing past Main Street and down Fair Street toward the hospital. Ariel trotted along behind her, hoping the brief walk would settle Sheila's nerves. The town was small, and so was the hospital.

The Nantucket Cottage Hospital was a two-story structure with a receptionist in the lobby and an elevator to the second floor. Sheila bypassed the receptionist, who was helping a patient, and sped through the hallways and up the stairs. Ariel followed. The stairs opened on to the nurses' station.

Sheila approached their desk. "What room is Frank Johnson in?"

"Are you family?" the nurse asked. She was older, with curly gray hair and tortoiseshell glasses that framed careful eyes. Her name was Marleen, and Ariel guessed that this woman had grown up on the island, knew everyone who lived here, and spotted Sheila as a summer person immediately.

"No, not exactly, but yes, sort of," Sheila stammered, impressed by those wary eyes.

"His wife is with him now," Marleen said. "You and your friend can wait in the waiting room down the hall. I'll tell his wife you're here. What's your name?"

Sheila froze.

"Evie," Ariel said, stepping in front of Sheila. "Her name is Evie Lovelace."

"Very well." Marleen made a note on a Post-it and stuck it to her desk.

Ariel pulled Sheila down the hall and into the waiting room, where several dark green faux leather sofas sat against the walls. Side tables held old issues of *People* and *Sports Illustrated*.

"Sheila, we have to leave," Ariel said.

"I want to see his wife," Sheila insisted.

"Do you want *her* to see *you*?" Ariel asked.

Sheila looked helplessly at Ariel. "I can't believe he's still married."

"Here's what I'll do," Ariel said. "I'll walk down the hall and if I see a man in bed and a woman sitting with him, I'll tell you what she looks like."

Sheila shook her head. "No. No, you don't have to do that. If that Marleen says his wife is with him, then I guess I believe he's still married. But, Ariel, he told me he was divorced."

Ariel took her arm and gently guided Sheila out of the room and down the stairs to the main entrance. They stepped out into the summer sun, and the sudden difference between the bright, warm day and the dim hospital space was almost shocking, like stepping from a dream into reality.

The two women walked together toward the Sand Palace.

Sheila said, "Evie? Evie Lovelace?"

Ariel laughed. "Okay, *you* try to come up with a believable name in two seconds."

Sheila linked her arm with Ariel's. "Thank you for going with me. Without you, I think I'd still be standing in that hospital corridor, frozen like a statue."

"You'll be fine," Ariel said. "I think I'd punch him in the face if I ever saw him, not that I know what he looks like."

"He's handsome," Sheila said sadly. "He's charming, and smart, and funny, and he treated me with such . . . gentleness. Until last night anyway. He said he loved me. When he looked at me, I believed he loved me."

"He probably did love you, Sheila. People can love two people at the same time. I mean, you still love Hank, don't you?"

"Oh, God." Sheila buried her face in her hands. "Hank can never know about this. It would break his heart. I'm such an idiot!"

Ariel could tell that Sheila was on the edge of a crying jag. It was a glorious Sunday morning, and people were out enjoying the day. Babies cooed, dogs barked, children begged for ice cream even though it wasn't lunchtime yet, men in Nantucket red trousers came out of the Hub carrying *The New York Times,* and flocks of people were crowding up the stairs and into St. Mary's church. Ariel said, "Sheila, *hush.*"

Sheila pulled herself together and didn't cry as they walked to the Sand Palace. But once they were in the dim corridor of the building, the tears started to fall again.

Helplessly, Sheila turned to Ariel. "Will he ever contact me again? How can he? How can he do anything when his wife is with him? Ariel, he said he *loved me.* I thought he told me to run from the accident because he didn't want me hassled by the police and all the red tape. I thought he was trying to take care of me. Instead, he didn't want his wife to know he had a girl with him." Tears streamed down Sheila's face. "Every time I think of this, it seems worse."

"You're exhausted, Sheila, and an emotional wreck. You need to get back in bed and rest."

"I know. Thank you, Ariel. You've been wonderful."

"Listen, you're going to get past this. It was a summer romance, and it never could have lasted. Be glad you had it. You were special to him. He probably did love you, but it was a fling. You've got Hank waiting for you at home, and Hank is a genuine good guy, right?"

"Right." Sheila began to sob. "I've been so bad. Hank can never know about this."

Ariel gently but insistently moved Sheila into her room, where she fell down on the bed, dissolving into tears.

"I'll see you later," Ariel said, and left the room, closing the door behind her.

She returned to her own room, trying to gather her thoughts. Often on Sunday mornings, while the guys slept late, Ariel and Sheila went out for huge calorie-filled breakfasts. She felt sorry for Sheila, but she felt hungry, too. She still was shy about eating alone in a restaurant. She decided to walk down to the strip and get a takeaway muffin and juice.

Love was such a complicated mystery. Sheila loved Frank, who was obviously *not* making long-term plans with Sheila. Ariel loved Wyatt, and she wanted to make love with him, too, but because she was pretty—she knew she was pretty, she'd certainly learned that—lots of men and boys over the past few years had wanted to be with her. Ariel was holding out for true love.

She did love Wyatt. She believed his love was real. She believed he wanted to marry her. Still, this disaster with Sheila and Frank had unsettled her. Ariel sat on a bench staring out at the water, wondering what to do on this beautiful day.

Two women walked past her, heads leaning together as they talked.

"Did you hear that a man *died* in a car accident last night?" one woman said.

"Oh, no, that's terrible! Who was he?"

"I don't know, but at least it's not someone we know. Our husbands are safely at the beach, surf casting."

"If they catch anything, *they* can clean it. Let's go shopping."

Ariel couldn't get her breath. She went cold all over. Had Frank died? Dear God. She tossed her muffin into a barrel and hurried back to the Sand Palace. She should be there when Sheila heard.

Nick always experienced a pull of emotions when he went to the magnificent house on Main Street to see Francine. Part of him was a little boy, full of envy and a fear of not being good enough. Most of him was a grown, competitive man, full of determination to someday have the money to buy a house as good as this or better.

Francine opened the door herself. She was in very short shorts and a halter top. Barefoot. Her blond hair pulled into a ponytail.

"Nickie!" She flung her arms around his neck when he entered the foyer. "You're here!" She tried to kiss him, but he pulled away. "Your father."

"He's in New York today. Or someplace. Natalie has gone to the mainland to visit friends. It's just you and me."

"Well, then . . ." Nick kissed her, pulling her against him.

Francine whispered in his ear, "Would you like to see my etchings?"

Nick said, "Oh, yes."

She led him up the stairs, down the hall, and into an unexpectedly modern bedroom. He thought Francine would have a canopy bed and roses on her carpet. Instead, everything was modern, structural, the colors muted gray and a cream so rich he thought he could taste it.

They fell onto her unmade bed together. Francine tore off her clothes. Nick quickly undressed. He no longer thought of interior décor but only of Francine's lithe, slender body pressing against his.

They made love slowly, memorizing each other's bodies, stroking, kissing, and lingering here and here and here, and afterward, covered in a sheen of sweat, they smiled at each other.

"*Je t'aime,*" Francine murmured.

Nick's breath caught in his throat. "Did you just say you love me?"

Francine ran her fingers over his chest. "I did."

"I don't say that frivolously," Nick told her.

"Nor do I," Francine said, and tugged on his chest hair, hard. "Don't take me for a fool."

Nick rolled over on top of her, supporting himself on his elbows, and cupped her face with his hands.

"I love you, Francine. I seriously love you."

She smiled. "That makes me so happy."

They rested, side by side.

After a while, Francine said she was hungry, so they pulled on clothes and went down to the kitchen where Francine served Nick strong coffee in a large cup. She made eggs and bacon and toast and bowls of cut fruit. While she cooked, they chatted about the island, the Sand Palace friends, local gossip.

When they had finished eating, Francine said, "Nickie, my sweet, tomorrow I'm going to France for a week. Maybe two."

"You are? Why?"

"A good friend is getting married. The wedding will be in the country, an entire weekend of celebrations. There will be other parties, before and after."

"Two weeks?" Heat rose up Nick's neck and flushed his face. "That's a lot of the summer."

"*Chéri,*" Francine said, "I assume you and I are going to be together after the summer."

"Will we? I'll be working for your father, but you—you'll be able to go wherever you want."

"True. That's what happens, Nick, when you love a rich girl."

She touched his arm lightly. "I think you and I are going to be together for a long time."

Nick shook off her hand and stood up. "Francine, you and I haven't even *been together* for a short time."

Francine rose and came close to him. "These plans were made months ago. I had no idea I would meet you. Lise is a dear childhood friend. I have to go. There will be so many parties, events, lunches with grandparents, and, yes, dancing at nightclubs."

"I will miss you," Nick told Francine. He was too proud to admit how he felt, although they had said those serious words, *I love you*. But she was French. Maybe she said that easily, to many men. He was confused, and hurt, and too self-respecting to tell her he was hurt by the news . . . and afraid that she might not come back.

"I will miss you, too," Francine said. "But now I must pack."

"Of course." Nick walked away from her, pausing to say in the nicest tone he could achieve, "I hope you have a good trip."

Then he went down the hall and out the door.

It was after eleven when Wyatt got up, but he always slept late on Sundays, often later than this. His room still held the coolness of night, and the fan purred along quietly, stirring the air gently. He'd yanked the curtains over the window to keep out the light, and his room seemed, for a while, like his own private world. He sat on the side of his bed, trying to decide what to do with his free day.

He had dreamed that Ariel and Sheila were singing. Now he heard them enter the Sand Palace. Sheila was crying. Ariel was comforting her, speaking in a low, sympathetic voice. He couldn't hear their words, only the sad music of their voices. Wyatt didn't know whether to go out and see what was happening or let them have their privacy.

He rose, dressed in board shorts and a T-shirt, and pulled up his sheets in a half-assed effort to tidy his bed. He tried to read a paperback mystery, but couldn't concentrate. Finally, he heard the women's voices in the hall.

Wyatt stepped into the hallway. Sheila was going back into her room, shutting the door softly.

Wyatt said, "Ariel, are you okay?"

"Oh, Wyatt." Ariel came toward him, and she was crying and shaking. "Something terrible has happened."

He put his arm around her and guided her into his bedroom. "Sit down. Tell me. Are you okay?"

Ariel nodded. "I'm fine. But Sheila's broken-hearted. She was dating a man and last night they were in a car accident on the Milestone road, and Frank's car—the man's name is Frank—he turned too fast and collided with a station wagon with a family in it. Frank is in the hospital, but the father in the station wagon *died.*"

"God. How awful."

"I know. Plus, this morning Sheila discovered that Frank is *married.* His wife had flown to the island to be with him in the hospital."

Ariel broke down, sobbing wholeheartedly. Wyatt wrapped his arms around her and held her tight. He kissed the top of her head as if he were a parent comforting a child.

Actually, he had no idea what to do now. His parents had always been sparse with their emotion, and when he became a teenager, it was a sign of weakness to cry. He was sorry for Sheila. It was tough to find out someone you're dating had lied to you. He wasn't sure how he felt about Ariel's reaction. She wasn't really involved. She was extremely kind and sympathetic, but she'd been crying against him for a long time, and he didn't understand why she was so upset about what had happened to Sheila.

He was more concerned with what was happening to him now, in this room, with this woman in his arms. Her hair smelled like flowers and her skin was so soft. He wanted to make love with her, not to have sex, but to embrace her body and soul with his love and protection, with his promise to never cheat on her. He wanted to embrace her with passion, and so he put his hand on her chin and lifted her face to his and kissed her. Her cheeks were wet with tears, which he found unbearably sexy. She kissed him back, whimpering, and he gently leaned her back on his bed and pulled her on her side, so that their bodies touched.

"It's okay," he whispered. "It's okay."

He put his hand on her breast.

She struggled and pushed him away. "Wyatt, stop."

"Ariel—" He tried to hold her back.

She shoved him away, twisted so she could stand up, and drew her hand across her mouth, as if wiping away his kisses.

"How can you at a time like this?" Ariel asked. "Is sex all you care about? God, you men!" She stormed out and he heard her enter her room, and lock the door. *Click*. What did she think, that he'd storm after her and force himself on her?

Now *he* wanted to cry. What had just happened? Girls could get so dramatic. He'd seen them weep and hug one another if their football team lost a game. Wyatt was sorry for Sheila, and really sorry that a man had died last night, and sorry that that guy Frank had lied to Sheila, but why was Ariel so upset with *him*?

And his day just got worse.

He rode his bike to the Jetties and swam for a long time. The sheer effort kept him from thinking about Ariel. When he returned to the hotel, he was hungry, so he showered and shaved and walked into town to have breakfast, or, more likely, lunch. The sun was right overhead, and he thought it was the hottest day of the summer. He stopped at a takeaway on the strip, bought two cheeseburgers and two iced cans of Coke, and returned to his room. He read his mystery while he ate, then went back to bed and the oblivion of sleep. He was tired, he was confused, he was furious at Ariel and at himself.

When he woke, it was almost four o'clock. He'd wasted his day off. In Columbia, he lived with his parents, and usually on Sunday afternoons he watched a baseball or football game and enjoyed one of his mom's Sunday roasts. He wished he could go somewhere with Ariel, but he heard no sounds from her room or from Sheila's.

A knock came at his door.

Nick stuck his head in. "Hey, man. Let's go to the AC and have some brews."

Wyatt thought Nick was irritating with his cool dude persona. The AC instead of the Atlantic Café, as if Nick and the restaurant were close buddies. But Wyatt was glad to have company and he knew a "brew" would make him feel better.

This time when he left the Sand Palace, the wind had come up and the sky was clouding over. As they walked, Nick talked incessantly about Francine.

"She's the one, man," Nick said. "I know it. I just know it. I've met her family. They're snobbish, but we get along. I'm going to work for her father after the summer. But this is not about Mr. Bruel. I have serious feelings for Francine, and she's leaving for Paris tomorrow and I'll miss her like hell. I hope she misses me."

They sat at the bar right at the front of the restaurant and ordered beers.

"Have you seen Ariel or Sheila?" Wyatt asked Nick.

"Not today," Nick said.

Wyatt filled him in on Sheila's disastrous evening, and how she discovered her boyfriend was married, and that a man had died in the accident.

"Damn, that's awful," Nick said. "Poor Sheila. Wow. That's, like, epic."

On a TV above the bar, a baseball game was in progress.

"Who's your team?" Nick asked.

Wyatt was shocked that Nick would jump immediately from the accident to a baseball game, but then Wyatt had come to learn that Nick liked skating on the surface of life. Plus, Wyatt had moved fast from the accident to making love with Ariel, and now she was mad at him. What they said was right: Men and women were different. They watched the game and ordered another beer.

"I want to play polo someday," Nick was saying. "I can sit a horse pretty well and I'm good at hockey, so when I get rich enough to do it, I'm going to try. What about you?"

Wyatt laughed. Nick was such a prick. *Polo.* "I've ridden a lot, in Missouri. Friends have horses and I go out with them. Quarter horses. Western saddles. Sometimes guns in case we come across rattlers." Wyatt was trying to sound as Midwestern as he could, because Nick was all about being continental, and he knew this would irritate Nick.

Four young men entered the bar. They wore button-down shirts with the tails hanging out over their madras shorts, loafers without socks, Rolex watches, and fifty-dollar haircuts. They were tanned and handsome and laughing, and Wyatt hated them on sight. They were such a *type.*

And what a surprise. They knew Nick.

"It's the Nickster!" one of them yelled.

They surrounded Nick in a swarm of arrogance, pounding his back, shouting everything they said, ignoring everyone else. Finally, Nick introduced Wyatt to them, and they all found a waitress who pushed two tables together for them.

"I went to school with these guys," Nick told Wyatt.

"Where'd you go to school?" a man asked Wyatt.

"University of Missouri," Wyatt said, knowing what was coming.

"Missouri? What's that? Is that a place?"

"Do they serve that as a drink?" a guy asked.

Much laughter and back-pounding took place. Wyatt knew they weren't trying to be rude, but by the time the drinks were served, and then the nachos, he was tired of them. They were obnoxiously loud, as if trying to call attention to themselves, to their wealthy, tanned, private club selves. Nick got into an animated discussion with them about a teacher they'd all had who had just retired, and Wyatt tossed back his third beer, or maybe it was his fourth.

"Excuse me, guys. See you later." He slipped away from the group, and no one tried to stop him.

———

He walked slowly through the small town. It was a hot August night and people were out having fun. On Easy Street by the harbor, a couple sat on a bench kissing passionately. Lucky kids. Wyatt knew he was being an asshole, he knew it was the heat and craziness of August that was throwing him off, but he couldn't stop brooding over Ariel refusing to make love with him. She'd told him she loved him, she would marry him, but she wouldn't have sex with him. Okay, this morning after she told him about the accident, he had moved too quickly, wanting to have sex, but wasn't that one way people consoled each other when they heard about a death?

Whatever. He didn't like himself much, and right now he was enjoying a good sulk. He shut himself in his basement room, took the latest *Marine and Petroleum Geology* journal, and lay on his bed, reading. Soon his emotions disappeared as his mind disappeared into the mysterious solace of science.

twenty

This Summer

"Look," Liam said.

Penny was bent over her iPhone, checking for messages. She sensed that the boat had stopped moving. When Liam spoke, she rose to look toward the west.

"Ohhhh," she said, enchanted.

"That's Boston," Liam told her. "We won't enter her harbor. Too crowded right now. But I wanted you to see it."

The sun shone down on the towers of the city, a long cluster of skyscrapers seeming to rise from the water. Boats were entering and exiting the harbor. Majestic cruise ships were slowly moving forward among small sailboats, their white sails skimming the blue.

"It looks like a golden city," Penny said.

"It does."

"It's magic." Penny couldn't look away.

"I thought you'd like it."

Liam put his hands around Penny's waist and she leaned against him. For a long time, they stood together. Occasionally, Liam would point out a building that blazed in the sun's light. The tall, blue-glass-windowed Hancock building. The historic Boston Custom House Tower with its clock and triangular peak. The glittering windows of commerce.

"I'm in heaven," Penny said.

"Just wait until I prepare your breakfast," Liam told her.

She settled on the deck, watching the ever-changing view, and Liam prepared scrambled eggs and bacon and brought them to her.

"With service like this," she joked, "I may never go home."

"I hope you don't," Liam said.

She knew she couldn't take him seriously. And really, she didn't want to.

Later, he told her to watch her head while he came about, so that the long wooden boom didn't hit her. The sail billowed with air, Liam turned the wheel and adjusted the sheets, and slowly they sailed south, returning to Nantucket. Penny washed their dishes in his dollhouse kitchen sink, then returned to the deck. Now she took pictures without hesitation, photos of the coast, and the sun on the water, and Liam, tall and suntanned and handsome.

Liam pointed. "See that land in the south? We're near the tip of Cape Cod."

"Oh." Penny shook her head. "Almost back."

Liam recognized the yearning in her voice. "We could drop the anchor and go below."

She turned to him, put her arms around him, and smiled up at him. "Yes, please."

After they made long, slow, lingering love, they lay curled together in the bunk.

Penny asked, "Could we have dinner, on land, tonight?"

Liam shifted slightly, but kept his arms around her. "I've got to be in Newport this evening. Maybe another night."

"Ah." Her disappointment made her brave enough to ask, cheerfully, "Are you the man with a girl in every port?"

Liam was quiet. Then he said, "I don't have to be."

"We leave tomorrow," Penny told him.

"Do you have to?" Liam asked.

Penny blinked. "Maybe not. Maybe I could stay on the island for the summer . . . I could get a job . . ."

Liam gently put his thumb beneath Penny's chin and tilted her face up so she could meet his eyes.

"You should get a job. You should stay on the island."

Friday morning, Jade-Marie and Jason came down the corridor from their rooms and met at the elevator.

"Hi," Jade-Marie said, sounding, she thought, way too chirpy. That was how she felt, though. Penny was gone, leaving Jade-Marie and Jason alone, the only two newbies. Jade-Marie thought she looked good in her tiny polka-dot pink-and-white dress and flip-flops. Her dark hair was pulled back in a high ponytail. Her face was bronzed by the sun.

"Hi," Jason croaked. He wore board shorts and a rugby shirt and flip-flops. He hadn't shaved yet, and the second-day beard looked good on him. "You look nice."

"Thanks," Jade-Marie said. "You look . . ."

"Like I need a shower," Jason admitted. "I promise I'll take one after I have breakfast."

The elevator door opened. Jade-Marie stepped inside. Jason joined her. And there they were, only two of them, alone in the small space.

"I'm glad you'll be here all summer," Jade-Marie told him.

Jason smiled. "I'm glad you'll be here all summer, too."

"There are lots of fun things to do on the island," Jade-Marie said, and started to apologize for sounding so lame.

Jason interrupted her. "I can't wait." He stepped close to her, close enough to kiss. "I mean it. I—"

The doors slid smoothly open. Jade-Marie and Jason stepped out, grinning.

They walked together to the bistro bar and piled their plates high with scrambled eggs, bacon, and fruit. And *coffee.* Jason almost inhaled his. They sat next to each other at the empty table.

"Maybe we should go swimming this morning," Jade-Marie said. "Just the two of us. I mean, Penny is off sailing with Liam."

"Good idea," Jason said.

The elevator pinged. The door slid open. Jade-Marie's parents came toward the long table of breakfast foods.

"Good morning, *chérie.*" Francine kissed the top of Jade-Marie's head. "Good morning, Jason."

"I've got good plans for today," Nick said. "I'll wait until your parents come down, Jason, to announce them. You kids might want to go with us."

"Dad, I think Jason and I will just hit the beach," Jade-Marie said.

Her father frowned. The elevator pinged again and Jason's parents arrived.

"Good morning, sweetie," Ariel said, kissing his cheek.

His father didn't say a word to Jason. Clearly, Wyatt was still furious about Jason's decision to work on the island this summer. Jason watched the way his mother fluttered around her husband, bringing him a napkin and extra little plastic cups of syrup for his pancakes. Wyatt showed the intensity of his anger by going Antarctica cold. It seemed that his father lowered the temperature in the room simply by being there.

"Okay, troop!" Nick said cheerily. "The plan for the day is to go to Tuckernuck. For you young ones, Tuckernuck is a small island to the west of Nantucket. It's really natural, environmentally pure, trees, grasses, deer, great beaches, and a lagoon. You all will be some of the very few people in the world ever to set foot there."

"I don't think I want to go to Tuckernuck," Francine said. "The Nantucket Historical Association is giving tours of the most famous old houses on the island, built by whaling captains, furnished with gorgeous antiques. Maybe you'd like to go with me, Ariel? And Jade-Marie, too? The men can go tromp through the bushes and use up some of their testosterone."

"Do we need tickets?" Ariel asked.

"We can get them at the door. Then we can go out to the Summer House in 'Sconset for lunch. It's on the water. The climbing roses will be everywhere on the small cottages. After that, maybe pedis and manis? I'll call Sheila and ask if she wants to join us."

Jade-Marie spoke up. "Jason and I are going to have a beach day."

"Well!" Ariel said.

"Ooh-la-la!" Francine said, laughing. Nick looked crestfallen. "All right, Wyatt. Want to go to Tuckernuck?"

Wyatt said, "Absolutely."

Sheila lay in blissful silence in her room, drinking a Diet Coke and eating several candy bars she'd bought from a machine yesterday. The sun was so bright it hurt her eyes, but she was too comfortable to get up and pull the heavy curtains closed.

But really, she should get up.

Or not.

This was the rarest of times, being absolutely alone, with no household duties to perform, no sons to root for at some sort of ball game, not even a daughter to attend to. She hoped Penny was having a good time with Liam. She really did. Now that she'd had a night to sleep on it, she understood how romantic Penny's adventure was. Sailing alone with that handsome Irishman? Penny would remember it all of her life.

Sheila's friends had warned her that she worried too much, but how could she not? She was raising four children in a difficult world. And it was unsettling to be here, where she'd once worked as a chambermaid, and now was the guest of a man who owned a *chain* of hotels. She liked the other women, although Francine was still a snob. Jade-Marie seemed nice enough, especially for a child with Nick's genes.

Sheila had wakened this morning and made a decision. Today she would spend in bed. She'd doze and watch television and eat like a teenager. She had this lovely, beautifully furnished, private hotel room wrapped around her like her own personal fort.

She could rest.

Her phone rang. Sheila wasn't going to answer it, and then she thought: *Penny!* She had to rise from the bed and dig her phone out of her purse. The caller ID named Francine. She let the message go to voicemail.

That afternoon, as they arrived back at the hotel, Wyatt was in an unusually good mood. He'd enjoyed the outing more than he'd expected to, and felt tanned and toned after their expedition through the high grasses.

Most important, as they were in the Jeep riding back to the hotel, Wyatt's phone had buzzed. One of his interns had figured out the problem they'd been having with the computerized print-out of an experiment with a specimen of a geologic deposit. It would take a few days to resolve, and by the time Wyatt returned to the lab, it would be ready.

"Listen," Wyatt said. "I want to treat us all to dinner tonight. I'm going to make a reservation for all of us at, what, seven-thirty? Eight? Let's go to Dune. Their menu looks interesting and we can sit outside if we want."

Nick said, "That sounds great, Wyatt. Thanks."

A few minutes later, Wyatt said, "Reservations made. Seven-thirty. I'll text everyone."

Sheila stepped out of the shower, pulling on the thick white terrycloth robe as steam billowed around her. Just as she entered her bedroom, a knock came on the door. She looked out the small peephole.

"Penny! You're back!" Sheila threw the door open. "Come in. Tell me everything!"

Penny was radiant. "The trip was wonderful, Mom. *Liam* is wonderful."

"I want to hear all about it, but first I have to tell you that we're all going to dinner tonight at Dune. Wyatt is taking us."

"That's nice," Penny said. "I'll have time to shower, won't I?"

"Yes, but quickly, do you like Liam?"

"Oh, Mom, I like him a lot." Penny followed her mother over to the mirror where Sheila was brushing her hair.

"Ask him to join us for dinner," Sheila suggested, wondering which dress she should wear.

"He's going on to Newport tonight." Penny sat on the end of the bed.

"So, you'll never see him again," Sheila concluded. She walked across the room, sat on the bed, and hugged her daughter. "It's all right, darling. There are lots of fish in the sea."

"I'm sure I'll see him again. I'm going to get a job on Nantucket and he'll be back and forth."

Sheila felt a twinge of anxiety, remembering her summer experience. Still, she said, "Summer loves are so sweet."

Penny groaned. "It's not a summer love, Mom, and it's not like *love*. It's not serious. I'm not going to tie myself to a husband and children so soon. I want to explore, live my life."

"I understand, Penny, but let me warn you. Summer loves are often life-changing." Sheila paused, wondering if she should tell Penny about Frank.

"Well, this summer love isn't changing *my* life," Penny announced. "He's wonderful, but I'm young."

"When I was your age, I had a summer love," Sheila began.

"Of course you did," Penny said carelessly. "I'm hungry. I'd better go shower and change. What time is dinner?"

Sheila relaxed. "We're meeting downstairs at six-thirty."

All of them, five parents and three adult children, sat at the long table at the back of Dune's patio. It was the perfect summer night, warm and slightly humid as fog drifted onto the land from the warm evening sea. Everyone except Sheila was glowing from the day's sun, and Sheila, even with her creamy-white skin, was bright-eyed and rosy from the day's rest.

The excellent cocktails and food had kept them happy and talkative. Nick described the men's hike over the small wild island of Tuckernuck as if he were Jim Cantore from the Weather Channel.

Francine raved about the décor of the house tours, the vases and chinoiserie wallpaper inspired by the whalers' visits to the Pacific.

As they were finishing their desserts, Ariel said, "Hey, everyone, remember Hump Night?"

"Hump night?" Jade-Marie repeated.

"Not in *that* way," Ariel replied. She was a little tipsy after all the cocktails and wine and champagne. "That's what the four of us called it when we were working here. Because it meant the work week was half over. Everyone uses that expression now."

"Oh, I remember," Sheila said. "Back then, Nick's hotel looked nothing like it does now. It was under renovation so there were only a few rooms on the ground floor with lights and electricity, like Sharon Waters's office. We scavenged a table and every Wednesday night the four of us ate dinner there."

Ariel added, "We alternated cooking. Men versus women. Obviously, Sheila and I made delicious dinners. The men heated up beans and franks from cans. I'm not sure they ever served anything green."

Jade-Marie laughed. "It seems you all survived that summer nicely."

Francine asked, "Penny, tell us, how was your trip with Liam?"

Penny blushed. "It was perfect. From the water, Boston looks magical."

Jade-Marie grinned. "And was Liam magical?"

Penny absolutely did *not* want to talk about sex in front of her parents, so she blurted out the first thing that came into her mind. "Liam is nice. But he had an odd childhood. When he was a little boy, he was on Nantucket, riding in a car with his father and mother, and his dad's car and another car ran into each other. His father died."

Sheila and Ariel looked at each other.

"How terrible," Ariel said. "What was his father's name? I mean, was he a summer person?" Hastily, she added, "Not that it matters."

"Liam's birth father's name was Harrison. But when his mother married again, when Liam was only six, she legally changed his last name to Miller."

Sheila frowned. "Let me get this straight. Penny, you went sailing with Liam Miller, whose father was killed in a car accident on the island when Liam was a child."

Penny nodded. "That's right. It's so sad. But Liam loves his stepfather. Well, he calls him his father. He always has."

"Very tragic, but happy ending, right?" Francine said, trying to lift the mood at the table.

"Oh, God, I feel sick." Sheila pushed her chair back. "Excuse me." She left the table, hurried to the sidewalk, and headed for the Lighthouse.

"What's wrong with her?" Wyatt asked.

"I'll go with her." Penny pushed back her chair.

Ariel said, "No, Penny, you stay. I think she ate a lot of sweets today while Francine and I were touring historic homes. Now she's probably paying for it. *I'll* go with her."

Ariel left the table and hurried away. She glimpsed Sheila far ahead of her, almost running, and even though Ariel called her name, she didn't stop or slow down.

By the time Ariel reached the hotel, she saw Sheila vanishing into the elevator. Ariel took the stairs and caught up with Sheila as she was unlocking the door to her room.

"Sheila. Let's talk, okay?"

Sheila pushed the door open, let Ariel enter, then shut and locked the door. She spun to face Ariel. "I never told Penny about Frank Johnson. I didn't want her to think badly of me, that I was a slut—"

Ariel grabbed the overwrought woman by the arms. "For God's sake, Sheila, you weren't a slut. You were a young woman in love. You did nothing wrong."

"A man *died*." Sheila pulled away from Ariel and strode to the window, looking out, as if she were looking back through the years of her life.

"Have you told Hank about—"

"No, I didn't tell Hank about it. I never told anyone but you. I thought it was all over. It *is* all over. But what if Penny *marries* Liam, the son of the man who died in the collision?"

"Sheila, Penny only went sailing with him. Maybe she has a crush on him. Maybe they're in love. But it's a long leap from summer love to marriage."

"But do you think I should tell her?"

Ariel pulled a chair away from the small round table.

"I can't answer that, Sheila. She's your daughter. The two of you seem close. Also, you made a pretty dramatic exit from the table this evening. Penny's bound to check in with you, see if you're okay."

"I tried to tell her earlier. I told her I had had a summer romance, but she wasn't interested. She doesn't *seem* head over heels with Liam. She wants her freedom and I understand that. Maybe she'll get serious with Liam. Maybe not. Whatever, I don't want to ruin it for her. I'm going to wait awhile. See how it goes. Maybe I'm a coward."

"Or maybe," Ariel said, "you're wise."

twenty-one
That Summer

Nick left Fanshaw's at five, as usual, and for the first time in weeks, he wasn't rushing to clean up and then meet Francine. Francine had gone to France.

The day had been cloudy off and on, and a breeze puffed through the air. He didn't want to go to the Sand Palace and sit in his room, so he walked to the A&P on the harbor and bought himself some sandwiches, then up Main to Murray's to pick up a six-pack of Bud. He headed down to the Brant Point lighthouse.

Waves were slapping at the shore. Boats tied to buoys were rocking back and forth. Families were leaving the beach because sand was flicking their faces. Nick found shelter on the land side of the lighthouse. A nervous energy skipped in the air and Nick liked it. It was how he felt.

From the first moment he saw Francine, he'd been in love with her, and she'd made him feel she was in love with him, too. He wanted to trust her. But two weeks was a long time in the summer.

He knew he wasn't really in her league. She probably knew dukes, diplomats.

"Hi, Nick!"

He turned to see Sheila approaching him.

"Hi," Nick said. "What are you doing out here?"

Sheila shrugged. "Walking. Getting some fresh air. I can't force myself to spend the evening in that hole of a room."

"I hear you."

"Do you mind if I hang out with you?" Sheila asked.

"Of course not. I have cold beer and sandwiches."

"Cool."

For a while they ate and drank in silence.

Sheila said softly, "It all looks like a dreamworld. But that's not true."

"Come on, Sheila, sometimes it is. No place can be a dreamworld all of the time."

"I know, Nick." Sheila cried quietly, tears rolling down her cheeks.

"Want to talk about it?" Nick asked half-heartedly.

"Thanks, but no." Sheila sniffed and dried her face with her hands.

Nick leaned over and hugged her. "You'll be okay. This, too, shall pass."

"I've always been a good girl," Sheila whispered.

"You're still a good girl," Nick told her. "You're tired. So am I. Come on, let's go back. We both could use a good night's sleep."

Sheila kept pace with him as he walked. She didn't try to hold his hand. She didn't talk. Once she yawned.

At the entrance to the Sand Palace, Sheila said, "'Night, Nick." She went past his room and into her own.

Nick fell on his bed and wished Francine were with him.

The August afternoon was punishingly hot and humid. Wyatt and Don Cabot were in the shop. Don was wrenching something on an engine. Wyatt was unpacking new deliveries from UPS. Somewhere in the bowels of the shop a fan whirred, stirring the air, but the sun was strong through the doors and windows.

"What's wrong with you, son?" Don Cabot asked. "You're making a hash out of those gear sets."

"I'm making a hash out of my life," Wyatt grumbled. He hadn't slept for the past two nights. When he went to bed, he could hear Ariel going down the corridor to the bathroom. When she returned to her bedroom, her sweet fragrance drifted into his room. He wanted to talk to her.

Cabot laughed. "Girl trouble, is it?"

Wyatt stared at the older man. "How did you know?"

"It's either girl trouble or money trouble. Girl trouble is a summer tradition on Nantucket."

Something about Cabot, how honest he was, how forthright, inspired Wyatt to tell him. "I want to marry her."

"Is she an island woman?" Cabot asked.

"What? Why?"

"Because if she's an island woman, I'm going to tell you to leave her alone or I'll make you sorry you were born."

Wyatt gave his boss a sardonic stare. "Thanks." He focused on the cardboard box full of small metal bits in plastic packages.

Cabot persisted. "Well, is she?"

"No." Wyatt shook his head. As tough and perceptive as Cabot was, it took all Wyatt had not to cry. "Her name's Ariel. She's from Boston. She's really pretty and smart."

"You met her here this summer?"

Wyatt nodded. "She's like an angel. Plus, she's sophisticated, and I'm just a guy from Missouri. But she told me she loves me."

Cabot turned back to the engine he was working on. He could do this, quit a conversation and immerse himself in work. Wyatt realized he was pretty much that way, too.

But not totally that way. He'd never felt for any woman what he felt for Ariel. He'd certainly never asked another woman to marry him. And Cabot was smart, a genius with boats but smart about people, too.

"What should I do?" Wyatt asked.

Cabot's back was to him now. "What do you want to do?"

"I want to marry her."

"How did you ask her?" Cabot banged something metal with a wrench and the sound reverberated through the air.

"Uh, I didn't actually, um, propose. We talked about getting married, kind of."

"Wyatt Smith, you can't be so stupid. Did you have an engagement ring?"

"Well, no. Like I said, we talked about marriage."

"So let me get this straight." Cabot stood up and leaned against a boat. "You think you love this woman enough to live your entire life with her and first thing, right off, you can't even be romantic enough to offer her an engagement ring."

"Why are you being so tough on me?" Wyatt demanded.

"Because I like you, Wyatt, and I get how you are. Smart, but dim. Wyatt, women like romance. They like a *memory*. If I were you, I'd leave work right now and go buy an engagement ring and get down on my knee and propose properly."

Wyatt nodded. "Okay. Okay. Where should I buy a ring?"

"Not on Nantucket, they're expensive here, especially in August."

"I don't have much money."

"Get a ring."

Wyatt nodded. He didn't know what to do next.

Cabot sighed. "It would be cheaper for you to take a boat to Hyannis and find a jeweler in their mall. Go on now, you might make the five o'clock Hy-Line."

"Great. Thanks, Don." Wyatt raced out of the shop and down along the sandy beach toward the wharves. Sand flew up behind his feet as he ran. He thundered up the rocky shore onto the boardwalk and headed toward Straight Wharf. He could see the fast ferry still at the dock. He ran faster.

———

The Sand Palace was empty. No one was there, and that sense of disturbed air, a kind of invisible wave from people passing through, wasn't around.

Ariel went up the back steps to Sharon Waters's office to use the phone. Sharon had left for the day, and Ariel was glad. She found the phone book lying beneath the phone—Sharon was practical—and drew her finger down the page of *C*'s until she discovered the number of Cabot's Marine.

A gruff voice answered. "What?"

Ariel almost dropped the phone. "Is Wyatt Smith there?"

"No, darlin', he left early. He went off-island." The man disconnected.

She almost fell as she ran down the stairs. Had Wyatt left the island for good? He wouldn't do that without telling her, would he? The door to his bedroom was unlocked. She threw it open and stood on the threshold looking around. All his stuff was still here. The pajama bottoms he slept in had been tossed on the unmade bed. His plaid bathing suit was hanging from a chair. Books and papers and letters littered his desk and for one moment Ariel was tempted to scan the letters to see who had written him. But she wouldn't do that, and with a sigh, she pulled the door closed.

In her own room, she dropped her bag on the desk, flopped onto her bed, kicked off her shoes. Where was Wyatt? Why hadn't he told her where he was going? Why *should* he tell her where he was going?

But he was coming back. He had to come back. All his things were here. Ariel kept her clothes on, listening for sounds of Wyatt returning. After an hour, she fell asleep.

Wyatt sat on the deck of the slow ferry with the ring box in his hand. Out here, benches lined the wall, and you could lean against the back and tilt your head up and see the entire sky sparkling just for you. He thought it would be cool to give Ariel the ring at night, somewhere outside, under the stars.

The ferry was crossing the sound, chugging along in a grumbling rhythm as it cut through the water. When they neared the harbor, the boat slowed its speed, and in the harbor, it crept along inch by inch. Sensible, Wyatt supposed. The ferry was big and the other boats small in comparison, and there was always some nut in a kayak obliviously paddling across the ferry's path. Wyatt thought he'd get to Ariel faster if he dove off the ship and swam to shore.

The ferry finally docked at ten-fifteen. As he walked down the ramp and onto the sidewalk, he noticed that his heart rate had increased. It was booming in his ears. Was he nervous? Yes, he was nervous. Science was easier. If one experiment didn't work, you readjusted the variables and tried it a different way. People were harder. You never could count on what they would do. He hadn't counted on falling in love this summer, and certainly he'd never counted on falling like a penny dropped off the Empire State Building, so unexpectedly, so surprisingly, so fast and so deep. He'd had girlfriends before, of course. He knew he was good-looking in his own way, not glamorous like Nick, but not a dog. As a senior in high school, he'd sat in a steamy car on a cold night listening to a girl weepily explaining how much she loved him and begging him to be more demonstrative, more spontaneous. In college, he'd tried to date only girls who were in his science classes, but those girls were as saccharine and needy as the liberal arts girls.

Ariel was definitely a liberal arts type, but she wasn't dreary. She had a wonderful laugh. She liked listening to him talk about his experiments and she tried to understand what he told her. She wanted to write, for a magazine or even fiction, but she had told him she could do that anywhere, practically writing it out in capital letters: I WILL FOLLOW YOU ANYWHERE.

As he walked, his thoughts were coming fast and piling up on one another, making little sense, and not curbing his nervousness. He knew he could understand lust. He didn't think he'd ever understand love.

The odd skyline of the nearly demolished building came into view. Much of it was mounds of stone and dirt and wood dumped where a hotel once stood. At the far end, safety lights illuminated the narrow structure housing Sharon Waters's office and the steps down to the Sand Palace.

Wyatt fumbled around in his pocket to be sure the ring box was still there.

It was.

His mouth was dry. He entered the corridor leading to the bathroom and the four bedrooms. No sounds. It wasn't even eleven, but either people had gone to sleep or were out partying. With Nick it was certain to be partying. He hoped Sheila was asleep.

Wyatt rubbed his sweaty hands on his jeans. It was humid outside, but he admitted to himself that he was nervous. He knocked very quietly on Ariel's door. What if she didn't answer? What if she wasn't there? Or what if she was so soundly asleep it would be wrong to wake her? Then he'd have to get through this night and the next day before he could properly propose to her and end his crazy obsession.

He turned the handle. The door wasn't locked, which seemed like a good sign. Maybe she was expecting him. Although, he suddenly realized, he hadn't told her that he was going off-island. Did that matter? Could he do *anything* right in the bizarre interaction of courtship?

He opened the door far enough to see Ariel on her bed. She was curled up in a ball with all her clothes on.

She looked like an angel, too beautiful to touch.

Wyatt stood frozen in terror. Love was a cruel, piercing thing. A sword, a knife, an arrow through the heart, just like those drawings of Cupid showed. Wyatt could do anything, he could comprehend the solar system, he understood volcanic tephra. But this, this *love* thing, was so messy, so intricately tied into other bits of life, like need, like adoration.

She stirred and stretched.

"Ariel?"

"Oh," Ariel said. "Wyatt? Come in. I guess I fell asleep. Hot day."

Wyatt entered the room. "Hi. Um, can we go outside, maybe?"

Ariel sat up, looking puzzled. "Go outside?"

He didn't want to propose in this humid basement room. "Yeah, get some fresh air. Maybe sit on the bench."

"Okay," Ariel said. "Let me change into some shorts."

"No. No, you look beautiful. Perfect. Come right now. You'll . . . you'll see."

"Okay, mystery man." Ariel got off the bed and went to her bureau. She brushed her hair. "Do I have to wear my heels?"

"Uh, no." He touched the box in his pocket, as if it might have evaporated from his sheer nervous energy.

Ariel slid on her sandals. "Okay?"

"Okay." This was taking way too long. What if she refused? Wyatt took her by her hand and walked with her out of the Sand Palace and over to the bench by the flowers. "Sit down."

"Yes, sir!" Ariel sat. He had to do it now. He knelt on the grass in front of her, held out the red box, and said, "Ariel Spencer, will you marry me?"

Her smile opened his heart. He rose and sat beside her.

"Oh, yes!" She opened the box. "Oh. Wyatt. This ring is beautiful."

"You're beautiful," Wyatt said. He coughed then cleared his throat. "I need to tell you something, and I know I'm not the most eloquent man. But I want you to know that I fell in love with you the moment I saw you and I've loved you every moment since. I want to live with you. I want to have babies with you. Or not have babies with you. Whatever."

"I do, too," Ariel told him. She threw her arms around him in a fierce hug. "Yes, Wyatt, yes, I'll marry you."

"Thank you," Wyatt said.

Ariel's laugh was bubbly and light, and Wyatt felt more intelligent, hopeful, and even more handsome than he'd ever felt before in his life.

"One thing," Ariel said. "I've been accepted in the writing program at the University of Iowa. Starting this September."

Wyatt froze. He said nothing.

"I suppose the drive between Iowa City and Columbia isn't too long, maybe four or five hours."

Wyatt still didn't speak.

"Wyatt?" Ariel prompted.

"You can write anywhere," he said. He wouldn't meet her eyes. "I'm sure they've got creative writing workshops at the University of Missouri. I thought . . . I want to get married right away. Get an apartment near the campus. I'll work and you can stay home and write."

"Iowa's program is prestigious," Ariel said. She was on the point of tears. "It isn't easy to get in."

"So it's the prestige you want."

"No, Wyatt. Well, yes, of course, it might help when it comes time to try to sell a story or a book, but—"

"Books can take years to write. The work my father and I are doing is of groundbreaking importance," Wyatt said. Quietly, as if confessing a crime, he said, "Ariel. I *need* you." He took her hand in his. "I can't do it without you."

Ariel said nothing aloud, but her mind was racing. She could write at home. Writing a book could take years. Who was she to think she could ever get anything published? This summer, she'd seldom had time to write anything in her notebook. She was young. She needed to learn more, read more, write more, before trying to write a novel.

And she did love Wyatt.

"So you want to get married this fall?" she asked Wyatt quietly.

"I want to get married tomorrow," Wyatt joked, and now he looked at her, and his eyes were warm and loving.

"Okay, then," Ariel said. "I'll write the director of the program to tell him I'm unable to attend the program because of an urgent family problem."

Wyatt put his arms around Ariel and held her close. "I'll give you an urgent family problem."

Ariel laughed. "Let's go home as soon as we can. Let's tell our parents."

"Let's get married," Wyatt said.

"Yes," Ariel replied. "Let's do that."

twenty-two

This Summer

At the restaurant, the ones left behind sat in confusion.

"What was that about?" Penny asked.

Wyatt responded with a shrug. "Women. Who can understand them?"

"My mom worries that I'll have a 'summer love' and get my heart broken," Penny said.

Francine smiled. "Oh, that happens to everyone."

"Mom worries about everything," Penny mused aloud. "Especially when I'm driving a car. *Look both ways! Don't run a red light! Don't text and drive.* Sometimes she makes me crazy."

Nick said kindly, "I'm sure you make her crazy sometimes, too."

Wyatt was sulking. "Jason has definitely made me crazy. I can't believe he's giving up a prestigious scientific career to do manual labor."

Jason took a deep breath. "Dad, Don Cabot is a good guy.

Smart. You know that. I know I can learn a lot from him when I work for him this summer."

"A lot about boats," Wyatt shot back. "Nothing about science."

Francine said, "Not all children are fated to follow in their father's footsteps."

"You can say that, Francine, because you have never had to worry about money or success."

"Did you envy me, Wyatt?" Francine aimed her charm at Jason's father. "I envied you all. When you were living in the Sand Palace, you four had each other. You fought, sometimes, but you were like a club, a fellowship, living almost as a family. I didn't *choose* to be wealthy. I had no idea the dinner I invited you to had aroused such strong feelings."

Wyatt couldn't meet her eyes. "I apologize. I suppose I've felt guilty all these years because Nick asked to borrow three hundred dollars to take you to dinner, and I refused to loan it to him."

"Ooh-la-la!" Francine was completely surprised. "I never knew this." She looked at her husband.

Nick said, "I never told you. I was worried that I couldn't give you the kind of life you already lived."

"Oh, my darling," Francine said. "All I wanted was life with you."

Penny cried, "They're coming back!"

Everyone at the table watched as Sheila and Ariel cut their way between tables to return to their own party.

"Sorry about that," Ariel said smoothly. "Women's problems."

"Are you okay, Mom?" Penny asked.

"I'm fine. Sorry to leave so abruptly." Sheila reached over to pat her daughter's hand.

Nick cleared his throat. "In that case, now that we're all here..."

He stood up. His curly black hair was glossy, his amber eyes almost the same color as his tan. He looked like a beautiful god.

"Ariel, I have something for you," he announced.

Ariel blinked. "You do?"

"I do. Something quite substantial, I think."

"Is it a bird? Is it a plane? Is it Superman?" Sheila joked.

Nick took an envelope out of his breast pocket. He looked at Ariel, but he was well aware of the others watching him. "It's a check for thirty thousand dollars."

"What?" Ariel lurched back, shocked.

"We were just talking about it," Nick said smoothly, smiling, "that summer in the Sand Palace. I asked Wyatt if I could borrow three hundred dollars so I could take Francine to a nice restaurant."

"And I refused," Wyatt said forcefully.

"But your wife didn't," Nick told him. "Of course, she wasn't your wife then."

"Ariel?" Wyatt's eyes flew to his wife.

"Oh, this is silly," Ariel said. "Nick, I'd forgotten all about that."

"You gave Nick three hundred dollars?" Wyatt's face was stormy.

Nick answered for Ariel. "She did. She left before I could pay her back, so I put three hundred dollars in a savings account. Later, I put it into stocks. This is what those three hundred dollars turned into over twenty-five years."

Wyatt shoved back from the table. "My wife does not need your money."

"Wyatt." Ariel put a gentle hand on his arm.

"Why don't you let your wife decide," Nick said. "She's the one who loaned me the money."

Wyatt strode to the head of the table. Nick stood up, glaring. The two men scowled at each other.

"You're a social climber and a money-grubber," Wyatt said.

Nick's mouth quirked in a half-smile. "Okay. But *you* are boring."

Wyatt's face turned red. "I ought to—" He raised his fist.

"I want the money." Ariel rose from her chair. "I've been struggling to build an online club for aspiring writers. I want to attend more writers' workshops and haven't had the money. I deserve the money, Wyatt. I want it."

Wyatt froze. He turned to face his wife, and he looked completely confused, lost, like a man coming out of a coma.

"You never told me you wanted to do that," he said.

"I *did* tell you. You didn't *hear*."

Wyatt said, "You never told me you loaned Nick three hundred dollars."

"No," Ariel said. "I didn't tell you."

Nick folded his arms over his chest and stared at the floor, trying to keep a taunting expression off his face.

Wyatt walked away from Nick, as if Nick didn't matter. He stood before his wife, his beautiful and adoring wife, and he was humbled. "I'm sorry I didn't hear you. I know I tend to have tunnel vision about my work."

"You'll never change," Ariel told her husband. "I don't want you to. I'm proud of you, of the work you're doing. But I deserve this money, and I want you to be proud of the work I can do."

Wyatt nodded. Ariel sat, and Wyatt took the chair next to her.

Nick returned to his seat. He slid the envelope down to Francine, who passed it to Sheila, who passed it to Ariel. Ariel put it in the pocket of her capris.

Wyatt grumbled, "Where's the waiter? It's time to go."

Jade-Marie kicked Jason's foot under the table.

Jason shared a glance with Jade-Marie. "We're going to skip out now and leave you oldies with the check. It's a beautiful night. We want to walk on the beach."

Nick said, "Wait, we'll be ready as soon as—"

Francine put her hand on his. "Darling, let them go."

The moment they were out of the restaurant, away from their parents, Jade-Marie twirled in a circle.

"Now I can breathe!"

"Let's go to the beach."

Jade-Marie and Jason walked through the town, down toward the Brant Point lighthouse. They passed boutiques, restaurants, homes, and were away from it all, walking next to a large swath of open land, tall grasses swaying in the slight breeze. The moon was high in the sky tonight and somehow it made the sky seem even wider, higher, more inviting, as if the universe was larger than they had dreamed.

"I'll never understand the world," Jade-Marie said.

Jason nodded. "Haldane—he was a scientist—said that not only is the universe stranger than we imagine, it's stranger than we *can* imagine."

Jade-Marie smiled. "I love that." After a moment, she said, "I want to go to bed with you." Jade-Marie stared up into Jason's face as she spoke. She knew she was being daring, but *there*. She'd said it.

"I want to do more than that," Jason said, his voice low.

Jade-Marie's heart thumped. "More than go to bed?"

"Yeah, like, make love. Get to know each other. Make love again. Spend lots of time with each other. Make love again. Like that. You know how I feel about you, Jade-Marie. You must. I mean, the way we danced out at Cisco's . . ."

"You're only going to be here a week."

"No, I'm here for the summer. I got a job at Cabot's Marine, remember?"

"Oh, right. Your father's angry about that."

"He's always mad at me. I'm an adult. I can do what I want."

"Can you? Are you? I mean, if you're going to work at Cabot's, don't you need to at least let the university know you're quitting? That would be the mature thing to do. Not just let your father deal with it."

"You're right. I should tell them. I'll do it tomorrow," Jason said.

They came to the beach by the lighthouse and walked silently to the water's edge. Boats dotted the harbor with circles of light. The sea was calm. They sat down together on the sand.

Jason said, "You're thinking I came to the island and got all island-happy, right? Like I've been transported to fantasyland."

Jade-Marie nodded her head, smiling. "Lots of people feel that way when they get here."

"Right. Like you. You're working here this summer."

"Maybe the winter, too. I'm ambitious, Jason. I'd like to run a hotel, especially this hotel. The hotel business is what I know, and I like the size of this hotel, the challenge of off-season possibilities. I love this island and I hardly know it. But I'm not set in concrete. Working here this summer will be a good testing ground for me. I've got a lot to learn. And believe me, *working* for a hotel instead of *staying* in one is not in any way a fantasyland." She paused, reflecting. "One thing I know for sure is that I'm not going to let my work, my ambition, get in the way of being with my family. I mean my husband and children, when I ever get around to having a family. I'm like my father, yes, but not totally like him."

"Yeah, I get that," Jason said. "When I get married and have children, I want to be in their lives. I want to show up at their recitals and teach them how to ride a two-wheeler bike. I want to be, I don't know how to say it, with the *real* moments."

Jade-Marie said, "I know, like when she's got the flu and throws up or the first time at the dentist or gets a kitten."

"Or a puppy."

Jade-Marie said, "Yeah."

Jason turned to face her. In the darkness, he could see the white flash of her teeth as she smiled, and the way she was looking at him.

Slowly, he put his hand on the side of her face. He could feel the warmth of her skin. Jade-Marie slowly turned her head and kissed the palm of his hand. He cupped the back of her head and brought her mouth to his. Her breath was warm and sweet. She put her arms around him. He felt her body yielding, and together they lay on the sand, pressing their bodies together, kissing. And kissing more, longer.

When they drew apart, they lay side by side, looking at the stars. Jade-Marie's head was nestled on Jason's chest.

"I came all this way to find you," Jason said.

Jade-Marie said, "And I came all this way to be found."

"We won't be rash and rush things," Jason said.

"Right. We'll see how the summer goes."

"But," Jason said, and his mouth went dry with fear and hope, "if we want to make love, we will."

"Oh, yes," Jade-Marie replied, her voice light. "I think we need to have lots and lots of sex before we decide we belong together."

"I think it would be a good idea to start now," Jason said.

"I think so, too. But not out here. Too many people."

"Too many people in the lobby of the hotel," Jason said. "They'll see us, stop us, and want to talk."

"Yeah, but, Jason, guess what. I have the key to the back entrance."

Jason sat up. "You might be the perfect woman for me."

Jade-Marie sat up next to him. "I certainly hope so."

Jason stood. He reached out his hand to pull Jade-Marie to her feet. They held hands as they walked back to the hotel.

twenty-three

That Summer

The summer was coming to an end. Sidewalks were no longer congested with people and baby strollers and dogs. Restaurants weren't overbooked. The Rose Hotel had empty rooms. Occasionally a cool breeze drifted in from the sea.

At the end of the day, Sheila removed her apron and put it into the closet with her supply caddy. She searched for Mrs. Reardon and found her in the kitchen, drinking tea and studying her reservation book, a woeful expression on her face.

"Mrs. Reardon?" Even though the door was open, Sheila knocked lightly.

The older woman looked up. "Oh, Sheila. Come in, dear, sit down."

Sheila pulled out a wooden kitchen chair and sat. She was braver now than she had been at the beginning of the summer and needed to be honest more than likable. "I wondered how much longer you'll need me."

Mrs. Reardon nodded sadly. "I'm afraid I need to let you go now."

"Now? That's a week earlier—"

"Yes, but that charming Mr. Johnson has made a miserable mess of things for me."

"Oh, dear. I suppose he's not returning to the hotel after his accident."

"More than that, Sheila. Never mind that he had booked into September and I was counting on that income and I turned down reservations because he was staying. *Said* he was staying. He owes me for a month. Almost two months."

Sheila twisted the hem of her shirt. "Maybe he'll send a check once he leaves the hospital . . ."

Mrs. Reardon shook her head. "When his wife came here to collect his things, I told her that he owed me for more than a month, but of course she was worried about him and I didn't press it because she seemed nice. She told me the police consider both drivers at fault, so she's not worried about legal matters. First of all, she has to concentrate on helping Frank recover. She was too distraught to talk about money."

"I'm so sorry." Sheila didn't know how to console her employer. She was on the verge of tears herself.

"No, I'm sorry," Mrs. Reardon said. "I know I told you I'd give you a bonus if you worked to the end of August, but now I've lost his September reservation and he owes me for August. I can't give you a bonus. My financial affairs are a mess."

Sheila sagged in her chair.

"I wish things were different, Sheila." Mrs. Reardon's tone softened. "I like you. You've been a good, steady worker for me. I don't want to let you go, but it's only a week early, and thanks to that accident—"

"You're letting me go today?"

"I hate it more than you do," Mrs. Reardon said. "I'll have to clean the rooms I do have rented. But I can't pay you for another week."

Panicked, Sheila raised her voice. "But that's not our agreement! That's not fair!"

The landlady gave Sheila a cold stare. "Life's not fair, Sheila. And this island isn't perfect just because it's pretty. We year-rounders have to scrape to get by in the winter. We count *on every penny we make*"—she pounded the table with each word—"to help us pay for heat and food in February. If losing a bonus and one week's salary is a tragedy for you, you're lucky."

"I'm lucky," Sheila echoed. She stood up, shaking. "Goodbye, then."

"Goodbye, dear. I'm so sorry."

Shattered, Sheila left the kitchen, walked down the hallway, opened the door of the Rose Hotel, and stepped out into the afternoon.

She composed herself. What could she do now? It was after five. At the Sand Palace, Sharon Waters would have left, locking her office with the telephone in it. She'd started doing that when unknown numbers showed up on her bill. Ariel was undoubtedly with Wyatt, and Nick was probably drinking with friends. Sheila was alone on this island, and she always had been.

At the corner of Main and Union, behind the Lion's Paw, was a small parking lot with a bank of pay telephones. Sheila headed in that direction, walking faster as she got closer, until she was almost running, as if for her life. She reached the phones. For once, no one else was using one. She took up the receiver from the phone on the end. It was dead. No signal. Sheila let the receiver dangle and hurried to the phone at the other end. It worked. She put some quarters into the slot, dialed the operator, and asked to make a collect call.

Hank might not even be there.

"Hello?" He was there, his voice as lovely and husky as she remembered.

"Oh, Hank," Sheila cried. "I'm so upset. My employer just let me go, without my summer bonus, because one of her guests didn't pay her, and it's the end of the summer, and people are going home, so I won't be able to get another job, and I don't know what to do!"

Hank hesitated.

Sheila's heart sank to the bottom of her shoes. Had he met someone else during the summer?

His voice came over the phone, sure and strong. "I'll tell you what to do. I'll have to work tomorrow, but then I can take a few days off. You pack up. Day after tomorrow, say goodbye to that place, and take a boat to Hyannis. It's about seven hundred miles from here to Hyannis. About twelve hours. I'll gas up the car and start driving tomorrow evening. I should be there sometime Wednesday morning. You take the boat over and I'll pick you up in Hyannis and we'll come home."

Sheila burst into tears. "Oh, Hank. Oh, Hank, I've missed you so much. I can't wait to see you."

"I can't wait to see you, sweetheart."

She couldn't stop crying. "But, Hank, you should come to Nantucket. I mean to see the island, to see how beautiful the ocean is. You could stay with me for a day or two and then we could go home."

"Sheila," Hank said. "All I want to see is you."

Business was slow at Fanshaw's. Dead, really. That was probably a good thing, Nick thought, because he was in a shit of a mood. He hadn't heard from Francine. Of course, he wouldn't. She would be too busy with her friends. A postcard would be nice, but that would take time to arrive, and anyway, Francine wasn't the type for postcards.

It was early afternoon when the store phone rang.

"Nick, it's Jean-Paul Bruel. How's business?"

Nick's heart lurched at the sound of the man's voice. "Rather slow," Nick answered. He tossed the "rather" in because he thought it made him sound aristocratic.

Jean-Paul Bruel chuckled. "I'm not surprised. Listen, I'm here in New York where they're gearing up for the autumn season.

Floods of tourists flocking in to see the newest hits on Broadway. The newest fashions at Bergdorf's. So on. What would you think of leaving Fanshaw's early and coming down to the city?"

Nick hesitated. This was the devil's tightrope, the razor's edge. If he said yes, he would be admitting he was the type of guy to quit a job before the arranged date. If he said no, he might endanger his relationship with Jean-Paul Bruel.

"I'd like to check with Mr. Fanshaw," Nick said. "If Steve is staying, it might be fine if I leave early."

"Good man," Mr. Bruel said. "Do that. Let me know."

Toward the end of the day, when no one was in the shop—and no one had come in for hours—Nick phoned Mr. Fanshaw. He was nervous, not wanting to provoke an argument, but wanting very much, more with every hour, to leave the store and the island and start his real life in New York.

"Of course, you can leave early," Mr. Fanshaw bellowed over the phone. "Most of our customers have already left the island. I'll mail your check to your home address, shall I?"

"Thank you, Mr. Fanshaw." Nick was surprised and delighted, and he spoke with honesty when he said, "I've very much enjoyed working for you this summer, sir."

"Well, you did a fine job. If you need a reference, I'd be glad to give it."

It was odd, Nick thought, as he hung up the phone, how exhilarated he was to leave this job, when at the beginning of the summer he'd been thrilled to start it. This was how he was, he learned this about himself again and again. He liked change. He like challenges. He liked climbing the professional ladder in the same way Hillary liked climbing Mount Everest.

He didn't like failing.

Entering the humid Sand Palace felt like failure to him. Ariel and Wyatt, practically swooning with happiness, were engaged. They were leaving the island on Wednesday, going to have a wedding at the town clerk's office in Wellesley, and getting married, with their parents attending. Then they would fly to Missouri, where Wyatt would work toward his PhD and teach freshman classes. Ariel planned to make them a cozy home and write brilliant novels in her spare time. Nick wished them well, but he secretly doubted that he'd ever see them again.

Sheila was leaving Wednesday, too. Nick had a hollow space in his gut that could be loneliness. He wanted the Sand Palace group together one more time.

But no, he didn't really need to see them again. He needed Francine.

Where was she? Why hadn't she called or written to him? Had he been only a toy for her? He had thought she loved him. He certainly loved her.

He wasn't a natural letter writer. In fact, he knew his spelling was horrendous. He'd been told so many times.

Still, he went to his rickety desk and sat down. A pen and hotel stationery headed ROCKERS was in the desk drawer. He'd never used it before, but he was glad to have it now. The paper was creamy and thicker than what he was used to. He marked out the word ROCKERS and wrote in SAND PALACE.

He wrote: *Dear Francine,*

He stopped writing. He looked at the two words. Oddly, just seeing her name in his handwriting made him feel closer to her. He felt less alone.

I miss you so much. I think about you all the time. It's odd to know that while I'm here at my desk in this horrid basement room, you are half the world away, probably sleeping in a luxurious Paris flat.

I told you that I love you, and I do. It seems I can't stop loving you, even though you've left me and gone to Paris. I'm sure that if I never see you again, you will be the woman I love for all of my life

Nick put down the pen. He stood up so suddenly his chair rocked backward, falling on the floor.

He couldn't stay in this rat hole blithering away with pity for himself and love for a woman he didn't deserve.

Nick left his room and stormed out of the Sand Palace. He headed toward the Atlantic Café. People there at least knew his face. He'd flirt with a woman, have a couple of beers, maybe run into some old friends. He'd cheer up.

It was still early, but the restaurant was filling up. The AC was a popular place, with great food and a friendly waitstaff. Nick found a spot at the bar and ordered a Heineken. He chatted with the guy next to him, an Irishman who'd painted houses all summer and was going home with a fat wallet.

"My girl's waiting for me," the Irishman said. "We're going to marry and get a flat in Dublin and save up for a house in Kilkee, where we come from. Sure, it's on the west side of the island, on the mouth of the Shannon, a beautiful place, you never saw such a beautiful place."

The Irishman nattered on and on about his lovely fiancée and their lovely plans to live on the lovely mouth of the lovely Shannon, and Nick ordered Irish whiskeys for them both and was glad for the slug of heat hitting his lungs. Nick could almost see the dream the Irishman described, and when he had to leave, Nick was sad, as if he'd lost a good friend.

He ordered another whiskey. All around him, people laughed and chattered. He was all alone.

"I'd like one of those."

The girl who approached him was Nick's age, more or less. She was pretty and had an easy laugh. Her name was Christi. She was down for the summer, returning for her last year of college in Boston. She'd been cleaning houses with a group of friends, and working for a babysitting service most evenings. When she laughed, she tilted her head back and her wavy chestnut hair fell down her back, almost touching her waist. Her throat was as white as a swan's feather.

"What about you?" Christi asked. "Why are you here this summer?"

"I came with some friends," Nick said, and caught himself. He'd come alone. He'd made friends, perhaps, but the truth was, at the end of the summer he was as solitary as he'd arrived. Often before, he'd entertained a woman with a humorous story about the odd little cave they called the Sand Palace. Now, if he wanted, he could tell Christi about Francine, this la-di-da French girl who thought she was too good for him.

But he couldn't say that. He couldn't even think that. He remembered Francine whispering that she loved him, saying that they would be together for a long time.

"I'm sorry," Nick said to Christi. "You're a beautiful woman, but I've been going through a bad breakup. I'm not fit company."

He put a twenty on the bar, stepped off the stool, and left the restaurant. It was quieter outside, but families and friends were in clumps at the Juice Bar, at the Dreamland theater, on the streets. As he walked, he watched the others with envy. It didn't matter, he told himself. He'd go back to his room, pack all his belongings, and take the first boat away from here tomorrow.

The entrance to the Sand Palace was dark. He'd forgotten to leave a light on for himself. He was used to one of the others having a light on. He stumbled into the corridor, flicked on the bald overhead lightbulb, pushed open the door to his room, and went in.

The sun was setting early now, but pale light came through his window to illuminate his room. His desk, with his letter on it.

His bed, where Francine lay curled, her head on his pillow, sleeping.

"My God," Nick said.

Francine stirred voluptuously. She peeked through her lashes. "There you are."

"I'm sorry to wake you." Nick stood by the side of the bed. "I can't believe you're here."

"I did not like being away from you," Francine said. "I'm so glad you wrote me a letter."

"I didn't send you a letter," Nick told her.

She laughed, deep in her throat. "Yes, but you wrote that letter." She pointed to the desk.

Nick nodded. "I did."

Francine patted the side of the bed. "Sit down."

Nick sat. The warmth of her body and the fragrance of her perfume drifted next to him. "I don't want to lose you, Francine."

"I don't want to lose you," she replied. "We must be careful, you and I. We're so much in love and yet so cynical. We know each other deeply and yet in many ways we don't know each other at all."

"Oh, I think we know each other very well," Nick said. "But I have to go wherever your father directs me, and I don't know where you'll be or how I'll find you."

Francine was quiet for a moment. "I will go where you go, Nick. You've told me I will be the woman you'll love all your life." She saw his confusion and smiled. "In your letter, Nick. There on your desk. And you will be the man I will love all my life."

Nick struggled to keep calm. This day—this summer—had been overwhelming. He wanted to tell Francine that, and he wanted to promise her he'd love her forever, and he kind of wanted to tell her that a girl named Christi just tried to pick him up at the AC and he'd refused because he loved Francine even though he didn't know if he'd ever see her again. He didn't know where to start.

Francine watched him. She lay back down on his bed. She pulled the covers back. "Come, my love," she said. "Lie down with me and rest."

Nick lay down. She snuggled against him.

Francine said, "Let's sleep. Now everything is all right."

Ariel, Sheila, Wyatt, and Nick walked to the Brant Point lighthouse, carrying their picnic dinners and drinks in their hands. They'd discussed going to the AC or the Brotherhood for their last dinner together, but decided, instead, to be frugal. Besides, it was a perfect summer evening. The wind had dropped and the sea rolled gently, like a blue whale turning over in its sleep. The sailboats in the outer harbor looked like paintings.

Wyatt had asked the town clerk for permission to have a fire pit on the beach, but she said that wasn't possible. Nick wanted to argue—he'd been to many beach parties with fires, but they were all on the other side of the island, far out of town. Anyway, Ariel had pointed out, it was too hot for a fire.

They had spent the day packing and cleaning their rooms. They'd returned their rented bikes and the rented Jeep. Tomorrow they'd catch a boat to the mainland, and the summer would be over.

They found a spot near the lighthouse where they could watch the boats come and go. The sand was warm, the tide going out, leaving behind a woven line of seaweed.

"We should have brought a blanket to sit on," Ariel said as they settled onto the beach.

"Yes, because we always remember to do that," Nick joked.

"We haven't had that many meals on the beach," Wyatt said. "We've had Wednesday nights together, but usually at the Sand Palace."

"And that one time at Francine's," Sheila added.

"Did you invite Francine to join us tonight?" Ariel asked Nick.

"I did. She said she thought tonight should be for just the four of us." Nick popped open his beer and the liquid hissed into the air.

"She's right," Sheila said. "I'm glad she's not here. She's a snob."

Ariel uncorked a bottle of white wine, poured the wine into two plastic cups, and handed one to Sheila. "Be good, Sheila. Francine is nice. You can't hate her because she's rich."

"I'll drink to that!" Nick said, touching his can to Ariel's cup. "Because if you hate rich people, you're really going to hate me."

Sheila laughed. "I'd never hate you, Nick. And I hope you do get rich."

"We came here with such dreams," Ariel said.

"I wanted to make a lot of money and have an adventure." Sheila drew a wandering line in the sand with her finger. "I made a lot of money—a lot for me, not for someone like you, Nick— and I had an adventure. It certainly wasn't what I expected."

"That's what makes it an adventure," Nick said. "It's something you don't expect."

"I bow to your wisdom, O Wise One," Wyatt said, opening his own beer.

"Are you glad you had an adventure?" Nick asked Sheila.

She still gazed down and swirled the sand with her finger. "I suppose I am. I probably grew up a little because of it."

Ariel touched Sheila's arm. "I bet you realized how wonderful Hank is."

Now Sheila looked up, and she was smiling. "You're right. Maybe this island is like Oz, and after spending time here, I realize how fortunate I am to have Hank waiting for me and—"

"Don't go any further with that metaphor," Nick said. "I adamantly decline to be a scarecrow, tin man, or lion. Although actually, I guess I wouldn't mind being a lion."

"You are a lion," Ariel told him. "Nick, you absolutely are a lion."

"Hey," Wyatt called to Ariel. "The lion in Oz was cowardly."

"All right, all right. Nick is not a cowardly lion."

"Did you ever wonder," Sheila said dreamily, "if the tin man was the first robot?"

"No, Sheila," Nick said, very earnestly, "I never did."

"Are you drunk already, Sheila?" Wyatt asked.

"Are you still boring, Wyatt?" Sheila responded.

"Way to go, Sheila!" Nick applauded. "You've grown a spine since you've been here."

Sheila grinned, pleased. "I guess I have."

"Have some more wine." Ariel refilled both their cups. "Really, you guys, when I think about it, we're all lucky."

"Did you write your novel?" Nick asked.

"I can't believe you remember that I want to," Ariel told him. "And no, I didn't. But I certainly collected plenty to write about."

"And you collected me," Wyatt joked.

Ariel leaned over and kissed his cheek. "I did."

"Oh, that's so romantic," Sheila cooed.

"I'm like you in a way," Wyatt said to Sheila. "I enjoyed being here. It's a beautiful place. But I know more than ever that I want to work at the university. It's a huge honor and responsibility to work with my father."

"Ariel, I hope you like Wyatt's father," Nick said, half joking.

"I hope he likes me," Ariel shot back.

"Come on, you guys!" Nick shouted. "We can't all be so pleased with ourselves."

Sheila protested, "But, Nick, we should be! I mean, you met Francine and her father here. You made an amazing connection, a kind of miracle, you have to know that."

"Yeah," Nick agreed. "I guess I do. I have been lucky."

Wyatt said, "On the downside, we'll probably have a long-term lung disease from all the mold and mildew in the basement."

Ariel said thoughtfully, "I wish I'd gone to more of the island's museums."

"You can always come back," Nick told her.

"Yes, but will I? Once we get back to our real lives, this place will seem like a dream."

"Oh!" Sheila held up her tote bag. "That reminds me. I have photos for all of you." As she took separate envelopes out and passed them around, she said, "Most of them are of sunsets or yachts, but look, there the four of us are the first night we were here."

"We're all so pale we look like we have tuberculosis!" Ariel cried.

"And here's a photo I took one night before we went to a party. We were dressed to kill."

"What a dreamy photo of you, Nick," Ariel said. "You've got your bedroom-eyes look going on."

"He was probably drunk," Wyatt snapped.

"Do you have your camera?" Nick asked. "Why not snap a shot of the four of us now?"

Sheila searched the beach for a likely volunteer. "I'll just go ask them."

She walked across the sand to a trio of women with their feet in the water and beach towels around their shoulders.

"I'm sorry to bother you," Sheila said, "but could I ask one of you to come take a photo of me and my three friends? We've worked here all summer and we're leaving tomorrow."

"Sure." One of the women stood up and followed Sheila back to the pack.

The four of them squeezed together, said "cheese," and the woman snapped several shots. Everyone thanked her, and the woman strode away to her friends.

Ariel whispered, "You guys! Do you know who that was? *Jane Curtin!*"

"Right," Nick agreed. "She was on *Saturday Night Live* forever."

"Oh, and she was in that comedy series *Kate and Allie,*" Sheila said. "Wow!"

"Never heard of her," Wyatt said.

The other three laughed.

"You don't see anything unless it's under a microscope," Nick said.

"Look at the boat with the red sail!" Ariel cried, pointing.

The four went quiet as they watched a very beautiful schooner glide out of the harbor.

"We should all meet again here someday," Nick said.

Wyatt snorted. "Don't count on that happening soon. I've got a lot of significant work to do."

"Maybe in ten years," Ariel suggested.

"Maybe in twenty," Sheila said.

"Maybe we'll all come back here the day I own a hotel on the island, and you'll be my guests," Nick said.

Ariel laughed. "What a wonderful idea, Nick!"

"You're such a dreamer, Nick," Wyatt said, shaking his head.

"Yes," Nick agreed. "Yes, I am."

twenty-four
This Summer

At the bistro, most of the group were seated around the table, eating. Francine prepared a dark coffee for herself and sat down next to her husband.

"Good morning, everyone," she said.

A chorus of replies came toward her.

"My darling," Francine said to Nick, "what are your plans for us today?"

Before Nick could respond, Sheila said, "I think I'll go home. I miss my boys, and I have so much to do."

Ariel touched her husband's hand. "Actually, Wyatt and I are considering going home today, as well. As you might have noticed, Wyatt becomes slightly neurotic when he's away from his work, and you haven't seen Wyatt when he really gets lonely for his core samples and computers."

Nick glanced around the table, shocked. "Oh, I don't think you all need to scatter this morning. We're scheduled for a round of golf at the Nantucket Golf Club. That's the one Bill Clinton played on. And—"

"Dad!" Jade-Marie hurried into the bistro. Penny was right behind. "You know how Karla was having trouble with her computer spreadsheets? *Penny fixed it!*"

The two young women stood beaming at the table and they almost seemed like twins, one with red hair in a pale green dress and one with dark hair in a pale blue dress. The women were young, fresh, crisp, and absolutely glowing. They were obviously pleased with themselves; they were like angels announcing a miracle.

And wasn't it a miracle, Sheila thought, that her daughter was so brilliant and competent that she could fix a hotel computer? Wasn't it a miracle that Penny was even here on the earth, in all her youth and beauty and hope for the day?

Nick studied Penny. "What was your degree in?"

Penny folded her hands in front of her and lifted her chin. "Business administration and IT."

Nick said, "I'd like to offer you a job."

Penny asked, "Do you mean for the summer? Here? Temporary?"

"I'll start you here, Penny," Nick said. "And yes, here for the summer for a paid internship. In the fall we'll evaluate whether you should stay here and work, or transfer to another of my hotels."

Penny held her breath and looked at her mother.

Sheila clenched her hands beneath the table and calmly said, "What a wonderful idea, Penny. What a wonderful opportunity."

"That means all three of you kids are staying on the island," Nick said. "I'm glad."

Wyatt glared at his coffee cup. Ariel put her hand on his arm. "One word of advice, Jason," Ariel said. "Don't let Penny and Jade-Marie share a place with you."

Penny and Jade-Marie shrieked with laughter.

Jason said, "Don't worry, Mom. Cabot's renting me a place

above his shop. It's a complete pit. Penny and Jade-Marie wouldn't want to enter it, and there's not enough room for two people."

"Penny can stay with me," Jade-Marie said. She looked at Penny. "Hotel rooms go for five hundred a night in the summer, so we can't give you your own room. I know I told you the room is small, but we can trade the queen bed for two twins."

Penny's face went pink with pleasure. "Wow. Thanks, Jade-Marie!"

Sheila smiled at her daughter. "Well, you have your adventure at last!"

"I want to see your apartment!" Jade-Marie told Jason.

"Sure," Jason said. "Sometime."

"Now," Jade-Marie insisted. "It's not far, right? It's above the shop?"

"Yeah," Jason said. "Okay. Whenever you're ready."

"Could I go, too?" Penny asked.

"Sure!" Jade-Marie and Jason spoke at the same time.

"Use the hotel bikes," Nick suggested.

"Good idea!" Jade-Marie said. She kissed her father's cheek as she headed for the door.

"I'll be back before you go, Mom," Penny told her mother.

"Yeah, me, too," Jason called to his parents as he followed the girls out the door.

The air of the room was suddenly silent.

Sheila broke the tension. "I remember, the first day I was here, I was frantically worried about biking in my bathing suit."

The others laughed. Nick said, "And that was only the *beginning* of the summer."

Ariel said, "When I try to remember those months on Nantucket, it's all a blur."

"I have more—" Sheila began, and then stopped, her face red. "I brought my photographs of that summer with me. They're not good photos. I only had one of those throwaway cameras. I guess I was trying to be artsy."

Francine frowned at Sheila. "Should we be worried?"

"Absolutely not." Sheila took a deep breath. "These are pictures of the beach, hydrangeas, ferries. Like that." She took a
thick envelope from her purse and handed the photos around.

Ariel and Wyatt, Francine and Nick, studied the photos. Their
faces lit up.

"The Atlantic Café!" Nick yelled. "Nachos and brews!"

"Remember when we drove out to the Great Point lighthouse?"
Ariel asked. "I almost touched a seal."

"Look at the four of us." Sheila pointed to the photo of the
group standing near the base of the lighthouse.

"We were so young," Nick said.

"We were so thin," Sheila added. She slipped another photo on
top.

"Sharon Waters, still the hotel manager!" Wyatt said. "She's actually smiling. You should show her this picture."

"What a dump this place was," Nick said. "You've got to admit
I've turned it into a palace."

Ariel pulled Wyatt close and they both stared down at a photo
of the four of them at the beach. "We were babies."

"We were *full of hope*," Nick said.

"I wish the kids were here to see these," Sheila said.

"They've got better things to do," Nick reminded her. "They're
heading into their own Nantucket summer."

"I envy them," Ariel said.

Sheila nodded. "Me, too."

They sat smiling, together again, gazing down at photos of the
summer when they were young.

About the Author

NANCY THAYER is the *New York Times* bestselling author of more than thirty novels, including *Summer Love, Family Reunion, Girls of Summer, Let It Snow, Surfside Sisters, A Nantucket Wedding, Secrets in Summer, The Island House, The Guest Cottage, An Island Christmas, Nantucket Sisters,* and *Island Girls*. Born in Kansas, Thayer has been a resident of Nantucket for nearly forty years, where she currently lives with her husband, Charley, and a precocious rescue cat named Callie.

nancythayer.com
Facebook.com/NancyThayerBooks
Instagram: @nancythayerbooks

About the Type

This book was set in Garamond, a typeface originally designed by the Parisian type cutter Claude Garamond (c. 1500–61). This version of Garamond was modeled on a 1592 specimen sheet from the Egenolff-Berner foundry, which was produced from types assumed to have been brought to Frankfurt by the punch cutter Jacques Sabon (c. 1520–80).

Claude Garamond's distinguished romans and italics first appeared in *Opera Ciceronis* in 1543–44. The Garamond types are clear, open, and elegant.